TEMPLE

TEMPLE

ROBERT SWARTWOOD

RMS PRESS

For Darrell Stotz

The question isn't who is Temple—no one knows that —but rather what is Temple. Is he a hero? Is he a vigilante? What Temple most certainly is not is a communist, as the junior senator from Wisconsin has recently suggested in a press conference. The mere idea is preposterous, and the senator has no valid evidence to support such a claim. Earlier, the senator asked, "Upon what meat does this, our Caesar, feed?" Had he looked three lines earlier in Shakespeare's *Caesar*, he would have found this line, which is not altogether inappropriate: "The fault, dear Brutus, is not in our stars, but in ourselves."

—from Edward R. Murrow's broadcast of
See It Now, May, 9, 1954

Today a bill has been passed in the Senate to require Temple to turn himself in to the federal authorities. I am coming before you tonight to tell you that I will veto any legislation of this kind that passes my desk. It is not the opinion of this office that Temple poses any risk to our national security. The complete opposite is true, in fact, as this office maintains that Temple is a hero and a patriotic American. As long as I am

President, I will make sure he is protected just as he protects our country.

—President John F. Kennedy,
October 21, 1963

76 DEAD IN CENTRAL PARK BOMBING. HAS TEMPLE FORSAKEN US?

—*New York Post* headline,
July 17, 1997

PART ONE
FORTRESS OF SOLITUDE

1

I didn't know what day it was, only that the temperature was dropping outside, and there wasn't much firewood left. I grabbed the axe leaning against the wall and opened the cabin door, letting Zelda exit first. She trotted past me out onto the porch and down the three wooden steps, her tail wagging with excitement. I followed, axe in hand. Several yards away, a pile of logs was stacked next to a tree stump. Zelda headed straight for it, knowing what the axe meant. She liked when I chopped wood. She'd sit and watch and then pick up what slabs she could and drop them in the rusted wheelbarrow.

But today, halfway to the stump she paused, tilted her head to the side. Stood still for a half second before a low growl started up at the base of her throat. She moved then, low and cautious, toward the side of the cabin. She stopped at once and growled again.

The day was cold and crisp, the sky thick with clouds. The valley stretched out before us, a mixed carpet of blue spruces and pine trees and junipers, looking as beautiful and boring as it had the first time I viewed it twenty years ago. Our closest neighbor was over ten miles away. Harper, the nearest town, was fifteen miles.

The temperature was somewhere in the forties and I wore a flannel shirt and jeans, scuffed workman boots. My grip on the axe handle tightened as I stepped toward Zelda and glanced at what had caught her attention.

An animal lay in the shade of the cabin.

It was a red fox, large for its size. It just lay there for a long moment, its black eyes staring glassily. Then it blinked. Rose onto all four paws. But it didn't run. It stayed where it was, now facing Zelda. Baring its teeth.

"Zelda, stay."

Zelda stopped growling. She sat at attention. Not once did her gaze flick toward me. It remained focused on the fox.

The fox moved again, shifting in its place, and I understood something was wrong with it. Even in the shade of the cabin I could see the darkness on the animal's side. Blood. It had gotten into some kind of scuffle with another animal and had ended up beside the cabin. Not the most ideal place to rest, but it wasn't the first time a wild animal had ventured from the trees into the clearing.

Zelda started growling again.

The fox hissed.

I said again, "Zelda, stay."

She stayed. She didn't want to—that was clear by the wildness in her eyes—but she stayed.

I placed the axe on the ground and started toward the fox. It backed up a step, hissed again, but didn't bolt. Like Zelda, it had a wildness in its eyes, only the fox's wildness was more intense.

Fifteen steps away. Ten steps. Seven.

The fox kept its ground. Hissing again. Still baring its teeth.

The blood looked fresh. The animal favored its rear leg, not putting any pressure on it. That explained why it hadn't bolted yet, though I was surprised it hadn't at least tried.

The distance between the fox and me was barely five feet. I started to crouch down. Behind me, Zelda growled again, and despite everything I had taught her over the years, all the training that made her as obedient as she was, she sprinted forward to protect me from the animal.

It happened in an instant, but I saw it happening before it actually did, I knew exactly what the fox meant to do, and before it could even launch itself at Zelda, I leaned down and put my arm between the two animals.

Despite the heavy flannel fabric, the fox's teeth tore into my skin and held on.

With my free hand, I grabbed the fox's nape and yanked up, hard enough for it to let go. It kicked, hissing again, and I realized what the wild intensity in the fox's eyes meant.

The animal was rabid.

Already my body had begun to heal itself. Where the fox's teeth pierced my skin, an itching sensation had started. Many, many years ago the process would take no more than a couple seconds. Now it would be minutes. It was something I had gotten used to over the years, a reminder that I was no longer a young man.

Zelda was going crazy, barking as she tried to get at the fox, the fox hissing back at her and swinging its paws.

My truck was parked on the other side of the cabin. I started toward it. Circling the front of the cabin, I diverted my direction and headed up the three wooden steps to the porch. I looked around the cabin for a frantic moment before I spotted the surplus duffel bag I used for laundry. Half of it was filled with dirty clothes. I dumped the contents out and shoved the fox inside.

It scratched my hand.

The scratch wasn't nearly as deep as its teeth had been. Blood appeared, but it was minimal, and at once the itching started up as my body began to heal the scratch.

I cinched the duffel bag closed and set it aside. The fox was frantic. Zelda wasn't much better. She went right up to the bag and continued to bark.

"Zelda, stop!"

She looked at me, looked back at the moving bag, then back at me again. She sat at alert and glared down at the bag.

I stripped out of the flannel shirt. Used it to wipe the blood off my arm. The scratch wasn't quite healed yet, but it was getting there.

I tossed the shirt on the floor, put on another one. Picked up the duffel bag and grabbed the single key from the hook by the door.

Despite her earlier disobedience, Zelda continued to sit at attention, watching me.

I said, "Let's go."

Five minutes later, coming down off the mountain, the pickup bouncing on the rutted drive, Zelda's head out the window with her tongue lolling, the fox in the duffel bag in the rear cab, I checked my arm and hand. Besides some residual blood, the skin in both places was whole again. As if the fox had never attacked me in the first place.

2

A new girl was working the counter, or at the very least I had never seen her before, though it had been more than a year since I was last here. She shifted her gaze from the moving, hissing duffel bag to me then back to the moving, hissing duffel bag. She barely even acknowledged Zelda, sitting at attention by my side with no leash.

I repeated my earlier request.

"Is Dr. Snyder available?"

The girl kept staring at the bag. She licked her lips.

"What's in there?"

"A leprechaun."

The girl's mouth opened.

"Really?"

"No. It's a red fox. It's injured. Now can you please call Dr. Snyder?"

There were two other people in the waiting room of the veterinarian clinic. An old woman with a white cat. A middle-aged man with something in a plastic crate. Christmas decorations spotted the walls. A daily flip calendar on the counter announced that today was December 17.

The girl picked up the phone and dialed a number, murmured into the receiver. Her gaze didn't leave the moving, hissing duffel bag.

The old woman and middle-aged man didn't say anything either. They both watched with the same wide-eyed fascination.

A minute later Dr. Snyder came out from one of the back rooms. At once Zelda's tail began thudding the floor. Dr. Snyder patted her head, scratched her behind the ear, and looked down at the duffel bag.

"So, Eli, what did you bring me this time?"

I opened the duffel bag just a bit, enough for her to peek inside.

She sighed and motioned toward the back rooms.

"Let's go."

Zelda and I followed her through the doors into a hallway. Barking echoed from a room farther down. A pet hospital is never a quiet place.

"I think I scared your new girl out there."

Dr. Snyder peered back at me.

"Why do you say that? Because you look like a wild mountain man who hasn't shaved in over a year?"

It was true—I looked rather disheveled. When you live by yourself in the middle of nowhere, you become lax about your appearance. No real reason to shave or cut your hair. The few times I trek into civilization, I make sure to clean myself up the best I can, look presentable. But this, of course, had been an unscheduled trip.

We came to a room at the end of the hallway. A medium-size cage sat off to the side. Dr. Snyder held out her hand as she approached the cage. I handed her the duffel bag. She opened the cage door and then opened the duffel bag and deposited the fox into the cage.

The fox immediately cowered back in the corner, hissing at us.

Dr. Snyder stepped back, crossed her arms as she studied the fox.

"It's rabid."

"How can you be so sure?"

"Call it a gut instinct. We could do a blood test, but I'm not sure it would be worth the time. We're going to have to put it down."

I nodded, took a deep breath.

"I was afraid that would be your answer."

"But still you brought it anyway."

She didn't say this in an accusatory way, merely a statement.

"Where did you find it?"

"Beside the cabin. It looked like it had gotten into some kind of scuffle."

"It certainly got into something. It didn't bite or scratch either you or Zelda, did it?"

"Thankfully no. It tried, but I managed to get it in the duffel bag before it caused any serious damage."

She eyed me for a second, as if she wasn't sure whether she should believe me. She was in her late thirties. About the same age as my daughter, which maybe explained why I always found a reason to visit her. Visiting my daughter was out of the question, so Dr. Snyder seemed a likely replacement.

The last time I was here she had been wearing her wedding ring. She'd been married for some time. Now her finger was bare. Part of me wanted to ask what had happened, but I knew it wasn't my place.

Dr. Snyder tilted her head at Zelda.

"How's she doing?"

I patted Zelda's head.

"As fine as can be. She's still energetic, but it comes in

spurts. Fact is, I think she might have the start of arthritis in her legs."

Dr. Snyder knelt and held her hands out to Zelda, who immediately wagged her tail and approached. She loved Dr. Snyder. After all, the woman had been the one who nursed her back to health nearly ten years ago. By that point, I had been bringing in the occasional injured animal. Dr. Snyder told me I could use a friend and suggested I check out the dogs in the kennel. There were seven dogs to choose from, and all of them looked as if they could use a home, but Zelda caught my attention. She was two years old, a black Labrador mix. Her owner had beaten her badly, and because her owner had been a male, Dr. Snyder said the dog was afraid of males. But that hadn't stopped me from approaching her cage, bending down, and extending my hand through the bars. She slunk back against the far wall, watching me, growling. I didn't move. I just waited. I would have waited all day, but Dr. Snyder suggested I pick another dog. I told her I didn't want another dog. She said then I should come back tomorrow. So I did. I did the same thing as the previous day. Crouched in front of her cage, my hand extended through the bars. Still she didn't approach. Still she slunk against the far wall, growling. I came back the next day. And the next. It took eight days before she finally approached me. Sniffed my hand. Hesitated. Licked it.

I didn't take her home that day. I came to visit the next day. Then the day after that. Dr. Snyder asked what it was about this particular dog that caught my attention. I shrugged, told her I wasn't really sure. But I knew. Out of all the dogs in the kennel, she was the most scared. She was the one in the most need of saving. And to be honest, I missed that. I missed being able to save others.

A week later I adopted her. Even then she was scared. She had come to accept the cage as part of her life. Once she was taken away from it, she began to tremble. I didn't rush her. I let her take her time. Leading her outside. Helping her up into my truck.

Eventually she adjusted, but it took a long time. Sometimes at night she would whimper in her sleep. I never knew dogs could have nightmares. Every time I woke her out of those nightmares, softly petted her head, soothed her until she fell back to sleep.

Dr. Snyder asked, "Would you like me to examine her?"

I shook my head.

"To be honest, at this point I'd rather not know."

Dr. Snyder nodded slowly, smiled down at Zelda. Zelda leaned forward, licked the vet's chin.

In the cage, the fox hissed again.

I said, "Sure there's nothing you can do about him?"

Dr. Snyder stood back up, crossed her arms again.

"I'm afraid not. But it's a good thing you brought him in. Don't want him infecting other animals if we can help it."

"Still, it's a shame he has to be put down. He looks young."

"That's just the way it goes. You know that."

She placed a hand on my arm, forced a smile.

"You can't save everything, Eli, no matter how hard you try."

3

Harper, Colorado, is a tiny town about fifteen miles west of Durango with no more than five hundred residents. Zelda and I lived in a cabin in the middle of nowhere, about fifteen miles outside Harper. The vet clinic was in Durango, twenty-five miles away from the cabin. Which meant, on the drive back, we passed through Harper.

Whitman's General Store sat along the highway, just like almost every other business in Harper. And the highway wasn't really even a highway at all. It was more like a heavily traveled two-lane road. Most people only saw Harper in passing as they breezed past at sixty miles per hour.

When we pulled into the lot, there were two motorcycles parked out front. Not Harleys, but those flashy crotch rockets the kids liked to ride.

I opened my door and stepped out, and Zelda crawled across the seat and jumped down from my side. Her nails clicked loudly against the asphalt. It made me want to kick myself for not asking Dr. Snyder to trim them during our visit. Next time.

In front of the store was a pile of firewood, shovels, rock

salt, the usual winter fare. Sale signs hung over each product. Like most mom and pop stores, Whitman's couldn't undercut the major retailers, but Darrell still liked to put as many items on sale as he could. Even if it was only a few cents, he wanted people to know he cared.

I placed my hand on the doorknob, but before I could even turn it, I heard the voices inside. Loud voices. Angry voices.

Beside me, Zelda growled. A soft growl, kept back deep in her throat.

I looked down at her. She looked up at me.

I said, "It's okay."

And opened the door.

"Bullshit. Complete, fucking bullshit."

There were two of them, kids just like I had suspected, no older than twenty-one. One had his head shaved to the skin. The other had a close-cropped mohawk. Both had tattoos and earrings and studs sticking out everywhere. Their appearance wasn't what bothered me about the two. To be honest, I could have cared less how they were dressed or what they'd done to their bodies. But acting like assholes to other people, especially friends of mine? That didn't fly.

Darrell's voice quivered.

"Again, I'm sorry, but there are signs clearly stating—"

Skinhead cut him off.

"Who gives a fuck? It's still bullshit."

There wasn't a bell above the door signaling new arrivals, but still our entrance was apparent to Darrell and his two customers. Both of the kids glanced back over their shoulders, uncertainty in their eyes, but when they saw it was just an old man with an old dog, they continued like we weren't even there.

Darrell said, "I don't know what you want me to do."

He was about my age, a light-skinned black man, tall and frail. Some days it seemed like a strong wind could knock him over.

Zelda stayed put beside me. She didn't sit at attention but stood on all four paws. She growled again.

Mohawk looked back at us.

"If that dog bites me, I'm gonna kick its fucking head in."

I said nothing. I was tempted to give some kind of rebuttal, but that was what this punk wanted. Any excuse to cause even more trouble.

Skinhead said, "Just what kind of fucking business is this?"

I asked, "Everything okay, Darrell?"

Mohawk said, "Everything's fine."

I ignored him, keeping my gaze on Darrell.

Darrell nodded, slowly, and swallowed.

"Everything's fine. These two, uh, gentlemen are upset that I only accept cash."

Skinhead snorted.

"Cash. Who the fuck uses cash anymore?"

Darrell was traditional in the way he did business, and he got by just fine. Like he told the two punks when Zelda and I first walked in, there were signs all over the place. On the door leading in, and several posted around the store, all announcing that Whitman's General Store did not accept credit cards. Cash, check, money order, sure, but no credit cards.

Darrell's voice still quivered.

"I don't know what you want me to tell you. There's an ATM at the bank down the highway a bit. You can take cash out there."

Mohawk said, "All we want is some sodas, and you think we're going to run to a fucking ATM for cash?"

Darrell didn't say anything. There was nothing to say. It was not entirely clear what these two punks wanted other than to complain, but whatever it was, they weren't going to get it here.

Beside me, Zelda's growling grew louder. She didn't like these two at all.

Mohawk eyed us again.

"Seriously, old man, you better keep your dog in check, or I'm going to crush its skull with my boot."

I don't care for bullies. Not one bit. In the past, I dealt with the bullies in an appropriate manner ... and sometimes in a not-so-appropriate manner. Part of me wanted to respond with something smart, something to get this kid's goat, but punks like them were a dime a dozen. Let them talk themselves out, and they'd go away. It was that simple.

Skinhead tapped the sodas with his finger.

"You know, we could just take these. I figure at this point we're owed that much for having to put up with this bullshit. I mean, Christ, it's only, what, three dollars for the two of them?"

Two 20oz bottles of soda currently stood on the counter between Darrell and the punks.

Even from where I stood across the store, I could see the slight hesitation in Darrell's eyes. He was considering it. Thinking that giving them the sodas would be the easy solution. Just send them on their way and hope to never see them again.

Darrell glanced at me, and I shook my head slightly, just enough for him to catch my meaning.

Don't do it.

There was a silence. Even Zelda had stopped growling.

Finally Darrell cleared his throat.

"I'm sorry, but it will be three dollars for the sodas. And we only take cash. Or a check if you have one."

Mohawk said, "Fuck this."

He hit his friend on the arm, nodded toward the door.

"Let's go. I'm tired of this place."

But Skinhead didn't move. His back was to me, but I could tell he was staring down Darrell. Or at least trying to stare down Darrell. It's hard to do that with people who have been to war. Like me, Darrell was a Vietnam vet. If either of these two punks were veterans, it was from a video game war.

Skinhead said, "You know, it would be a real shame if something were to happen to this store of yours."

Darrell didn't say anything. To his credit, he stared back at Skinhead, didn't look away.

Mohawk hit his friend's arm again.

"Come on, let's just go."

Skinhead still didn't move. He kept his staring contest up for another couple seconds, then finally shook his head, blew air out through his teeth.

"Fucking ridiculous."

He turned and started toward the door.

As the two punks approached, Zelda moved to hide behind me. But still she growled.

Now it was Skinhead who glared down at her.

"That thing bites me, I'm going to sue the shit out of you."

I knew I should remain quiet, but I couldn't help myself.

"Then for my sake let's hope she doesn't bite you."

Skinhead looked at me again with renewed interest. He squinted, took a step forward.

Zelda, peeking at the punks from behind my leg, growled even louder.

Skinhead said, "You want to start something, nigger?"

I saw what he planned to do before he even did it. It's one

of my abilities. It was like with the fox, how I knew when it was going to strike right before it did. My body may be growing old, but still my mind works just as it always has. I knew exactly what Skinhead planned to do next. So when he leaned forward, jerking his head toward my face, I was already closing my eyes and turning my head away. It was the response he wanted, after all, the punk needing to show dominance. I could have just as easily stood there without reaction, not flinched at all, because I also knew based on his body language he wasn't going to follow through with the threat. But that would have created more problems. And right now the only thing I wanted was for the two punks to leave.

Skinhead laughed.

"Yeah, that's what I thought."

He pushed through the door.

Mohawk started to follow his friend outside but paused. A spinner rack stood next to the door, small bags of pretzels and chips hanging on the pegs. Mohawk eyed the rack for a half second before he made his decision. With one smooth sweep of his arm, he knocked the rack over and, with a laugh that matched his friend's, walked outside. The door closed behind him, and seconds later both motorcycles started up.

Zelda growled again, moving out from behind my legs. I placed a hand on her head. She was trembling.

I whispered to her.

"It's okay, girl. It's okay."

As the motorcycles' engines faded away, so did her growls.

4

Darrell grabbed his cane, a broom and scoop, and hobbled around the counter and down the aisle toward us. I'd already set the spinner rack back up. Most of the bags hadn't stayed on the pegs and were scattered everywhere. Three of them were split open, pieces of chips and pretzels littering the floor. Zelda, being the good obedient dog she was, refrained from having a free-for-all with the snacks.

"Goddamn punks."

Darrell mumbling, his face twisted in frustration.

"Just who the hell do they think they are? They're what's wrong with this country—or no, just part of the problem. I see punks like that, it makes me worry about Phil and Thomas. I can't even begin to imagine what I would do if they turned into such pieces of shit like those two."

Phil and Thomas were Darrell's grandsons.

Darrell paused before the mess, shook his head. He set the cane aside, used the broom to sweep up the scattered chips and pretzels into the scoop. While he did this, I slid the bags back on the pegs. Zelda just sat there, watching.

Darrell continued to mumble as he worked.

"Is this why we did it, Eli? Why we risked our lives? Why we gave up our youth? So that we would someday put up with assholes more than half our age who have no respect?"

Darrell did that sometimes. Went off on tangents, especially about Vietnam. We both served over there, young men in our early twenties. Darrell started out in the infantry, but eventually ended up working as a medic. He had no formal training and simply learned on the fly. It helps when half your company gets blown up and pieces of shrapnel lodge into your hip. When there's no other option for survival, you create one. That's how Darrell became a medic, and why decades later he needed the cane.

I said, "How are the grandkids doing these days?"

"What's that?"

He blinked, looking first at me, then down at Zelda. He smiled, leaned forward, scratched Zelda behind the ear. Zelda let Darrell do it because she had come to love him. Anybody else besides Darrell or Dr. Snyder tried it, she might have snapped off their fingers.

"Oh, the grandkids are fine. Michael sent me some pictures. Keeps telling me to sign up for that Facebook thing, says that there is a load of pictures on there. I have no use for it. I keep telling Michael that, and he keeps telling me I need to embrace the new technology. You have it lucky all the way up on the hill by yourself. You don't have to deal with any of this crap. Like my satellite bill this month? Nearly two hundred dollars! I don't even know what all I'm paying for. I only watch two or three channels as it is."

He grabbed his cane again and, with the broom and scoop, wandered through the store back toward the counter. Zelda and I followed him.

Darrell lowered himself down onto the stool behind the counter. It was a wooden stool with extra padding on top. Darrell had had it so long the faux-leather top had started to wear years ago, a problem he'd remedied with duct tape.

"So what brings you two off the hill anyhow? Here to pick up supplies before the first snowfall?"

The hill. In any other part of the country, the elevation where I lived would be considered a mountain. But not in Colorado.

"It's supposed to snow tonight?"

He chuckled.

"If you weren't so disconnected from the rest of the world, you wouldn't have to ask that question."

"How much snow?"

"Not much—only a foot. Say, you want to stick around for dinner?"

"We don't want to put you out."

"You wouldn't be putting me out at all. I've got some extra steaks. Zelda, you like steak, don't you?"

She barked, though I was pretty sure it wasn't in agreement so much as because Darrell just directed that last question at her. Though she did love steak.

Darrell, like most old men, could get lonely at times. His children were over a thousand miles away, one on the east coast, the other on the west coast. He rarely saw his grandchildren. Hardly ever talked to them. But Darrell did see people from Harper on a regular basis, even if they were stopping in for a few quick groceries. At least he got that sociability. It was something I'd never much cared for, which is also why life on the hill suited me. But to be honest, there were times when I got lonely too, which probably explained why I'd sometimes drive almost thirty miles to see Dr. Snyder.

I looked down at Zelda.

"What do you think?"

She barked again.

I shrugged at Darrell.

"You heard the boss. I guess we're coming to dinner."

5

Despite the twenty-degree weather, Darrell wanted to cook on the grill outside. He opened the top and squirted lighter fluid, threw in a match. The thing puffed up in flames. He put first one steak on, then another, then a smaller steak for Zelda, and shut the top of the grill and sat down on the picnic table next to me.

"Want a smoke?"

He pulled a pack of Pall Mall from his jacket pocket.

I said, "We've known each other now for, what, fifteen years?"

"Give or take."

"And in all that time have you ever seen me smoke?"

"I keep offering, you keep declining. Figure one of these days you'll take one just to shut me up."

"If that's all it took, I would have done that years ago."

He chuckled as he lit his cigarette, blew a stream of smoke into the air.

I said, "Those things are going to kill you one of these days."

"Old age is going to kill me. These—"

He held up the cigarette and squinted at it like it was an alien object.

"—these are helping accelerate the process."

A silence fell between us then. Zelda lay on the patio floor beside us. The sky was gray and low and expansive. Occasional traffic could be heard out on the highway, as Darrell's house sat right behind the General Store.

Darrell struggled to stand up, limped to the grill, and flipped the steaks. He lowered himself down beside me with a grunt.

"Gonna snow tonight."

Sometimes it was difficult to know if Darrel liked reiterating himself or if he really didn't remember recent conversations. It hadn't always been that way, just something in the past couple years. More than once I'd thought about mentioning it to him, but I knew he would only wave it off, tell me to mind my own goddamn business.

"How many inches?"

"The weatherman is calling for a foot, but I'm thinking it'll be less. Maybe … eight inches."

If I were a betting man, I would have placed all my money on Darrell. For as long as I'd known him, he was never wrong about the weather. And it was not like he checked the forecast first; he only checked it after to confirm what he already knew. Felt it in his bones, was the way he put it to me once, and I didn't doubt it. If Darrell said we were getting eight inches tonight, we were getting eight inches.

"On second thought, make that ten inches. And believe me—"

He threw a wink in my direction.

"—I know what ten inches looks like."

We both laughed, hearty chuckles, because that was what old men like us did. But Darrell's laughter didn't sound good.

It hadn't for a while now. There was something deep inside that sounded congested.

"You should quit smoking."

He took one last drag, smashed the butt out in the ashtray on the table.

"And you should mind your own goddamn business. You're not my doctor."

"No, of course I'm not your doctor. I'm your brother."

He chuckled again.

"That's right—my brother from another mother."

I grinned.

"That's what the kids say. Or at least that's what you tell me the kids say."

It was true. For years now Darrell had been making the joke, and I had been going along with it, because while we may not be actual brothers, we were very close friends. Probably the only friend either of us had.

Slowly, like paint drying, Darrell's smile fell off his face. He stared off into the distance.

I said, "What's wrong?"

He blinked, frowned at me.

"Wrong? Nothing's wrong."

He got up again and flipped the steaks, lowered himself back down with a grunt. He was quiet for another several seconds, then let out a heavy sigh.

"Goddamned kids."

"Don't let them get to you."

"When we were their ages, we were in the middle of Vietnam. Shooting at Charlie. Killing Charlie. Those sons of bitches wouldn't know the first thing to do in a war."

I didn't say anything. When Darrell got like this, it was best to let him tire himself out.

"I heard what that little bastard said to you."

He shook his head, his face twisted in disgust.

"Fucking asshole."

"It's not the first time I've been called a nigger, and it probably won't be the last."

"I can't even remember the last time someone called me a nigger. In fact, they didn't even call me a nigger. They called me a half nigger, and I'm not sure if that was meant to be more insulting or less insulting."

He shook his head again.

"I'll tell you, nothing much has changed since we were kids. You're up on the hill without a TV or radio, you don't know how racist people have gotten. They said the Civil Rights Movement was going to end racism. Shit, it was just an intermission."

Darrell fell silent for a moment, brooding.

"Every night I go to bed, I worry about Phil and Thomas. That I'll wake up the next morning and find out one of my grandsons has been shot by a cop. Or that there was a shooting at their school. That shit happens all the time now. I know my son's terrified about it too. He's a good boy. I raised him right. I never knew my old man, so I always wanted to make sure I was a good father to my son, and because of it my son turned out okay. Not a complete fuck up like his old man."

Darrell chuckled, but it was a hollow chuckle as he stared off into space. He was quiet for another moment before he spoke again.

"Two percent."

"What's two percent?"

"That's how much the processing fee is for credit cards. At least the last time I checked, a couple years ago. Then there's the setup fee, the monthly fee ..."

He shook his head.

"If I wasn't so goddamned cheap, maybe those punks

wouldn't have acted like they did. It's all about the bottom line, isn't it? So goddamned cheap of me."

"Darrell, don't."

"Plus—and here's where I'm going to sound really paranoid to you, I know—there's the whole problem of the government knowing every single goddamned thing I do at my store. That's why they put those credit card machines in stores in the first place, you know, so they can track everyone in the country. Know what you buy. Know where you shop. It's Big Brother, and it's just getting worse. Hell, some days I think you have it all figured out."

"How so?"

"Living off the grid like you do. Up there in your Fortress of Solitude."

He smiled when he said this, then started up another coughing fit. This one went on longer than usual, and when I placed a hand on his back, he waved me off.

"I'm fine, I'm fine. Just need another cigarette, is all."

Back on his feet, he flipped the steaks but didn't sit back down. He looked at me again.

"But I don't think I could actually go through with it. Living all by myself. No TV, no radio, no electricity, no phone. You don't even wear a goddamned watch. And sure, you got Zelda to keep you company—"

And here the dog's ears perked up at the mention of her name.

"—but what else do you got? Nothing. What's that saying, no man is an island? Not you, my friend. You are your own island. Your own goddamned continent. And sometimes it makes me so jealous it pisses me off."

"Do you want to switch?"

He let loose another laugh.

"And have you run the store? No offense, but I think Zelda

would be better suited. You're too much of a nice guy, you'd give everything away."

I wasn't sure why he said this. The truth was Darrell didn't know much about me. We were friends, yes, but that was about the extent of it. He knew I was from New York, but he didn't know what line of work I had been in. When he asked once, I told him it was so boring it wasn't even worth discussing. He hadn't brought it up since. He knew about my family, my children, and he'd ask every once in a while how they were doing, but he knew I didn't talk to them anymore, that I never saw them. It wasn't like I ever left my Fortress of Solitude, as Darrell liked to call it, except for once a month when I traveled down to Harper for supplies, or to take a wounded animal to the veterinarian clinic in Durango.

"It's not good being by yourself."

The good humor was gone from Darrell's voice. He stared into that distance again.

"And it's not just the social aspect, either. That's nice, of course, but I'm talking about ... well, what happens when you die? Have you thought of that? Say something were to happen to you up there on the hill, you have a heart attack or slip and fall and break your neck, who would know? Certainly not your family. Not right away. And just how long should I wait until you don't make your regular visits before I begin to worry? And then what about *Zelda*, for Christ's sake? Would she even know the first thing to do if something were to happen to you?"

"Darrell."

He blinked, frowned at me again.

"Hmm?"

"Why don't you flip the steaks?"

He hobbled over to the grill, and as he did, I glanced down at Zelda. She was looking up at me. She had no idea what it was we were talking about, but I sensed worry in her eyes, maybe asking the same thing. What would happen to her if something were to happen to me? Or, on the flip side, what would happen to me if something were to happen to her? Besides Darrell, she was my only friend in the world, and the sad, hard truth was that some day she would die, just like Darrell would die, and it would just be me by myself. Living all alone on the hill. My Fortress of Solitude.

"I think these are almost ready."

Darrell flipped the steaks one last time.

"Nice and juicy, just way you like it. Isn't that right, Zelda?"

She barked, her tongue now lolling from the side of her mouth, her tail thumping the wooden planks of the patio.

Darrell grabbed the oversized plate from the table, forked the steaks on top, then turned around, holding the plate high above his head like a sacrifice.

"Let's eat!"

6

By the time we arrived back to the cabin, it was nearly ten o'clock. The sky was overcast, but there was no snow yet. Ten inches, Darrell said. Maybe. Or maybe in his old age Darrell was finally starting to slip.

Before we had left, Darrell gave me a box of books. It was a heavy box, nearly twenty hardcovers, some paperbacks, and I huffed it up the steps to the cabin. Darrell made weekly trips to a used bookstore in Grand Junction. He was as voracious a reader as I was. When he finished the books, he passed them on to me. When I finished the books, I passed them back, and he returned them to the bookstore, where someone else would eventually pick them up. A book's circle of life.

There was some firewood inside by the stove, but not nearly as much as I would have liked. Today was supposed to be wood chopping day. That had been disrupted by our rabid furry friend. I wondered what had happened to him. Maybe next week Zelda and I would head back to Durango, see if Dr. Snyder had had any luck.

Zelda found her stuffed dinosaur—a bright green T-Rex— and took it over to the giant pillow in the corner. She lowered herself down and set the dinosaur beside her. It wasn't a chew toy. Or no—it *was* a chew toy, but Zelda never chewed it. It was her pet, in a way. Her puppy. She loved it. When I first got her, I picked it up not really sure why I had done so. It certainly wasn't a normal dog toy. But she had taken to it immediately. Ten years later, she didn't fall asleep without it.

I lit two of the kerosene lanterns and positioned them around the cabin to give me enough light. Darrell thought I lived up here with no electricity at all, and he was partly right. A decade ago I had gotten a generator, just in case. I sometimes used it when the temperature dropped and the stove wasn't enough. That's when I'd start the generator and it would roar to life and power a small space heater. But besides that, I usually used kerosene lanterns at night to read.

I sorted through the books. Most of it was commercial fiction, but there were some literary fiction and non-fiction too. I'd never been much of a reader growing up. Even after the war I hardly read. But after I came out here and decided I wanted nothing to do with TV or radio, there wasn't much else to do but read. Because I hadn't read much growing up, I was a slow reader at first. But the more I read, the easier it became. Soon it wasn't taking me a week to finish a book. Soon I was reading a book every day.

Zelda's namesake came because of books. When I first got her, I was going through an F. Scott Fitzgerald phase. Fitzgerald didn't publish much, but I was taking my time with his books, savoring the characters and scenes and places. I was reading *This Side of Paradise*, and I'm not sure why, but Fitzgerald's wife's name stuck with me.

I started a fire in the stove, adding three pieces of wood like usual. Zelda watched me from her spot across the room. She knew the bedtime routine. Start a fire, read a book. We lived a simple life.

I picked up one of the hardcovers—*Wild Child* by T. C. Boyle—and sat down in the chair by the kerosene lamp. It was a book of short stories, apparently, which was perfect for reading before bed. I opened to the first page but then closed the book. I looked over at Zelda, who was still watching me. She was waiting for me to go to bed first. Sometimes she'd fall asleep first, but that was only when she was exhausted. I would tell her it was okay, she could fall asleep now, but that would only encourage her tail to start wagging. She would think I wanted to talk to her, maybe play with her, though in truth we didn't play like we used to. I wondered if she missed it. I wondered if she yearned for those days when I would throw a ball or Frisbee and she would take off running. Maybe we'd do that tomorrow if it didn't snow. Even if it did snow, maybe we'd do it anyway. Zelda liked the snow, though I couldn't imagine she could run fast in ten inches of powder like she had years ago.

Darrell's words kept haunting me. Of course the knowledge that I'd someday die had entered in my mind more than once. How could it not? That was why I was here, why I'd come to this hill and this cabin. I'd come here to die. Taking my life was never an option. It would go against everything I'd always believed in. But now, in a way, wasn't living by myself in the middle of nowhere with nearly no communication with the outside world a form of suicide?

The reason I left my family was because I wanted to die. And I knew if I saw my grandchildren, listened to their jokes, played games with them, my will to live would grow stronger. I would want to live as long as I could, and if I lived longer than I was supposed to, it would start to raise too many questions among my children's friends. All of them wondering why their own parents were growing old and dying while their friend's father grew old but did not die.

That was why my own father had eventually taken off and disappeared. So questions like that weren't asked.

Currently I was sixty-five years old. I looked to be about fifty. Well, when my hair wasn't long and shaggy and my beard was trimmed. When I looked more presentable. But who cared about such things when they lived by themselves in the middle of nowhere? The truth was I was just waiting to die. But not yet. I couldn't do that to Zelda. I couldn't leave her alone like that. So now I was waiting for her to die. It sounded terrible, but wasn't that just how life is, everyone waiting for everyone else to die?

I set the book aside, took a low, heavy breath as I stood up from the chair.

"Ready for bed, girl?"

Zelda's tail thumped the pillow.

I grabbed one of the thick blankets and wrapped it around her, kissed the top of her head. She licked my chin. I stood back up and walked over to my bed.

"Sweet dreams."

I extinguished the lanterns.

7

n my dreams, I can fly.

I levitate off the ground like it's nothing out of the ordinary. I rise up past the buildings into the sky, past the clouds, toward the stars.

I can regulate my own speed. I can stop on a dime. I can hover in the air.

In my dreams, I'm back in New York City. Zooming between skyscrapers. People on the sidewalks crane their necks to see me. They point. They shout. They cheer.

I don't know why it is I have these dreams. Maybe it's my subconscious wanting to fly. I could never fly in my other life. I could run extremely fast. I could jump from one building to another, if they weren't spaced too widely apart. I could survive being shot and stabbed. But flying? It was never possible. And yet, still, sometimes in my dreams I will fly.

There is always a freedom to the act. The knowledge that nothing—not even gravity—can control me. That in the end the only thing that controls me is myself.

In the dreams, I never stop crime. I never stop the bad guys. I never save the damsel in distress. That's all for the movies and comic books. The eternal struggle of good versus evil. In reality, it's much more indistinct. Evil exists, just like good, but they've come to an understanding. A perfect yin and yang.

And yet, as I fly through my dream, I can hear a growling. This is something new. It's nighttime and the sky is clear and the moon is bright, reflecting off the millions of glass windows. I soar through the air, searching for the source of that low growling. Whatever it is, the sound signals danger. Maybe I will finally fight the bad guys after all. Maybe in my dream I will find my nemesis, my archenemy, my would-be destroyer.

Maybe I will just stand there and let him kill me, put me out of my misery.

But the growling doesn't grow louder, no matter how far or how fast I fly. It's almost like it doesn't exist. Like it's not part of the dream. Like ...

I opened my eyes.

The cabin was dark. There was still a fire going inside the stove, though it was beginning to taper off. The windows had no curtains and some moonlight from outside filtered in. It was hardly anything at all because the sky was overcast. Even in the dark, through the windows, I could see it was snowing. Some of it had begun to stick to the glass.

Zelda stood by the door, her hackles up, growling.

I pushed the covers off, placed my bare feet on the floor. The cabin had little insulation, and the wooden boards were freezing.

"Zelda."

She paused her growling, glanced back at me, then turned her attention back to the door. The growl started again.

I rose from the bed and crossed the room to stand by her. She couldn't see through the window at her level of sight, but I could. A fine powder had coated the world. Everything was white. Nothing was outside. No animals. Not even any tracks.

"What's wrong?"

She looked at me again, and in the dark I saw the fear in her eyes. Whatever was out there—or whatever she believed was out there—scared her.

She began growling again. I placed my hand on her back, meaning to comfort her, to stop her. But she kept growling. Her entire body vibrated with the sound.

"Stop it. There's nothing there."

She looked at me again, and in that instant I got the sense that she knew much more than me. And maybe she did. Animals have certain sensitivities that humans don't. My own senses had once been heightened more so than anyone else's, but there were still things I would miss. Things that animals like Zelda would not.

"Is something out there?"

The low growling stopped. Zelda looked up at me again. She didn't look away. It was all I needed to confirm she wanted me to open the door.

I debated it for several long seconds. We were five miles from the nearest road. Nobody ever came up here. In all the time I'd been on the hill, not even a hiker had stumbled across the cabin. There was no reason why anyone would be out there now. And besides, what time was it? I had no alarm clock on my bedside table. During the day, I judged time by the sun's position in the sky. My internal clock said it was the middle of the night. Maybe three, four o'clock.

Telling myself to ignore it, to go back to bed, let Zelda continue growling at the door all night until she wore herself out, I reached out and placed my hand on the doorknob. It was freezing cold, just like the floor. I waited a beat, suddenly feeling a strange sense of dread, and without thinking, I turned the knob and opened the door.

It was only a couple of inches, no more than that, but it was all Zelda needed. She nosed the door open even farther and pushed through. Took off down the steps into the front yard, running faster than I had ever seen her run.

"Zelda, stop!"

Always the obedient dog, she stopped at once, skidding in the snow. I was outside on the porch now, my feet freezing. About six inches of snow were stacked on the railing.

Zelda glanced back at me. Even from the distance of maybe fifty yards, I saw the same fear in her eyes. I knew what she was planning to do even before she did it, but there was nothing I could do to stop her. Suddenly she ran away, kicking up puffs of snow, and disappeared into the trees.

8

"Zelda, come back!"

She didn't.

I stood in the cold waiting. Whatever was out there, she'd get bored of it and come back soon enough. She'd scratch at the door, and maybe it would wake me up and I'd let her in. If not, she'd have to sleep on the porch. Oh, who was I kidding? I'd keep the door open just a crack so she could nose it open and curl up by the fire.

The snow continued to fall, big fluffy flakes. The world was completely silent. As if God was holding his breath.

I listened closely. I should have heard Zelda off in the distance, through the trees, her paws racing the light snow, but there was nothing. Total silence.

I took another step forward and surveyed the area. I looked out at the trees. The lighting wasn't good, and I could see nothing more than shadows.

The temptation to call Zelda's name again was strong, but I tamped it down. What I needed to be right now was quiet. And still. I couldn't move an inch.

But I needed to. I had no choice. I couldn't keep standing

out here. Pretty soon my feet would go numb. And so in one fluid motion I turned and stepped inside and closed the door. It all took less than a second. But I didn't keep the door open a crack. Instead, I locked it.

I moved through the cabin as quietly as possible. There were places on the floor that would sigh with pressure. I made sure to overstep those places.

I went to the dresser first. I opened the bottom drawer, slowly and quietly, and dug through the pants and shirts and underwear to the pistol hidden beneath.

Generally people keep their guns in lockboxes or safes. This is smart because most people live with other people, what are probably loved ones. There is always the fear a child will stumble across the gun. You don't have that problem when you live by yourself. And if you live with a dog as your only companion, it's a safe bet the dog isn't going to stumble across the gun and pull the trigger by accident.

I'd kept the gun empty all this time. I had, however, loaded the magazine. It was a Smith & Wesson 5946, the weapon of choice before I retired from the police force. When I left, I took the service weapon with me. I hadn't used it in years. It hadn't been cleaned. It hadn't been oiled. For all I knew, it wouldn't even shoot. Even if it did shoot, would I still have my marksman's eye? Because of my heightened senses, I was always able to calculate the exact distance to my target and aim appropriately. But it had been over twenty years, and there was a very good chance I had become rusty.

Despite all those concerns, I silently inserted the magazine and pulled back the slide.

I kept the gun in my right hand as I moved to the chair in

the corner. I sat and placed the gun on the floor and quickly pulled on thick socks. Next was a pair of jeans, the same trousers I'd worn that day. Finally, I threw on a sweatshirt. I considered putting on my boots, but they'd make noise on the floor, no matter how quietly I walked across the wooden boards.

Maybe I was being paranoid. Maybe it was nothing. But Zelda had never growled like that before. She had never taken off into the night. She had never disobeyed me. And when I was standing on the porch, watching the snow, listening to the silence, I had felt something there in the night. Whatever it was, I wanted to be prepared when it came.

It was another twenty minutes before I heard it.

A soft step in the snow outside, barely even audible over the wood crackling in the stove and my heart beating in my ears.

It wasn't Zelda. Wherever she had gone, I had no clue, but it wasn't her making the sound outside.

Another step in the snow.

I closed my eyes. Did everything I could to heighten my senses. When I was younger, it would happen automatically. Now I had to will it to happen, and even then it wasn't one hundred percent.

Another step.

Another step.

Whoever was outside, there was more than one person. They were walking slowly, trying to make as little noise as possible. If I were asleep, I wouldn't hear a thing. But I wasn't asleep. I was sitting in this chair, the Smith & Wesson in my hand aimed at the door.

I thought about the gun, how it hadn't been used or cleaned in years. Did I want to chance it backfiring? No, I didn't. Not when I wasn't sure what I was dealing with. Not when I wasn't sure *who* I was dealing with. If whoever was out there was a lost hiker, they wouldn't be slowly approaching the cabin like this. I could have easily glanced out a window, but I didn't want to risk exposing myself.

I wished Zelda were here. She would be growling, no doubt, and there was a chance I wouldn't be able to control her if push came to shove, but I didn't like to think what had become of her. She should have returned by now. She could be anywhere. She could be dead.

My eyes had adjusted to the dark within a minute of waking. My gaze skipped now around the interior of the cabin, searching for anything else I could use as a weapon. It took two circuits before landing on the axe leaning against the wall, right where I had placed it earlier today.

I leaned forward in the chair and gently stuffed the gun in the back waistband of my trousers.

I stood, just as quietly, and crossed the room, making sure to step over the loose wooden boards. I stayed low. The urge to rise up, enough to see out the windows, was strong, but I kept moving forward until I'd reached the other side of the cabin.

I took the handle of the axe in my hand, squeezed it tight.

9

I t was another five minutes until someone placed their weight on the first porch step.

It creaked, and suddenly there was silence. The rest of the steps stopped at once.

Another minute passed in silence. A second minute. A third.

Then the person outside continued up the porch steps. There were only three of them. Neither step creaked like the first, but I could still feel the slight differential in weight. An average person wouldn't have felt the slight change in pressure, but I wasn't an average person. That was why I was crouched here now, the axe gripped in both hands.

Soon a second person had reached the top of the steps. They were on the porch now. There was just enough moonlight outside to see their shadows.

Outside, on the other side of the cabin, others were quietly stepping through the snow. Two others, maybe more. Four in total at least.

The doorknob began to turn, slow and silent, but it wouldn't make any difference. The door was locked from the inside. When the person outside realized the door would not open, the doorknob stopped moving. There was another moment or two of heavy silence, and then suddenly the door was kicked open, shards of wood flying everywhere.

Because I knew there were two of them on the porch, I waited for the first one to enter the cabin before making my move.

He was dressed in black tactical gear and wore night vision goggles. He carried a rifle, its barrel immediately sweeping the entire room as he took another step inside.

The second man entered after him, and that was when I rose up, swinging the axe back over my shoulder like a baseball bat and bringing it forward so the blade dug into the second man's chest.

The first man spun fast. There was a flashlight on the table right beside the door. I grabbed it and flicked it on and aimed the beam at his face. He turned his head away, his finger impulsively squeezing the rifle's trigger. It wasn't a bullet that exited the barrel, but a large dart that stuck into the wall. A tranquilizer dart.

I yanked the axe out of the second man, started toward the first man, when I remembered the others outside. I wouldn't be able to take them all out with the axe. In my younger days, maybe, but not today.

Still, I couldn't stay in here any longer. I swung the axe again, this time throwing it at the first man. It arced end over end through the air until its blade slammed into the man's face. As he fell, I turned and started running through the door, just as two men outside opened fire.

I dove headfirst, somersaulting over the porch steps, landing hard on my back. I managed to slip the gun out from my waistband, aimed it at the closest man, pulled the trigger.

Dry click—jammed.

The men opened fire at me again. The ground spit up puffs of snow. I rolled away, scrambled to my feet, but one of the men shot me in my shoulder. I spun away, hit the ground again. There wasn't much pain, but it was clear the bullet got me good. In fact, judging by the level of pain, the bullet was still inside. Already I could feel the itching sensation as my body started to heal itself. I tried to sit up, but both men were standing over me, their rifles aimed at my face.

Neither one spoke. Both wore night vision goggles so I couldn't see their faces.

I said, "You're trespassing."

The one man tilted his head toward the other man.

"I'm going to check on Sam and Tyler."

The other man shook his head.

"They're dead."

"I still need to check. Keep him covered."

The man started away. He didn't walk quietly as before. The snow kept falling around us, as indifferent as the wind. I stared up the man with night vision goggles holding a semiautomatic rifle on me.

"Who are you?"

He didn't answer.

"Why are you doing this?"

Nothing.

I wasn't surprised. I hadn't been expecting an answer. The only reason I'd asked in the first place was to distract him. Because I could hear more steps through the snow. Only it wasn't from a human, and it wasn't coming slowly. It was from four legs, and it was coming fast.

The man finally spoke.

"You're bleeding."

I said, "So are you."

Because the night vision goggles covered his eyes, I could

only see the bottom of his face. His mouth downturned into a frown.

"No, I'm not."

"Give it a moment."

A moment was all Zelda needed. She was moving just as fast as she did earlier when she had taken off into the trees. Now she came right at the man, growling, and launched herself at him.

The angle was from the side, and it knocked him over. Zelda immediately went for his throat. It was such a savage, animalistic act, so unlike her. Except I realized it wasn't. This was what she'd done in the first year of her life before she was rescued and taken to the kennel. Not only did the men beat her, but they'd also had her fight other dogs. And that was why she lasted as long as she did. Even as a puppy, she was vicious.

The man screamed. He tried pushing Zelda away, but that only enraged her more. He swung his fists, flailing them, and one connected with Zelda's head. It stopped her only for an instant, but it was enough time for the man to bring the rifle up and fire off a round.

By then I was back on my feet, charging toward the man. I was distantly aware of Zelda crying out. I was distantly aware of the man up in the cabin running out onto the porch. But all of it was background. The only thing I needed to focus on right then was the man in front of me, swinging his rifle in my direction.

And just like that, I suddenly felt like I did in my prime when I was on the top of my game. Even in the lack of light, even with the snow falling around us, I could see every tiny movement. Every movement signals another movement, which signals another movement, so much so that I knew what this man was going to do before he did it. That was how I was able to duck to the left as he fired, then duck to the right as he fired again, both bullets missing me by mere centimeters, and then my feet were no longer on the ground as I launched myself at the man.

We both hit the ground at the same time. He'd lost his rifle in the scuffle. It lay only feet away. I reached for it, but the man under me grabbed my throat with his gloved hand. I didn't have time to waste, so I did the only thing I could right then: I made a fist and drove it into his face, right in the middle of his forehead, with enough force that it cracked his brain. His gloved hand fell away from my throat. I rolled to the side, grabbing the rifle and coming up into a kneeling shooter's stance. I aimed up at the cabin and fired off three rounds. The man on the porch stood motionless for a moment, stunned, then raised his own weapon. None of my bullets had hit him. I blinked, shook my head as if to clear it, and then aimed again right as the man aimed back at me. I squeezed the trigger, placing a round in the man's throat. As he stumbled, then fell to his knees, I fired two more rounds into his head.

Behind me, Zelda whimpered.

I was back on my feet in an instant. Running over to Zelda, crouching down beside her. Despite the darkness, I could see she had been shot in the stomach. The blood kept coming. She lay on her side, breathing short, shallow breaths.

"It's okay, girl. It's okay."

I placed my hand on her head, wanting to comfort her, wanting to take away her pain. But there was nothing I could do. Tears stung my eyes. I blinked them away, telling her that it was okay, that she would be okay, while at the same time I knew it was all a lie.

That was when I heard the distant roar of an engine, coming fast up the drive.

10

The vehicle came without lights. Based on the four dead men in tactical gear, I had to assume the driver —and whoever else was inside—wore night vision goggles. I considered grabbing the goggles off one of the men, but that would take too much time. The vehicle would be here any second.

Grabbing the rifle, I stood and turned toward the drive. The pickup was parked directly ahead of me, and I angled to the side for a better view. Flakes of snow swirled around me. The SUV's engine—because that's what it had to be, a four-wheel drive SUV coming this fast up the drive in this snow—roared angrily. In another couple seconds, the SUV would appear and I would have perfect aim at the driver. One bullet would be all it took. One simple squeeze of the trigger and he'd be dead.

Behind me, Zelda whimpered again, her quiet and desperate pleas just barely heard under the SUV's approaching engine, and as the SUV appeared in the dark, I began walking forward, slowly, taking careful aim. I fired at the windshield, right where the driver would be, and I fired at the two front tires, and I fired at the grill before firing at the windshield again. I exhausted the entire magazine. And still the SUV pushed forward, its engine growling even louder though it was suddenly clear the driver was no longer in control of the vehicle. I imagined the driver dead, a bullet through his head, his foot heavy on the gas pedal. The SUV barreled forward, not slowing, swerving not toward me but toward the pickup truck.

The SUV was going maybe fifty miles per hour when it smashed into the pickup truck. Glass in both vehicles shattered. Despite the fact there was no more room for the SUV to go any farther, its engine continued to growl.

I flung open the passenger side door. The passenger—still stunned by the impact, his reflexes slow—fired his weapon at my head. I jerked my head to the side, allowing the bullet to pass by me, and I reached up into the SUV—noting the driver was dead—and grabbed the passenger by his neck and threw him from the vehicle.

He hit the ground, but his grip on the gun was solid. He turned over and attempted to let off another round, but I kicked the gun to the side just as it went off, sending the bullet into the air. I bent and twisted the gun out of his hand and then twisted his hand farther back, snapping the bone. The man cried out in pain. I leaned down and with my other hand took hold of his throat.

"Who are you?"

The man didn't answer.

"Who do you work for?"

Again no answer. I realized a second later I was squeezing his windpipe. Another ounce of pressure and I could snap it altogether. I loosened my grip just enough to let him suck in a gulp of air, and asked my question again.

"Who do you work for?"

The man still didn't answer. I tore off his night vision

goggles, but his face wasn't familiar. He glared up at me, his lips pressed together in a tight line. He was the last one still alive. I didn't think there would be any others coming. I could take my time with him. I could break every bone in his hand, in his arm, in his entire body, until he answered all my questions. But part of me didn't think he would answer my questions. Whoever this man was, he was a professional. All of these men were professionals. None of them would have given me answers, even under extreme duress. No sense keeping him alive, I decided, and applied that extra pressure and crushed his windpipe.

I stood back up, letting him gasp out his last couple breaths. I returned to where Zelda lay on her side. She was still alive, but barely. I picked her up as gently as I could, though this caused her extreme discomfort, so much so she growled at me. She didn't mean it, though. I knew she didn't. It was simply instinctual.

I whispered to her again as I carried her back toward the cabin.

"It's okay."

I stepped over the body on the porch, then the bodies just inside the cabin entrance, and I took her over to her pillow in the corner. I placed her down on the pillow and laid one of the blankets on top of her and set the stuffed T-Rex beside her, and I sat with her, my hand on her head, petting her gently, while Zelda continued her short, shallow breaths, while the wood continued to pop and crackle in the stove, while outside the snow continued to spit those fat, fluffy flakes.

"It's okay, girl."

Fighting back the tremor in my voice, more tears stinging my eyes.

"Everything will be okay."

11

I didn't bother knocking. It was after four a.m. and knocking would probably go unnoticed. So I let myself in the back—I had to break the window to do this, reach inside and unlock the door—and then sat down at the kitchen table. I didn't move for several minutes. I let my heart rate slow. I let my breathing become calm. Finally, I got up and grabbed a glass from the cabinet and poured myself some water. It was then I heard the creak on the stairs as Darrell made his way downstairs.

"What the hell?"

He stood in the doorway in his robe, an old hunting rifle in his hands.

"I thought you were an intruder."

I didn't respond to this. In many ways, I was an intruder. I finished off the glass and filled it again and returned to my seat.

Darrell squinted at me in the dark.

"What's that at your feet?"

"A duffel bag."

"What's in the duffel bag?"

"Stuff."

"Don't be a smart-ass."

He set the rifle aside and went to flick the switch for the lights.

I said, "Don't."

"Why not?"

"It's best the light stays off."

He wandered deeper into the kitchen. He didn't have his cane and had to hold onto the counter for support. When he was close enough, he squinted again.

"What's that on your clothes?"

"Blood."

He didn't even blink.

"Your blood?"

"Some of it."

He didn't question this and lowered himself down on one of the chairs across from me.

"What happened?"

"I need a favor."

"I'm listening."

"Actually, I need a couple of favors."

"I'm still listening."

"I need to take a shower. I need to shave. And I need some clothes."

"Is that it?"

"For now."

"I think I can allow that. Now are you going to tell me just what the hell is going on?"

"It's probably best you don't know."

"Like hell it is."

He paused, sniffing the air.

"Why do you smell like smoke?"

I smelled like smoke because I'd stood close enough to the cabin while it was going up in flames. Despite the snow, I wanted to make sure the fire was controlled and didn't spread into the trees. I'd left the men's bodies where they were in the snow. Zelda I had buried in the front yard.

"I think I'd like to take that shower now."

"Sure. I'll make sure to put chocolate on your pillow while you're at it."

Despite everything that had happened tonight, I found myself smiling.

"Thanks, Darrell."

"No problem. Though I would like to know what the hell is going on."

And just how was I supposed to explain it to him? My friend—my only friend in the world—wanted to know what had happened, and just what was I supposed to say?

"Okay, I'll tell you."

This seemed to surprise him.

"Really?"

"Yes, but I also need another favor."

"What's that?"

"I need your sharpest steak knife."

I glanced at the stack of dishes in the sink.

"Preferably one that's clean."

The bathroom light was stark and bright. I pulled off the bloodstained sweatshirt.

Darrell said, "You brought me up here for a striptease?"

I held out my hand for the knife. He placed it in my palm, handle facing toward me. Under normal circumstances, I would disinfect the blade, but it wasn't like it would matter. Not for me. The blade could be covered in a dozen different diseases and none of them would affect me.

Without a word, I stuck the blade in my shoulder. Darrell cried out in surprise. I pushed the blade in deeper and twisted it until I could feel it connect with the bullet. Very gently I dug the bullet out with the tip of the blade until it was close enough to the surface. I set the knife aside, pinched the bullet out with two fingers, and dropped it in the sink. The clatter of the round on the porcelain in the silent house was just as loud as a gunshot.

Darrell leaned forward, looked into the sink, then incredulously looked at me.

"Someone shot you?"

"Many someones."

"Why?"

"That's what I wanted to show you."

"Show me what? Christ, aren't you going to do anything about that? You're bleeding!"

It was such an obvious statement, but Darrell looked at me in disbelief. I wasn't even flinching in pain. Blood trickled down my chest and side, but it wasn't much. By now the bleeding had stopped. The itching was in full force as the skin began to stitch itself back together.

I ran the water in the sink, soaked a washcloth, and wiped the blood away. Where I had sliced my skin moments ago, there was only a slight scar.

The incredulous expression hadn't left Darrell's face.

"What ... how ... I don't understand."

"In another couple minutes the scar will be completely gone."

Darrell shook his head slowly, at a loss for words.

"I'm going to tell you the basics. I can't tell you the whole story because we don't have time, and quite honestly, I don't think you'd believe me anyway."

He swallowed, his eyes still wide.

"I think at this point I'm apt to believe just about anything."

"Some men came up to the cabin tonight. They were professionals. The lead guy's rifle had a tranquilizer dart loaded. I think they meant to abduct me, and when that failed, they meant to kill me."

"What men?"

"I'm not sure. I searched each of them, but none had any identification on them. There wasn't even anything in their vehicles."

Another SUV had been parked a mile down the drive, cold and empty.

Darrell frowned.

"Speaking of which, how did you get here anyway? I didn't see your truck outside."

"I got here on foot."

"On *foot*? It's practically fifteen miles!"

He paused again as something occurred to him.

"Where's Zelda?"

I only shook my head.

He cursed, sighed, bit his lower lip.

"I feel like there's something you're leaving out."

"There are a lot of things I'm leaving out. The main thing is I need to take a shower, and while I do, I want you to pack."

"Pack?"

"Pack as much as you can. You need to disappear."

"I can't do that. Who will run the store?"

"Darrell, your life is in danger."

"How so?"

"You're a known associate of mine."

"What the hell is that supposed to mean?"

"I have no idea how these men found me, but somehow they did. And if they found me, they probably knew I was friends with you. And if they knew that, the people who sent them know it too."

"People that sent them?"

He shook his head as if to clear it.

"You're not making any sense."

"I don't want you to die. Does that make enough sense for you?"

He didn't answer right away. He just stared back at me. I was sorry to do this to him, but I didn't have any choice. I cared about him too much to let him become collateral damage. Zelda had been more than enough.

Finally he nodded.

"Okay, I'll start packing. I have no idea where to go, though. Maybe I'll—"

"Don't say it. I don't want to know. Don't tell anyone where you're going. Just go."

He nodded again.

"I'm hoping that's your last favor."

"There's only a few more."

"Good God, what more can you ask of me?"

I looked at myself in the mirror. The shaggy hair, the unkempt beard. Like Dr. Snyder had said, I looked like a mountain man.

"Can I borrow your razor?"

12

When I stepped out of the shower, some clothing was stacked on the floor outside the bathroom. Underwear, undershirt, trousers, sweatshirt, socks. Despite the fact Darrell was a couple inches shorter than me, the clothes fit fine.

I found Darrell downstairs in the kitchen, sitting at the table. He'd brewed a pot of coffee and sipped from a mug.

"Well, don't you clean up nice."

His good-natured tone quickly turned solemn.

"I've been thinking about it, and I'm not going to leave."

"It's not up for discussion."

"I very well think it is. I have a business to run. The people of this town depend on me."

The people of this town did not depend on Darrell, but I didn't need to tell him this. He could close the store tomorrow and everybody would get along just fine. I suspected he knew this but was too bull-headed to accept the truth. As an old man, he didn't have much left in his life, and what little he did have—the general store—he intended to hold on to for as long as he could.

"You understand the risk?"

He didn't answer. Didn't even meet my eyes.

"If you stay, there's a chance you might die."

"And if I leave, there's a chance I might die too. I might end up in a car crash somewhere. You remember those punk ass kids from yesterday? The road's full of them punks nowadays. You can't very well go more than a mile without encountering them. They don't give a shit. They'll run you right off the road."

It was at that moment something occurred to me. In all the time I'd known Darrell—fifteen plus years—he'd never once gone more than twenty miles outside of Harper. His family might visit him on those very rare occasions, but he never once left to visit them. It reminded me of what Dr. Snyder said when I first adopted Zelda. How some animals become so accustomed to their cages they're terrified to leave. That was what had become of Darrell. His entire life was in Harper, and he wasn't going to leave it even if it meant he might die.

"I don't want to be responsible for your death."

He shook his head, waved a dismissive hand.

"You're being too overdramatic."

"Have you already forgotten about the men I told you about?"

"Of course not. I haven't forgotten what I saw earlier, either. And I've been thinking about that."

He swallowed.

"Are you … an alien?"

I couldn't tell if he was serious. His face was a blank slate. He stared at me, waiting for my answer. I wasn't sure what to tell him. Initially, I wanted to tell him the truth—tell him everything—but I wasn't sure just how he'd take it. Besides, I'd already spent more than enough time here. I needed to get going.

Before I could answer, Darrell's face cracked and he burst

out laughing. He even went so far as to slap the table with the palm of his hand.

"I'm just messing with you."

Though there was something in his eyes that said he wasn't, that said from now until the day he died he would never fully trust me.

"I'd love to know more, but something tells me you ain't gonna say a word."

"I could."

"You could, sure, but you won't."

"It's for your protection."

"Is it?"

He squinted at me now.

"Or is it for your protection?"

Good question.

I said, "You don't have a computer, do you?"

"Of course I don't. What—I want another thing for the government to spy on me?"

He paused.

"Why do you need a computer?"

"I need to check the Internet."

"For what?"

I paused a beat, still not sure what all I wanted to tell him. In the end, it didn't matter. He shifted in his seat, took another sip of coffee, and waved his hand again.

"You want to use a computer, you should go to the library. Or the mall. Or, hell, Walmart's open twenty-four-seven and will have computers."

"I also need your car."

He squinted at me again.

"Where are you going?"

"It's best if you don't know. But I need transportation."

"What happened to your truck?"

"It's ... currently out of commission."

"And you think my truck will get you to where you want to go?"

Darrell drove a worn-down GMC from the 1990s. He hadn't had the thing inspected in over ten years.

"I'm not talking about your truck."

Whatever ghost of a smile lingered on his lips, it was now completely gone.

"You can't be serious."

My bag was on the floor, right where I left it. I picked it up and reached inside and pulled out a strap of twenty-dollar bills. I tossed it on the table, along with four other straps.

"That's ten thousand dollars."

He stared at the money for a long moment, then looked up at me.

"But it's a classic."

"And it hasn't been run in over a decade, I bet. Look, if you want more money, I'll give you more money."

He squinted at the bag.

"How much more do you have in there, anyway?"

He looked at the money on the table again as if for the first time.

"Where'd you get all that cash in the first place? Did you rob a bank? Is *that* why those men came after you?"

The stacks of bills had been hidden underneath one of the floorboards at the cabin. Nearly eighty thousand dollars in cash. I'd stuffed all the stacks in the bag before I set the place on fire.

When I didn't answer, Darrell released a heavy breath.

"This is big, isn't it?"

"Yes."

"How big is it?"

"Something deep in my gut tells me it could be global."

"*Global?*"

His eyes went wide for a quick moment, then he studied my face.

"Am I ever going to get the full story? You know, what's really going on?"

"It's possible. Unless I get killed beforehand."

He grabbed his cane and pushed himself out of the chair.

"Well, then, follow me."

13

A single light bulb hung suspended from the middle of the garage ceiling. It was an old light bulb, edging toward the end of its life, the filaments inside almost retired. It flickered for the first few seconds after Darrell hit the switch, but then it stayed on, though it wasn't very bright. It didn't even begin to do the car parked beneath it justice, but neither did the tarp currently hiding it.

I asked, "So this will run, huh?"

Darrell hobbled over and grabbed one end of the tarp. He threw the tarp aside, placed his hands on his hips, and stepped back to marvel at the car's beauty.

"It'll run. Question is, how far will it take you?"

The car in question was a 1970 Dodge Charger. The color was all black. Most importantly, the engine was a 440 Six Pack. With three two-barrel carburetors and 390 horsepower, it didn't stack up to many of the cars nowadays. Still, it was a classic, Darrell's pride and joy, having made it his very first purchase when he returned from the war and he had kept it ever since.

The sentimentality in Darrell's eyes gave me pause.

"If you don't want me to use it, I won't."

"You already paid for it."

"Consider it collateral. I'll make sure you get it back."

He didn't answer, just kept staring down at the car.

"Darrell, I'm serious. I can find other transportation."

"Did I ever tell you why I never got rid of this car? It's the car I drove when Janice and I had our first date. It's the car I drove us to the beach one summer day a year later, and where I proposed to her. It's the car I drove our son home from the hospital in. I don't know why—I know it's stupid—but this car had always been there for every pivotal point in my life, I just could never bring myself to sell it."

"It's not stupid."

"No? Tell me what's really going on."

"I can't."

"Yes, you can."

"If all goes well, someday soon I'll bring this car back and we'll crack a beer and I'll tell you everything."

"You promise?"

"Yes, but I wish you would consider leaving too. These men are trained professionals. They won't think twice to kill you."

He nodded, staring down at the car again.

"I'll think about it. I promise I will. You know how stubborn I am. Have to convince myself it's my own choice. But I appreciate you looking out for me."

He turned and held out his hand. I shook it. The man had a firm grip, even after all these years.

"I'm putting her in your care."

"I understand."

"I trust you."

"I know."

"Do me one favor."

"What's that?"

He forced a smile.

"Don't get yourself killed."

The Charger had only a quarter-tank of gas left, so I stopped at the first gas station I came to just before Durango to fill up.

Big fluffy flakes of snow still kept falling. The road crew was already out, plowing the major roads.

It wasn't even six o'clock in the morning, but the gas station was moderately busy. Several tractor-trailers were parked in the side lot, a few with their running lights on. Since I didn't own a credit card, I went inside to pay and waited behind two truckers before it was my turn. I placed two twenties on the counter and told the kid working the register my pump number.

He rang it up, chomping on a piece of gum as he did, barely even making eye contact with me. He had a magazine open beside him on the counter, some sports rag, and it seemed he couldn't wait to get back to it.

"Question for you."

He gave me a tired look. Didn't say anything, but the expression on his face indicated he was waiting for me to ask my question. An echo of what Darrell had said came to me: *goddamned punk.*

"What's the easiest way for me to check the Internet?"

The kid didn't do a good job of hiding his disdain. He literally rolled his eyes.

"Uh, your phone."

"I don't have a phone."

"Then your computer."

"I don't have a computer."

The harsh bright fluorescents in the ceiling spotlighted the acne and grease and furrow on the kid's brow. He couldn't be more than sixteen years old, and judging by his current position and the time of year, he was a dropout.

"I don't know. What do you need the Internet for? Wanna look at some dirty pictures?"

I didn't even bother dignifying his question with a response. I turned and started for the exit when the kid spoke.

"The Apple Store."

I glanced back at him.

"What's that?"

"The Apple Store. We don't have any around here, but when I was up in Colorado Springs last month, I stopped by and played around with their stuff."

He shook his head, offered up an embarrassed smile.

"But that's because I like Apple products. You might as well use the Walmart in Durango. They'll have computers too."

The Walmart in Durango was the most obvious choice, and that was exactly why I needed to avoid it. There was no telling just how far the reach of the people hunting me went. My best bet was being as unpredictable as possible.

The kid watched me, seeing if this would make up for his earlier disrespect. He sincerely looked like he wanted to help. And it was because of that I nodded, said thank you, then continued toward the exit again. But then I stopped and turned back around, asked one final question.

"What exactly is an Apple Store?"

14

By the time I reached Colorado Springs, it was eleven o'clock in the morning and the snow was finally starting to let up.

I had to stop at another gas station for directions, but soon I was back on the road and headed for the Apple Store. It seemed foolish to go to such lengths, but I had to be sure. Any father would. I could call, but there was a chance the phone numbers I had memorized were out of service. And if they weren't, there was a chance the people who came after me might be listening in to the phone calls.

Eventually I'd have to head east, toward New York. The best way to do that was driving straight east. Instead, I'd driven north for nearly five hours. Out of my way, maybe, but I didn't want to take any expected routes. I had to assume the people who came after me had other people out there. People who would soon learn what had happened to their friends, if they hadn't already figured it out. They'd be looking for me. Again, being predictable was not the best option right now.

When I walked inside, an employee in a blue shirt smiled

and said hello and asked if there was anything she could help me with.

I hesitated, taking in the computers spread out around the place, people at all the tables handling devices. I returned her smile and shook my head, told her I was just looking and continued toward the computers.

They were much bigger than I remembered computers being, as least in terms of their screen size. They were also much thinner and compact. The mouse wasn't even connected with a wire. At first I didn't think it would work, but when I touched it, the arrow on the screen moved. Okay, that was a start. But now what? All these images and pictures confused me. Just how did I get to the Internet?

A young boy, no older than twelve years old, stood at the computer beside me. He moved the mouse around and typed on the keyboard like he was a pro.

"Excuse me."

I lowered my voice for my next question, suddenly embarrassed.

"How do I get to the Internet?"

He turned his head slowly, frowned at me.

"What?"

"It may seem silly, but I haven't used a computer like this before."

He looked around, maybe searching for his parents.

"Is this a joke?"

"It's no joke. I haven't used a computer in years."

He turned then, and I saw his T-shirt. He wore jeans and a parka, so much of the T-shirt was hidden, but it was what was on his chest that drew my attention and made me catch my breath.

The boy asked, "Are you okay?"

I blinked, looked back up at him, and nodded quickly.

"Yes, I'm fine. Just the perils of being old, I guess. Now do you think you can help me?"

He started toward me, and I looked again at his T-shirt. It was mostly black, except for a gray circle on the chest with a capital T in red in the center.

"What?"

There was caution in the boy's eyes now. He looked around once again, this time no doubt searching for his parents. They might be watching us now. How would any parent in his or her own right mind leave their child alone like this? But this was how the world was now, I thought, and mentally kicked myself for sounding like Darrell.

"Your T-shirt. It caught my attention, is all."

He beamed down at it.

"Yeah, it's a Temple T-shirt."

"A Temple T-shirt."

Nodding his head now, excitement in his voice.

"Yeah, Temple. You've heard of Temple, right? He's amazing!"

People were watching us now. Or maybe I was being paranoid. People were all around us, but they were mostly focused on the devices. Where were this boy's parents?

I cleared my throat.

"Interesting. So the Internet …"

"Yeah, here."

The boy touched the mouse and the arrow on the screen moved, clicked an icon, and suddenly a window appeared.

"There you go."

He started to turn away.

"If I want to find something, what do I need to do?"

The boy gave me that cautious look again. He glanced around the store once more.

"Are you sure this isn't some kind of joke?"

"Please."

He thought it over for a couple long seconds, then sighed.

"What is it you want to find?"

"Not what—who. Two people. How do I do that?"

"What are their names?"

"Excuse me?"

"Their names."

The boy's fingers now hovered above the keyboard.

"What's the first one?"

"Aisha Shepherd. Assuming she didn't get married."

He typed the name into the computer, smacked a button, and suddenly the screen was full of words and pictures.

"Whoa. She's pretty."

Yes, she was. The very first picture was a headshot, my daughter smiling at something past the camera. The last time I'd seen her she was in her early twenties. Now she was in her early forties, but time hadn't changed her much at all. She was beautiful.

"Looks like she's pretty important."

The boy scanned some of the text on the screen.

"She runs some kind of foundation, it says here."

"Is she okay?"

"Huh?"

I paused a moment, thinking how to properly word the question.

"Are there any recent news articles about her?"

The boy moved the mouse again, typed some more, then shrugged.

"Yeah, it says here she's hosting some kind of gala soon."

"But that's it?"

The boy gave me a sidelong glance.

"Mister, what are you looking for exactly?"

I wasn't sure. That was the problem.

"Can you search another name?"

"Sure."

The boy's fingers hovered over the keyboard again, waiting.

"James Shepherd."

The boy typed and smacked that same button again.

"It looks like there's a couple James Shepherds."

"What do you mean?"

The boy tapped the screen.

"A writer, a lawyer, a former rugby player. Which one are you looking for?"

None of them, actually.

"I'm thinking of a different James Shepherd."

"Then you need to be more specific."

"Can you search for a James Shepherd in New York City?"

"What's the time frame?"

"I'm sorry?"

"The search parameters. Like, how far back do you want the search to go?"

Good question. I still wasn't sure what it was I was looking for.

When I didn't answer immediately, the boy spoke.

"How about I make it a week."

He moved the mouse again, typed some more, and suddenly more text filled the screen.

The boy's mouth fell open.

"That's not good. I hope you're looking for a different James Shepherd."

"Brian?"

A middle-aged woman stood a few yards away. Clearly the boy's mother, she had a concerned look on her face.

"Is everything okay?"

"Yeah, Mom. I was just helping this guy out."

"Don't say guy. It's disrespectful."

"This ... gentleman."

"Your son was very helpful."

I said it with a smile, trying to relieve the tension, but it didn't seem to work. The woman motioned the boy toward the front of the store.

"Brian, let's go."

Brian looked at me, shrugged, then started away. I called thank you to him, and he waved back, but then his mother grabbed his arm and pulled him forward.

I turned back to the computer. I stared at the text on the screen. The first thing that came up was a news article. It may have been a long time since I'd last used a computer, but I was not a complete novice. I'd watched how the boy interacted with the computer, and I moved the mouse now, clicking it to change the screen. The full news article came up. As I read the text, my stomach began to churn.

According to the article, police were called Saturday evening to a disturbance at a home in Crown Heights. When the officers arrived, the door was broken open. They entered and found a woman and two children dead. The details of their deaths had still not been released. The police had issued a statement that they were currently looking for James Shepherd, the husband and father. James had been missing since Saturday, police said. While they had not stated that James was a suspect, they did wish to speak with him immediately.

There wasn't much there, but it was still enough to cause my world to tilt and sway and pitch forward. I wanted to sit down. I wanted to cry. I wanted to scream. I wanted to do *something* other than just stand there under all the bright lights around all these cheerful people playing with their toys.

But what could I do? Not much right now. And quite honestly, I didn't even know what all was going on. There wasn't much information in the article, but what was there was unsettling.

Someone had murdered my daughter-in-law and grand-children.

And my son—who the rest of the world knew only as Temple—was missing.

INTERLUDE
ORIGIN STORY (I)

I n the fall of 1943, my father came to Pennsylvania in the most unusual way.

He was driven directly from Tennessee in a military sedan operated by a tall soldier with a buzz cut who barely spoke five words to him the entire ride. They drove nonstop. When they arrived at the mansion—because that was what it looked like to my father, who had never seen a house so big in his life—it was six o'clock in the morning and the sun was already beginning to rise.

Up until that point, my father had never been anywhere north of the Mason-Dixon line. He had never been outside the eastern end of Tennessee.

He was seventeen years old.

The mansion sat in a wooded area. It was three stories tall but stretched out wide enough to contain over fifty rooms.

The soldier with the buzz cut never left the sedan. He parked in front of the mansion and another soldier hurried down the steps and opened my father's door and shook my father's hand and told him it was an honor to meet him and thanked my father for coming all this way because Hitler was a menace and every bit helped. He ushered my father inside the mansion, which was as ornate inside as it looked on the outside. My father felt very out of place, and he couldn't help staring at the grand staircase and the brass chandeliers and the marble floors and the old portraits hanging on the walls.

The soldier led my father through the first floor to a large room which contained two dozen cots. Half of them were occupied. The young men in them were my father's age. Some were still sleeping, while others were sitting up, stretching and wiping the sleep from their eyes.

The soldier announced breakfast would be in 0100 hours and that he expected everyone to be ready by then.

"We're here to win a war, aren't we?"

All the young men, now on their feet standing at attention, answered loudly.

"Yes, sir!"

The man left my father in a bewildered state. He looked around the room at the other young men, many of whom nodded their hellos. Only one of them drifted over to meet my father.

"Where you from?"

"Tennessee."

"Where in Tennessee?"

"Friendsville."

"*Friends*ville?"

The young man snorted a laugh.

"You must be joking."

My father said he was not. He said that he had been born and raised there and hadn't traveled outside the town until just recently.

The young man said, "Why's that?"

"My mama died."

"Aw, I'm sorry."

The young man stuck out his hand.

"Name's Eugene Smalls. My friends call me Short Stack."

My father shook Eugene's hand.

"Henry Temple. Why do your friends call you Short Stack?"

"Because growing up I loved short stack pancakes. Still do, whenever I can get them. Can't you tell?"

He patted his stomach and chuckled, which didn't make much sense to my father because Eugene didn't look like he had much of a gut.

"What if I want to call you Eugene?"

"You can do that. But like I said, my friends call me Short Stack, so if you don't call me Short Stack, I guess we ain't friends."

My father, who had never had many friends, decided to call Eugene Short Stack.

Short Stack led my father around the room and introduced him to the other boys. There were ten of them, and my father got their names mixed up almost immediately. He had never been a fast learner, which was one of the reasons he had dropped out of school. As his own mama had once told him, he was smart, just not *book* smart.

The only boy my father hadn't been introduced to yet approached him. He was tall and muscular and had an angry face.

"You got any family?"

Short Stack sighed.

"Tyrone, give it a break."

Tyrone stared hard at my father.

"Well, do you?"

My father looked at Short Stack, then at the rest of the boys who were watching him. He shook his head.

"No aunts or uncles or cousins?"

My father, afraid to speak, shook his head again.

"How'd you end up coming here?"

My father looked at Short Stack for help, but Short Stack looked down at his feet.

Tyrone said, "Well?"

My father cleared his throat.

"I ... my mama died. She'd been sick a long time. And, well, I had nowhere else to go, no money, so I went to sign up for the army."

Tyrone squinted at him.

"How old are you?"

"Seventeen."

"That what you tell the army people?"

"No, I told them I was eighteen. But they didn't believe me. They told me to go home, but I told them I didn't have no home anymore. That's when one of them started asking me questions. Like about whether my mama and dad were still alive. My dad, he gone run off when I was just a baby, so I have no idea where he's at. And I had no aunts or uncles, no cousins, not even any grandparents. That's when the man made a phone call and spoke into the phone for some time and then hung up the phone and smiled at me and told me there was an opportunity to fight in the war."

Tyrone listened carefully as my father spoke, nodding slowly with each word. When my father finished, Tyrone stood silent for a long time, processing this, before turning to the other boys and shaking his head.

"This don't smell right."

"What doesn't smell right?"

All the boys turned to face a uniformed man with close-cropped brown hair and the shiniest shoes my father had ever seen. The boys immediately stood at attention, their shoulders back, their arms straight down at their sides. My father quickly did the same.

The man entered, his footsteps echoing on the floor in the spacious room. He approached my father. My father, not sure what to do, just stood there with his hands at his sides, before Short Stack, standing beside my father, whispered to him to salute.

My father saluted.

The man smiled.

"New recruit. That's okay. First day is always nerve-racking."

He stepped over in front of Tyrone, his smile fading.

"What were you saying doesn't smell right?"

Tyrone said nothing.

The man's voice went hard.

"Recruit, don't make me ask again."

When Tyrone spoke next, his voice had lost the edge it had when he questioned my father.

"None of us know why we're here."

The man tilted his head so his right ear was pointed at Tyrone.

"Say that again?"

"None of us know why we're here, sir. None of us have family. No parents, no siblings. Nothing."

The man nodded.

"I see. The answer will be clear soon enough. You've been handpicked for a very important reason. The world is at war, gentlemen, and the United States is the only country that can save it. Hitler is a menace and needs to be eliminated, and you soldiers—*you*—will help us accomplish that. Am I clear?"

Only a couple of the boys nodded.

The man said, "*Am I clear?*"

The boys shouted, "Yes, sir!"

Without another word, the man turned and left the room. Everyone watched him in silence. Nobody moved. Nobody even breathed. When the door closed, everyone seemed to release a sigh of relief.

One of the boys—Michael?—whispered to Tyrone.

"You better be careful."

Tyrone's face had hardened once again. He shrugged it off.

"I don't care. It don't smell right. Especially since all they seem to be collecting are black boys."

The boys dispersed after that. Short Stack nudged my father, told him he'd show him to a cot and the extra uniforms they had for new arrivals.

My father asked, "You have no family either?"

Short Stack shook his head.

"Who was that man?"

Short Stack said, "That was the Colonel."

Breakfast was served in a large dining room and was more food than anything my father had ever seen. Pancakes, eggs, bacon, sausage. As expected, Short Stack had several short stacks before patting his stomach and saying that he gave up.

Which probably wasn't the best idea for Short Stack, as the next several hours my father and the rest of the boys spent training. They ran around the mansion grounds, following one of the sergeants who set the pace. They did pushups and sit-ups and pull-ups until their bodies couldn't take it anymore. The whole time the sergeant shouted at them and told them that they weren't working hard enough and they were pussies compared to the German soldiers.

That night my father was exhausted. All he wanted to do

was sleep. After all, he had been up now for over twenty-four hours, too anxious to sleep on the trip from Tennessee.

His cot was right next to Short Stack's, and as they got ready for lights out, Short Stack asked him a question.

"Did you bring anything from home?"

"What do you mean?"

Short Stack looked around the room as if there was an audience he didn't want to hear him.

"You know, something personal."

When my father still looked confused, Short Stack did another one of his looks around the room before slipping his hand underneath his pillow and bringing out a crinkled comic book.

While my father could read, he had never been much for books, though one time in the local dime store he'd paged through the comic books on the rack before a clerk ran him out. Despite that, he'd never had much interest in comic books. The one Short Stack showed him had CAPTAIN AMERICA in loud yellow letters at the top, with Captain America punching Adolf Hitler.

"This one is my favorite, which is why I brought it along. I mean, jeez, Captain America is the whole reason I wanted to become a soldier!"

Some of the other boys nearby chuckled at this, but Short Stack didn't seem to hear, or if he did hear, he didn't seem to care. He paged through the comic book, his eyes going wide as he grinned and mouthed the words.

My father sat down on the bed across from Short Stack. He didn't realize his eyes had begun to tear up until one fell down his cheek.

Short Stack noticed my father wiping at his cheek and paused from his reading. He squinted at the tears in my father's eyes, then a sort of understanding crossed his face. He set the comic book aside.

"When did your mama pass?"

"What day is today?"

"Wednesday."

"Then two days ago. There was no money for a funeral. We were just renting, and my mama was behind on the rent. I was working any job I could to bring in money, but it wasn't nearly enough. When she—she—she died, Mr. Jensen demanded his money or else he was going to call the police. I had no choice. That's why I went to sign up for the army."

"I'm sorry."

Short Stack smiled.

"But look on the bright side. Maybe you'll be the one who kills Hitler. Maybe you'll be the one who saves the world."

Colonel Strickland—my father had finally learned the man's name—made an appearance the next morning. He only ever made appearances in the morning, my father came to realize, giving the boys a pep talk about how they were going to win the war and that the boys in this room—his gaze shifting to each of them in turn—were the ones who would help defeat Hitler. Then without another word he turned and disappeared and wouldn't be seen until the next morning when he came to deliver the same pep talk.

A new boy arrived that afternoon. His name was Etan and he was from Georgia and Tyrone was more careful this time when he questioned him, and just as Tyrone had suspected, Etan had no family. Tyrone looked around at the rest of them with his suspicious gaze. That was all he needed to do. It was clear something was going on, and that it indeed did not smell good.

Every day they ran ten miles each carrying a full pack and did sit-ups and push-ups and pull-ups, and my father's body was sore every night, but as the days passed his muscles and endurance began to build. Still, he was exhausted at night, just like everyone else, except Short Stack for some reason, who always wanted to talk about one thing or another.

"Where do you want to live?"

This was three nights after my father had first arrived. By then two more boys—Joshua and Daniel—had arrived, both of whom had no family.

My father lay on his back, staring at the ceiling despite the fact lights out wasn't for another twenty minutes.

"What do you mean?"

"Once the war is over—once we defeat Hitler and the Nazis—where do you want to live?"

"I haven't thought about it. I've never been outside Tennessee before. I honestly don't know what's out there."

"Me, I want to live in New York. It's the greatest city in the world. You can be anything there."

Another night after two new arrivals came, Short Stack lamented that he should have brought along more comic books. He said he loved Captain America, but it got boring looking at the same panels and reading the same words every night.

"You know what I always wondered?"

Short Stack could have been talking to anyone, but my father—lying on his cot, staring at the ceiling—knew otherwise.

"What?"

"Why there ain't no Negro superheroes."

Tyrone, several cots away, snorted.

"That's easy. Ain't nobody want to read about a Negro superhero."

"That's not true."

"Who do you see buying comic books? White kids. You think white kids want to read about a nigger saving the world?"

He snorted again, lay down on his cot, shaking his head.

"You're dreaming."

The next day they had two new arrivals. The day after three new arrivals. Then the day after that two more.

That brought their number to twenty-four. Now every cot was filled.

The next morning, the Colonel announced that it was time for them to start their training. He stood with his shoulders back, his hands on his hips, his gaze skipping around to each boy as he smiled widely.

"Make me proud."

At midnight on the dot they loaded into smalls trucks—six boys to a truck, four trucks in total—and rode for almost an hour until they came to a naval base. Short Stack sat next to my father, his knee bouncing in anticipation. Every time my father looked at Short Stack, Short Stack was grinning, and despite my father's nervousness, my father found himself grinning too. It seemed everything Short Stack did was infectious.

The trucks drove through the naval base to the docks, where a ship was waiting for them. The ship had no lights on it, and even the men directing the boys had no flashlights. Fortunately, the sky was clear and the moon was bright enough to see their way. The boys had been told previously that once they arrived they were not to make a sound. They were to follow the men onto the ship as quietly as possible and go below deck to their assigned locations.

Tyrone had raised the obvious question: What were they going to do on a ship, as none of them had had any training?

He wasn't given an answer.

My father was directed toward the front of the ship, or maybe it was the rear of the ship—he quickly lost his sense of direction—and he ended up in one of the engine rooms with a lot of machinery that meant nothing to him along with Tyrone and Etan.

Once they were left alone, Tyrone muttered.

"This don't smell right at all."

After a while, the engines started up. The machinery around them roared so loudly my father could barely think. The ship began to move, slightly at first, as it pushed away from the dock. Soon it straightened out as it headed down the river.

Eventually the machinery suddenly stopped, as did their forward progression.

My father whispered, "Do you think we're on the ocean yet?"

He had never seen the ocean before.

Across the room, Tyrone frowned but said nothing.

Etan looked around the room, suddenly nervous.

My father looked around the room, too, not sure what to do. They hadn't been told anything other than to stay in their specified locations. My father opened his mouth, meaning to ask a question, when a buzzing sound caught his attention. It was low at first, then grew in pitch. My father flinched.

Tyrone asked what was wrong.

"Can't you hear that?"

Tyrone only shook his head. Then, suddenly, he flinched too, clamping his hands over his ears.

Etan did the same thing.

The buzzing had become a high-pitched whine, shooting up several decibels.

By that point, my father had clamped his hands over his ears as well, but it didn't seem to do any good. The buzzing was now inside his head.

Etan shouted and fell to the ground, his body convulsing.

Tyrone started to hurry forward, toward where Etan had fallen, but then his body went rigid and his eyes went wide and he stared around at the room.

My father stared too. The steel wall next to him had begun to ripple. At first my father thought he was hallucinating, but it was clear Tyrone saw the same thing. Then the high-pitched whine increased—my father's head began to feel like it was going to explode—and the entire engine room began to ripple. A vibration had started up in the air, faint at first but growing stronger. Every tooth in my father's mouth felt like it was going to break loose. The tiny hairs on his arms stood up on end.

Tyrone screamed on the other side of the engine room.

"What the fuck is happening?"

Etan kept convulsing on the floor—until, suddenly, he was no longer on the floor. He was *in* it. Or only half of him was, the top half, while his legs stuck up through the floor, scissoring in place, kicking wildly.

Tyrone screamed. At first my father thought he was screaming by what he saw, but my father realized Tyrone hadn't even noticed what happened to Etan. Instead he was focused on the floor, at the rippling steel floor, as his body began to sink into it like the floor was made out of quicksand. Tyrone tried to step out of it, but his legs were stuck. He looked wildly around, searching for something to grab onto, but there was nothing nearby as he sunk lower and lower into the floor.

My father looked down at the floor, which was rippling right beneath him. The solid support of ground beneath his feet began to lessen. He stepped right, then left, thinking that if he moved his feet, he wouldn't get stuck. There were some pipes above him and he jumped up and grabbed them and tried to hold on, but they, too, were rippling, and his fingers slipped through them and the floor tried to suck his shoes in, just like it had done to Etan and Tyrone, and my father kept moving, turning back and forth, searching for some escape— until, just as suddenly, the rippling stopped. Every surface below and above and around him was solid again.

That was when the high-pitched whine became, somehow, even more intense. And with its intensity, my father found that he could no longer move. As if the high-pitched whine had frozen his body in place, just as it had frozen Etan, whose legs were no longer kicking, and Tyrone, who was now halfway through the floor with his face blank and his eyes glassy. My father could not even take a step forward.

In the end, none of it mattered anyway, because after another second the sound became too much, and my father's head exploded.

My father became aware of the buzzing first. It was faint, distant, almost imaginary. But it was there, ever persistent. Soon it became louder, closer, to the point he knew that whatever it was, it was very close to him in the dark.

That was when my father opened his eyes.

Bright, blinding whiteness hit him at once. His body convulsed as if it had been shot. His eyes snapped shut, and he cried out.

The buzzing was even louder now. Closer. Somewhere right beside him. Above him. Everywhere.

He opened his eyes again and the brightness was still there, glaring into his face, the intensity so brutal he was afraid it would burn his skin off.

My father cried out again. He tried to move.

He was aware of his legs kicking out, of his arms flailing around. He was aware of pounding somewhere in a room, something akin to footsteps but these were stomps, like a giant had somehow gained access to wherever he was trapped, and a voice shouted—*screamed*, really, screamed as loud as any voice had ever screamed—for help.

Soon there was more stomping, more screaming. The buzzing continued. And my father's head began to vibrate again.

Tyrone and Etan, my father thought. What happened to Tyrone and Etan? What happened to Short Stack?

He clamped his hands to his ears, but the noises persisted —they wouldn't stop—and he began to yell himself, one constant shout to rival all the other noises bombarding him.

Hands grabbed at him, their touch sharp, like knives, leaving tiny cuts with every point of contact.

My father shouted again.

The hands grabbed at him again.

Someone shouted at him to calm down.

Someone else shouted that everything was all right.

My father kept shouting.

The buzzing kept buzzing.

The world swelled with so much brightness that my father was certain it would explode in another moment, filling up and up with more and more light until it reached a point when it would burst everywhere, killing him and everyone else on the ship.

But he wasn't on the ship anymore. This much he knew, blinking fast enough to make out the white room and people around him.

Something else touched my father's arm, something even sharper, penetrating skin, and my father swung his arm on instinct, simply self-defense. He watched a man in a white coat go sailing through the air until he smacked against a wall and fell crumpled to the floor.

Sorry, my father said or wanted to say or maybe he just thought, stuck there with all different kinds of hands holding him in place, while something else poked him in his other arm and the light began to darken and the buzzing began to lessen and the edges of the world around him began to take on subtler, blurry edges, until all those edges fell together and combined and everything went black again.

At some point later—hours, days, maybe even weeks—my father opened his eyes again.

The brightness was there, just like before, only it wasn't as intense.

The buzzing was present too, but its intensity had also lessened.

My father tried to sit up but couldn't. Straps tied him to the bed. It wasn't just one or two straps either, but several straps. Even his arms and legs were bound to the bed.

He wore a white undershirt and white boxer shorts.

My father shouted, "Hello? Is anybody there?"

There was no immediate answer. The room was still and quiet. And small. And clean. And bright. Very bright. The linoleum floor must have just recently been washed (there was an antiseptic smell), and the lights in the ceiling reflected brightly off its surface.

My father tried again: "Hello?"

In the distance, stomping. Or was it really stomping? The

noise was loud, yes, but so had been the buzzing—what my father understood now were the lights in the ceiling—only the buzzing had decreased to a more tolerable level. At least it was just quiet enough for him to think, try to get his thoughts straight. Like what had happened to him? And where was he?

The door opened and in walked a young woman. She was pretty and blonde. She didn't smile at my father, didn't even say a word, but stood by the door and held it open. My father wasn't sure why until a moment later he heard more stomping —footsteps—and a man entered the room. This man was old and had dark hair sprinkled with gray. He wore a long white coat with a stethoscope wrapped around his neck. It made my father think of the man from earlier, the one he had seen go flying through the air before hitting the wall. Thinking of this now, his eyes shifted toward the wall in question. An indentation marked the spot where the man had struck it.

The man in the long white coat walked toward him.

"Yes, that was where Dr. Hogan landed."

"Is he okay?"

"He broke his spine, but he'll live. Now, what about you? How do you feel?"

My father wasn't sure how he felt. He felt the same but somehow different. He couldn't even begin to try to put it into words.

"I don't know."

The doctor nodded, consulting a clipboard.

"You're talking, so that's certainly an improvement."

"What about the others?"

The doctor peered at him over the clipboard.

"What others?"

"On the ship."

The doctor didn't answer. He set the clipboard aside and put the stethoscope in his ears to listen to my father's chest. The metal part was freezing. The doctor moved it around my father's chest and then nodded and pulled the stethoscope from his ears.

"Are you hungry?"

"Why am I here?"

"We'll get you something to eat. Maybe some soup would do you good."

The doctor and the woman started toward the door.

My father said, "Why am I tied to this bed?"

The doctor and woman hesitated. Stood motionless for a long moment, and then continued forward, stepping out of the room and closing the door quietly behind them.

Not long after that, Colonel Strickland came to see my father. His shiny black shoes echoed off the bright linoleum floor.

"Hello, Henry."

The Colonel stood with his hands clasped behind his back.

"Glad to see we didn't lose you."

"Where are the others?"

The Colonel sighed, his face all at once solemn.

"I'm afraid they didn't make it."

"What ... what happened?"

"All in good time."

The Colonel smiled and touched my father's shoulder.

"I'm happy you made it."

My father didn't like the smile on the Colonel's face or his hand on my father's shoulder, but my father knew better than to let the Colonel know this.

"Yes, sir."

Colonel Strickland nodded.

"I should let you rest."

The Colonel started toward the door.

My father said, "Sir?"

The Colonel turned back.

"Yes, soldier?"

"Why am I tied to this bed?"

The Colonel smiled again.

"All in good time, soldier. Don't worry—you're in good hands."

And with that the Colonel turned and left the room, which went all at once silent. The buzzing from the lights was still there, but my father had learned to listen past it. He was aware of its presence, but he had forced the buzzing to become background, barely even a whisper. What he strained to hear now was the Colonel out in the corridor. The sharp click of his heels. A question being asked by someone already in the corridor—the doctor—and the Colonel answering.

"What are your thoughts?"

"I think he's hiding something."

"Maybe he should be told the truth."

"Absolutely not. He's just a stupid nigger. He wouldn't be able to understand."

"But he's special now."

"Obviously he's special. It's incredible that he survived this long. We need to find out why."

"We're studying the blood samples, but we haven't been able to determine a reason yet."

Colonel Strickland was quiet for a moment.

"Then we might have to dissect him sooner than planned."

The doctor came to see him again, along with the pretty nurse. The doctor asked how he was feeling and checked his vitals and asked if he was hungry. My father said he was not.

"Are you sure? I know last time we only fed you soup, but we can see about getting anything you'd like."

"I'm not hungry."

The doctor frowned slightly and jotted something down on his clipboard. Then he and the nurse started to leave the room.

My father said, "Can I call my mother?"

The doctor and nurse paused. The doctor turned back, an even larger frown on his face.

"Your mother?"

"Yes. I want to let her know I'm okay."

The doctor jotted something else down on his clipboard.

"We'll see if we can arrange that."

He turned and left the room along with the nurse.

Alone in the room, my father strained to hear past the faint buzzing to the voices outside in the corridor.

The doctor: "That's very strange."

The nurse: "What's strange?"

"There must be something wrong with his memory. His mother is dead. He has no family. What's the use of having a guinea pig with a family?"

Colonel Strickland smiled down at my father.

"How are we feeling today?"

"Tired."

"Haven't you been getting much sleep?"

"The lights are always on."

"Ah, yes. We'll make sure to turn them off for a couple

hours tonight. I apologize about that. The doctor told me you asked about your mother."

"Yes. I want to make sure she knows I'm alive."

"Sure, I understand. But the thing is, Henry ... your mother is dead. She passed away two weeks ago."

The Colonel studied my father's face.

"Don't you remember?"

My father closed his eyes, issued a long, deep sigh.

"Yes, I remember."

"Good. I'm sorry it happened, but it's good you remember. Do you remember anything else? Like what happened on the ship?"

"My mother ... she was a good woman."

The Colonel was quiet for a moment. It was clear this wasn't the direction he wanted the conversation to go.

"I'm sure she was."

"She would be very disappointed to hear what happened."

"Of course. Regarding what?"

"How her son was used as a guinea pig by the Army."

My father had always been told to respect white people, especially those in authority. This was a fact that had been drilled into my father from a very early age, and he knew better than to disrespect or raise his voice to a white man. But, strangely enough, that fear had all but vanished. He was no longer afraid of the Colonel. He was no longer afraid of anything. Of course he knew his mother had died two weeks ago—he had only asked for her to see what reaction it would bring. The gentle, naïve boy had died on that ship; what had emerged was someone sharper and more calculating.

Without a word, Colonel Strickland turned and started toward the door. He only paused when my father spoke again.

"I remember everything that happened on that ship. But I'll never tell you."

Colonel Strickland stood motionless for a moment. Then he turned and walked back toward my father. His face had become stone.

"You're goddamned right you're a guinea pig. All of you boys were. The fact is we didn't expect there to be any survivors. But you proved us wrong. So we're going to do whatever we need to do to find out what makes you special. Either you help us or you don't, it doesn't matter. We're going to get the answers we need because there's nothing stopping us."

The Colonel leaned in close, his face red, his voice a harsh whisper.

"You're nothing. You're dirt. No—you're less than dirt. The world doesn't care about Henry Temple. It doesn't know you're here. It doesn't even know you exist. Do you understand? You belong to us. We own you. And very soon, when the time comes, we're going to take your life."

When the doctor came to visit my father again, he found that my father was dead. At least, that was his first impression. He walked into the room with the pretty nurse and asked my father how he was feeling. My father didn't answer. He lay on the bed, his eyes closed, his head tilted to the side. He wasn't breathing. The doctor and nurse rushed forward. The doctor checked my father for a pulse. He didn't find one.

The doctor said, "Get Colonel Strickland."

The nurse hurried out of the room, yelling for assistance.

Footsteps thudded in the corridor. Two uniformed men entered, pistols on their belts. One of them asked what was wrong.

"He has no pulse!"

"How long has he been dead?"

"I don't know! But we need to move him as soon as possible if we want to do the dissection."

The men approached the bed. They began loosening the straps keeping my father secured. And as they did this, my father began breathing again, only slightly, and his heart started to beat. How he had been able to make them cease for as long as he had, he didn't know, but when he realized it was possible, he had come up with an idea.

The doctor shouted, "We need a gurney!"

One of the soldiers ran out of the room while the other soldier finished loosening the straps. He leaned over my father, his body pressing into my father's side. The pistol was right on the guard's belt, inches away from my father's limp hand. My father had never fired a pistol before, but he understood the basic principles of operating one. So when he opened his eyes, reached out, snatched the pistol from the soldier's holster, he knew that a squeeze of the trigger would cause a bullet to shoot out of its barrel into whatever place he aimed the pistol.

My father fired two rounds into the soldier's chest, sitting up as he did, swinging his feet off the bed, and as the doctor shouted out in surprise—from the gunshots or the fact a dead man was rising from bed or maybe both—he turned and started running for the doors, and my father sprinted forward, moving faster than he ever had in his life, meeting the doctor halfway across the room within seconds, and he grabbed the doctor by his hair and held the barrel of the pistol against the doctor's back.

"Where are we?"

The doctor said nothing.

"*Where are we?*"

Footsteps pounded out in the corridor. More soldiers. It sounded like there were four, maybe five coming.

Holding the doctor in front of him as a shield, the barrel of the pistol still digging into the doctor's back, my father pushed the doctor out into the corridor.

Colonel Strickland and four soldiers blocked the corridor. The Colonel was at the front of the pack, and he raised his hand up to halt the men.

"What do you think you're doing, Henry?"

The corridor was short. At the end was the elevator. Unfortunately, Colonel Strickland and the soldiers blocked that elevator. Behind my father and the doctor was a dead end.

"I'm leaving."

Colonel Strickland held his gaze.

"That isn't an option."

"If it isn't, then the doctor dies."

The doctor's voice rasped at the Colonel.

"David, don't let him kill me."

Colonel Strickland said, "Relax, Richard. He's not going to kill you."

The Colonel raised his own pistol.

"I am."

He fired a bullet into the doctor's chest.

The doctor became dead weight in my father's grip. Before he'd had a living human shield to use to his advantage as a means of escape. Now he had a dead human shield, which did him little good.

Except, my father realized, living or dead, the doctor's body was still a shield, and any shield was better than no shield.

The Colonel said, "Kill him."

The two soldiers directly behind the Colonel stepped forward. They raised their pistols at my father.

And, suddenly, time seemed to slow. My father's heartbeat slowed. His breathing slowed. *Everything* slowed. In the space of an instant, my father saw what the soldiers planned to do before they even did it. As if he could anticipate their every movement.

The soldier to my father's left was younger, stronger, smarter. It was clear that he would fire his pistol a half second faster than the soldier on my father's right. So the soldier to my father's left was the one at whom he flung the doctor's body. As the doctor's body flew through the air, my father pointed the pistol at the other soldier's head—his aim precise and steady—and fired two rounds. As the soldier's head snapped back and he fell to the ground, my father sprinted forward. Colonel Strickland and the other soldiers tried tracking him with their own weapons, but my father was too fast. Within a second he was standing in front of the Colonel and punched him in the stomach with his free fist. The Colonel bent forward, and my father fired over his back at the two other soldiers, two bullets each, and then turned to the last soldier, the one who was currently trying to grapple with the doctor's dead body, and as the soldier pushed the body away, my father aimed his pistol at the soldier's head and pulled the trigger. Nothing—the pistol was empty. The soldier raised his own weapon but my father jumped forward, slamming the back of the soldier's head into the wall, and as the soldier's entire body shook from the impact, my father went to grab the pistol from the soldier's hand. The soldier, however, did not want to let go, no matter how hard his head had been slammed into the wall. In that same instant, my father heard something behind him, a slight rustle of clothing as Colonel Strickland started to stand up straight, a soft, almost silent smack as the Colonel's finger touched the trigger of his own pistol. My father ducked just as the Colonel fired, and the bullet intended for my father went straight through the fourth soldier's forehead. My father rolled backward and sprang to his feet right beside the Colonel, who was still trying to catch up, moving too slow, and with two sharp jabs to the Colonel's side, my father managed to free the pistol from the Colonel's grasp and shoved the barrel of the pistol into the Colonel's side.

Everything had happened within the space of seven seconds.

My father said, "Move."

"You won't get out of here alive."

"*Move.*"

My father shoved the Colonel down the corridor, past the dead bodies, toward the elevator.

They went past an open doorway and my father saw movement and raised the pistol but it was only the pretty nurse, crouched in a corner, so my father kept going, pushing the Colonel forward, until he heard movement behind him and spun back just in time to see the nurse with a rifle, aimed right at my father's head.

My father fired two bullets into the nurse's chest. Two spots blossomed like roses on the flawless white of her uniform as she slumped to the floor.

At the distraction, the Colonel tried to free himself from my father's grasp. But my father was too strong, keeping him in place, and shoved him right at the elevator. There was only one button on the wall, and with the barrel of the pistol my father pressed the button.

The Colonel said, "How many others do you intend to kill? A dozen more? *Two* dozen more?"

The elevator door opened. My father had prepared for there to be more soldiers on it, but it was empty. He shoved the Colonel inside and stepped in after him, keeping the pistol aimed at the Colonel's chest, and then pressed the only other button on the panel. The door closed, and the elevator began to rise.

"You're making a mistake. We can help each other. Think

about what you did to those men in a matter of seconds. Just imagine what you could accomplish against the Nazis."

My father watched the elevator door.

"Shut up."

"Henry, in twenty seconds that door will open and there will be a dozen men waiting with guns. There's no way you're getting out of here alive."

The elevator began to slow. My father grabbed the Colonel and pressed the barrel of his pistol into the Colonel's side.

"We'll see about that."

The elevator door opened and my father pushed Colonel Strickland forward, out toward the dozen soldiers with guns waiting for them—the dozen soldiers with guns who weren't there.

The corridor was deserted. No soldiers with guns. Not even one soldier with a gun. Nothing.

Suddenly it made sense to my father. The only reason Colonel Strickland and those other soldiers had come downstairs was because word had been sent that my father had died. Then, in the corridor, they'd heard gunshots. They hadn't known what had happened, just as my father hadn't known what he was going to do. As far as my father knew, no further word had been sent out regarding the escape. Which meant right now my father only needed to deal with Colonel Strickland.

"Last chance, Henry. You can make this right. You can be a hero."

My father ignored the Colonel and directed him down the corridor. It looked nothing like it had downstairs—which, my father realized belatedly, must have been the basement. Here the floors were marble and shiny brass chandeliers hung from the ceiling and portraits covered the walls.

"I know where we are."

"Do you?"

The Colonel sounded amused.

"This is the mansion. And if I remember right, there weren't many men stationed on the mansion grounds. Which makes me think there are no more soldiers."

"If you're so sure about that, why don't you let me go?"

My father pushed the Colonel forward. They went down one long corridor, down another. The mansion was so big, and the boys had only been sequestered in one section, that it was like walking through a maze. Until they turned a corner and my father recognized the front foyer with the grand staircase farther ahead. There were windows here that overlooked the mansion grounds. It was pitch-black outside. The middle of the night.

A door was closed on their right as they continued down the hallway. My father paused, pulling the Colonel to a stop. The door was familiar to my father. Of course it was. Through that door was where he'd found the other boys when he'd first arrived at the mansion. Short Stack and Tyrone and all the rest.

"Open it."

Colonel Strickland didn't move.

My father dug the barrel of the pistol into the Colonel's side.

"Open it."

The Colonel said, "What do you expect to prove by me opening that door?"

"Do it."

The Colonel hesitated another moment, then reached out and turned the brass knob and pushed the door open.

The lights were off, but there was just enough light

streaming in from the hallway to illuminate the cots inside. They looked just as they had the first time my father saw them. Only then there had been nearly a dozen boys occupying those cots. Now there were two.

One of the boys stirred awake. He rose slightly from the bed, propping himself up on an elbow, and squinted toward the door.

"Sir?"

My father shoved Colonel Strickland inside the room. He flicked the lights on.

The other boy stirred away, wiping the sleep from his eyes.

My father said, "You need to leave."

The boys didn't move.

"They're going to kill you!"

The boys didn't respond.

Colonel Strickland spoke in his loud, authoritative tone.

"Recruits, listen carefully. This young man is confused. He has something wrong with his head. He wanted to join this operation but was denied, and now he's come here to exact his revenge."

My father said, "He's lying."

"Boys, our only focus here is to defeat Hitler and the Nazis. You know that. And now this deranged individual is trying to stop us."

My father had had enough. He shoved Colonel Strickland forward and fired a round at the ceiling. Both boys jumped to their feet. My father aimed at the boys, back and forth.

"Get out now. Save yourselves."

The boys looked to the Colonel briefly, as if for advice, and then they hurried toward the door. My father stepped back to allow them to pass and watched as they headed down the hallway.

Colonel Strickland chuckled.

"That wasn't smart. Now the other men on the grounds will be here within seconds."

My father turned back to the Colonel. He'd listened to just about enough from the man. So far he had only killed in self-defense, but right now the desire to kill this man was almost beyond my father's control. Would it be murder? Probably, but at that moment my father didn't care.

Before he could pull the trigger, though, something sharp dug into his side.

My father cried out.

One of the boys had returned with a small knife, which he used to stab my father in his side.

The boy stepped back, surprised, and dropped the bloodied knife.

My father, fueled now with rage, punched the boy. Like Dr. Hogan, the boy flew through the air before slamming into a wall. My father heard more than one bone snap.

The Colonel sighed.

"You just killed one of the boys you tried to save. How does that make you feel?"

Out in the hallway then, footsteps. Not many, but there were enough.

The place where the boy had stabbed my father had started to tingle. There had been a flash of pain, but that was it. Now the tingling was followed by itching. My father would only come to understand later that this was the sensation he felt when his body started the process of healing itself.

The footsteps in the mansion were getting closer. The men would be here in seconds.

My father said, "I'm not a killer."

And shot the Colonel in the leg.

He turned and stepped out into the hallway. Men hurried toward him from both directions. They paused when they saw him, raising their rifles. My father knew he didn't have enough bullets to protect him from the rest of these men.

One of the soldiers shouted.

"Put it down!"

My father looked left and right. Then he looked forward. At the window. At the pitch-black outside.

Another soldier shouted.

"Get on the ground!"

My father ran forward, jumping and diving through the window. Shards of glass cut at his arms and face as he fell, and then he rolled on the grass and sprang back up to his feet and kept running. The wounds already tingling, already itching. His body already starting to heal itself. While behind him the soldiers fired out the windows, trying to stop him, trying to slow him. One bullet clipped my father in his shoulder, and he stumbled forward, nearly lost his balance, but managed to stay on his feet. He ran, as fast and as hard as he had ever run in his life, and with bullets flying after him, with an alarm going off signaling other soldiers to follow, my father disappeared into the night.

PART TWO
SENTINEL

15

L ike many bars in New Jersey, the Third Quarter was a dive. Or no—calling it a dive was too generous. What it really was was a piece of shit. Located in Union City, not too far from the train tracks, it was the kind of place where you'd expect a stabbing or shooting at least once a week. It wasn't the kind of place I'd expect to find my old partner, but it had been almost twenty years since I had last seen him, and I knew more than anyone else that things change.

It was almost two o'clock in the morning. The parking lot was half full, which was surprising for the amount of snow falling from the sky. A foot had already fallen, and the snow kept coming.

When Hector Sanchez had entered the bar a half hour ago, he had been wrapped in a parka with a wool hat on his head. Now he exited the place with the same parka and hat, only now he carried a black gym bag.

He trudged through the parking lot toward the Crown Victoria parked ten spaces away. It was an old model, probably a retired cop car which had since been put to pasture and sold on the cheap. Sanchez had probably gotten it for a steal. He had probably also gotten it because he couldn't get comfortable behind the wheel of any other car. Once you drive a particular car for so long, everything else just feels wrong.

As Sanchez approached the Crown Vic, I stepped out of the Charger and quietly shut the door.

He opened the back door first, tossed in the gym bag, then went to open the driver's door. That was when I slipped up behind him. I'd moved soundlessly enough, but still he paused, cocked his head slightly to the side.

"Whatever you plan on doing, do it quick. Otherwise, I reach for the piece I have holstered on my belt and put you down."

This wasn't at all what I had expected him to say. Not that the situation might not warrant it, but I'd never known my partner to say such things. For a second, I wondered if maybe I had the wrong guy. But no—it was his voice. Aged twenty years, yes, but it was his voice.

"That any way to say hello to your old partner?"

He stood still for a long moment, almost as if he didn't hear me. Then he turned, slowly, wiping away the snow falling on his face, and squinted at me.

"Eli?"

"Been a while."

"What ... what are you doing here?"

Pussyfooting around had never been something either of us cared for, so I cut to the chase.

"I need your help."

The door to the bar opened and pounding heavy metal poured outside as people left. Sanchez watched them for a moment, his expression all at once guarded, then lowered his voice.

"We shouldn't be talking here."

"Then let's go."

"Where?"

But I wasn't sure what to tell him. Not yet. I motioned at the car.

"How about you drive. I'll explain on the way."

"On the way to where?"

"In the car."

"Eli, I haven't seen or heard from you in twenty years. Not one word. And suddenly you show up and expect me to help you with something?"

I didn't know why, but his reluctance hurt a bit. For some reason, I'd expected more out of him. Then again, it had been twenty years. Loyalty only lasted so long.

"We're partners. *Were* partners, yes, but I'm hoping that's enough."

"Hoping what's enough?"

"It's about my son."

"What about your son?"

Clearly he didn't follow the news. Or if he did, he didn't remember my son's name.

"James's wife was murdered. His children were murdered. He's currently missing."

Sanchez's mouth dropped open a bit. He stared for a long moment, then took a deep breath.

"Fine, get in the car. I'll give you as much help as I can, but don't expect it to be much."

I started around the car to the passenger side.

"Thank you."

Sanchez opened his door.

"You can fill me in on the way."

"On the way to where?"

But he only shook his head, dropped down behind the wheel.

I slid into the passenger seat. The car's interior reeked of the ghost of stale cigarettes and coffee. It may have been years since it was last used in service, but it was clearly a retired cop car.

"How many miles are on this thing?"

"Too many."

He started the car, and the engine didn't sound nearly as healthy as it probably had a decade ago.

"Buckle up. The weather as bad as it is, it's going to be a bumpy ride."

16

We drove in silence for several long minutes. Because the streets weren't plowed, Sanchez went more slowly than normal, only twenty-five miles per hour. There was only a handful of other cars on the road.

I decided to break the silence.

"It's really coming down."

He nodded but said nothing at first, just drove with both hands on the wheel. Finally, he cleared this throat.

"They're calling for another foot by tomorrow. There's talk the governor will issue a state of emergency, which is going to royally piss everyone off with Christmas days away."

"It's sorta like déjà vu."

"How so?"

"The two of us in a Crown Vic, riding the streets."

He snorted a laugh.

"Yeah, I guess it is."

"Only we're in Jersey."

He nodded but said nothing.

"Where'd you get the car, anyway?"

"They were getting rid of them. Got a great deal. Plus, to be honest, it always felt weird riding in anything else."

He paused, shook his head.

"Eli, what are you *doing* here?"

"I told you, my daughter-in-law and grandchildren were murdered."

"Right, right. I understand that, and I'm sorry to hear it, I am, but what are you doing here tonight? Were you following me?"

I hesitated a beat.

"I was, yes."

He glanced at me, his eyes narrowing.

"Why?"

"To be honest, I didn't know who else to turn to."

"There's the police."

"Right, and tell them what exactly? I haven't been in contact with my son for almost twenty years. Besides, my daughter-in-law and grandchildren murdered and my son missing? He's a prime suspect."

Sanchez didn't say anything to this, his focus back on the street, but I knew what he wanted to say.

"Go ahead and say it."

"What?"

He glanced at me again, stared for a moment, then shook his head.

I said, "Say it. Get it off your chest."

"Christ. Fine—how can you be so sure he didn't do it?"

"That's a good question. To be honest, I don't know, but I have a hunch."

"A hunch."

"I don't want to get too much into details right now, but I have a suspicion my son is being set up."

"You're shitting me."

"That's why I need some extra eyes on the scene."

Sanchez paused.

"Say that again?"

"How many murder scenes did we work together?"

"You can't be serious."

"You've been retired now, what, fifteen years? You have any buddies still on the force you could call in a favor, find out some information?"

"No."

"Exactly. That's why you and I need to do this ourselves."

"The place is going to be locked up. There'll be crime scene tape everywhere. Besides, how long ago did this happen? Whatever evidence there may have been will be long gone."

"I still want to check it out. Look, if you don't want to help me with this, that's fine. I don't want to force you into anything. But I could use the help."

He sighed, shaking his head again as we merged onto the highway headed east, toward Manhattan.

"Goddamn it. How do you always talk me into this shit?"

"My charming good looks."

"Yeah, right. Look, I don't know just what kind of help you think I'll be, but I'll do what I can to help you. First, though, I need to make this stop. It's only going to be a minute, that's all, and then we can be on our way. Where's the scene, anyway?"

"Crown Heights."

He shook his head again.

"I can't believe we're doing this."

"Sanchez, can I ask you something?"

"I suppose."

"What's in the bag?"

I watched his face by the glow of the dashboard, and I saw it tense, just briefly, but then he shook his head.

"Dirty underwear. Why, you got a pair you want to get rid of?"

I didn't press the issue. It had been twenty years since I'd seen him last. His life had changed, just as my life had changed. He had secrets, just like I had secrets. No use digging into something that would cause a rift.

We entered the Lincoln Tunnel. No other cars ahead of us.

Sanchez said, "Hold on tight."

He slammed on the gas.

17

Out of the Lincoln Tunnel, Sanchez directed us into Hell's Kitchen. The streets were as bad here as they'd been in Union City. Pretty soon he turned off into an alleyway. At the end of the alleyway was a small parking lot. An SUV sat facing us, its lights off, exhaust pluming from its tail end.

Sanchez pulled up beside the SUV, lowered his window.

The SUV's driver's side window lowered, and a large man with a Russian accent spoke.

"You're late."

Then ducking his head and squinting at me.

"Who the fuck is that?"

"Nobody. Just a friend."

Someone was in the passenger seat of the SUV. I could see that much from my vantage point. There was movement inside, and the passenger door opened, briefly illuminating the SUV's cabin. The door slammed shut and another man trudged around the front of the SUV. He stopped at the back of the Crown Vic, tried to open the door, but it was locked.

"Open the door."

Rarely had I known Sanchez to show fear. Now it was evident in his voice.

"Why?"

"Open the goddamn door."

Sanchez hit the button for the automatic locks. Every door clicked as the locks disengaged. The man slid inside, the whole car shifting with his weight.

"Who's your friend?"

The accent—it wasn't Russian, not quite. It was familiar, but it had been so long since I last heard anything similar that I couldn't place it.

"Nobody."

"You already said that."

"He's just a friend. I ran into him at the bar. He'd had way too many and I didn't want him to drive."

"Ever hear of a taxi?"

"Viktor, he's okay. I vouch for him."

Viktor snorted a laugh through his nose.

"Vouch for him. You *vouch* for him?"

He laughed again, then shouted out the window.

"Yuri, the spic says he vouches for him!"

Yuri seemed to think this was just as funny. He even went so far as to slap the SUV's steering wheel.

Then, all at once, Viktor went silent and suddenly a gun was in his hand, placed against the back of Sanchez's head.

"The instructions have always been simple. You come alone. No friends. No strangers. Nobody."

Sanchez stared into the rearview mirror, his face frozen. Despite the cold temperature and the snow falling outside, sweat had begun to bead his brow.

Viktor said, "Now what? Cat got your tongue?"

But Sanchez didn't even look capable of responding to the taunt.

I cleared my throat.

"I didn't mean to cause any trouble. I just needed a ride. I'll let myself out here and walk home."

Keeping his gaze on Sanchez, Viktor asked me a question.

"Where do you live?"

I didn't answer.

His eyes shifted toward me. It was clear forcing him to ask the question again wasn't an option.

I said, "Crown Heights."

He stared at me for a moment, then he nodded slowly and turned his attention back to Sanchez.

"You were taking your friend home?"

Sanchez whispered, "Yes."

"You were taking your friend home all the way to Crown Heights?"

Again, a whisper: "Yes."

"What a good friend you are. Yuri, isn't the spic a good friend?"

Yuri said, "It seems that way."

"The only thing I don't understand is how your friend ended all the way over in Union City. Can you explain that, spic?"

Sanchez said nothing.

From the SUV, Yuri said, "Viktor asked you a fucking question."

Ukrainian, I realized. That was the accent. It was slight, but it was clearly Ukrainian.

Which meant the situation was worse than I'd feared.

Sanchez swallowed.

"No."

I opened my mouth to answer, but Viktor shook his head at me.

"No, no. You don't speak. I don't want to hear your fucking voice until I tell you I want to hear it. Understood?"

I nodded.

"Good."

Viktor leaned back, taking the gun away from Sanchez's head.

"I'm going to ride back here while you follow Yuri."

Now Sanchez's lips had begun to tremble.

"Where ... where are we going?"

"Follow him."

Viktor nodded once to Yuri, who put the SUV in gear and rolled past us down the alleyway toward the street.

Sanchez didn't do anything at first, just sat there dumbly behind the wheel. It took another hit in the head from Viktor's gun to snap him into motion. Placing the Crown Vic back in drive, negotiating a three-point turn, and following the SUV.

18

We drove for a while. Through the Theater District, past Times Square, through Midtown. Signs of Christmas were everywhere. In every shop window. On nearly every billboard that wasn't half-covered with snow. Eventually, we came to Gramercy. Viktor didn't say anything the entire time. Neither did we. The only sound was the wipers screeching back and forth and the warm air blowing through the vents.

We followed the SUV off the street and down a ramp into an underground garage. The place was only half-lit, a few emergency lights spaced around along the ceiling making it just bright enough to illuminate the two vehicles already parked there. They weren't in any spaces but just sitting out in the main section. One was another SUV, the other a black Mercedes.

Yuri parked beside the Mercedes. His tail stuck out while the Mercedes' and the other SUV's noses were aimed toward us.

Viktor said, "Stop right here."

Sanchez stopped the car. He shoved the gear in park but kept the engine running.

"Why are we here?"

Viktor ignored the question.

"Turn off the car."

Sanchez turned off the car.

Viktor said, "Give me the key."

"What?"

But Viktor did not repeat himself. He just held out his hand, palm up, waiting.

Sanchez reluctantly placed a small ring of keys in his hand.

"Now get out of the car."

Viktor stepped out with the black gym bag and slammed the door shut. He waited for Sanchez to follow, but Sanchez didn't move. Just sat still behind the steering wheel, staring ahead at the vehicles twenty yards away. Two men had emerged from the SUV, stood beside Yuri.

Sanchez whispered, barely moving his lips.

"Eli, I'm sorry about this."

Viktor didn't rap on the Sanchez's window so much as slammed his fist against it.

"Now!"

Unclipping his seat belt, opening his door, stepping out—Sanchez did it all as slowly as humanly possible. Viktor wasn't so patient and grabbed Sanchez by the arm to hurry him along. He leaned down, pointed at me.

"You—get out too."

I stepped out and followed Viktor as he led Sanchez toward the Mercedes and SUVs. Yuri and the three men had fanned out. They all wore suits. Based on the slight bulges underneath their arms, each man had a holstered weapon.

Viktor pulled Sanchez under one of the emergency lights. He let go of him and tossed the gym bag at the three men.

"Count it."

One of the men picked up the bag and opened it and began pulling out bundles of money. Fifty bundles in all, most of them packs of twenties. Judging by their thickness, they were strapped by two thousand dollars each. Meaning that in the bag there was one hundred thousand dollars, if not more.

Two of the men started counting the packs. One of them was faster than the other, shuffling the bills like he was a casino dealer in Atlantic City. The other took his time, even going so far as to lick his thumb every couple of seconds so he would have a better grip on the bills.

Yuri said, "Shit, don't you know how fucking dirty money is?"

The man ignored him and continued with his counting. It didn't take long. In only a few minutes, they'd set the packs back in the bag.

One of the men said, "It's all there."

Sanchez said, "Of course it's all there."

Viktor said, "Shut up."

He still had the gun in his hand, held at his side. He nodded toward the Mercedes. For a moment I thought he was signaling one of the men standing by the SUVs, but then the Mercedes' driver's door opened and another man dressed in a suit emerged. He opened the back door, and a man I hadn't seen in over twenty years stepped out. He too wore a suit, though his was clearly more expensive than the other men's.

"Well, well, well."

Roman Vyhovsky stared hard at Sanchez.

"Looks like we have ourselves a problem, don't we, Detective?"

19

Back when I was a detective, Roman Vyhovsky was one of the most dangerous men on the streets. It was rumored that over one hundred people had died by his hand, both men and women, but there had never been any substantial evidence. Sanchez and I had brought him in countless times for questioning. It had become our mission to make something stick. Nothing ever did. Even the few times there were witnesses those witnesses eventually changed their stories or went missing.

To Roman, it was a game. After all, he was the head enforcer for the Ukrainian mob in New York. He had grown up in Ukraine and killed countless people in his country before coming to America. It was said on his first day—within the first hour of his feet touching U.S. soil—he had strangled a man to death. There had never been a body, but that didn't mean it hadn't happened, though part of me had always wondered if Roman had started that story to create his reputation.

Somebody in the DA's office had once called Roman "The Magician," and the name had forever stuck. Because whether it was bodies or evidence, Roman always managed to make them disappear.

Roman had been in his early thirties the last time I saw him. Right after Shalissa passed away. Right after the Central Park Bombing. Just before I left the city and my old life behind for good.

Now, twenty years later, it seemed Roman Vyhovsky had graduated from head enforcer and become the head of the mob.

And he was staring right at me.

"Who the fuck is this?"

Sanchez answered.

"Nobody."

"Shut up."

Viktor smacked Sanchez in the back of the head with his gun. He answered Roman.

"Spic told us he's just a friend. Had too many to drink, didn't have money for a taxi. But his friend said he lives in Crown Heights."

"What was he doing in Union City?"

Viktor said, "That's what we want to know."

Roman squinted. He stared at me for several long seconds, and then recognition filled his face.

"I know who it is. Detective Shepherd, it has been a long time, has it not?"

I said nothing.

Now it was my head that received the wrath of Viktor's gun.

"Answer him."

"I'm not a detective anymore."

Roman nodded.

"No, of course you are not. Neither is Hector. But that

does not matter. In my memory, you are still both detectives. How many times did you bring me in for questioning?"

"That depends. How many people did you murder?"

I expected another blow from Viktor's gun, but it didn't come. Maybe the man was too stunned to do anything.

Roman shifted his gaze at Sanchez.

"Spic, do you know why you are here?"

"No."

"Yes, you do."

Sanchez said nothing.

Roman looked at me again.

"Your old partner has been stealing from me. Not a lot, mind you—he no doubt did his best to hide it—but stealing is stealing. And nobody steals from me."

He took off his suit jacket. He held it off to the side and his driver took it and draped it over an arm like a loyal butler. Roman began to roll up the sleeves of his dress shirt as he approached Sanchez. His hand slipped into his pants pocket, came back out gripping a thick pair of brass knuckles. He slid the knuckles over his fingers, flexed his hands.

"My original plan was to teach you a lesson. I was not going to kill you—I do not kill cops, even retired ones—but I was going to make you bleed quite a lot. However, the appearance of Detective Shepherd has given me a change of heart."

He stepped up close to Sanchez, grazed the brass knuckles across Sanchez's face.

"I go to work on you just as I had planned. You spend a month or so in the hospital, then come out and continue working for me. Only now your debt has tripled. Or—"

Roman glanced at me.

"—I go to work on your old partner. He spends a month or so in the hospital. You keep working for me just as you have been doing, and your debt stays the same."

Roman patted the side of Sanchez's face, smiled and stepped back.

"I will give you a moment to make your decision. But only a moment. I do not have all night."

I glanced at Sanchez. He was already looking at me. He shook his head, almost imperceptibly, and whispered two words.

"I'm sorry."

Roman laughed. He raised his hand and motioned his men toward me. The two from the other SUV marched over. They stripped me of my jacket, held onto my arms to keep me in place.

"I have always wanted to tell you something, Detective Shepherd."

Roman massaged his hands as he approached me.

"You were always a nuisance. I understood you were doing your job, but you always seemed to hold a grudge against me. Your questions were always a little more hostile than your partner's. Every time I sat in an interrogation room, I would look at you and wonder what it would feel like to bash your face in. And now, all this time later, I finally have my chance. Is that what is called serendipity?"

The men holding me had grips as tight as vices. I didn't bother trying to struggle with them. I stood there, staring back at Roman.

"Before you start, let me just say two things."

He held my gaze for several long seconds, then tilted his head for me to proceed.

"First, you've always been a spineless piece of shit. Second, I've had a couple bad days so far. I lost my dog—my only friend in the world—and right now I need to be somewhere else. So this little show you're putting on? It's delaying what I need to do. So either let us go now and we'll be on our way, or

I'll put each and every one of your men in the hospital for at least a month."

At first Roman made no reaction. He stared at me, his stern face blank. Then, like before, the corners of his lips rose.

"Nobody likes a funny nigger."

He stepped forward, cocking his fist back, and threw a punch.

And like that, the world began to slow. Just as it did back in Colorado, everything took on an extra sense of texture. My heart rate slowed. My breathing slowed. *Everything* slowed.

Roman's fist came right at my face, but in slow motion.

I leaned back as his fist swiped past my nose. I pulled the man holding my right arm forward, directly in the path of the fist. Roman's brass knuckles tore into the man's face. His grip loosened on my arm, enough for me to yank it free. I turned in toward the man gripping my left arm, kneed him in the groin, and as he bent forward I extracted his weapon from his holster, used the butt of the gun to hammer the back of his head, and then shot Viktor twice—once in the arm, once in the leg—and turned and did the same to Yuri and Roman's driver. All the men hit the ground, their weapons clattering away. Yuri reached for the piece he had holstered to his ankle, and I shot him once more, right in the hand.

The two men holding me were back on their feet. They charged at me, and I shot them twice too. Both fell to the ground.

Everyone was down except for Roman Vyhovsky, who had grabbed Sanchez and now used him as a shield. He still had the brass knuckles on the one hand, and in the other hand he held a gun at Sanchez's head.

"I'll kill him."

I didn't bother responding. The piece I'd taken off the guy was a Glock 17. Assuming it had been fully loaded before I took possession, its magazine held fifteen rounds. I'd already exhausted eleven rounds, which meant there were still four rounds left.

I stood beneath one of the emergency lights in the damp garage. With a flick of my wrist and a slight squeeze of the trigger, the light bulb disintegrated. As Roman looked up, startled, I hurried forward. Not as fast as I had moved in my prime, but it was still fast enough. When Roman turned his attention back to me, I was standing right beside him, the barrel of my gun pressed against his head.

"Let him go."

He released his grip on Sanchez, who wriggled free and stepped away.

"Hector, take his gun."

Sanchez approached, hesitant, and took Roman's gun.

"Now go secure the others."

He looked at me like I was crazy. But it was only for a moment and then he hurried over to the others. A few had tried picking up their weapons, but Sanchez ordered them to put them back down. He picked up several guns, shoved them in his jacket pockets, keeping Roman's gun on the men to keep them in place.

Roman glared back at me, confusion on his face.

"Who the fuck *are* you?"

I leaned close, my voice going low, staring deep into his eyes.

"An old friend."

"Temple?"

He frowned, shook his head.

"But that … that's impossible. Temple's supposed to be dead."

I looked past Roman at Sanchez and the men still on the

ground. Yuri tried to get up, and Sanchez kicked him in the ribs to stay down.

"Sanchez, come over here."

He hurried over.

"Yeah?"

"Frisk him."

Sanchez looked reluctant, but we'd already come this far. He crouched down and started with Roman's left leg, then his right leg, patting all the usual spots. He pulled out a wallet and a cell phone.

"That's it?"

He nodded.

"Toss them. And get in your car."

He started toward the Crown Vic, paused, then turned toward the SUV with the bag of money resting on its hood.

I said, "Leave it."

His shoulders dropped. He stared at the bag for a moment, then continued toward the Crown Vic.

I pushed Roman toward the Mercedes.

Sanchez shouted, "What are you doing?"

I called back over my shoulder.

"Just follow me!"

As we reached the Mercedes, I shot out one tire on each SUV. The slide hadn't kicked back, which meant I had one round left.

I snapped my fingers at the driver of the Mercedes.

"Give me the keys."

He grimaced in pain.

"Fuck you."

I pushed Roman forward. I opened the driver's door, checked and saw that the keys were still in the ignition. I pulled the lever for the trunk to disengage and shoved Roman toward the back of the car.

Roman said, "What the fuck are you doing?"

The trunk was completely bare. Good.

"You're not putting me in there."

Again, I didn't bother responding. I punched him in the stomach, and as he bent forward, I shoved him into the trunk and slammed it shut.

As I went to slide behind the wheel, I paused and surveyed the bodies moving about the garage. None of them were dead, but all of them were out of commission.

I slipped inside and started the Mercedes. The engine purred like a kitten. After days of driving the Charger with its ravenous engine, it was like night and day.

I put the car in gear and glided past the SUVs and bodies and Sanchez. I paused only briefly to make sure Sanchez was following, and then I accelerated up the ramp.

20

Sanchez was out of his car before I even turned off the Mercedes's engine. I opened the door and he was standing right there, less than a foot away, his voice going low and quiet despite the fact there was nobody around to hear him.

"What the fuck are you doing? Have you lost your fucking mind?"

I moved past him toward the trunk.

"It's okay."

He grabbed my arm, spun me back around.

"The fuck it is. Do you have any idea what you've done?"

I stared at him for a beat, then glanced down at his hand on my arm. It took five seconds before he got the hint and released his grip.

Sanchez took a breath, reached up and massaged the back of his neck with his hand.

"I don't know what the hell happened back there, but as bad as things may have seemed, you've just made them a thousand times worse. Why'd you leave them all alive? You should have killed them."

I shook my head and continued toward the back of the Mercedes.

The trunk was silent. Roman Vyhovsky was not one to panic. He rarely showed fear. Being stuffed into the trunk of his own car was not going to break him. I knew that. That's why I had something else in mind.

I popped the trunk, and he lay on his back inside, staring up at me. He said nothing. I didn't expect him to. I grabbed a fistful of his shirt and yanked him out of the trunk. Now he began to fight back, one hand on the arm gripping him, the other trying to reach for me. When that didn't work, he attempted to kick me, but I jabbed him in the throat, enough to cause him to start coughing, and I dragged him toward the edge of the lot.

Roman didn't realize where we were at first. Maybe he was too disoriented from being in the trunk. Maybe his sudden rage had clouded his vision. Or, more likely, he was still trying to catch his breath after I'd just hit him. In the end, it didn't matter. By that point we were almost to the edge. We were on the top portion of a parking garage. It was seven stories tall and deserted at this time of night. Now here we were, me and Roman Vyhovsky, Sanchez trailing nervously behind, as I dragged Roman toward the edge of the platform.

He stopped struggling and let me drag him toward the edge.

"You do not have the guts."

"That remains to be seen. Why did you say Temple was dead?"

He squinted up at me.

"You are not Temple."

I didn't have time to play games. I shoved him to the side. He immediately went up on one foot, pinwheeling his arms to stay balanced. Gravity had other ideas. Roman began to fall. I grabbed him at the last second. I had him by the ankle and he was upside down, his body twisting and turning.

"I'd stay calm if I were you unless you want me to lose my grip."

It took a moment, but he settled down.

Roman craned his neck to look up at me, his eyes wide with panic.

"*What the fuck are you doing?*"

"Asking you a question. Why did you say Temple was dead?"

"I do not know anything about it."

"You said Temple was dead."

"That is what I heard."

"From who?"

"I do not know! The word on the street. One of my men heard it from someone, who heard it from someone else. Nobody has seen Temple for at least a week!"

I glanced at Sanchez. He just stood there, staring down at Roman Vyhovsky. He looked mortified. It was hard to say who he was more scared for, Roman or himself.

"How many people, Roman?"

"What?"

"Since you came to this country, how many people have you killed?"

He was quiet for a long moment, and I didn't think he was going to answer. He just swung there, staring down at the street seven stories below.

He said, "I lost count after two hundred."

Everything in me wanted to drop him right there and then. Watch him fall those seven stories until he went splat on the concrete below. Granted, some of the snow would catch his fall, but it wouldn't be enough for him to survive. There was a perverse pleasure in wanting to watch him die, something I had never experienced before, but Roman Vyhovsky wasn't the reason I had returned to the city.

I looked at Sanchez again.

"You got tape in your car?"

He blinked at me.

"What?"

"Tape. In your car. You got any?"

"I think so, yeah."

"Get it."

As he hurried toward the Crown Vic, I pulled Roman Vyhovsky back up and tossed him aside.

He lay on the ground for several seconds, taking deep breaths, before his glare found me.

"I will fucking kill you."

"Maybe, but not tonight."

Sanchez returned with a roll of duct tape. He held it up.

"Now what?"

"Tape his wrists behind his back, then his ankles."

Roman's glare burned into me.

"You have a family, yes? I will kill them. I will kill your family's family. Their family's family."

I said to Sanchez, "First tape his mouth shut."

Sanchez tore off a strip of tape and pressed it over Roman's mouth. He secured Roman's wrists and ankles. He stood back, the roll of duct tape at his side, flakes of snow in his hair.

"You need me to help you carry him?"

I shook my head and grabbed Roman's shirt and dragged him back to the Mercedes, shoved him in the trunk again.

Roman glared up at me, like before, and like before he didn't bother to struggle.

I slammed the trunk shut and turned to find Sanchez now glaring at me.

"Problem?"

He opened his mouth. Shut it. Kept it shut.

I held out my hand.

"Give me your keys. I'll drive."

21

L ike before, we drove in silence, only this time I was behind the steering wheel. Sanchez sat slumped in the passenger seat, shifted so he was staring out his window at the passing buildings. It had been five minutes since we left the parking garage and neither one of us had spoken yet. But that was okay. I knew Sanchez—or I had known him, once upon a time—and it didn't take long before he finally broke the silence.

"I never took anything from him. Not a dollar. Not a fucking cent. You probably think I worked for him, but I didn't. Not for that son of a bitch. It all ... it's just complicated."

I said nothing. Kept driving.

"The gambling debts just became too much. At first it wasn't too bad—a few hundred here, a few hundred there—but it started adding up. Fast. The vig got out of control. Soon I was five grand down, then ten grand. I knew it was getting bad, but I also knew it was possible to win that money back. To, you know, dig myself out of that hole. But then my marker became fifty grand, then seventy-five."

He shook his head, still staring out his window.

"When it reached one hundred grand, they finally cut me off. Wouldn't let me even try anymore. Word got out I was a bad investment. Clearly I wasn't a good gambler, but even a bad gambler isn't wanted when he has no money. And I had no money. I tried to get a third mortgage on the house, just to pay off the first mortgage, but none of the banks would bite. That's how they knew to approach me, I guess. They knew a desperate man when they saw one."

The Crown Vic's windshield wipers kept moving back and forth, clearing those large fluffy flakes.

"The job was simple. Cake, really. I was a courier. Not even a glorified courier. They didn't even give me a gun, but they expected me to carry one. There was always the worry that someone would try to jack the money, but most people knew who the money belonged to, and they knew better than to mess with me. Besides, I wasn't the only one. Roman has been using cops to do the runs for years. Some of them are still active, but most of the others are retired. We all have that card in our wallets that helps us get out of tickets, stay out of jail. It was exactly what Roman wanted. All of us had debts, some larger than others. I heard about this one guy who was down a half million dollars. I mean, Christ, how stupid can you be to be down that much money?"

He snorted, shook his head again.

"Shit, listen to me. I'm the fuck-up here. I'm the one who should have known better. But it was my only way out. My only way to pay the money back. Not that I was ever going to pay the money back. I could live another fifty years and never pay the money back. That's the thing. You never pay the money back. Roman never wants that to happen. He likes keeping people on a tight leash. But not that anybody ever told me that. I never even saw him until tonight."

"How much did you take?"

He jumped, startled at the sudden sound of my voice.

"What?"

"How much did you take?"

He watched me for a long moment, on the verge of saying something, then turned away again. He spoke to his window.

"Not that much. It didn't even occur to me at first I could take anything at all. I mean, you saw the bag. They don't even fucking lock it because they know nobody would be stupid enough to steal from them."

"But you did."

He nodded, slowly, still staring out his window.

"Yeah, I did."

"You're an idiot."

He issued a harsh, desperate laugh.

"Don't you think I know that? But I had no choice. I needed the money."

"No one needs money that badly. Not when you're stealing it from a psychopath."

He shrugged, waved his hand.

I asked, "When did Maria pass?"

This time, his entire body froze at the question.

"What's that?"

"Maria. You know, your wife?"

He was silent for a long moment, then sighed.

"Five years ago. A stroke. How did you know?"

"After what happened tonight, a caring husband would want to call his wife first thing, tell her to leave the house and go somewhere safe. But you haven't mentioned her at all, which means you're either divorced or she's passed away, and from what I remember about you and Maria, the two of you would never divorce. You drove each other crazy, fought all the time, but you loved each other. Nothing but death would split you up."

He slumped down in his seat, stared out his window.

I said, "When did Roman take over?"

Sanchez shrugged.

"Not really sure. When I retired, I stopped paying attention to that kind of stuff."

"I'm surprised he managed to stay out of prison this long, or at the very least didn't end up dead."

Sanchez shrugged again.

"You know how it is with the Magician."

"Does he still run Maksim?"

Maksim was a Ukrainian restaurant located in the East Village, right in the heart of Little Ukraine, where Roman had stationed himself once he arrived in America and set up shop. On paper, he was the restaurant's owner, but everyone knew he used the place as a base for his illegal activities.

"Yeah."

"Remember that time we went there to have lunch?"

Sanchez barked out a laugh.

"Of course. We wanted to get on his nerves. Instead, we ended up pissing him off even more, and he put out that supposed hit on us, but then Temple ..."

He paused.

"Eli, what happened tonight?"

"What do you mean?"

"You know exactly what I mean. Back in that parking garage. Then on the top of that *other* parking garage. Are you..."

He squinted at me in the dark, searching for the right words, then shook his head.

"No. No way is it true."

"No way is what true?"

"You're not Temple. There's just no way. I know you. Or at least I did. We were together for hours every day. We were partners. Friends. Just—"

He shook his head again.

"—there's no way you could have hidden that from me. No way at all."

I got onto the Williamsburg Bridge, glancing at the rearview mirror as I'd done this entire drive to make sure we weren't being followed.

"You're right. I'm not Temple. Not anymore."

22

The row houses along the street were dark and quiet. A few had lights on inside, though it didn't appear as if anyone was awake yet. Maybe in another hour or so people would begin to rise. According to Sanchez, there was talk the governor would issue a state of emergency, and, in that case, the city would essentially be shut down. Trains wouldn't run. Only emergency personnel would be allowed out on the streets and highways. For now, many people would still be expected to go to work, no matter how bad the weather was or how much worse it was expected to get.

"How do you know that's the one?"

Sanchez stared out at the house halfway down the block, one of the few disconnected from the rest of the row houses by a narrow walkway. We were parked at the curb on the opposite side of the street. Even in the dark the crime scene tape across the front door was evident.

"The address was in the papers. I drove past it earlier today. I'm not going to be able to enter through the front. There's an alley around back. I'll go that way."

"And what do you want me to do?"

I was silent for a beat.

"Keep an eye out. Obviously I'm not going to be able to turn on the lights inside, but I'm sure any slight disturbance will be noticed sooner or later. A concerned neighbor will call the police. You notice anything, you signal me."

"How do you want me to do that?"

"If you see anything, honk the horn once, then get out of here. I'll slip out the back and head down the alley."

"I thought you wanted me to work the scene with you."

"I changed my mind."

"Why?"

When I didn't immediately respond, he realized the reason.

"Because of what happened earlier? I'm sorry about that. I, well, what do you want me to say? I'm a coward."

I said nothing.

"Come on, Eli. You haven't worked a crime scene in twenty years. Even if you had, what good would any of this do? You expect to find something the other detectives missed? Even if you did, none of it would hold up in court."

"Who says I expect anything to go to court?"

"I'm sorry this happened to your family, I am, but I don't understand what the point is."

"You know how I said I wasn't Temple anymore?"

"Yeah."

"I was Temple, a long time ago. Just like my father before me. When I left, the role of Temple was passed on to my son."

Sanchez was quiet for a moment, soaking this in.

"Nobody's seen Temple for at least a week."

"That's what Roman said too."

"You don't think your son did this to his family, do you?"

Now it was my turn to be quiet. The possibility had always been there. The paternal part of me had refused to accept the possibility, while the detective part of me knew never to rule out anyone in a homicide, especially the spouse.

Sanchez said, "Fuck this. I'm going with you."

"No, you're not."

"Yes, I am. Two sets of eyes are better than one. Besides, how many times did we work scenes together and I spotted something you didn't?"

"It was rare."

"But it still happened. We'll make it quick. In and out. If we hear engines outside, we'll run for it. Besides, after what I witnessed tonight, I don't think a pair of patrol officers stand a chance against you. Tell me, Eli, when was the last time you saw your son?"

"I'm not quite sure. At least twenty years ago."

"So you never even met your grandchildren?"

"No."

"Never saw any pictures?"

"No."

"How is that possible?"

"I never called. I never visited. I stayed out of their lives altogether."

"Why?"

"I had my reasons."

"What about your daughter?"

"I checked on Aisha as soon as I arrived in the city."

"You spoke with her?"

"No, I watched her from a distance. She seemed safe. Part of me thinks whoever did this to James's family may not even be aware of her. If that's the case, I want to keep it that way. My plan is once I figure out what happened to James, I'll contact Aisha."

Sanchez looked around the still dark and quiet street.

"If we're going to do this, let's do this."

I turned the ignition, cranked the wheel, and slowly coasted out into the street.

We parked two blocks away and trudged down the alley. There wasn't much light, so we moved through the shadows. Because no vehicles had gone through here in a while, the snow had piled up to almost a foot high.

The backyard was tiny, almost nonexistent. No garage. No swing set. No slide. Nothing but a waist-high chain-link fence that Sanchez and I easily climbed over. Here the snow was flawless. For some reason, I didn't want to disturb it. Nothing should be put out of place.

Sanchez looked over at me.

"What's wrong?"

I shook my head and continued forward, across that flawless snow which came up to our knees, and then up the porch steps. Sanchez and I glanced around to make sure nobody was watching us. Here on the door was another notice from the police that no one should trespass on the premises.

I knew the knob would be locked but tried it anyway. It didn't move in my hand.

Sanchez whispered, "How do you want to do this?"

The options were simple: pick the lock or break a window. If there was an alarm set, it would go off either way. Best not to waste any more time than was necessary.

I used my elbow against the lowest pane of glass. The first hit cracked the pane. The second hit shattered it. I reached in, ignoring the glass shards—if any of them cut me, I'd heal in minutes—and unlocked the door.

Seconds later, Sanchez and I were inside.

We wiped our shoes on the mat just inside the door,

stomped our feet as quietly as possible to loosen the snow clinging to our pants.

Sanchez said, "Smell that?"

I did. I had expected no less. Not after what I'd read about in the news. The murders had sounded brutal enough, and they had only been five days ago. The bodies were gone, of course, but not the blood. There was no need to clean up the blood, at least not yet. Eventually, the house would be cleaned up. Everything inside would be taken out. The house would be put on the market and someone would buy it, either knowing what happened here and not caring or someone completely oblivious to recent events.

The windows were covered. Curtains closed, blinds shut. The police wouldn't want anybody to see inside. Especially the press. Which gave us an advantage.

I pulled a small penlight from my pocket, flicked it on.

Sanchez brought out his cell phone and used the glow of the screen to light the way.

The kitchen was a mess. Some dirty dishes in the sink and on the counters, but that wasn't the worst of it. If the kitchen was any indication, the house had been ransacked. Pots and pans and Tupperware containers and boxes of cereal and crackers and bags of chips were scattered around the floor. Every cabinet had been cleaned out. So had the cupboards. Cans of soup and vegetables were just as numerous. One can of vegetables caught my attention, a name brand of lima beans. Growing up, James and his sister had *hated* lima beans.

The fridge looked as if it had been ransacked as well. Cans of soda and bottles of juice were on the floor. Some pictures were scattered across the fridge that looked untouched, which seemed a small blessing. Some of James and his wife, Yolanda. Others of my grandchildren. A few of all four of them together. Some drawings done in crayon and marker. One math test with a circled A+ in bright red ink. The name printed at the top said *Ashlee.*

"Look at this."

Sanchez stood by the wall, the glowing screen of his cell phone pointed upward.

On the wall was a plastic clock. The clock itself wouldn't have been that strange, but it was what the clock featured. Temple. Or at the very least it had that red T in the center of the black clock.

I did another sweep of the kitchen. I noticed a basket on the counter, and in the basket were several envelopes. They'd been scattered about, just like everything else, but I recognized what they were at once. Overdue bill notices.

We continued deeper into the house.

The next room was the dining room. Like the kitchen, the dining room was a mess. There had been less here to ransack—only a few cabinets—but stuff littered the floor and table. It didn't matter anyway. What we focused on was the carpet, which didn't appear stained.

Besides, the smell was coming from the next room. The living room.

Sanchez said, "Are you sure you want to see this?"

"How many murder scenes have we worked in the past?"

"Yeah, but none of them was your own blood."

I didn't know why, but I only expected there to be a little blood. There wasn't. There was a lot.

Sanchez sucked in air between his teeth.

"Holy shit."

I shined the penlight across the floor. The carpet's color was a sort of beige. Much of it was now stained dark with blood. Not just the carpet, either, but the couch and recliner. I moved the penlight and found that even spots of blood dotted the walls.

An artificial Christmas tree lay on its side in the corner. That, too, was spotted with blood.

Sanchez shook his head.

"Not a gun. Not with this much blood."

I shined the penlight toward the other end of the living room, toward the foyer. The floor there was wood, and there didn't appear to be any spots of blood marking the surface.

I said, "Whoever did this was a family friend or associate."

"What makes you say that?"

"The front door doesn't look like it was kicked in. Which means the killer was invited in. They waited until they were in the living room. This was where my daughter-in-law was killed."

"Are you sure?"

"From where the blood stained the carpet, it looks like it came from just one body. And besides, that's too much blood for a child."

"So what about the children?"

I shifted the penlight's beam at the stairs. I dreaded the idea of going up there. Stepping into rooms of dead children who I had never hugged, let alone even spoken to.

"How do you know for sure it's a family friend or associate?"

"What do you mean?"

"Eli, I know it's difficult to accept the idea that your son—"

"He didn't do this."

"I know that's what you want to believe, and I want to believe the same thing, I do, but we can't rule him out. Christ, he's disappeared. When a husband disappears after his family is murdered, what does it usually mean?"

"He didn't do this."

Sanchez placed a hand on my shoulder.

"Stop kidding yourself. I don't want to believe your son did this any more than you, but you can't look at this subjectively if you refuse to accept that it's a possibility."

I pushed his hand off my shoulder, nodded toward the steps.

"We should check upstairs."

Sanchez didn't move at first. He just stood there, staring at me. It was clear he wanted to say something but wasn't sure what to say. Then he frowned, studying my face.

"What is it?"

"Don't you hear that?"

Of course he didn't hear it. His ears weren't as finely attuned as mine. But that didn't matter. A few seconds later he did hear it—the deep growling approach of engines—and his eyes narrowed.

"Maybe it's just a plow truck."

I moved to the closest window in the living room—one that looked out at the street—and spread the blinds just enough to peek outside.

A black SUV had pulled up. Before it had even stopped moving, the doors opened and people dressed in black spilled out.

I reached for the Glock in my jacket pocket.

"We have company."

23

There were four of them, including the driver. Their uniforms didn't quite match the men's from Colorado, but that didn't mean anything. Then again, after another glance at the SUV, it was clear the vehicle wasn't the same either. Still, didn't mean anything. But the four—three men and a woman—each had pistols holstered to their sides. None of them had reached for the weapons yet, but again, that didn't mean anything.

Two of them headed for the front door while the other two stayed on the sidewalk.

I turned away from the window.

"Out the back."

Sanchez followed me through the house. The fridge caught my eye again and I wished there was something I could take, some kind of memento of the two grandchildren I never knew. But I kept going, straight for the back door.

Even before I opened it, I could hear another SUV idling in the alleyway.

I parted the curtain, just slightly, and saw two more men in black trudging through the snow toward the porch. No doubt there were two others keeping lookout in the alley.

Sanchez whispered, "Police?"

I stepped back from the door, shaking my head. These weren't police. At least not the police I was familiar with. I remembered one time Darrell complaining that recently the police had become more militarized, that they were practically a militia unto themselves, and maybe that was the case. Maybe this was how police operated in this day and age. Sanchez would know better than me, but we didn't have time to discuss the recent changes.

My grip tightened around the Glock. I'd since loaded a fresh magazine, so there were fifteen rounds to work with. More than enough to take out these six intruders, assuming it took no more than two rounds each. But that also assumed they were the only ones. Maybe others were coming. Maybe others were already here, waiting down at both ends of the street.

Sanchez touched my arm, gently, and shook it to get my attention.

"What do we do?"

I thought about those men in Colorado. The tech they wore. The night vision goggles. The heavy artillery. Just how much planning their failed operation must have taken. The time it took for them to sneak up on me as they had.

Then again, this team had been called out at a moment's notice. Whoever had sent them wanted the job done as quickly as possible, no matter what it took.

My grip tightening even more on the Glock, I peeked through the curtain again.

The two men had advanced through the tiny backyard, but they had not come up onto the porch. They stood in the snow

now, their backs to the house, handguns held at their sides. As if they were guarding the house.

The doorbell rang.

Sanchez and I traded glances. We stared at each other, both completely still and silent. The plastic Temple clock hanging on the wall ticked.

The doorbell rang again.

Another glance through the curtain showed me the two men again, still standing with their backs to the house, guns at their sides.

I let the curtain fall back into place and retraced my steps through the house, this time to the front door.

Sanchez kept pace beside me.

"What are you *doing*?"

I didn't answer. It was obvious what I was doing, but that didn't appease Sanchez's incredibility.

In the front foyer I paused, my hand on the doorknob. I could peek out the nearest window, see who was on the other side, but it wouldn't matter. Not at this point.

I opened the door.

The man and woman stood on the stoop. Large flakes of snow had begun to lie on their shoulders.

The man said, "Elijah Shepherd? I'm Agent Palmer with Homeland Security. This is Agent Njeim. We need you to come with us."

The man was tall, well built, in his late-forties with a full head of hair. He had the face of a leader. The woman was late-thirties, Middle Eastern, short black hair and dark eyes.

I kept the Glock hidden behind my back.

"Why are you here?"

Agent Palmer said, "We believe your life is in danger."

Sanchez said, "How would you know that?"

Agent Palmer glanced at him, as if for the first time.

"And you are?"

Agent Njeim answered.

"Hector Sanchez. He was Mr. Shepherd's partner when he was a detective."

Sanchez said, "How did you know *that*?"

Agent Palmer ignored the question, his gaze back on me.

"Sir, I understand this situation is confusing, but if you come with us, we'll explain everything."

"I'm not sure that's a good idea."

Both agents said nothing. More and more flakes of snow fell on their shoulders.

Agent Njeim tilted her face toward Agent Palmer.

"Call him."

Agent Palmer stood motionless for a moment like he didn't hear her. Then he addressed me again.

"Mr. Shepherd, I have a cell phone in the left pocket of my jacket. I'd like to take it out if that's okay with you."

"Go ahead."

The agent opened the pocket and took out a cell phone. He touched the screen, dialed a number, and put the phone to his ear.

He was quiet for a long moment, listening to the phone ring, and then he said his name and gave some kind of clearance code.

"I need to speak with him. Yes, I know what time it is. But this is important."

Agent Palmer clicked off the phone, touched the transmitter in his ear.

"Bring me a tablet."

Behind him, on the sidewalk, the SUV's driver moved at once. He went to the back of the vehicle, opened the door, leaned in, came back out and started up the walkway.

The driver handed Agent Palmer the tablet before promptly

turning and heading back to the sidewalk, where he took up his previous position.

Agent Palmer pressed a button on the side of the device, and its screen began to glow. He started tapping the screen in several places, then waited, staring at the screen.

Nobody spoke. The snow kept falling. Agent Palmer kept the device tilted so the snow didn't touch the screen.

A minute passed in silence. Then finally a voice from the device spoke.

"Yes?"

Agent Palmer said, "Sir, I have Elijah Shepherd here."

The agent flipped the device around so I could see the screen.

The voice from the device spoke again.

"Good morning, Elijah. It's an honor to meet you."

For a moment, I wasn't sure what to say. I knew technology had advanced at a rapid rate since I had hidden from the world. Often Darrell would decry its relentlessness. So on one level I was shocked to be seeing someone from a device that was thinner than a book. On another level, I was also shocked by who this certain someone was. I may have hidden myself away from the world for the past twenty years, but that didn't mean I wasn't familiar with important world leaders. I may not have voted for him—I hadn't voted since 1996—but that didn't mean I didn't know who he was.

"Thank you, sir. It's an honor to meet you too, Mr. President."

24

The President of the United States wiped the sleep from his eyes. The device only showed his head and shoulders. He wore an undershirt. No doubt he had been awakened just minutes ago by Secret Service or whoever had answered Agent Palmer's call.

"I heard what happened to your daughter-in-law and grandchildren. I'm very sorry. But please trust me when I tell you Agent Palmer and his team are doing what they can to not only track down the people responsible but to also find your son. The world needs him more than ever right now."

I didn't know what to say, so I just nodded.

"Elijah, once this is all over, I'd like to meet you in person. It would be an honor."

I nodded again.

"Yes, Mr. President."

The president said, "Agent Palmer?"

The agent flipped the device around so the screen faced him.

The president said, "You take care of this man. Understood?"

"Yes, sir. Thank you, sir."

Agent Palmer tapped the screen and the glow went out. He looked up at me.

"Will you please now come with us?"

I looked out past him at the street, at the two men standing guard by the SUV. Besides them, the street was still and quiet.

"Would you come inside first? I have a question to ask you."

"Sir, we don't have the time—"

Agent Njeim touched his arm. She said to me, "We would be happy to."

Sanchez and I stepped back to allow the agents into the foyer. I closed the door and they began stomping the snow from their boots. Since there was no more need to hide, I flipped the switches by the door. The foyer light and living room lights came on. The light made the blood on the carpet even more evident.

I asked, "How did you know we were here?"

Agent Palmer was annoyed, but he did a good job trying to hide it.

"Everything will be explained to you once we return to the Vault."

"The Vault?"

"It's what we call our base. Now, please, if you would just—"

"Agent Palmer, I need to know now."

"May I ask where you've been all this time?"

"I was out west."

"Were you aware of all the changes that have happened to this country since 9/11?"

"I've heard of some."

"Since passing the Patriot Act, it has been our focus to stop any forms of terrorism, either domestic or international.

Because of this, we had been granted access to all communication, whether telephone or the Internet, as well as video feeds."

Sanchez murmured, "Illegal access."

"Be that as it may, one day someone decided to use this surveillance to track Temple. It wasn't easy, and it took many resources, but they were finally able to determine who he was."

I said, "How long ago was this?"

"Seven years, give or take. At least that was when they finally determined your son was Temple. Before that, it was maybe five years of research."

"And then?"

"Nothing. It was ultimately decided that we were never supposed to intervene. All we would do was monitor. If there ever came a situation that appeared too dire for Temple—wherein he may have died—we had been given permission to intervene, but nothing until then."

"Were there ever cameras inside this house?"

"No. But we did secure a house down the block as a surveillance point. The city also has cameras on almost every block. We monitor those feeds constantly."

"Then if my daughter-in-law and grandchildren were murdered in this house, you know who did it."

For the first time, Agent Palmer looked to be at a loss. He glanced at Agent Njeim, who answered.

"Unfortunately, whoever murdered them was aware of our surveillance. The cameras for a five-block radius had been temporarily shut down. The stakeout house down the block had been broken into, and the two agents on shift had been murdered. The Vault had been notified at once that the cameras in this sector had gone down, and when they could not reach the two agents in the house, two teams were sent out. By the time the teams arrived, your daughter-in-law and grandchildren were already dead."

"And my son?"

Agent Palmer said, "There has been no sign of him for the past week."

"Is there a chance—"

"That your son was the one who killed his wife and children? It's certainly a possibility, but we don't believe so."

"Do you have any suspects at this time?"

Agent Palmer shook his head.

I glanced at Sanchez, who suddenly looked smaller than he had before, weaker. Scared.

"Agent Palmer, do you have access to the police reports of this murder scene?"

"We do."

"Then before I come with you, I want you to walk me through the murder, step by step. I want to know exactly what happened here."

25

Agent Njeim walked us through the crime scene while Agent Palmer stepped away to make a phone call.

The official police report more or less matched what I had assumed took place.

The killer had not broken in. There were no signs of forced entry. Whoever the killer was, my daughter-in-law had known him or at least been somewhat familiar with him. At least that would explain why she would open the door at almost eleven o'clock at night and invite the killer inside. Because the killer didn't strike immediately. The killer waited at least a couple seconds, enough for my daughter-in-law to lead the killer into the dining room. That was where the killer plunged the knife—what police believed was at least an eight-inch blade—into my daughter-in-law's back.

"The police think the killer walked up right behind her, placed a hand over her mouth to muffle her scream, and stabbed her."

Agent Njeim's tone was indifferent. She was merely relaying a report she had no doubt read countless times.

"There were over thirty stab wounds in total, half of which

were to her back. Then the killer sliced her throat. As she fell to the ground, the killer stabbed her in the stomach."

"And then?"

Agent Njeim hesitated.

"And then the killer beheaded her."

This gave me pause. Everything else I had predicted from the bloodstains and from what little I read in the news, but not this.

Sanchez's voice cracked when he spoke.

"Beheaded her?"

Agent Njeim said, "Yes, just as the children were beheaded."

I said, "That wasn't in the news."

"No, it wasn't. We made sure the police suppressed that information."

"How?"

"We told them it was a potential terrorist attack."

"It's been almost a week. The news hasn't leaked yet?"

"We're Homeland Security, Mr. Shepherd. If we don't want something printed in the news, it doesn't get printed. And besides, we were on the scene almost immediately. We let the police do their investigation, but we had complete oversight."

Agent Palmer had been in the kitchen, talking on his phone. Now he entered the dining room, slipping the phone into his jacket pocket.

"Are we ready?"

I shook my head.

"Not yet. Show me the upstairs."

Agent Palmer didn't accompany us upstairs. He headed back outside to regroup with the other men and prepare our convoy.

The house itself was at least fifty years old. The stairs were hardwood and creaked with almost every step. The second floor hallway was tight and narrow. Some pictures hung on the walls, photographs of my son and daughter-in-law and grandchildren. Like the few photos on the refrigerator in the kitchen, they looked happy.

The second floor had three bedrooms and a full bath. Agent Njeim skipped the master bedroom. She opened one of the children's rooms and flicked on the light.

This had been my granddaughter's bedroom.

The walls were white but had posters lining the walls. Some of movies, some of pop musicians.

She had been only eleven years old.

Like the living room downstairs, blood stained the carpet and some of the wall. Also the bed. The bed was soaked with dried blood.

"The police believe she was first. She was most likely asleep when the killer entered the room. The killer stood over her and held her mouth shut as he stabbed her repeatedly. All said there were just over thirty stab wounds. Then he cut off her head."

I looked around the room one last time. I had been to countless murder scenes, had seen my share of terrible deaths, but nothing like this. A father is not supposed to outlive his children, and he is most certainly not supposed to stand in the room where his grandchild was beheaded.

"What about the number of participants? What do your analysts predicate about that?"

"At this point it's still undecided. Clearly at least one person was responsible, and we believe there were multiple people involved, but regarding the murder itself? We aren't entirely sure."

"My granddaughter's name was Ashlee. I only know this because I saw her math test on the refrigerator downstairs. I'm almost embarrassed to ask this, Agent Njeim, but what was my grandson's name?"

"Trevor."

I nodded.

"Please show me Trevor's room."

Agent Njeim turned off the light and closed Ashlee's bedroom door behind her and led us to the next room. She opened the door, flicked on the light inside.

Just as the previous bedroom had clearly belonged to an eleven-year-old girl, this bedroom had belonged to a boy.

There wasn't as much blood on the bed as in my grand-daughter's room. Most of it was on the carpet and the wall closest to the door. A desk was stationed against the wall, a large, bulky computer on top. Those too were spotted with blood.

"He wasn't killed in his sleep, was he."

I didn't bother making it a question.

"Based on the position of his body, police believe he was awoken when the killer entered his room. He may have panicked, cried out—that part we don't know, of course—but it is clear that he jumped out of bed. Maybe he tried to hide, or maybe he tried to rush past the killer. In the end, it didn't matter. The killer stabbed him at least forty times. Then beheaded him."

I closed my eyes. Despite the fact I had never actually seen my grandson in real life and the only face I knew of him was in the pictures I had just seen tonight, I saw it all playing out in my mind.

"You told the police this was a potential terrorist attack?"

"Yes."

"Is that mere speculation or is there actual evidence to make that case?"

Agent Njeim said nothing for a moment, and that was all the answer I needed.

"My son?"

"We have him leaving this house at seven forty-five that evening. There were several emergencies in Manhattan that he may have been responding to, but as far as we can tell, he never showed up to any of them."

"So as far as you know, he's disappeared."

"Yes."

Agent Njeim's phone vibrated. She looked at the screen, then up at me.

"Agent Palmer wants to know if you're ready."

I looked down at the stained carpet one last time.

"I'm ready."

26

As we made our way outside, Sanchez asked if he was free to leave.

Agent Njeim shook her head.

"I'm afraid not, Mr. Sanchez. At this point, it's best if you stay with us."

Sanchez opened his mouth to protest, but then gave it another second's thought and nodded. He followed us down the walkway toward the street.

Agent Palmer stood beside the SUV. He opened the back door and motioned for us to get in.

Sanchez climbed in first.

I started to get in after him but glanced back at Agent Njeim.

"You're not coming?"

"Not enough room. Agent Rachman and I will squeeze in elsewhere."

Even as she spoke, headlights splashed us as another SUV turned down the street and headed our way.

I climbed inside, and Agent Palmer shut my door. I watched him outside speaking briefly with Agent Njeim before she started toward the approaching SUV, and Agent Palmer opened the passenger door and slid into his seat.

Sanchez looked around the SUV.

"Huh. I always wondered where my tax dollars went."

The driver put the vehicle in gear and we headed down the street, the SUV with Agent Njeim inside behind us. At the intersection, another SUV was waiting—this one from the alleyway, presumably—and it pulled out in front of us so that our envoy now included three.

"I'm sorry about your grandchildren, Mr. Shepherd."

Agent Palmer had the tablet open in his lap, swiping at the screen.

"I have three children of my own. One's already a teenager, another is twelve years old. My youngest is seven and obsessed with Temple. He has all the toys."

"There are toys?"

Agent Palmer turned his head to grin at me.

"Of course there are toys. You can't have a superhero if you don't have toys."

I remembered the kid from the Apple Store, the red T on his T-shirt.

"Where did the red T come from?"

Agent Palmer shrugged.

"Probably some marketing executive. As you well know, the real Temple never wore any symbol or logo, but that probably doesn't help sell toys."

"How long have there been toys?"

"I don't know. Maybe ten years now? Someone finally decided to ramp up the merchandising. It wasn't like Temple was a copyrighted or trademarked figure. There's T-shirts, lunchboxes, comic books. There was even a cartoon that lasted a year or two before it was canceled."

"What was it about?"

"I have no idea. I never watched it. But the way I understand it, Temple was given this bizarre backstory about being from space."

"From space?"

"Either that or something from space fell to the earth and Temple encountered it. Again, I never watched it, but my son always talked about it. The way I understand it, there's been talk about doing a full-length feature film, but the studio hasn't found the right director yet."

I thought about my son's house. The overdue bills on the kitchen counter. His family barely able to scrape by.

"Where does all the money go?"

"Corporations, no doubt."

We drove for another minute in silence. Light was beginning to grow in the east. Despite the early hour, the streets were dotted with cars. A few large dump trucks with plows attached to their front ends roared past laying salt.

Agent Palmer shook his head at the cars.

"These people are going to be pissed when the governor announces a state of emergency in the next two hours."

The SUV in front of us slowed for the next turn, and then we were headed onto the Manhattan Bridge.

Agent Palmer kept swiping at the tablet in his lap.

"So my son, he's obsessed with Temple. And it's tough because I can't tell him what it is I do all day. I'm almost never home as it is, so when he sees me I'm like a stranger to him, and sometimes I feel that if I could just have one thing to connect with him he would think I'm the coolest. But I can't. And that's okay, but just imagine his face if I told him that it's Daddy's job to protect Temple."

Sanchez said, "Only you let his family get murdered."

Agent Palmer set the tablet aside. His shoulders seemed to drop, and he shifted in his seat to look back at me.

"Yes, that did happen. I could try to make excuses, but the fact is our whole purpose was to keep an eye on your son and his family. And we failed. There's no arguing that. That's why right now we're doing everything we can to find the people responsible. That's why right now we're doing everything we can to find your son. And that's why right now we're doing everything we can to protect you."

We were moving at maybe forty miles per hour over the bridge. The snow was thick and some of the smaller cars ahead of us were driving even slower.

The city rose up ahead of us, the overcast sky and flurries making it look like something out of a snow globe.

I said, "They found me."

"Who?"

"The people who killed my daughter-in-law and grandchildren. They somehow managed to find me and came for me in the middle of the night."

The SUV ahead of us switched lanes to bypass a slower-moving car. Our SUV followed directly behind, just as the SUV behind us, as if we were connected by invisible wire.

Agent Palmer said, "How many were there?"

"Six. They were heavily armed. Very well trained."

We were halfway across the bridge now, directly over the East River.

"What happened to them?"

"They're dead."

I let that hang heavy in the air for a moment.

"Whoever these men were, they found out where I lived. The thing is, Agent Palmer, nobody knew where I ended up. Not my son. Not my daughter. Nobody."

The sun continued to rise in the east, its soft glow playing shadows off the wire cables hanging from the compression pillars.

I glanced out the window and watched the churning water of the East River.

That was when the helicopter appeared.

It rose up from under the bridge, already flying parallel with us. It wasn't a police helicopter. It was a Black Hawk. Sikorsky Aircraft had introduced the first ones to the U.S. Army in 1979, well after my time in the military, but still I recognized it at once.

For a second, I thought the Black Hawk was our escort. Just another precaution Homeland Security had sent to ensure we arrived safely at our destination. Then the side panel opened and a man was crouched there with an RPG launcher resting on his shoulder.

Agent Palmer grabbed a walkie-talkie on the dashboard, shouted into it.

"We have hostiles, three o'clock!"

The man fired the RPG. One second it was in the launcher, the next second it hit the side of the SUV in front of us. The SUV exploded.

Digging his cell phone from his pocket, Agent Palmer shouted at the driver.

"Keep going!"

The driver shifted lanes, pressed on the gas. The SUV's engine roared, but the vehicle didn't pick up as quickly as it normally would have without the snow.

We passed the SUV, the thing in flames.

Agent Palmer spoke into the phone.

"We're under attack. On the Manhattan Bridge, headed into the city. We need support ASAP."

He flung the cell phone away, pulled out his gun.

The helicopter kept pace beside us. Another man appeared to help reload the launcher with another RPG.

I leaned forward in my seat.

"Any spare weapons?"

"In the back."

Agent Palmer shifted in his seat, checked through the rear window at the trailing SUV.

It was following directly behind, fifty yards away.

I took off my seatbelt and twisted in my seat to reach into the back. A large plastic container was there. It was positioned so the clasps could be accessed from the tail of the vehicle, once the hatch was opened. I shifted the container around, undid the clasps, and opened the lid.

Inside, enclosed in gray foam, were four 9mm Sig Sauer P226 pistols, two H&K MP5 submachine guns, and several loaded magazines.

I pulled out one of the pistols, checked to make sure the mag was fully loaded, and handed it to Sanchez.

He was already on edge. He stared down at the gun as if he didn't know what to do with it, then swallowed and nodded.

I grabbed one of the MP5s, confident its magazine was also fully loaded, and passed it up front to Agent Palmer.

He already had his seat belt off, was positioning himself in his seat to shoot out his window.

I took the other MP5 and positioned myself in the same way.

The driver was pushing the SUV as fast as it would go in the snow. We were already doing sixty, almost off the bridge.

In the helicopter, the RPG launcher had been reloaded.

The driver, without having to be told, lowered both passengers' side windows.

Agent Palmer and I opened fire.

The helicopter jerked as bullets tore into it and then steadied out. The man who had helped reload the RPG launcher reappeared with a submachine gun. He fired at us as the other man aimed the launcher at the SUV behind us.

Like before, it took only a second for the man to fire the missile.

But the trailing SUV's driver had anticipated it. Already going sixty miles per hour in the snow, he slammed on the brakes and jerked the wheel. The SUV skidded forward and began to drift in a 360 just as the missile was fired. The missile overshot the SUV by mere yards and exploded on the other side of the bridge.

Agent Palmer and I kept firing at the helicopter. We exhausted the mags. Sanchez had already gathered extra magazines for us, and we loaded them just as the driver took us off the bridge. The arch and colonnade were coming up on the left.

We leaned back out our windows, fired up at the helicopter, but it was no longer flying parallel.

It banked and rose up, hovering in one spot.

Agent Palmer and I both stared up at it, unsure of what this meant.

That was when we reached the end of the bridge.

When the dump truck came out of nowhere and smashed into us from the side.

27

The dump truck hit us at an angle, and with just enough force, so that the SUV's side tipped up and sent us on two wheels. The SUV rolled, first on its side and then on its roof. It slid for several yards in the snow before coming to a halt.

Suddenly noises were evident: the continuous thudding of the helicopter's rotor blades, yes, but also several high-pitched whines. They reminded me of the motorcycles the two punks had back in Harper. Only these weren't motorcycles. They were snowmobiles.

Up front, Agent Palmer groaned. Because he'd taken off his seat belt a minute before, he had been tossed around by the impact.

I hadn't been wearing my seat belt either, but Sanchez had. He had grabbed me at the last second and tried to hold me in place. It hadn't done much, but at least the impact hadn't thrown my body around like it had Agent Palmer's. For me, a few bumps and bruises would heal within minutes. For Agent Palmer, it could be weeks. If we managed to get out of this alive.

Agent Palmer said, "Everyone okay?"

The pain evident in his voice.

Halfhearted murmurs greeted this, stating that we were.

I twisted so my feet were on the ground. I ducked down and grabbed the MP5 I'd dropped during the collision.

"Mr. Shepherd—"

Agent Palmer groaned even as he said the words.

"—I must ask that you to stay in the vehicle."

"You're joking, right?"

Outside, the high-pitched whines had stopped. The snowmobiles had arrived. By the sound there were at least three of them, maybe four.

Gunfire started up.

I ducked down and watched through the rear window as the other SUV had come to a halt. The agents poured out and opened fire on the dump truck and the men on the snowmobiles.

Problem was, the SUV wasn't much cover with the Black Hawk still in the air. The man with the submachine gun was already raining fire down on the agents. The other man was busy reloading the RPG launcher.

Agent Palmer said, "Backup will be here soon."

I watched Agent Njeim sprint for the colonnade. Two other agents followed her, just as the man in the helicopter launched the third RPG.

This time, the SUV didn't have the luxury of trying to outwit the missile. The thing was a sitting duck. The missile hit its target dead on.

One of the agents hadn't made it away in time for the explosion. Half of him was on fire. He hit the ground and started rolling around. The man in the helicopter, no doubt with more malice than compassion, sprayed several bullets into his writhing body.

I said, "Agent Palmer, soon all of your people will be dead."

Agent Palmer had managed to right himself. He had the MP5 in his hands.

The driver too had managed to right himself, a gun in his hand.

Sanchez had the Sig, held at the ready.

Agent Palmer did a three-count and we opened our doors and stepped out into the cacophony.

The four snowmobiles had entered the intersection from three different points: two coming up Canal Street, another coming down Canal Street, and the fourth coming up Chrystie Street.

Each man now stood in front of his snowmobile, submachine guns aimed.

Like back in the parking garage, my body went tense. Time seemed to slow down. My heart rate slowed. My breathing slowed.

I focused on the man by the closest snowmobile. I squeezed the trigger twice, placed two bullets between his eyes, and then spun and fired several shots at the two men from the dump truck.

The driver got hit in the shoulder. He dropped his rifle, bent to pick it up, but another one of my bullet's caught him on the side of the head.

The Black Hawk circled in the air. The man with the submachine gun fired down at us. Bullets punched through the undercarriage of the SUV.

Agent Palmer returned fire, but they were wasted rounds. What was worse, his attention was focused on the helicopter for a second too long. A bullet from one of the men on the snowmobiles took out the side of his head.

Agent Njeim and the other agents were busy firing at a second dump truck.

I bent and checked Agent Palmer, just to be safe, but he was dead. I fired up at the helicopter as it continued to circle until the magazine was exhausted. I didn't have time to crawl back into the SUV, find another magazine, so I tossed the MP5 away. Bent down and grabbed Agent Palmer's Sig Sauer.

I circled the SUV. Both the driver and Sanchez had been shot. The driver fatally, Sanchez in his shoulder. He was on the ground, dazed, the gun in his hand aimed at two of the men on snowmobiles. The men were approaching but paused when they saw me. I shot them both in the head, one after another.

I crouched down next to Sanchez.

"How bad is it?"

"I'll live. Palmer?"

"Dead."

"What about the other agents?"

"One's down. Not sure about the others."

"Didn't Palmer say there was backup coming?"

"He did, but there's no telling how long that will take."

The Black Hawk continued to circle. The man with the submachine gun saw us but didn't open fire. The helicopter went in a wide arc over the colonnade, and the man with the submachine gun opened up on the agents down there.

I said, "They're here for me."

"What?"

"These men are here for me."

"So?"

I glanced over at the closest snowmobile.

"So I think I can buy you guys time."

Before Sanchez could protest, I stood and hurried over to the snowmobile. Someone fired at me and I turned, focused on one of the men by the dump truck, and shot him in the throat. I turned back to the snowmobile and climbed on.

I hit the throttle and twisted the handlebars so I was aimed down Canal Street. I looked up at the Black Hawk, to see whether anyone noticed me. One of the men was raining fire down at the agents at the colonnade.

I squeezed the gas, the engine screaming a whine. The snowmobile jumped forward, halfway down the street.

I looked back up and saw the helicopter making a wide turn. Headed directly for me.

I kept going down Canal Street.

A few cars were out on the streets, some of which were completely oblivious to the mayhem happening several blocks away. I swerved around them, hoping they didn't end up as collateral damage as the Black Hawk gave chase. For several blocks, it kept pace with me and then flew ahead, circling so one of the men had a good aim. He fired down at me, but the shots were at the street, his purpose to keep me from moving any farther west.

I made a right on Broadway, headed north.

It was one-way coming in my direction, but there were so few cars it didn't matter. I swerved from one lane to the next, the helicopter right above me. I knew staying on the same street for too long would give the Black Hawk enough time to overshoot me and then fire down, so at the next intersection I turned left, then right, then left again.

The pilot expertly handled the Black Hawk in the blizzard. He tried to stay with me the best he could, but every other block he'd lose sight of me for a few seconds. He took the helicopter up high but then dipped back down.

Back up Broadway, I made a right on Houston Street and headed back east.

The Black Hawk trailed me several yards back, dipping closer and closer to street level.

It had been decades since I was last in the city, but I had worked here, had spent most of my life here, so I still knew the streets. I made a left on Avenue A and headed up several blocks, then crossed over to Avenue B. Tompkins Square Park was only a block away. With luck, it would be deserted at this time of morning.

I zoomed right up through the park entrance.

Trees hid me from the Black Hawk momentarily. The Black Hawk banked to the side, searching for me. Which was just as well. It also gave me time to double-check Agent Palmer's Sig Sauer. The mag was fully loaded.

I headed to the other side of the park, toward the multipurpose courts. Here there would be enough opening in the trees for me to see the Black Hawk. And, more importantly, for the Black Hawk to see me.

I circled the snowmobile in the open space, making myself an obvious target.

The pilot spotted me in seconds.

The Black Hawk dipped down and headed straight for me. The pilot turned the helicopter so the man with the submachine gun had an undisturbed line of sight.

I stared straight back at him.

My mind instantly calculating the distance and wind and air being pressed down by the Black Hawk's rotor blades, I aimed and squeezed the trigger.

Even with the distance and the height, I saw the man jerk as the bullet entered his body.

The Black Hawk immediately turned, trying to protect the other man—the one with the RPG launcher.

As it did, I had a direct aim at its pilot.

There were two of them, actually, the pilot and copilot, and I squeezed off four rounds.

The first bullet was enough to penetrate the glass.

The second bullet was enough to hit the pilot in the face.

The same with the third and fourth bullets with the copilot.

The pilot slumped forward. The Black Hawk began circling, faster and faster. It seemed to waver toward the buildings on East 10th Street but then tilted back toward the park. Dipped even closer to the ground until it crashed straight into the trees.

There was no explosion. The Black Hawk just simply crashed, maybe one hundred yards away.

I left the snowmobile and trudged through the snow toward the Black Hawk. There had been four men on board, from what I could tell. I had killed three of them. One of them, if he was lucky, had survived the crash.

The fourth man had not survived the crash. I saw his body as I entered the trees. He had fallen from the Black Hawk as it fell to the ground and half of him had been crushed.

Confident that the Black Hawk wouldn't explode, I climbed inside.

Back at my cabin, the men had had nothing on them, no tech other than their weapons. I was hoping that would be different here. I wasn't expecting their wallets to be filled with their IDs and credit cards, but at least something. This was a Black Hawk, after all. No way they would be in it without any kind of communication.

It took two minutes to properly search the Black Hawk.

All I found was a cell phone on the copilot.

Better than nothing.

I pocketed the cell phone and headed back to the snowmobile, hoping Sanchez and Agent Njeim and the others were still alive.

28

Despite the early morning and the heavy snowfall, a loose crowd had begun to form around the destruction just off the Manhattan Bridge. A few police cars were parked along the streets, officers bundled in their winter uniform coats and hats trying to keep the crowd back. Beyond them were several ambulances as well as several black SUVs, men and women that were clearly Homeland Security agents moving from dead body to dead body. A helicopter circled in the air. It wasn't a police chopper, and it wasn't a news chopper, which made me think it too was from Homeland Security.

I approached down Canal Street on the snowmobile. A block away I hesitated. Even though police and agents swarmed the area, that didn't mean the people who attacked us weren't there either. Maybe they were hiding in plain sight, just part of the crowd. Waiting until I showed up before they whipped out their weapons and even more people died.

I spotted Agent Njeim. She was over by the colonnade, speaking to a group of other agents, but when she heard the snowmobile, she turned and saw me and said a few parting words to the agents before heading my way.

A police officer stood between us by his car, its hood lights flashing red. He was already shaking his head, waving for me to stay back. Agent Njeim came up behind him, touched his arm, said something to him. The officer nodded and, with an annoyed look on his face, waved me forward.

I turned off the snowmobile and climbed off it.

"How's Hector?"

"He's fine. He's being treated as we speak."

She motioned at one of the ambulances.

"What happened to the Black Hawk?"

"It crashed in Tompkins Square Park. No survivors."

"Was anything salvageable?"

I hesitated. I wasn't sure whether I should tell her about the cell phone. It still wasn't clear who I could trust.

But then I remembered how she had walked Sanchez and me around my son's house, repeating the police report she had undoubtedly read countless times, the thing practically memorized. The care she had taken when she opened my granddaughter's and grandson's bedroom doors.

I pulled the cell phone from my pocket.

"This was on the copilot. I doubt it will be useful, but that's all there was."

She took the phone from me and immediately stripped off the back, peeled out the battery and withdrew a tiny chip.

"What are you doing?"

"Making sure whoever else may have access to this phone can't trace it or listen in to our conversation. I'll have the analysts look at it when we return to base. In fact—"

She waved at an agent by the colonnade, who nodded and started toward one of the SUVs.

"—we should leave. It's best you don't stay around here too long. This is already starting to trend on social media. We're doing our best to suppress it, but it won't last long."

"Sanchez?"

"He'll be taken to the hospital."

"I'd prefer he came with us. After what just happened, I'd like him to stay with me."

"I'm afraid that won't be possible."

"Agent Njeim, he's the only friend I have right now. I need to keep him close."

She stared at me for a moment, then nodded.

"I understand."

"I saw one of the agents from your SUV was killed. The others?"

"Agent Sobreiro was killed. Agent Rachman took a bullet to the leg, but he'll live."

"I'm sorry about Agent Palmer."

She nodded solemnly.

"I'm going to have to tell his wife at some point today. Not sure when I'm going to find the time."

The chopper continued to circle above us. The cops kept trying to get the crowd to disperse. Even as the people began to drift away, there were those in the nearby buildings watching from windows. Many had their phones out, snapping pictures.

An SUV pulled up.

Agent Njeim opened the back door, motioned me inside.

"If you want to get in, I'll go get Mr. Sanchez and we'll be on our way. Mr. Davidson is eager to meet you."

"Mr. Davidson?"

"He's the director of the Vault. He's been involved since day one."

A minute later Sanchez crawled into the back of the SUV. One of the medics had put his arm in a sling. He winced in pain as he settled in. He glanced at his seat belt, considered attempting to put it on, and then sighed and leaned his head back against the headrest.

I asked, "How do you feel?"

"Been better."

He kept his eyes closed for a long moment as the driver got us moving. Agent Njeim was in the passenger seat, typing at her cell phone. Then, as we passed the barricade of police cars, Sanchez tilted his face toward me and opened one eye.

"I'm sorry to say it, Eli, but I'm starting to wish you hadn't returned to the city."

I stared out my own window at the passing buildings.

"Me too."

We headed uptown. There were no emergency lights on the SUV, but the driver moved us through the streets like he had a bar on the roof flashing. Another SUV trailed us, no doubt our escort. For a moment I was surprised the helicopter wasn't also following us, but then I realized that there was a good chance wherever we were going was not public knowledge. It was one thing for two SUVs to be driving through city streets, even if those streets were mostly deserted because of the snow, but an entirely different thing if a helicopter were circling above wherever we were headed.

Several blocks and several minutes later, we entered Midtown and I had my confirmation.

A Bank of America took up the corner of the block. Beside the bank was the entrance to an underground parking garage. The idea of entering another parking garage after having just been in one was a bit unsettling, but something told me this one wouldn't be full of Ukrainian mobsters.

"A bank?"

Agent Njeim shifted in her seat to look back at me.

"People don't question black SUVs and sedans coming out of a parking garage next to a bank. They just assume it's business. If we were next to a dry cleaner's, on the other hand, that might raise some eyebrows."

I remembered what Agent Palmer had called their headquarters and nodded.

"I get it now. The Vault."

Agent Njeim smiled.

"Exactly."

A gate blocked the entrance to the parking garage. The driver paused before the entrance, leaned forward to stare out the windshield. It was difficult to know what he was looking for, but based on what Agent Palmer had told me two hours earlier, there were probably cameras stationed somewhere outside.

The gate began to lift.

The driver took his foot off the SUV's brake and coasted us over the sidewalk and into the entrance. The SUV behind us followed. We went down a ramp into a much better lit garage than the one where Roman Vyhovsky and his men had been waiting. It made it easy to see the armed guards waiting at the base of the ramp.

There were four of them. Three of them had submachine guns strapped over their shoulders. A fourth held a German shepherd on a short leash, and as the driver stopped the SUV, the man led the dog around the vehicle one time, letting it sniff for explosives. Even with this measure done, another man used a stick with a mirror on its end to check the belly of the SUV.

Agent Njeim said, "Normally security isn't so tight. But after what just happened, Mr. Davidson isn't taking any chances."

Beyond the four guards were a half-dozen other black SUVs parked against one wall, a handful of black sedans parked against another.

Once the guard with the mirror waved us forward, the driver accelerated several yards and parked near the other SUVs.

We got out as the guards inspected the second SUV.

Agent Njeim led us toward an elevator. She pressed her thumb against a pad on the wall and the elevator doors slid open.

We stepped inside—just the three of us, the driver staying back.

I asked, "What floor?"

She pressed the only button on the panel.

"Basement."

The doors slid shut and we began to descend.

29

When the elevator doors opened again, a man was waiting for us in a wide corridor. He looked to be in his late sixties, his hair gray, his face showing signs of many years of wear. He wore slacks and a button-down shirt, the top two buttons undone. He adjusted the horn-rimmed glasses on his face and stepped forward and extended his hand to me.

"Elijah Shepherd, I'm Roger Davidson. It's an honor to meet you."

First the President of the United States, now this guy. It felt not only strange but somehow also wrong under the circumstances. I shook his hand anyway.

"Good to meet you, Mr. Davidson."

"Roger—please, call me Roger."

I motioned at Sanchez.

"This is Hector Sanchez."

Roger hesitated, staring at Sanchez.

"Agent Njeim, what is Mr. Sanchez doing here?"

I said, "I made her bring him."

Roger said, "He doesn't have clearance."

"Neither do I."

Sanchez said, "I'm standing right here, you know."

Roger shook his head as if to clear it.

"I apologize, Mr. Sanchez. It's just after what's happened, we're on high alert."

He extended his hand, and after a moment, Sanchez shook it.

Roger said, "I'm glad you were both able to arrive safely—or at least as safe as can be considering."

"Yes, I'm sorry about the men you lost."

His face went all at once solemn.

"As am I. Agent Njeim, thank you for escorting them here."

She nodded. She slipped the cell phone and its battery and tiny chip from her pocket, held the pieces out to Roger.

"Mr. Shepherd managed to take this off the copilot of the Black Hawk."

Roger took the pieces from her, gingerly, as if they were live explosives.

"Thank you, Agent Njeim. I'll have Taylor take a look. We're headed that way now."

Agent Njeim cleared her throat.

"Sir, about Agent Palmer—"

He held up a hand, cutting her off.

"Yes, I know. I'll take care of the notification. I'll do it for all the agents who lost their lives today."

Agent Njeim only nodded.

Roger motioned us down the corridor.

"Now, shall we?"

We followed him down the corridor into a large, expansive room. Long tables scattered about, people sitting at the tables on computers. Many tables had more than one computer set up. On the wall facing the tables were several large screens, and one massive screen, maybe ten feet tall, twelve feet wide. Currently on it was aerial footage of the attack's aftermath at the end of the Manhattan Bridge.

A few stares greeted us as we entered the room. A couple seconds, nothing more, and then the men and women shifted their focus back to their computer screens.

Roger spoke as he led us to the back of the room.

"This is our control center. We have a dozen analysts working at any time."

Sanchez asked, "Working on what?"

"We're Homeland Security. They work on whatever keeps our country safe. But their main focus is—or I should say, was —on tracking Temple."

He shuffled over to a table occupied by just one analyst. She looked to be in her late twenties, short blond hair, a nose ring. A half-dozen empty cans of Red Bull were scattered next to the monitors.

Roger made the introductions.

"This is Taylor. Taylor, this is Elijah Shepherd and Hector Sanchez."

Taylor didn't acknowledge us. She stared at her computer screen, typing at a rate that was almost inhuman.

Roger stepped forward, tapped his knuckles briefly on the table beside her.

She jumped. Looked at us. Stared for a long moment, then recognition filled her face and she quickly extracted the earbuds in her ears and stood up.

"Sorry."

She wiped her palms on her jeans.

"You're Elijah Shepherd."

She stared at me with a kind of awe, which I found very

unsettling. Before, when nobody knew who Temple was, I never had to deal with people treating me like a hero. She wiped her hands again and extended her hand.

"It's an honor to meet you."

I shook her hand.

"I wish everyone would stop saying that."

Taylor's gaze shifted over to Sanchez. There wasn't as much awe in it, but there was still excited recognition.

"And you're Hector Sanchez."

Sanchez shook her hand, and tilted his head to whisper in my direction.

"Nobody ever says it's an honor to meet me."

Roger set the pieces of the copilot's phone on the table beside her.

"This was the only salvageable item from this morning's attack. It was taken from the copilot of the Black Hawk. Agent Njeim will fill you in."

Agent Njeim said, "Whatever's on there, it's no doubt encrypted."

Taylor nodded.

"If anybody can break the encryption, I can."

Roger said, "Then we'll leave you to it."

He patted her on the shoulder and started past her, motioning for Sanchez and me to follow.

"Are either of you hungry?"

Sanchez said, "I'm starving."

"We have a chef on staff. He'll make you whatever you want within reason. When we get to my office, I'll call and order us breakfast."

We left the control center and entered another corridor.

Roger motioned at the doors ahead of us.

"We have a conference room, a medic station, a small arsenal. We also have quarters for our analysts, as well as showers.

Most of them work twelve-hour days, sometimes longer, and some never have a chance to go home. They crash here, grab a few hours of sleep, and then get back to work."

A staircase was off to our right. Roger started up it.

"There's an elevator to my office, but I prefer to take the stairs. At my age, any exercise helps."

The stairs led to another corridor, this one shorter than the one below. Roger went to the first door and placed his thumb on a scanner on the wall. The red button on the panel turned to green, followed by the sound of the door unlocking. Roger pressed down on the handle and pushed open the door and waved us through.

A large wooden desk dominated the room with a trio of chairs placed in front of it. Behind the desk was a two-way mirror. From up here Roger could watch the control center without the analysts down below knowing.

Roger closed the door, and all at once his body seemed to go through a transformation: the forced smile faded, his shoulder went back, his face became more severe, and his voice, when he spoke, took on an edge.

"There's a mole in this organization, gentlemen, and I need to find it before more of my people die."

30

oger Davidson fell back into his leather chair with a tired sigh. Sanchez and I each took one of the chairs facing the desk.

"Breakfast."

Roger saying it suddenly as if just remembering.

"You both said you'd like breakfast, didn't you?"

Neither one of us said anything.

Roger leaned forward, picked up the phone beside his computer and pressed a button.

"Louis, please do me a favor and make some breakfast for three. Yes, that's right, bacon and eggs will do. Thank you."

He cradled the phone and leaned back in his chair.

"It should be right up."

I leaned forward in my seat.

"You said there was a mole."

His elbows on the armrests, Roger folded his hands and steepled his index fingers and held them in front of his lips.

"That's right. I've suspected it for a while now, but nothing could be confirmed until your son went missing."

"Abducted."

Roger frowned.

"I'm sorry?"

"My son was abducted by the same people who came after me."

"How can you be so certain?"

"The point man who entered my cabin had a tranquilizer dart loaded in his rifle."

There was a silence as Roger digested this.

I said, "Regarding the mole, do you have any suspects in mind?"

"None. The agents here, the analysts—they've each been here for well over a year. The most recent analyst came in fourteen months ago. As you can imagine, we require a certain level of secrecy for this outfit. Transfers aren't acceptable. Once you're in, you're in. And believe me, it's extremely tough to become part of the team. The background checks are the same as those for Secret Service who detail the president. No stone isn't overturned."

"What about the men who attacked us—any idea who they are?"

"It's too early to tell. Our people haven't even had time yet to examine the bodies, let alone try to identify them."

"What does your gut tell you?"

Roger hesitated.

"Based on the beheadings of your daughter-in-law and grandchildren, we're pretty confident that there's some Islamic involvement. Al-Qaeda, ISIS, Hezbollah, just to name a few."

"But the men who attacked us tonight weren't Middle Eastern."

"They don't have to be. ISIS has done an impressive job of recruiting Americans to do their dirty work for them. But from what I've been told, the group that attacked you this morning was too well equipped, which leads me to believe they were some sort of mercenary group."

There was another silence, all of us letting this sink in.

I glanced at Sanchez.

"What do you think?"

He was staring forward, past Roger, out through the two-way mirror at the dozen analysts below.

"Hector."

He blinked, looked at me.

"What do you think?"

He said, "It's unbelievable."

Roger Davidson asked, "What's unbelievable?"

"You government spooks are constantly blaming everything on Islamic terrorists, even when there's no connection."

"That's not true."

"Bullshit it's not. Every major holiday the government issues alerts of possible terrorist attacks, but none of that shit ever happens."

"That's because we manage to diffuse—"

"Cut the bullshit. Everyone knows what's really going on."

There was an edge to Roger's voice.

"Meaning?"

"It's all about funding, right? You need to justify all the ridiculous money you guys spend."

Roger's face was stone.

"Are you done?"

"And *that*—"

Sanchez pointed at the control center beyond the two-way mirror.

"—I'd always heard that shit existed, but a part of me didn't believe it. Even after Edward Snowden, I was still skeptical to think the government has that much control over everyone's lives."

I asked, "Who's Edward Snowden?"

Both men answered at the same time.

Roger: "A traitor."

Sanchez: "A whistleblower."

The men glared at each other for a moment, and then Sanchez frowned at me.

"You don't know who Edward Snowden is?"

"The name doesn't sound familiar."

Sanchez kept the frown.

"Man, where have you *been* the last twenty years?"

Roger said, "Yes, I wanted to ask you the same question. Where have you been hiding?"

My first instinct was to lie. Give them a location that was nowhere near where I had spent my time for the past two decades. Maybe even tell them I was in another country. But then I realized there was no point trying to maintain the location's anonymity—I was never going back there, at least not to live. To see Darrell again, make sure he was okay, return his Charger, but not to live.

"Harper, Colorado. There was a cabin that my father had built when he left the city. He had purchased the land and set it up so that the taxes would be paid every year out of a trust. There was no electricity, no running water. I was ten miles away from my nearest neighbor."

"What happened to your father?"

"No idea. He had come to see me a decade before I left the city myself. He told me about the cabin, exactly where it was, and that he would be waiting for me whenever I decided to retire. He even told me to bring my wife, though he admitted she might not want to live out in the middle of nowhere. The truth was I didn't think I would enjoy it either. And for the first year or so it was difficult to adjust. But then it got easier."

"So the cabin was empty when you got there?"

"There were signs that my father had once been there, but there was no sign of him. No note. Nothing that would suggest what happened to him."

Roger said, "Tell me more about these men who came for you."

"There were six of them. They were as well equipped as the men who came for me this morning."

"What happened to them?"

"I killed them."

"Their bodies?"

"I searched them, but there was nothing on any of the bodies to identify them. But like the men tonight, none of them were Middle Eastern."

"When did these men attack you?"

"Three nights ago."

"How did they find you?"

"I have no idea. As I told Agent Palmer, nobody knew where I lived. Not my son or daughter. Nobody."

"And where was this exactly? You don't happen to know the longitude and latitude, do you?"

"No, but I can show you on a map."

Roger leaned forward and tapped his keyboard and his computer screen lit up. He shifted the monitor so that I could see the screen, clicked his mouse and brought up a web browser. He typed "harper colorado" and then a map of the town appeared on the screen.

I rose from my chair and approached the computer and stared at the screen for several long seconds before I pointed at a section of wooded area.

Roger said, "You're sure?"

I nodded.

He hit a button on his phone and it rang once before a voice answered.

"Yes, Mr. Davidson?"

"Nate, I'm emailing you coordinates."

"What am I looking for?"

"A cabin."

I said, "What's left of a cabin. After the attack, I burned the place down."

"The bodies?"

"I left them where they were. They're probably snowed over by now if wild animals haven't already gotten to them, or other men came to take them away."

Roger said, "Nate, I need you to send a team out there ASAP to search the grounds for anything useful."

"Yes, sir."

"Also, how long will it take to get a satellite in position to view the area?"

"I'll have to check to see which satellite is closest and have it redirected."

"Do it."

Roger disconnected the call and leaned back in his seat. Nobody spoke for the longest time. Then Sanchez cleared his throat.

"I have a question."

His focus now on me.

"Just who the hell *are* you?"

31

shifted in my seat so I could give Sanchez my full attention.

"I'm Eli Shepherd. I was your partner for fifteen years. We worked together almost every day. What more do you need to know?"

"Just ... at the same time you were also Temple?"

"Yes. I mean, no. I mean, I was Temple once my father finally decided it was time to retire. Then I took his place."

"How did your father become Temple?"

Roger said, "I can explain that."

He paused, waiting to see whether he should continue. I nodded, mostly because I was curious what he had to say.

"Back in World War II, our government was working on many different projects. We had received word that the Nazis were conducting experiments on total camouflage, known as the invisibility quotient, and teleportation. We had no choice but to try to keep up. Over the year, there were several experiments conducted on ships from the Philadelphia Naval Shipyard. One of those test runs included several young men. It did not go well. Elijah's father was the only survivor."

He looked at me.

"At least I've come to assume the sole survivor was your father."

"How do you know this?"

"Because of my position I was able to access several thousand classified documents. We basically went back to the beginning, to when Temple first appeared. Then we tried to determine what might have caused this ... this change in your father. After all, it was clear—and still is—Temple's strength and speed and agility are almost superhuman. Even the best athletes in the world couldn't compete."

"It's a bit of a stretch, though, isn't it? That you would narrow down my father as Temple?"

"Not really. After all, your father's surname wasn't Shepherd, was it?"

I said nothing.

Roger smiled and shrugged as if to say it was the only obvious conclusion.

Sanchez asked, "What does that mean?"

"My father's name was Henry Temple. After everything that happened—the failed experiment—he took off and started a new life in New York. He called himself Temple because the man who wanted to dissect him told him that nobody would ever know he existed, would never know his name. So by announcing himself as Temple, he was essentially giving that man—and the military in general—the finger."

"*Dissect* him? What are you talking about?"

"Tell him, Roger. You must have read the files. You know the reason my father was picked for the experiment."

Roger said nothing.

Sanchez said, "What's going on here?"

I shifted in my seat again to look at him.

"The reason my father and the other boys were picked for

the experiment was because they were black. The government was okay with making black boys guinea pigs. They hadn't even told any of the boys what the experiment was about. Hell, none of them even knew it *was* an experiment."

Roger leaned forward in his chair, folded his hands on the desktop.

"Obviously mistakes were made, but—"

"*Mistakes*? It's pretty clear the government never had much faith in the project as it was, otherwise they wouldn't have used just niggers."

Roger winced at the use of the word.

"That's all my father and the other men were to the government. Niggers."

Roger had been maintaining eye contact with me this entire time. Now he blinked, looked away, seemed to gather his thoughts. Finally shifted his gaze back to me.

"I apologize for what happened to your father. I apologize for what happened to the rest of those boys. As you no doubt know, I personally had nothing to do with the project—hell, I was just a baby at the time—but if you're looking for an apology, that's the best I can do for you."

"I'm not looking for an apology. I just want you to understand that I've grown up with a certain lack of trust in the United States government, especially the military. Despite that, I still served two tours in Vietnam, and I'll be honest with you, Roger, the army didn't treat its black soldiers any better then either. I mentioned that I've been out of contact for the past twenty years or so. That's true. No TV, no radio, no Internet. But I still read a lot of books. Mostly classics, like George Orwell's *1984*. And my God, from what I've witnessed so far, and from what little Sanchez has said, the government has become very Orwellian. Practically a surveillance state. No, let me rephrase that—it *has* become a surveillance state."

"Times change. Ever since 9/11, we've had to—"

"Stop. Agent Palmer already gave me the same line about how the government had no choice but to begin spying on all its citizens. This isn't the country I remember."

"You're right, it's not. This country has changed, because the world has changed. There are radical terrorists who want nothing more than to destroy our way of life. And yes, Mr. Sanchez, the majority of those terrorists are Muslim. As the saying goes, not every Muslim is a terrorist, but every terrorist is a Muslim. That's just the way it is. As far as I'm concerned, if we have to monitor every citizen of the United States to keep them safe from terrorists, then that's just what we'll do."

A knock came from the door.

Roger, without skipping a beat, reached over and touched a button on the phone.

"What is it?"

From the speaker came a voice.

"The breakfast you ordered, sir."

Roger hit another button to unlock the door.

A large man entered, carrying a tray with three covered dishes.

"Leave it on the table there, Louis. Thank you."

Roger waited until the chef had left before he cleared his throat.

"I think we got sidetracked there for a moment."

He adjusted his glasses.

"Mr. Shepherd, I understand with everything that's happened recently—and everything that's happened in the past —you have trouble trusting me. I understand that. But I promise you I am not the enemy here. I want to know who these people are just as badly as you do. I want to find your son. I want to find the people who murdered your daughter-in-law and grandchildren and make them pay. So please, tell me what I need to do to gain your trust."

"To be honest, I have no idea what you can do. I'm not a trusting person by nature."

The phone on Roger's desk beeped.

Roger pressed a button.

"Yes?"

Nate's voice came through the speaker.

"The satellite is in position, sir. There isn't much light yet, but I'm putting it on the screen."

Roger thanked him and stood from his chair.

I rose from my chair and circled the desk to stand next to Roger by the two-way mirror. A gray image appeared on the screen below. At first I wasn't sure what I was looking at, as most of the image was dark, and then I realized it was a wooded area. The trees and clearing surrounding the cabin—or what was left of the cabin. The image became lighter, making it easier to distinguish the trees. The image pushed in, zooming closer and closer to the cabin. The remains of the cabin and my pickup were there, but that was it.

The bodies and SUV were gone.

32

M aybe the snow covered the bodies."

Sanchez offered this in a small voice, as if he wasn't sure himself.

I stood with my arms crossed, staring at the screen through the two-way mirror. I thought about it for a moment and then shook my head.

"No, they're definitely gone. So is the SUV."

Roger said, "I'll have men on the scene within an hour. They'll inspect the entire area, try to find some clues."

I glanced at Roger.

"If everyone in the organization knew about my son and his family, they know about my daughter too, correct?"

Roger nodded.

"We monitor her, but nowhere near as closely as your son and his family. Since the incident, we've put a team on her twenty-four seven."

"Does she know?"

"About what—the team? Absolutely not."

"I need to see her."

"Of course."

He checked his watch.

"By now the governor should have made his official announcement of a state of emergency. The city will be shut down. The streets will be even more deserted than they had been earlier. We can make it there in no time."

"What's being done to find my son?"

"We've been scouring security footage throughout the city for days. Trying to backtrack his movements, but he just disappears. We've tried facial recognition, but nothing comes up either. We've even widened the search to the entire country. The system is actively monitoring everyone. If your son shows up, we'll know immediately. Now, let me ask you, is there anything my men in Colorado need to know about Harper?"

I thought about telling him about Darrell, to have his men check whether he had taken off like I'd told him to or if he had stayed. And if he had stayed, to put him in some kind of protective custody. But then I remembered what Roger said about there being a mole. The last thing I wanted to do was put Darrell in needless danger, especially after everything he had done for me.

"No, there isn't."

The phone on Roger's desk beeped again. He leaned down and pressed the button.

"Yes?"

This time, it was Taylor's voice that came through the speaker.

"I think I have something."

"Can you bring it up here?"

"Yes. I'll be right there."

Twenty seconds later a knock sounded at the door. Roger hit the button to release the lock, and then Taylor entered the office, carrying a tablet.

"What do you have?"

"The phone had almost a hundred encrypted files on it. It doesn't sound like much, but the encryption was something I've never seen before. I have the system working on it now, but I did manage to break twenty-two files so far. Most of the files are complete gibberish."

"But?"

"One of the files consisted of only the Quran."

"The Quran?"

"Yes. All 114 chapters, all in Arabic. I found an existing text of the Quran on the Internet and cross-matched it to this file. It matches except for one word found in chapter 49."

Taylor turned and pointed the tablet toward a large TV screen hanging off the wall. The screen blinked and a single image appeared in the center, white text against a black background:

خفير

Roger asked, "What does it mean?"

Taylor cleared her throat.

"Well, sir, here's where I think we have a problem."

"How so?"

"The word translates to sentinel."

At once the room filled with a strange sense of tension. Roger's body went perfectly still. He stared hard at Taylor.

"Are you sure?"

"I'm positive."

"My God."

Roger stared down at his desk for a long moment, thinking, then shot his gaze back up at Taylor.

"We need to verify all sites."

"I already have. All sites are secure."

"We need to add extra security to every location."

"I agree. The problem is most of our people are cleaning up the shootout off the Manhattan Bridge and the Black Hawk crash site in Tompkins Square Park."

"I'll make some calls. We'll have the National Guard brought in if that's what we need to do. Those sites need to be protected."

I asked, "What sites?"

Roger turned and looked at me for a moment without speaking. Then he sighed and ran a hand through his hair.

"I need to gain your trust, so I think it's best I show you."

"Show me what?"

33

Seconds later we were back in the control center, Roger
leading us toward the elevator.

Agent Njeim stood by Nate, leaning into his table
and whispering to him as he typed furiously on one of his
keyboards. He nodded every couple seconds, indicating that he
was listening. Beyond him, up on the screen, the satellite image
still showed the area where I had lived for the past twenty years.

Roger called to Agent Njeim as he moved through the
control center. When she looked up, he motioned her to
follow. She said a few parting words to Nate, who nodded
again, and then she hurried over and matched our pace.

Roger asked, "Did Taylor tell you yet?"

"About Sentinel possibly being compromised? She did."

"I'm taking Mr. Shepherd to Number Seven. I want him to
see what's at stake."

Agent Njeim glanced back at Sanchez and me.

"And Mr. Sanchez?"

"He'll be staying here. I need you to keep an eye on him."

"No."

I said the word at once and stopped walking.

Roger paused and turned back.

"What was that?"

"He comes with us."

"I'm sorry, Mr. Shepherd, but he shouldn't even be here right now. It was a mistake letting him access this location, and I'm not about to make that same mistake twice."

"If Hector doesn't go, I don't go."

Roger stared hard at me, probably weighing his options. Finally he sighed.

"Fine, we don't have time for this. Agent Njeim, you might as well come with us and babysit Mr. Sanchez."

Agent Njeim grabbed a small walkie-talkie from her belt.

"How many vehicles do you need?"

"Normally I'd say two, but after what happened this morning, let's go with three."

Agent Njeim nodded and spoke into the walkie-talkie as we entered the corridor.

Sanchez nudged my arm as we walked, whispered to me.

"Babysit? Who the fuck does this guy think he is?"

Without turning around, Roger answered.

"I'm the guy, Mr. Sanchez, who has a direct line to the President of the United States and every member of the Joint Chiefs of Staff. I'm the guy who stays awake twenty-four seven so that the rest of this country can sleep safely."

Roger came to the elevator, pressed his thumb on the pad. The doors slid apart and he stepped in, turning and leveling his gaze on Sanchez.

"I'm the guy, regrettably, that allowed Mr. Shepherd's son to be abducted and his family to die on his watch. And I'm the guy who is going to do everything in his power to make it right."

Our convoy drove through the nearly deserted streets, the snow just as heavy as it had been an hour ago. We were in the middle SUV of the three: Agent Njeim driving with Roger in the passenger seat, Sanchez and me in back.

Roger shifted in his seat to look back at us.

"We should be there in ten minutes. Mr. Shepherd, how much do you know about 9/11?"

"I'd say I know enough."

"Then as you know it was the worst terrorist attack on U.S. soil. Over two thousand people died. Over six thousand people injured."

Sanchez said, "It was also an excellent opportunity for the government to start spying on its citizens."

Roger was quiet for a moment.

"Mr. Sanchez, do you consider yourself an American?"

"Absolutely."

"Do you consider yourself a patriot?"

Sanchez snorted.

"Are you going to tell me that if I don't agree with the government abusing its power then I'm somehow not a patriot?"

"No, I'm going to tell you that you can't have it both ways. You want to live in a world where you aren't afraid of terrorists who want to kill you, then you need to give up some of your freedoms here at home."

Up ahead were three people on cross-country skis. They were bundled up and moving single file down the street, one forward step after another, each of them holding a pair of ski poles.

Sanchez said, "The problem is you have no oversight. You do whatever the hell you want and get away with it. Again, you violate people's privacy."

"We *protect* people."

I said, "Enough. Roger, what's the point?"

He cleared his throat.

"The reason I bring it up is that immediately after 9/11 it was decided that nothing like that can ever happen again."

Sanchez said, "Right. Hence your illegal spying."

"Call it whatever you like, our surveillance plays only a small portion in protecting the country. We realized that to ensure there would never be another attack on New York, we needed something more ... aggressive."

I traded glances with Sanchez.

"What does that mean?"

We came up West 13th Street. The SUV in front of us slowed at the upcoming intersection.

Roger said, "We're here."

I glanced out the window. Tall office buildings stood on both sides of us.

The garage door on the building on our left began to open.

Agent Njeim cut the wheel and steered us through the door, which began to close immediately after we entered. Down another ramp where four men were waiting, each holding a machine gun. Agent Njeim put the SUV in park and killed the engine, and the men performed the same inspection as the men did back at the Vault. Once they were done, we stepped out and Roger led us toward the elevator.

Sanchez asked, "Another underground command center?"

Roger pushed the button and the doors immediately opened and we crowded in. Despite the building having almost fifteen floors, the elevator panel only had two buttons, an up and a down.

Roger pressed the top button.

"No. This time we're going up."

When the doors opened again, two men were waiting for us. Like the men below, they also had machine guns.

Roger had mentioned something about there being a need for extra security, but this seemed like overkill. At least it did until Roger led us down another corridor and into a large room and gestured at what lay in the middle of the room, and all at once it made sense why security was so tight.

I was thinking it, but Sanchez whispered it first.

"Holy fucking shit."

34

R oger stood silent for a long moment, his hands on his hips, staring at the object in the middle of the room. Finally, he turned to us.

"This, gentlemen, is one of over a dozen surface-to-air missile launchers in Manhattan. This is part of the program we call Sentinel."

Because of the size of the missile launcher—it was fifty feet long at least—there wasn't much else in the room.

"This is the MIM-104 Patriot. They were first used in Operation Desert Storm and have been used in one way or another ever since. Typically they're fired off the back of trucks. Obviously the setup here has been tweaked. Raytheon was kind enough to build these so that each site contains two missiles. We figured for our purposes that would be more than enough."

Sanchez asked, "These are all over New York City?"

"That's right."

Roger motioned for us to follow him around the launcher.

"As you can see, it's resting on a rotating base. The ceiling above—the roof—will open and the base will rise up and the launcher will aim at its target within seconds."

Sanchez stared up at the ceiling.

"What target?"

"Whatever threatens the city."

I said, "How many are there?"

"Raytheon originally installed thirteen. Lockheed Martin, which took over production, installed the fourteenth on the top of the Freedom Tower just before completion. Each site is designated by number. This is Sentry Number Seven."

"When was it put here?"

"A week after 9/11. The first day after 9/11, a private meeting was held between the president and several of his advisors. The next day Raytheon began manufacturing these launchers. Within days the government had secured buildings around Manhattan and tore out the top floors to make room. These missiles have a range of over forty miles, but, in theory, they will never have to go that far. Basically, the purpose of Sentinel is to stop another 9/11. The airspace around Manhattan is continuously monitored. If anything larger than a helicopter enters that space, the closest missiles will be activated and blast it out of the air."

"Won't there be casualties?"

"Depending on where the debris lands, certainly, but that's a risk we have no choice but to take. We would rather lose a handful of individuals if it means we'll save hundreds, if not thousands."

"What about typical aircraft?"

"The system is aware of usual air traffic. Any irregularity sends up a red flag and the system analyzes it instantly."

"What if a helicopter brought in a nuclear bomb? Landed right down in the middle of Times Square. Your system wouldn't pick it up."

"Yes, it would. Every flying object within a mile of Manhattan is scanned for anything potentially dangerous such as a bomb. That's why the Black Hawk this morning wasn't taken out by one of the missiles. As far as the system was concerned, it didn't present a major enough threat."

"People still died."

Roger nodded solemnly.

"Yes, and I'm sorry that it happened. But in terms of a large scale terrorist attack from the sky, Sentinel is the best way to keep this city safe."

"And now the people who attacked us this morning are aware of the program."

"Yes, so you understand just what's at risk. If they're targeting one of these missiles ..."

Roger shook his head.

"God only knows what they have planned."

We were quiet for a moment. The room was silent. From my years of living in the city, I had grown accustomed to the constant noise outside. Traffic, honking, construction. It's something that quickly gets tuned out. When I left the city, began my life in my Fortress of Solitude, the sudden and deep silence had unnerved me for weeks. It hadn't felt right. Now, because of the storm outside, the usual city sounds were gone. It was like a vacuum. Like the entire city was dead.

Roger cleared his throat.

"I mentioned casualties earlier. It's actually much more than that. When those terrorists attacked us on 9/11, they just didn't kill thousands of people. They destroyed a symbol of our country. The World Trade Towers were among the tallest buildings in the United States. Quite honestly, sometimes that's all it takes to hurt a country. Not by killing any of its people, but by destroying one of its symbols. Mr. Shepherd, I know you weren't here during 9/11, but you were still in the city during the Central Park Bombing, correct?"

Something hollow opened up inside of me. I stared back at Roger and nodded slightly.

Roger said, "Then you know exactly what I'm talking about. Prometheus killed seventy people, injured over one hundred."

Seventy-six was the exact number of people who had died while one hundred fifteen had been injured, but I kept it to myself.

Roger was watching me, studying my face.

"I always wondered what happened that day. Why you weren't able to stop Prometheus."

I held his stare but said nothing.

Agent Njeim reached into her pocket and pulled out her cell phone. She put it to her ear, turned away from us.

Roger said, "I also always wondered—"

But then he stopped.

I said, "What?"

He shook his head.

"Never mind."

"Tell me."

"Well ... I always wondered about the next day. Jeffrey Solomon Harris turned up dead, and then over a million dollars was dropped into Times Square. Money literally raining from the sky—or, at the very least, from the top of one of the buildings."

Still I held his stare.

"What about it?"

"Were you responsible?"

I said nothing.

Roger said, "Harris was an awful man, no doubt about it, but him turning up dead like he did ... that wasn't typically how Temple acted."

"Harris blew himself up by accident."

Roger held my gaze.

"Did he?"

Before I could respond, Agent Njeim closed the phone and turned back to us.

"Sir?"

Roger glanced at her.

"Yes?"

"That was Taylor. She managed to break the encryption on a few more of the files."

"And?"

"One of the files contained three names. Two of the names are unknown to us, but Taylor assumes they're ISIS terrorists."

"Why?"

"Because of the third name. Abu Muhammad al-Naser."

"Is she certain?"

"Yes."

Roger was silent for a moment, letting this sink in.

I said, "Who's Abu Muhammad al-Naser?"

"The War Minister of ISIS. Or at least he was until we captured him."

"Where he is?"

"He's in one of our black sites."

"I want to see him. If this man has any connection to what happened to my son and his family, I want to see this man."

Roger nodded.

"That's fine. But I'm afraid Mr. Sanchez cannot accompany you this time. I'm sorry, but I must put my foot down on this."

I glanced at Sanchez, who didn't look like he was too disappointed not to be included.

"Fine."

"Good. Agent Njeim will take you to see Abu Muhammad al-Naser. I'll take Mr. Sanchez back to the Vault."

"Where is he? Let me guess—this black site of yours is somewhere in the city."

Roger smiled.

"Of course not, Mr. Shepherd. We keep the terrorists in Jersey."

35

Not much was known of Abu Muhammad al-Naser other than he was in his late-forties and that he was born in Syria. Before joining ISIS, he had been a prominent leader of the Taliban but left the group because he felt they were not aggressive enough. His high status in the Taliban helped him to rise through the ranks of ISIS until he became war minister. Or one of many. As Agent Njeim explained as we sped through the Lincoln Tunnel (just the two of us, Roger and Sanchez having returned to the Vault), the U.S. believed ISIS had several men working on the same level, so that when one was either captured or killed, another immediately took his place.

"How did they capture him?"

"One of our operations had been tracking him for months. They finally managed to extract him last week from Libya."

Without any traffic other than the SUV behind us for cover and with no snow slowing us down, we flew through the tunnel.

"How far away is the black site?"

"Just outside Edgewater. I've already called ahead. They'll have al-Naser waiting for us."

"Are we taking him anywhere?"

"Depends on what we can get from him. I'm told ever since he arrived he hasn't spoken once, even under extreme duress."

"You mean torture."

"Advanced interrogation."

Agent Njeim sighed, her shoulders dropping.

"Yes, torture. No matter what you want to call it, in the end it's the same thing."

"How did you end up here?"

"What do you mean?"

"In this unit. Don't take this the wrong way, but you don't sound American."

"That's because I'm not. I was born in Lebanon, grew up in Iraq. My father was a diplomat, my mother a professor. I was fifteen years old when Hussein's men came and executed my father for speaking out against him. They took turns raping my mother before slitting her throat. Two of the men had raped me before I managed to grab one of their weapons and shot at them. I don't think I killed any of them, but I certainly wounded them, and I escaped out a window."

We came up out of the tunnel into the snow.

I said, "Then what happened?"

"I was on my own for about a year. I stayed with friends, but it was dangerous. I knew Hussein's people were hunting me."

"Did they ever find you?"

"Fortunately no. I went underground for a bit to ensure my friends would stay safe. A year later I ended up working as an interpreter for the American soldiers."

It was midmorning now, and traffic was sparse. While New York's governor had issued a state of emergency, New Jersey's governor had decided the weather didn't warrant such an announcement. Already we had passed two multi-vehicle accidents and another accident in which a car had slid into a telephone pole.

"Some of the soldiers there learned my story. They were sympathetic. They trained me how to fight and how to use a weapon. Many of the officers were impressed how quickly I learned. They began using me in combat situations. That, I believe, is how I came to Roger's attention."

"So you hadn't worked with Roger previously?"

"No. But one day he contacted me and asked me to meet him to discuss a new opportunity in the U.S. As I had nothing keeping me in Iraq, I agreed."

"Had you heard of Temple before then?"

"Of course. The entire world had heard of Temple. But he was more of a distant celebrity than anything else. He never left New York City. Even back when I was a girl ..."

Agent Njeim paused.

"Never mind."

"What?"

Agent Njeim shook her head.

I decided not to push her. If she wanted to tell me, she would tell me. I stared out my window at the buildings sliding past and thought about how much courage and resiliency it took for a fifteen-year-old girl to be raped and beaten and manage to escape and become a soldier fighting men who raped and beat women.

When Agent Njeim spoke next, her voice was soft.

"When those men broke into our house, when they killed my father and when they ... when they did what they did to my mother and me, I wished Temple would come and save us. That Temple would kill those men. It was such a childish thought that I later hated myself for thinking it."

"Why?"

"Because I was just a worthless girl from Iraq. I was nobody special. Why would Temple save me?"

I said nothing. Based on what she had told me there was a chance that when those soldiers had broken into her house and killed her father and raped her and her mother, I had been Temple at the time, not my father. I had been in New York, saving the people there from killers and robbers and all other danger. People in New York had hope that they would stay safe while others in the rest of the world didn't have that privilege.

I wanted to say something to Agent Njeim, wanted to somehow apologize for not being there, but it was a ridiculous thought. I'd had the same thoughts growing up. I'd had the same conversations with my father, about trying to help more people than was even possible. He had sat me down and told me the obvious reality of the situation: We couldn't save everybody.

Agent Njeim flicked on the SUV's turn signal and slowed at the next intersection.

"We're almost there."

36

A Chinese restaurant sat at the end of a strip mall, and despite the nasty weather, it appeared to be open. Even more incredibly, three cars were parked outside. As we approached, the restaurant door opened and a man trudged out into the snow bundled up in his coat, his hood up, in his hand a plastic bag with a yellow face smiling on its side.

MOJO'S, said the marquee in red letters above the restaurant's overhang.

Agent Njeim drove past Mojo's and turned into the alley beside it. She braked in front of an abandoned garage.

One of the three bay doors opened as the SUV crawled forward.

Agent Njeim parked and shut off the engine.

I glanced out the window.

"No welcoming party?"

Agent Njeim kept her hands on the top of the steering wheel.

"No physical welcoming party, no, but we're being watched

right now. There are cameras and scanners all over this garage. Weapons, too."

Besides some trash and a couple steel drums, the garage appeared empty, but I wasn't about to question her.

Several seconds passed and then a light above the steel door ahead of us flashed green two times.

Agent Njeim said, "We're clear."

We stepped out of the SUV just as the door opened. A tall man with a serious face stepped out.

"Agent Njeim."

He nodded to her, then glanced at me and stared for a moment.

"Is this really him?"

"Yes."

The man held out his hand to me.

"Pleasure to meet you, sir. I'm Warren, the station chief."

I shook Warren's hand and then followed him through the door and down a set of stairs leading to a basement, Agent Njeim trailing directly behind.

"This place is under the Chinese restaurant?"

Warren said, "That's right."

"I'm assuming they have no idea what's beneath them."

"Of course not. This site's been here ten years. The restaurant opened six years ago. The only thing they know is that almost every day we grab takeout. Really, their crab Rangoon is spectacular. So is their General Tso's."

At the bottom of the steps was a narrow brightly lit corridor. Along the corridor were several steel doors. Warren led us to the door at the end.

"We have him waiting, but I'm not sure what you expect to get from him. We've done everything we can to make him talk. He knows our tricks. He knows exactly what to expect."

Agent Njeim said, "I understand, but we now have something al-Naser never expected."

She pointed at me.

"We have him."

The interrogation room was nothing like I'd ever seen before. There was no table, no chairs. There was nothing in the room except for a section ten feet by ten feet of floor-to-ceiling glass.

Warren said, "We call it the Tank. The glass is three inches thick. Bulletproof. Once the door is closed, it becomes a vacuum. We pump oxygen in, but if a prisoner is giving us a hard time, we can easily stop the oxygen flow."

We stood in the room next door, watching a bank of monitors. Judging by the screens, there were at least six cameras positioned around the room, maybe more. Abu Muhammad al-Naser stood in the middle of the Tank. He didn't look restless. He wasn't pacing back and forth. He barely even moved. He just stood there, staring ahead. Waiting.

I asked, "Does he speak English?"

"We're not sure. We assume he does, but none of our intel can say for certain, and he hasn't spoken since he arrived."

Agent Njeim asked, "Do you want me to go in with you? I can interpret."

I thought about it for a moment. My languages were limited to English and some Spanish.

"Let me have a go at him first."

I slipped off my jacket, laid it over a chair.

Warren spoke as I turned to leave.

"Just remember this guy has no rights. You give me the signal, I cut off his oxygen."

"Everybody has rights."

I pushed open the door.

Abu Muhammad al-Naser didn't react when I walked into the room. He didn't even blink. His eyes did shift to take me in and watched as I approached the Tank, but there was no recognition. For all he knew, I was just another interrogator come to ask him questions.

I had interrogated hundreds of people in my time as a police detective. Never once had I used physical force. Often intimidation was needed to persuade the perp to start talking, but I never once placed my hand on anyone. It wasn't that physical force wasn't allowed—almost everyone in the department would gladly turn a blind eye if it yielded results. But after my time in Vietnam, my outlook on physical force had changed. In the end, there was never any apparent result other than to prove who was more vicious.

But this man was different. If Agent Njeim was to be believed—and up until now I had no reason not to believe her —al-Naser was one of the worst terrorists in the world. Responsible for thousands of deaths. His men went in and looted towns. Raped and beat women. Beheaded people in the name of their religion.

Beheaded those like my daughter-in-law and grandchildren.

I stepped up to the Tank and stared hard at al-Naser.

"Do you know who I am?"

He made no reply. Just stood there, staring back at me.

"My name is Elijah Shepherd. But you may know me as Temple."

This caused the desired effect.

Al-Naser blinked. For an instant, confusion filled his face, and then immediately it became stoic once again.

"You do speak English after all."

He said nothing.

"I want to know what you did with my son."

Nothing.

"You do realize that, if I wanted it, your oxygen would be cut off. I'm guessing this isn't the first time you've been in this room. I'm guessing your oxygen has been cut off before. Tell me, what did it feel like?"

Al-Naser again made no reply.

"Your people made a mistake going after my family. You've made it personal now."

Still nothing.

I glanced up at one of the cameras. I wondered what Agent Njeim and Warren thought. Had they expected more from me? It had been two decades since I performed my last interrogation. Two decades since I had put on the mask and become Temple.

"Do you think Allah agrees with what you're doing? That when you die, you're going to be given one thousand virgins or whatever the hell it is you believe?"

Al-Naser did not move one muscle. His gaze stayed steady with mine.

Part of me wanted to follow through with my threat. Part of me wanted to snap my fingers and have the oxygen cut off inside the Tank. Part of me wanted to watch al-Naser's eyes the instant he realized there was no more fresh air. The instant he realized that he might die.

I turned away and walked back toward the door. I reached for the handle when al-Naser spoke behind me.

"Temple is an abomination."

Abu Muhammad al-Naser's voice seemed to echo in the

silence. He didn't speak perfect English, but his words were clear enough.

I turned back around.

Al-Naser stared at me.

"My son. What have you done with him?"

"You are blind to the Prophet's teachings. The end is coming."

I stayed where I was for another moment, waiting for him to say more. When he didn't, I turned back to the door.

Abu Muhammad al-Naser spoke again as I left the room.

"I will not be in here forever. I will find you. I will find your family. I will cut off their heads. And you will thank me."

37

R oger didn't meet us at the elevator when we returned. Nobody met us.

I followed Agent Njeim toward the control center. Every desk was occupied by an analyst. Taylor was busy staring at her screens. Nate, a few desks over, saw us and motioned to Agent Njeim, but then glanced at Taylor and shook his head.

Agent Njeim veered toward him anyway.

"What is it?"

He slumped down in his seat.

"Nothing. Just ... wanted to update you on some specs."

The young man looked nervous. Probably running on only a few hours sleep, an overload of caffeine, and the knowledge that if he and his team failed, they might let another terrorist attack decimate the city.

Agent Njeim waited for him to go on. He didn't.

I glanced at the large screens on the wall. When we had left, a satellite image showed my cabin and the area around it. Now the screens showed several different buildings around the city.

"You're monitoring the other Sentinel locations, aren't you."

I didn't bother making it a question.

Nate nodded. Now that his focus could shift to something else, he seemed to gain more confidence.

"Yeah, we're monitoring them, for what good it'll do."

"What do you mean?"

He hesitated a moment, thinking it over. Finally, he cleared his throat.

"If the enemy knows about Sentinel, then they probably know about our surveillance. Heck, they *do* know about our surveillance, based on what happened to your ... well, you know, your son's family. If that's the case, surveillance itself won't cut it."

"Positive thinking."

Agent Njeim patted him on the shoulder.

"You should try it sometime."

Nate snuck a glance at Taylor again. He looked like he wanted to say something, but that nervousness had returned. It was slight, but his hands were trembling.

Nate's phone rang.

He grabbed it, listened for a moment, nodded and replaced the phone in the cradle.

"Roger wants to see you upstairs."

We continued to the other corridor. We headed up the stairs and came to Roger's office. Agent Njeim knocked. A second went by, and then the lock disengaged.

Roger sat behind his desk. He turned toward us, swiveling in his chair.

"Well?"

I asked, "Where's Hector?"

"He's down in the cafeteria. Now, how did it go?"

Agent Njeim answered.

"Mr. Shepherd spoke with him, but he didn't say much."

"I know. I watched the feed. Typical Islamic bullshit. But what's your impression?"

He was directing the question at me. I wasn't sure what to say. I'd been thinking about it the whole ride here, back through the tunnel and through the deserted snowy streets. I'd faced my share of bad guys in the past, many of which were insane or evil, but this ... this was a kind of evil I had never faced before.

Before I could say anything, though, there was a knock at the door.

Roger frowned. He turned back to his desk, hit a button on the phone.

"Who is it?"

A voice from the speaker: "Nate."

Roger hit another button to unlock the door, and Nate entered the office. His nervousness was heightened. He was shaking more than ever now.

Roger said, "What is it?"

Nate strode straight up to Agent Njeim. His eyes intense. His voice a loud whisper.

"It's Taylor."

Roger frowned.

"What's Taylor? What are you talking about?"

Agent Njeim held Nate's gaze. He was still shaking, and she reached out and placed her hands on his shoulders to try to calm him.

"Are you sure?"

He pursed his lips, nodded quickly.

Roger said, "What's going on here?"

Agent Njeim said, "Before we left, I had Nate cross-reference every analyst's movement during the past week. Every click, every keystroke, I had him double- and triple-check everything, as well as search everyone's systems for irregularities."

"I already had Taylor doing that."

"I know. I wanted to get a second opinion, just to be safe."

Roger rose from his chair, stared hard at Nate.

"Are you positive?"

Nate nodded quickly. Then paused, considering.

"Well, I think I am."

"You *think*?"

"Ninety-nine percent positive. I mean, I think she definitely should be questioned."

Roger turned away from his desk to stare down through the two-way mirror at the floor below. From my angle, I could just see Taylor at her desk, typing away at her keyboard.

"Very well."

Roger sounded resigned.

"I'll call for security to take her to an interrogation room."

Agent Njeim shook her head.

"No. Let me do it. If you call, there's a chance she'll know. If she truly is the mole, she may be tapped into every line. You don't want to do anything now to rouse her suspicions."

Roger thought about it for a moment. He nodded.

"Go."

Agent Njeim turned at once, heading for the door.

I followed, Nate directly behind me.

Agent Njeim picked up her pace the moment she stepped into the corridor. She ran to the stairs and soundlessly flew down them, skipping two steps at a time. She headed into the control center but stopped immediately.

Taylor's desk was empty.

Agent Njeim addressed the room.

"Where is Taylor?"

All analysts turned to look at Agent Njeim, who hurried over to Taylor's workstation.

"Has anyone seen her?"

One analyst who sat next to Taylor absentmindedly pointed toward the other side of the control room.

Agent Njeim took off running, pulling her gun from her holster.

I hurried after her.

In the corridor, she paused, looking both ways.

Agent Njeim shouted at a security officer coming in our direction.

"Have you seen Taylor?"

"She didn't come this way."

"Initiate lockdown immediately!"

Agent Njeim was already moving down the corridor in the opposite direction.

We hurried through another door, which led to a stairwell leading up.

Agent Njeim paused just briefly, enough to allow a few seconds of silence to pass.

Above us, frantic footsteps on the stairs.

We started up the steps. Seconds later we reached the top and pushed open the door into the parking garage.

Taylor stood only a couple yards away.

Three guards stood around her, each of them aiming weapons at her.

Taylor had another guard held close to her with a gun to the guard's head. Her back was literally up against the cinderblock wall. She had nowhere to go, but she kept the gun in place.

One of the guards shouted at her.

"Drop it!"

Taylor didn't move. It was clear she had no intention of dropping the gun.

Agent Njeim approached slowly, her pistol aimed directly at Taylor's head.

"Don't do it, Taylor. We can work this out."

Taylor said, "Take another step and I kill him."

Agent Njeim paused, but she didn't lower the gun. She kept her aim steady on Taylor, as did the rest of the guards.

Taylor's eyes shifted around the garage. She knew she was trapped. She knew there was no escape. The only thing keeping her alive right now was her hostage. She had him right in front of her, a perfect human shield, and if anyone wanted to try to take her out, there was the chance they may hit the hostage by accident. At this point, none of them were willing to do that.

Still, it was clear to Taylor—just as it was clear to everyone else—that this was not going to end well for her. A tense moment passed, and then she said, "Fuck it," and shot the guard in the head. Almost instantaneously, Agent Njeim put a bullet through Taylor's face. Taylor fell back against the wall, slid down to the floor.

Agent Njeim rushed forward. Not to Taylor, but to the guard. She bent to inspect the wound, to check for a pulse, but the truth was clear enough. The guard, just like Taylor, was dead.

38

Roger held up a tiny microchip.

"This is a bug. They found it underneath my desk."

Three analysts currently circulated around the office, waving special tools at the walls and furniture and light fixtures.

Agent Njeim and I stood in front of Roger's desk.

"The last time I had this office swept was five days ago after the safe house was raided and your family was killed."

Roger shook his head.

"I was paranoid because it was clear to me there was a mole within the Vault. Then there had been no bug, so at some point in the past five days Taylor managed to sneak it in here."

Agent Njeim held a finger to her lips. We waited until the analysts finished up, and she took the microchip from Roger and handed it to one of the men.

"Analyze this. See if you can lift any prints. Anything."

The analyst nodded and followed the others out into the corridor.

Once we were alone, Agent Njeim lowered her voice to a whisper.

"There's a chance we may still be bugged."

Roger frowned.

"How?"

"We have to assume Taylor wasn't the only mole. There may be others."

Roger thought about this for a long moment, then sighed.

"Shit."

"Taylor must have been monitoring this office the entire time. She wiped all her computers, even the backups, but Nate is checking now to see whether anything is salvageable."

"How do you know Nate isn't a mole as well?"

"I don't, but at this point I don't think we have a choice but to trust he's on our side. At least, I trust he's on our side."

I said, "Taylor was the one who accessed the copilot's phone. She was the one who presented Sentinel as a possible target, and brought up Abu Muhammad al-Naser."

Roger said, "What's your point?"

"Why would she do that? If either Sentinel or al-Naser has anything to do with this, why would she lead us straight to them?"

Agent Njeim said, "He's right. We have to accept the possibility that either if not both were smokescreens."

Roger looked irritated.

"I understand that, but we can't outright ignore them either. I've already briefed the president on those developments. He's requested hourly updates moving forward. He's promised me any resource we need to make sure this whole thing ends well. And now, Christ, I have to call and tell him this."

Roger sank down into his chair, dropped his chin to his chest.

I asked, "Any word on the bodies from the Black Hawk attack?"

Roger shook his head.

Agent Njeim said, "How is that possible? There were over a dozen bodies. They can't all turn up not in the system."

"Oh, they turned up in the system, all right. They all turned up as deceased."

Agent Njeim frowned at me, then frowned at Roger.

"What do you mean?"

"Each of them comes up as someone who died decades ago. There's no rhyme or reason to it, as far as our people can tell. One of the men came up as a bank manager from Newport, Arkansas, who passed away in 1989. It's thrown everyone for a loop."

"Even dental records?"

"It's too early to try to match dental records, but they've already started with a couple of the bodies. It could be hours before anything comes back, but we're not holding out hope. Mr. Shepherd, may I ask you a question?"

"Go ahead."

"You were right there with Agent Njeim before Taylor took that man's life, from what I understand. Couldn't you have … well, saved him?"

"No."

Roger seemed surprised by the bluntness of my answer.

"Really?"

"Maybe in my prime I could have stopped her, but from where I stood I calculated the distance between us and all the possible outcomes. No matter what I did, that guard would die. Now let me ask you a question, Roger."

"Go ahead."

"Actually, it's more of a request. I need to see my daughter now."

Roger stared at me for a long moment, as if he didn't understand what I was asking, and then slowly nodded.

"Of course."

"I know you said you have a surveillance team on her, but with what's just happened, I think it's best I speak with her right away. She needs to know what's going on."

"I've always wondered something. Is your daughter—"

I cut him off.

"No."

"Are you sure?"

"Positive."

"How can you be so sure? They're twins."

Yes, they were twins. Aisha had been born eleven minutes before her brother. Growing up she had liked to tease him that, despite the fact they were twins, she was the oldest and he had to listen to her no matter what.

"I still have no idea how it works. What it is about my blood—my DNA—that makes me what I am. As it was passed on to me from my father, you'd think I would pass it on to my children, but it was only my son. My wife and I had countless conversations after the twins were born and as they grew older. We watched and waited for them to do something … extraordinary. By the time he was two years old, I knew my son was like me. But Aisha … she was just an ordinary child. Even the few times I tried to test her, to see what she would do, she reacted as any child would."

"So whatever it is that makes you … *special*, it doesn't pass down to females."

"I can't say for sure. It may very well pass down to females, but just not to my daughter."

Roger was quiet for a moment, thinking. He leaned forward in his seat, opened a desk drawer, and pulled out several black foldable cell phones.

"Agent Njeim, I would like you to take Mr. Shepherd to see his daughter. I'll have a team escort you. These, however, are just for us."

I asked, "What are they?"

Agent Njeim took the phones and handed me one.

"Disposables. In theory they can't be tracked."

Roger nodded.

"That's right. The current phones our teams carry have GPS, so they can be tracked by anyone internally. With these they can't be tracked, which means whoever is spying on us won't know where you are. Well, at least they won't know precisely where you are. It's not much, but it's a start."

I stared down at the phone, then glanced back up at Roger.

"I'll need another one for Hector."

Roger shook his head.

"He doesn't need one."

"Yes, he does. And I'll need to know its phone number, in case I need to contact him."

"Why?"

"He's going to come with us, and once we leave, he's going to stay with Aisha."

"Why do you think he'll do that?"

"Because he owes me."

Clearly not happy with this plan, Roger tossed me another one of the disposables. Then he rapped his knuckles twice on the desktop and nodded at us.

"Be careful."

39

The last time I saw my daughter, she was twenty-three years old and had just started graduate school.

Shalissa had been diagnosed with cancer the year before, and there had been several ups and downs in those twelve months. But then, out of nowhere, the cancer accelerated its campaign to take my wife's life.

From the time Shalissa went to the hospital to the time she took her last breath, eight days passed. And in those eight days the city had been terrorized by a man who called himself Prometheus.

That wasn't his real name, of course. His real name was Jeffrey Solomon Harris. He was a thirty-three-year-old retired veteran. He had been in charge of munitions during Desert Storm, and brought that knowledge back home where he quickly got divorced from the woman he had married before going on his first tour, couldn't hold down a steady job, and was arrested twice for aggravated assault.

It isn't clear when he eventually saw Temple as the cause for all his heartbreak and loss, but soon he found himself in Manhattan, hunting me. He knew the best way to catch my attention was to make an entrance, and so he had blown up a bus. Nobody had been on the bus at the time—it was in the middle of the night and the bus was parked in the depot—but he had written a note to the paper claiming the incident belonged to him and that next time he would blow up a bus with people on it if Temple didn't face him. As he didn't specify a place or time, it was nearly impossible for me to meet his demands, even if I wanted to.

Jeffrey Harris didn't seem to care about this point. Two days later, a city bus driving up Malcolm X Boulevard in Harlem exploded, killing eight people and wounding four others.

The city went into chaos.

Papers proclaimed that a terrorist was at work. TV and radio personalities questioned how Temple could let it get to this point. Hadn't the bomber explained his intentions, told Temple what would happen if Temple ignored him?

Another letter was sent to the newspaper, this time signed *Prometheus.*

The bomber had given himself a name.

My father once told me that whenever there's a hero, a villain will step up to challenge him.

Just like my father, I had only dealt with bank robbers, killers, arsonists, mobsters, and gangsters. Basically, anybody committing a crime that the police could not take care of on their own. Only one time before had a villain specifically challenged Temple, and that was the Reaper, one year after my father had managed to escape the mansion outside Philadelphia.

The Reaper had been sent to New York to hunt my father. My father had almost died because of it. But it was also because of the Reaper that my father met my mother, and that I was born.

But during my father's time as Temple, there were some in the world that viewed him as the enemy. Either he was something inhuman or he was a vigilante who needed to be apprehended by the police and brought to justice. This was, at first, a small group of people, but as the years passed and more pundits began to voice their say, the more public opinion began to shift. For the most part, the world viewed Temple as a hero. They understood that he was there to help, even though they may not have understood why he was there to help. But still there were those who didn't fully trust Temple. They questioned his motives. They wanted to know what he gained from doing everything he did for the city. Or, even more, why did he stay in the city? Why didn't he branch out into other cities? Other countries? Why was he being selfish?

The next thing Prometheus blew up was a subway car. He had timed it just right, as the cars were heading over the East River into Queens. Directly in the middle of the bridge, the two end cars.

Twenty-seven people died that day.

The front page of the *New York Post* the next day asked IS TEMPLE SCARED OF PROMETHEUS?

No, Temple wasn't scared of Prometheus. It was just that his focus was on his wife who lay dying in a hospital bed.

I took time off work to be with her. My captain and lieutenant understood. Besides, I had built up quite a bit of sick time over the years so that I could probably have taken the entire month off. Besides, I was a homicide detective. The people Prometheus had murdered had been killed, yes, but those scenes had called for different kinds of investigators. My information on the man was limited. And besides, my wife was dying.

My son wanted to go after Prometheus. He had already been training for three years. He was excited to take over for me, when the time came. But I kept putting it off. I didn't want him to take on the responsibility. Because once you took on the responsibility, it was nearly impossible to let go. Every day that went by, you wondered what would happen next. You worried about all the lives you might not save. You worried what might have happened had you focused more of your attention on one side of the city while the other side fell to ruin.

We took turns staying by my wife's bedside. We took shifts. We got little sleep. And meanwhile, the city was in chaos, trapped in fear of a man who wanted nothing more than to face Temple, to kill him.

My son wanted me to go after Prometheus.

My daughter wanted me to save her mother's life.

Couldn't I somehow transfer my blood to her? she asked. Couldn't whatever helps heal me help defeat the cancer?

It was a good question. Something I had wondered from the very first day we learned she had cancer. The problem was there were just too many unknowns.

Then, two days later, Prometheus took things to a whole new level.

He detonated a ten-pound brick of C-4 at the Delacorte Theater in Central Park. The bomb had been located right near the front of the stage, and all 1,872 seats were filled to capacity during the fourth act of *Romeo & Juliet* when it exploded. Most of the cast was killed, as were several of the audience. Seventy-six people dead, one hundred fifteen injured.

It was that same evening my wife passed away. Now nothing held me back. I was angry with Prometheus, yes, but the loss of my wife made me livid. I felt a rage I had never felt before.

That evening Temple tracked down Jeffrey Solomon Harris. Harris could have been brought to justice easily enough—

taken to the police, had his case heard before a jury of his peers —but that rage was still bubbling inside Temple.

Temple snapped Jeffrey's neck, then set up a bomb to explode five minutes later. Prometheus had been hiding out in an abandoned house in Greenpoint. As far as the rest of the world would be concerned, Prometheus had accidentally killed himself by one of his own explosives.

It was also that night I realized I could no longer be Temple. I needed to give it up. I needed to leave. But not before I finished an old score.

I faced off against Roman Vyhovsky. I beat up most of his men, tied Roman up, and took over two million dollars from his safe.

My wife's time in and out the hospital over the last year had drained most of our savings. Insurance had only covered so much. Her funeral needed to be paid. I made sure there was enough money to cover all of it, as well as something extra for my son and daughter, and I kept a little for myself because I knew I would be leaving and never coming back. The rest— well over one and a half million dollars—I dropped down into the middle of Times Squares.

As Roger had said, that day money literally rained from the sky.

The next day I resigned from the force. I gave my son my blessing to continue on as Temple. I didn't say goodbye to Aisha, though. Even now I'm not sure why. Maybe because I knew she would convince me to stay. Maybe because I would be reminded of just what I was giving up.

I couldn't let that happen, so I left.

Now, twenty years later, I didn't tell any of this to Sanchez or Agent Njeim or even the man currently driving the SUV. It was midday, and despite the governor's state of emergency, there were a few vehicles out on the street, more people with cross country skis out and about, kids throwing snowballs at each other. Another SUV trailed us, just like before, as we headed toward the Upper West Side and turned down my daughter's street and then, seconds later, pulled up in front of her brownstone.

I told them to stay in the SUV. I stepped out, looked up and down the street, and strode up the sidewalk and the steps leading to the front door. I rang the doorbell and waited, rang the bell again after several seconds passed, and I imagined my daughter dead inside, that the surveillance assigned to keep watch over her was also dead, killed by the group that wanted to kill me. But then there was noise behind the door, the soft shuffling of footsteps. Silence for a moment as the person on the other side peeked through the peephole. More silence as the person no doubt hesitated, deciding whether or not to open the door.

The door opened.

Aisha stood there, beautiful as ever, though her eyes were hard as they glared at me.

We stared at each other for a long moment.

Then she stepped forward and slapped me across the face.

40

didn't react. I saw her hand coming at me, knew what she planned to do even before she did it. I may be an old man, and my reflexes may have slowed, but I was still fast enough to step out of the way if need be, or even lean back so that her hand missed my face entirely.

But I didn't move. I just stood there and let her slap me across the face. First once. Then twice. Then three times.

Her face had darkened. She looked livid. She stepped back, her breathing heavy, tears in her eyes. I expected her to slam the door in my face. I expected her to lock it and never open it again. But instead she stepped forward, raising both hands this time. Even with my heightened senses, I wasn't sure what she planned to do. So it was surprising when she wrapped her arms around me and shoved her face into my shoulder and began to sob.

I stood there for a moment, not sure what to do. I tried to remember the last time I held my daughter. It had to have been on the night her mother died. I had held her much the same way I held her now, placing my arm around her, tilting my face down, smelling her hair briefly, that distinct odor that made up my daughter, the same odor she'd had ever since the day she was born.

"It's okay."

I said it just as I had said back then.

"It's okay."

I don't know how long we stood like that. It certainly wasn't very long, but time seemed to have stopped. As far as I knew, this was my only living family left in the world. I didn't want to let go.

Then, farther inside the house, there were footsteps, and a voice spoke.

"Everything okay?"

A man stood in the hallway. He wore sweatpants and a T-shirt. He looked to be about Aisha's age, tall and handsome, with almost obscenely coiffed hair. He held a mug in his hand, and even from where I stood on the stoop I could smell the green tea.

Aisha stepped back, wiping at her eyes.

"Billy, this is my, my father."

The hesitation was slight, but it was there. I wondered if Billy had caught it. Probably not. He looked annoyed by the intrusion. He stared at me for a long moment, then refocused past me through the door.

"Who else is out there?"

Aisha now noticed them too. She frowned at the two SUVs.

"Who are they?"

"Friends."

"Do you—"

Her face contorted, trying to fight back another sob.

"—do you know about James? About what happened to Yolanda and the kids?"

"That's why I'm here. I'm afraid you may be in danger."

"Wait—*what*?"

There was a strange sense of outrage in Billy's voice.

"What the hell's going on here?"

Aisha looked at him again. She opened her mouth, then shut it, clearly at a loss for words.

It was then that I noticed the diamond engagement ring on her finger.

"This is your fiancé?"

Billy answered for her.

"I am. Now what did you say about Aisha being in danger?"

The snow continued to fall on the street, flakes drifting inside.

"Maybe I should come in."

Aisha asked, "Who all is out there?"

"Nobody that you would know. Well, wait, that's not true."

I motioned at the first SUV. The back door opened and Sanchez stepped out.

The ghost of a smile touched Aisha's mouth.

"Uncle Hector?"

Billy said, "Uncle *who*?"

Sanchez trudged over the sidewalk and up the steps.

Aisha hugged him.

"What are *you* doing here?"

And then noticing the sling.

"What happened to your arm?"

Sanchez nodded at Billy, who hadn't moved from his spot where he stood sullenly.

"Who's the white boy?"

I said, "That's Aisha's fiancé."

"Is that right?"

He smiled at her.

"Congratulations."

She smiled, wiped again at her eyes.

"I still don't understand what this is about."

I forced a smile.

"Let's go inside."

Inside the brownstone, Sanchez asked Billy for a tour. Billy said he wasn't a tour guide. Sanchez, a thin smile on his face, said that he may be old but could still kick Billy's ass if he wanted to. Billy clearly didn't like hearing this, especially in his own home, but then he realized he had no choice but to comply. Grudgingly, tightly gripping his mug of tea, he led Sanchez deeper into the house.

A sitting area was positioned right next to the front door. A large oriental rug was spread out on the floor. Aisha directed me to a white leather chair.

I sat down carefully, so as not to disturb anything.

"Seems like an interesting young man."

"You never liked any of the guys I dated."

"That's a father's job, the way I understood it. How recently did you get engaged?"

Aisha, sitting now on a white leather couch that matched the chair on which I sat, looked away. When she spoke, her voice was soft.

"Five years."

"Say that again?"

"We've both been busy. And besides, essentially we're already married. Dated for two years when he proposed, and … like I said, we've just been busy."

I looked around the sitting area. The oriental rug seemed to clash with the otherwise modern style.

Aisha noticed me noticing.

"It's a family heirloom. Has been in Billy's family for nearly a century."

In that case, I almost felt bad standing on it with my wet boots. Almost.

"I remember you always said you wanted to live in a brownstone some day."

She smiled.

"Originally Billy lived in an apartment off Park Avenue. Corner apartment, looked out over Union Square Park. It was nice, but very ... sterile. So when we got engaged and he suggested I move in, I suggested he buy a brownstone. I was half joking, never thought he'd take me up on it. The next week we moved in here."

"So he seems to be doing well for himself."

"He works on Wall Street. His father is a hedge fund manager. Billy's typically a very nice guy, just the snow today is irritating him because of trading."

"And you? I saw you were the head of a charity organization. That's great."

She smiled again, this time reminding me more than ever of her as a girl, her embarrassed smile.

"It was something that came about because, well, I was getting frustrated by all the other foundations out there. A lot of them seem like they just want to collect money, none actually wants to find a cure. I mean ..."

She shook her head, wiped at her eyes again.

"I'm still mad at you."

"I figured as much based on your greeting."

"You just ... *left*. Didn't say goodbye. You weren't even there for her funeral."

"How was it?"

"What?"

"The funeral."

"What do you care?"

"Aisha."

"No. You fucking left. You couldn't even stay around to *bury* her."

"It was … complicated."

"Bullshit."

"Don't you think I regret it? Not a day goes by that I don't. But I … I couldn't stay. Not after what I'd done."

"What do you mean?"

Her voice flat.

"What you did to Prometheus?"

That wasn't quite right. Yes, there was the way I had tracked down Jeffrey Harris and murdered him—that was certainly something for which I could never forgive myself—but there was something else Aisha didn't know about, nor something I would ever tell her.

"You—"

Her voice cracked again, and this time she didn't wipe at the tear running down her face.

"—you didn't even try to save her."

To this, I said nothing.

"You didn't even *try*."

I didn't think I would find my voice but tried anyway.

"It wouldn't have worked."

"You don't know that."

"I'm not here to argue with you. Like I said before, I fear your life may be in danger."

"Because of James?"

"Yes."

"I don't know anything about that, other than what was in the news."

"When was the last time you saw or spoke to him?"

"It's been years. Maybe two years. We just ... fell out of contact."

I watched her, waiting for her to say more, because clearly she had more to say. But she just sat there, avoiding my gaze.

"What aren't you telling me?"

"Nothing. I just ... look, they had a lot of debt. James was working two jobs—he worked in a warehouse and worked as a garbage man—just to make ends meet on top of being Temple. It was running him thin. And then Yolanda and the kids ..."

She shook her head again.

"You never even saw them."

I said nothing.

"The kids were adopted. Both of them. Did you know that?"

I shook my head, suddenly at a loss for words.

"Yolanda couldn't have children. They'd tried several ways —even artificial insemination—but Yolanda wasn't able to carry. And having worked with special needs kids, Yolanda ... she wanted to help as many of them as possible. So they adopted Ashlee first, who was autistic, and then two years later they adopted Trevor, who had high-functioning Down syndrome. They were great kids, really sweet, but it took a lot to take care of them. Yolanda had to leave her job, which put even more stress on James."

"I saw they had several overdue notices."

Aisha frowned.

"How did you see that?"

"I was in the house."

"My God."

"I had no idea they were struggling so badly."

"I gave them some money. Actually, it wasn't even all my money. Most of it was Billy's. Twenty thousand dollars. James had missed payments on the house and on several bills and he came to me, asking for a loan, just a few thousand dollars if I had it. Of course I had it, so I asked him how much he was short."

"How much?"

"Seventy-five thousand dollars. Much of it was Yolanda's school loan, which she had been falling behind on too. They received some SSI for the kids, but it wasn't nearly as much as they needed. Had they lived anywhere else, maybe they would have been fine, but James didn't want to leave the city because … well, you know why."

Yes, I did know why. Of course I knew why. James didn't want to leave the city because New York was where Temple had started and where he would stay.

"Did he pay you back?"

"For a while he did, yes. A few hundred bucks every month. Then it started being just a hundred bucks. Then fifty bucks. Then a month would pass with no payment, and then the next month twenty bucks. I told him he didn't have to pay me the rest back if they were really struggling. We had an argument over that. The next week he returned the rest of the money. It was one of those cash advance checks. I was surprised he was even able to get a limit that high based on all his debt, but I deposited it and it went through. After that, we just never talked anymore."

I wasn't sure why this should surprise me, but it did. Hadn't Shalissa and I struggled when we were younger? Even after James and Aisha were born, we sometimes had trouble paying bills. She was a librarian; I was a detective. We didn't have great salaries, but they were decent, at least enough to get us by. Just as Aisha said regarding her brother, had we lived elsewhere, maybe we might not have struggled as much, but we couldn't leave the city. New York had become synonymous with Temple.

Being Temple, I realized, had killed my son in more ways than one.

Aisha said, "Did you know there are toys? Comic books? There was even a cartoon series. Everyone was getting rich off Temple except the one guy who *was* Temple. It drove James crazy. He hated all the merchandising, said it made the whole idea of Temple cheap. But it wasn't like he could come forward asking for a piece of the cut. And so ..."

She shrugged.

"He and Yolanda kept struggling month after month. By the way, who else is outside?"

"The government. Homeland Security. For years now they've been monitoring Temple. They knew who James was, and you. They've been watching you all this time."

"*What*?"

She sounded violated, which, of course, she had every right to be. I was beginning to understand more and more what Sanchez meant by a police state.

"The other night the agents they had watching James's family were killed. Soon after, so were Yolanda and the kids. James has been missing ever since."

"So ... why do you think I'm in danger too?"

"Simply because you're my daughter."

"But you don't know for a fact that I'm in danger."

"No."

"So what do you want me to do? Come with you?"

Just how much should I tell her? I'd told Roger that I wouldn't impart too much of the truth, and I had no intention of telling her about Sentinel and the black site—right now she didn't need to know about any of that—but she still needed to know why she wasn't safe.

"There are people out there that want me dead. They've either killed your brother or abducted him—we still aren't clear on that—but my fear is that if you were to come into Homeland Security's protection, you might be walking into their arms."

"How?"

"There was one mole that we know of who was feeding us false information. There may be others. I don't want to take that chance."

She looked stricken.

"So … what am I supposed to do?"

"Just stay here. I want Hector to stay with you too."

"And what is he supposed to do if someone comes to hurt me? No offense, but Uncle Hector is an old man."

Before I could respond, something in my pocket vibrated. I didn't know what it was at first until I reached inside the pocket and touched the cell phone Roger had given me. The disposable. I pulled it out and answered it.

Roger's voice sounded grave, and he didn't waste any time getting to the point.

"Mr. Shepherd, I'm calling about your son. We found him. Or, rather, we found what's left of him."

INTERLUDE
ORIGIN STORY (II)

Later, my father would come to realize New York City had always been his final destination. And it wasn't just what Short Stack had told him about it being his favorite city—though perhaps that got the ball rolling. What New York City had at that time in history was people. A *lot* of people. And with the military hunting him, my father knew the city was his best bet to disappear.

But my father did not go straight to New York. It was almost exactly one hundred miles away, after all, and my father had no money, no transportation. He had been able to escape the mansion easily enough—once outside he had taken off into the trees and never looked back—but now he was a wanted man, and like any wanted man, he needed to be careful.

Could he have returned to Tennessee? Perhaps. But there was nothing there for him except his dead mother and an irate landlord who wanted several months' back rent. That was it. My father had no other family, no friends. No one.

My father knew there was something wrong with him. At least that's how he viewed it for the first couple days, as if he were abnormal. Yes, he could move extremely fast, and yes, he could hear and see things with more clarity than normal people typically could, but the fact that his body could heal itself so quickly from having been shot? It scared my father. He felt like a freak. The kind of thing God turns his back on.

My father found clothes hanging from a line in someone's backyard. He felt bad about taking the clothes, but judging by the number of clothes on the line, he didn't suspect the owners would care, or even notice. A new pair of underwear, slacks, and shirt later, my father kept moving. He needed shoes. These, he knew, he would have to steal. Besides the clothes, my father had never stolen a thing in his life, and he hated that he had now become a thief, but he had no choice.

For the first couple days, after having secured a pair of shoes, my father worked his way north. Through Doylestown, then toward the New Jersey state line. He kept looking over his shoulder until he realized he didn't have to look over his shoulder. He allowed his heightened senses to take care of that. He was able to hear if someone was approaching. He was able to take in an entire space within a second to know whether or not there was any danger. My father had no weapon, and while at first he had worried that he needed one, he came to understand that he was himself a weapon.

In New Brunswick, New Jersey, my father performed his first heroic act.

It had been almost a week since he escaped the mansion. He knew the military was looking for him, but he hadn't seen anything since that worried him. Several police cars on the streets and highways, yes, but they seemed to be just doing their job.

It was evening and my father was in the white part of the

city. He had always known to stay out of the white part of the city, or else he would be arrested or beaten up. But the fear he'd always had toward white people was gone. He knew he *should* be afraid, but he wasn't. Besides, my father needed something to eat. He still had no money, refusing to steal any—the clothes and shoes he'd found had been bad enough—but he had come to realize that some restaurants threw away their leftovers, and so he figured that if he timed it right, he might find something fresh in the trash cans out in the alleyways.

That was where he was now, hiding in an alleyway, waiting for the kitchen staff to throw away food, when he heard a woman scream.

He hurried to the end of the alley and saw an elderly white couple across the street. The man was picking himself up off the sidewalk where he'd been pushed down. The woman had a lot of fancy jewelry—on her ears, on her fingers, even a flashy piece of jewelry on her jacket—and she screamed again at two boys, about my father's age, currently running away. One of the boys grasped a purse, the other a wallet.

My father gave chase at once. He didn't think twice about it. He sprinted down the street while the woman screamed for someone to help. My father caught up with the boys in no time. It was almost like they were running in slow motion. My father tripped one and then pushed the other into the nearest building. My father made sure not to use too much force, mindful of what had happened to the doctor and the boy back at the mansion. My father's intention was simply to stop these two, not kill them.

The boy who stole the wallet skidded across the sidewalk, his arms and face cut up from the concrete. He scrambled to his feet and came at my father, who easily deflected the punches. My father tossed him into the nearest building, where the boy fell in a heap next to his buddy, who still hadn't gotten back to his feet. My father collected the wallet and purse and left the boys there. He jogged back down the sidewalk and turned the corner.

Only the woman was there. She sat on the curb, wiping at her eyes with a kerchief. She was alone.

My father approached, the wallet and purse in hand.

"Ma'am? I believe these are yours."

The old woman looked up. Stared at my father for a second. And screamed.

For an instant, my father didn't move. He wasn't sure what to do. This wasn't how he had expected this moment to go. He'd expected the woman to smile, be grateful. Not look at him with terror and disgust.

Farther up the street, the woman's husband approached, along with two police officers. At the sound of the woman's screaming, the two officers started running. Directly toward my father.

The woman shouted, "Help!"

One of the police officers pulled his gun.

My father knew he could easily defend himself against these two men. But they weren't the enemy here, not like Colonel Strickland and his soldiers. The officers were simply doing their job. To them, my *father* was the enemy.

Tossing the purse and the wallet at the old woman's feet, my father turned and ran.

My father's second heroic act came in Newark, three days later. It was the middle of the night—two, three o'clock—and my father had begun to doze off to sleep when he heard a woman scream.

He opened his eyes. Didn't move. Just listened. For a

couple seconds, there was nothing but the ubiquitous city noises—traffic and a train off in the distance—and then the scream came again.

My father sat up. He was wrapped in a ratty blanket he'd found in the trash. He had gone from finding places to sleep on the ground to building roofs. He'd scale the fire escapes and then hunker down in a corner and sleep peacefully through the night, as there was never any reason for someone to come to the roof in the middle of the night.

The scream sounded once more.

My father flung the blanket aside and jumped to his feet. There was a slight wind that could have carried the scream, but my father was confident he knew from which direction it was coming. He jumped from one building to the next, the distance between the buildings more than ten feet, but it barely fazed him. As he ran, he listened past the city sounds to the origin of the screams, and he heard a woman's voice, begging someone to stop, and he heard another voice—deep, slurred, guttural—telling her to shut up.

The next building was positioned farther away than the others, this one more than twenty feet. He realized this after he had jumped and was already sailing through the air. He came down short but grabbed hold of the fire escape and hung suspended, his feet dangling, before he pulled himself up and scrambled back to the roof.

He was almost there. Just another block away. He jumped to the next building and crept up to the edge and looked down into the alleyway five stories below.

Besides the young woman, who had been thrown to the ground, her jacket ripped open, there were three of them. Two of them stood off to the side while the third knelt in front of the woman, his hand to her throat, his other hand working the zipper of his pants.

All of them were white.

My father surveyed the alleyway. No fire escape here. But on the opposite building was a metal ladder that led to the roof.

The woman begged, sobbing.

"Please. Please stop."

The man backhanded her across the face with the hand he had been using to free himself from his pants. He was clearly drunk, as were the other two. His coordination was off, forcing him to concentrate harder than normal to unzip his pants. His other hand still holding her around the throat, he worked at the zipper again.

My father backed away from the edge of the roof several feet, enough to give him a running start. He sprinted forward. He could have easily cleared the alleyway, but his intention was not to end up on the opposite building's roof. He grabbed hold of the metal ladder, but unlike the previous building's fire escape, my father headed down. He dropped one level, grabbed a rung, dropped another level, grabbed another rung, and then dropped the final two levels to land with his feet on the ground.

He didn't say anything to the three men. The three men said nothing to him. There was nothing that needed to be said.

The closest man attacked first. He rushed at my father, cocking his fist back, and my father quickly sidestepped the punch and grabbed the man's arm and threw him into the nearest wall. My father didn't care whether these men lived or died. Not after it was clear what they'd intended to do to the woman.

As the first man bounced off the brick wall, the second man charged my father. A knife had suddenly appeared in his hand, and he directed the blade at my father's face. My father ducked the knife easily enough, but the man kept coming, slicing the air back and forth, my father ducking here and there until he spun low and swept the man's feet out from under him. The man hit the ground on his back with a heavy thud.

The third man had given up trying to free himself from his zipper. He let go of the woman's throat and stood up straight. He was well over six feet, his face pocked with scars, his teeth crooked. The man glared at my father, snarling like a lion. Unlike his friends, however, the man didn't charge my father. He stood his ground, placing his body between my father and the woman, as if my father was the threat.

Behind my father, the others were coming to. He was aware of this just as he was aware of the sporadic traffic out on the street and a baby crying in a building three blocks away.

"She's ours."

The man immediately belched. At any other time, it may have seemed comical. The man certainly thought so, chuckling and wiping at the drool from his mouth.

My father said nothing. Despite not seeing the two men behind him, he knew where they were based on the noises they made. He could almost see them in his mind. The second man —the one with the knife—having gotten back to his feet. The first man—the one who hit the building—slowly attempting to sit up.

The second man came at my father from behind, and my father—watching in his mind's eye—stepped to the side. The second man stumbled forward. My father had expected the man to still be holding the knife, but both of his hands were free. Which meant—

The crunch of asphalt behind him as the first man stepped up close and plunged the blade into my father's back.

"You like that, nigger?"

The man twisted the knife.

My father fell to his knees. The blade had gone deep.

Already he could feel his body starting to heal itself, but with the knife still in his back, he doubted his body would be able to heal entirely.

A sudden rage filled my father.

What happened next happened within the space of five seconds.

My father reached up and grabbed the man's throat and flung him over his head. The man sailed through the air just like before, only this time he wasn't going to get back up. The man's spine snapped on impact with the wall. Rising to his feet, my father pulled out the knife from his back and threw it at the third man, the one still standing between my father and the woman. The blade plunged deep into the man's throat. As the man fell forward to his knees, his hands grasping for the knife, the final man turned to flee. My father was on his feet and running forward within an instant. He met up with the man several yards before the end of the alley, grabbed him by the arm, and threw him into the wall. The man's skull cracked open.

My father turned back to the woman. She was breathing heavy, staring wide-eyed around the alley. Fear flashed in her eyes, and for an instant my father thought she was scared of him.

"They stabbed you."

My father said nothing.

The woman climbed to her feet. She wore a white uniform that looked familiar to my father, though for a moment he couldn't place it. She took a step toward him.

"Don't."

My father's voice sounded strange to him.

"I'm ... okay."

"You were *stabbed*. You need to go to the hospital."

Except my father didn't. By then his body had already

healed itself. The damage that the blade had done to my father's body had all but disappeared, both internally and externally.

"I'm fine."

The woman looked at him as if he was crazy.

"You can't be fine. I saw him get you with the knife. You need help."

"It's okay."

Understanding entered the woman's eyes.

"I get it. You don't think they'll treat you at the hospital. But they will—I'm sure of it."

"Please …"

My father wasn't sure what to say.

"Please … I'm okay."

The woman looked around the alley again. She didn't seem concerned that the men were either dead or dying.

"I'm a nursing student. Let me at least treat you. Will you let me do that?"

My father wasn't sure what to say. The idea of going somewhere with this woman was beyond his comprehension—was this really happening?—but he nodded anyway.

The woman said, "Good."

She picked up her dropped purse and started toward the end of the alley.

"We better get out of here before the police show up."

She grabbed his arm, spun him around, and winced at the blood on his back.

"Here."

She took his hand and pressed his palm against his back on the spot in which the blade had pierced the skin.

"Keep pressure on it. My apartment's only three blocks away."

She lived on the fourth floor of an apartment building, and after she sneaked him up the four flights of stairs and got him inside, she directed him straight to the bathroom and had him sit down on the edge of the tub and told him to take off his shirt while she hurried around the apartment for anything she could use to disinfect the wound and help sew it up. When she returned to the bathroom, however, my father hadn't moved.

"What are you *doing*? You need to take off your shirt. That's the only way I'll be able to treat you."

My father said, "Why are you helping me?"

"Why did you help me?"

"Because you were in trouble."

"Well, there's your answer."

"But I'm a …"

"What, you're a Negro? That doesn't bother me. Growing up we had a maid who was a Negro. She was sweet and smart and treated me so nicely, and I was devastated when my parents let her go. They said they had done it for me, because they feared I saw her as a friend. Now here, take off your shirt."

She set the supplies on the sink—towels and a bottle of hydrogen peroxide and needle and thread—and grabbed my father's shirt and started to pull it up over his head.

My father stopped her.

"Please, no, I'm okay."

She ignored him and kept tugging at his shirt. My father allowed her to slip the shirt up over his head. She tossed it in the tub and told him to stand up and move in front of the sink where the lighting was better. She used the towel to wipe the dried blood away. Then she stepped back, her mouth agape, her face was full of confusion.

"But … I … I saw them stab you."

His back to the mirror, my father glanced over his shoulder to confirm what he already knew: there was no scar where the knife had stabbed him.

She took another step back, the confusion on her face morphing into fear.

"How did that happen?"

My father stared at her. He said nothing. He wasn't sure what to say. Until, finally, he realized he had no choice. He had to tell *somebody*. Otherwise the secret would drive him insane.

"My name is Henry Temple. I'm seventeen years old. I'm from Friendsville, Tennessee. My mother died not too long ago..."

He told her everything. For her credit, she listened. Never interrupted. Her face stayed calm the entire time, even when he told her about being on the ship and what had happened to Tyrone and Etan and how later Colonel Strickland had shot the doctor that my father had hid behind. When he was finished, having told her about hearing her scream several blocks away and running to her rescue, she barely even blinked. She was quiet for a moment, taking this all in, and then pointed at the towels and told him to take a shower.

"I'll make some soup."

She left him there, closing the door behind her. My father stripped off his clothes, stepped into the tub, turned on the water and had the first real shower he'd had in several weeks.

She gave him one of her bathrobes to wear and made chicken soup.

My father thanked her for what may have been the twentieth time.

"Thank you. This is very good."

She sat across from him at the small kitchen table. She had a bowl of soup in front of her but hadn't touched it yet.

My father said, "I don't know your name …"

This caused her to blink as if just waking up. Maybe she'd thought she was dreaming. She leaned forward, picked up her spoon, and began stirring the soup. And as she did, she told my father her story.

Her name was Vanessa Clark. She was nineteen years old. She attended Rutgers University as a nursing student and shared this apartment with a friend who also attended the university. Vanessa had stayed late at the hospital to cover another nursing student's shift because that student had called out sick, and instead of calling for a cab, Vanessa had decided to walk home. And ended up being dragged into an alleyway by those three men.

Where was her roommate now? Visiting family in Connecticut. Her roommate's brother had just come back from the war, missing one of his legs, and her roommate had gone straight up there to see him.

There was a silence, and then my father thanked Vanessa once again for her hospitality but said he should leave.

She shook her head.

"Nonsense. I need to at least wash your clothes. There's blood on your shirt. Besides, where are you going to go? You said you've been sleeping in alleyways and on rooftops."

My father said he would manage.

Vanessa shook her head again. No, she told him, she would get some blankets and he would sleep on the couch. It was the least she could do for him after he'd saved her life.

My father didn't sleep well that night. He had become accustomed to sleeping outside. Suddenly the soft, warm comfort of a sofa and blanket seemed alien to him.

In the morning, Vanessa made breakfast.

"I'm not going to my classes today."

She didn't elaborate. My father didn't say anything. They were quiet for a long time until finally Vanessa spoke again.

"Where will you go?"

My father said nothing.

"These people will hunt you wherever you go. You'll never be safe."

My father didn't answer.

"What will you do?"

My father shrugged.

"There's nothing to do. They're the military. I'm just one person."

Vanessa watched him for some time, studying his face.

"What do you *want* to do?"

My father answered immediately.

"I want to help people."

He told her about the old couple in New Brunswick. How helping them and helping Vanessa gave him a sense of purpose.

Vanessa smiled.

"You sound like the people in the stories my little brother reads."

"What stories?"

"The magazines with the pictures."

It took her a moment, and then she snapped her fingers.

"Comic books! You sound like one of those heroes."

My father thought of Short Stack.

"I'm not a hero."

"No?"

She studied his face again.

"But why can't you be?"

"I told you about trying to help that woman. She screamed when she saw me."

Vanessa waved a hand.

"That's because she doesn't like Negros. She saw you as a threat, despite the fact you had just helped her."

"There's nothing I can do about my skin."

Vanessa kept her gaze steady with his.

"No, but you can hide it."

Vanessa told my father to stay where he was, and she grabbed her purse and said that she would be back within an hour.

She left before my father could say anything. It didn't cross his mind until several minutes later that perhaps she had gone to get the police.

When she returned two hours later, she had two bags filled with clothes and fabric. Underwear, pants, undershirt, jacket. She had my father stand up tall and with a string measured the length of his legs and his arms and his waist. A Singer Sewing Machine was in the parlor room, that Vanessa said belonged to her roommate, and for the next several hours Vanessa cut and measured and sewed the fabric, often pausing to have my father try on one piece or another until evening came and she had completed what she said was a good prototype.

Vanessa had my father try on the outfit: black pants and shirt and a mask she had made to cover his entire head. She'd made eyeholes for the mask because obviously my father needed to see, but as she stood in front of him, taking it all in, she said his skin color could still be seen. She thought for a moment, then asked just how "heightened" his vision was.

"What do you mean?"

She raised a finger, told him to give her a moment, and disappeared into her bedroom. She emerged seconds later with a pair of sunglasses and told him to put them on, and as my father slipped them on—they were tight, which helped as his ears were hidden beneath the mask—Vanessa turned out all the lights and asked my father if he could see anything.

My father looked around the apartment. At first all he saw was darkness, but then, little by little, the room began to take on shape. Within seconds, he was able to make out everything in detail just as if the lights were on.

When my father told Vanessa this, she smiled and clapped her hands.

"You're still going to need shoes. Boots, more likely. Black boots. And gloves, of course. Black gloves. Here, come see yourself."

She led him into her bedroom where a full-length mirror leaned against the wall. My father stared at his reflection. Besides his feet and hands, no skin showed anywhere.

Vanessa said, "How does the fabric feel? We can always change it. It will probably get too hot for you during the summer. Again, it's just a prototype. But I think it will work."

"For what?"

She smiled at him.

"For you to be a hero. Isn't that what you want?"

My father said nothing. He didn't like to think of himself as a hero. He just wanted to help people.

Taking off the sunglasses, he handed them to Vanessa and then noticed a picture frame on the bedside table.

"What's his name?"

"Who?"

He pointed at the picture frame that held a photograph of Vanessa and a young man. Both smiled brightly at the camera.

"Is that your brother?"

Vanessa didn't answer. She'd gone all at once silent. Tears had begun to brim her eyes.

"That's not my brother. That's my fiancé. *Was* my fiancé. He … he was killed last week in action."

And with that, she fell into a chair sobbing.

***

His name was Justin, Vanessa told my father once she had calmed down and was finally able to talk about it. He had proposed to her before he left for Europe and of course she had said yes and of course she had missed him every day since he had been gone, always thinking of him, and then she received word just two days ago of his death.

It would be many years later before my father understood the dangers of depression, and it would only be then that he suspected Vanessa's careless walking home in the middle of the night might not have been entirely unintentional. She most certainly *hadn't* wanted to end up in that alleyway, but part of her may not have cared what happened to her life right then. Justin was dead, so she didn't feel like she had much to live for anymore.

My father said, "I'm sorry."

Vanessa wiped at her eyes. It was late at night and raining outside.

"He was such a wonderful guy. He would have been a wonderful husband. He would have made such a wonderful father."

They didn't talk after that. They just sat there, silent, and listened to the rain pattering against the windows, until finally

Vanessa got up and drifted into her bedroom, and my father lay back on the couch and stared at the ceiling and wondered what it truly meant to be a hero.

The next day Vanessa skipped her classes again, which gave her time to head back to the store for more material. When she returned to the apartment, she went straight to the Singer and got to work. She'd bought boots, too, black leather boots in my father's size, as well as gloves and dark goggles she'd found at a hardware store.

Standing once again in Vanessa's bedroom, right in front of the full-length mirror, my father stared at himself in the … was it a uniform? My father wasn't sure exactly *what* to call it, but it fit perfectly.

"Thank you."

"My pleasure. I told you I owed you. I think this will work. It's sad, but you'll be able to help more people this way."

Yes, my father thought, now his skin would not be seen and people would not focus on the color of his skin but on his actions.

"My roommate comes back tomorrow morning. As much as I'd like for you to stay longer, it would be best if you leave."

My father said he understood.

"But at least stay until it gets dark."

She smiled at him.

"I can make you some of that chicken soup you like."

My father stayed. He knew he should have left as soon as possible, but he stayed. He didn't know when it had happened exactly, but he had fallen in love with Vanessa. Or was it love? Maybe it was just infatuation. Whatever the case, my father never wanted to leave her side. She was kind and loving and did not seem to care at all that their skin did not match in color.

They sat in the parlor and talked. She told him about growing up, how her parents were wealthy and powerful and hated the idea of their daughter being a nurse, but that she didn't care because she wanted to help people. My father told her about growing up in Tennessee, how he had never known his own father and his mother had raised him until she got sick. He told her what segregation was like in the south. How the first time he was spit on he was four years old. How the white kids would throw rocks at him and his friends when they were walking to the Negro school.

Vanessa was quiet while he talked, her hand covering her mouth. Finally she shook her head and whispered.

"People can be so cruel."

For dinner, Vanessa again made soup. They sat at the small table and stirred their spoons, neither saying anything.

My father was afraid if he spoke, he'd tell her how much he loved her. That since the moment he'd met her he couldn't stop thinking about her. But again, was that love?

After they had cleaned up, my father announced that it was time for him to leave.

Vanessa packed the extra clothes she'd gotten him and the black uniform in a duffel bag, then dug twenty dollars from her purse.

My father shook his head.

"I can't take that."

She pressed the money into his hand.

"It's not a lot, but I hope it helps you get to New York."

She walked him to the door, opened it a crack, peeked out.

When she turned back, whispering to him that it was clear, a tear rolled down her cheek.

My father watched the course of that tear. He wanted to reach out, wipe it away. He wanted to lean forward and place his lips on hers. He had never kissed a girl before. Part of him knew if he did that, however, Vanessa might shy away from him. The image of that old woman in New Brunswick kept flashing through his mind, the fear in her eyes, the disgust, and he couldn't bear to live with the knowledge that Vanessa might feel the same way.

"Thank you."

"Good luck."

She leaned up on her tiptoes and kissed his cheek. It was brief, but it sent a flush through my father's face.

"I hope you help a lot of people."

"Goodbye."

My father walked out of the apartment.

He never saw Vanessa Clark again.

PART THREE
MONARCH

41

I had never been afraid of heights.

Even as a boy, twelve years old, I would drive my mother crazy by jumping from our apartment building to the next. My father had never encouraged this, but he had never discouraged it either. In a way, he knew that this was part of my training. Eventually he would have to tell me all I would need to know, so why not allow me to start figuring it out on my own? Then, during Vietnam, I parachuted a half-dozen times. Twice I ended up in trees and had to cut myself out of the straps, one time falling nearly fifty feet to the ground.

There was only one time I had been nervous of heights. It had been August 7, 1974. I had only been Temple for a year by then, my father packing his things and heading west.

At that time, I was still just a beat cop. It would be several years before I became a detective, and a few more years before I started working with Sanchez. News had quickly spread across the city about a man walking on a wire between the Twin Towers of the World Trade Center. Later the world would learn that this man was Philippe Petit, a French high-wire artist, but all that had been known at the time was that there was a crazy man up there.

Naturally, I hurried over to the Towers, changing into my Temple outfit in the elevator as it lifted me over 1,000 feet. It was clear once I made it to the roof that Philippe Petit was not crazy. Well, he was certainly crazy, but he was a special kind of crazy. This was clearly a stunt. He knew exactly what he was doing. He even recognized me and waved, shouted that he was a fan and hoped to shake my hand once he was done.

There was nothing for me or the cops up on the roofs to do but wait and watch.

And as I stood there on the edge, I stared down at the street below. Some may have considered me a superhero, but there was no way I would survive a fall that distance. My body would splat on the street just like anyone else's. Before, I had always known that I wasn't immortal and that many things could kill me, but right then I realized that, with just one misstep, I would die. It was terrifying. Meanwhile, Petit continued to cross back and forth on the wire, showing no fear whatsoever.

I thought about that now as I stood on the roof of the Freedom Tower. Roger stood beside me, staring off toward Liberty Island. The snow had let up some but was still coming down, and we were bundled in jackets, our hands in our pockets, our hoods up.

A helicopter circled the tower, a gunner positioned out the open side in case of another attack.

Roger spoke just loud enough to be heard over the helicopter.

"Look at it. Even from this distance she looks tiny, but she's beautiful nonetheless. When people think of America, they think of her."

The Statue of Liberty did not look majestic from this high

up in the air. Especially with the snow, she looked tiny and cold and alone.

"What if someone attacks her? Which Sentry is closest?"

"Here, actually."

Roger motioned toward the center of the roof.

"Sentry Number Fourteen was the last one installed. It protects this end of Manhattan. And the Statue of Liberty. And Ellis Island, though I can't imagine that would ever be a target. But we can never be too careful."

The helicopter circled again, the gunner staring at us from behind his sunglasses.

Behind us, Agent Njeim spoke.

"We're ready."

We turned around. Along with Agent Njeim, there were four agents bundled up in jackets. Two of them were crouched over the body near the center of the roof. Here, because of the scaffolding above us, not as much snow had piled up as it had down on the street. Still there was at least a foot, and the agents had needed to dust that snow off the body.

My son's body.

I recognized him even after all these years. A father always knows his son, no matter how much time has passed and how much his son has changed. And James had indeed changed, though it hadn't been any of his doing.

He was a husk. All the blood and fluids had been drained from his body until he was literally nothing more than skin and bones. His eyes were gone. They hadn't taken his head—no doubt for me to confirm his body—but they had opened up the back of his head to extract his brain.

Roger said, "Let's get him back to base. What have you found on surveillance?"

Agent Njeim said, "Nothing so far, but Nate is still

working on it and we're searching nearby cameras. Something had to have caught them placing him here."

Roger thought about this for a moment, then shook his head.

"No. These people know exactly where every camera is. They know how to avoid them, and if they can't avoid them, they can override them. You can keep looking, but nothing is going to come of it."

Behind Agent Njeim, the other agents had opened a body bag. They were going to place my son's body—his husk—in the bag and take him back to the Vault, where they were going to wait until he thawed and then perform an autopsy. But they wouldn't find anything. I was almost certain about this. The people doing this were playing games. They were leading us on a wild goose chase. The question was, why? Why did they bring his body up here?

Roger turned to me.

"What do you think?"

He was waiting. They were all waiting, but there was nothing much to see. Not with all the snow. They would need to eliminate the snow, shovel it aside, though there was no telling just how long James's body had been here. If there was any trace evidence, it was long gone, and if there *was* some still here, just how were we supposed to find it?

An hour ago, an alarm had gone off in the building, noti-fying security that the door to the roof was open. When a guard checked, he saw my son's naked body. He had alerted the head of security, and the head of security had dialed 911, but the call had been intercepted by the analysts at the Vault, who'd been monitoring all communication throughout the city. That was how Roger and his people were able to get here so quickly.

The people who did this wanted my son's body found.

I stared past Agent Njeim for a long moment. I tried to

focus on my son. I thought about this rooftop and how there may be trace evidence. I thought about the body being placed here for a reason and how we had been meant to find it, and it suddenly gave me an idea.

"Agent Njeim, once we leave here, can you take me back to my daughter's?"

She looked to Roger for permission, and when he gave her a slight nod, she said yes.

"Great. No need for an escort."

Roger cleared his throat.

"Mr. Shepherd, I would—"

"We'll be fine."

Roger said nothing, clearly not happy about it.

The helicopter kept circling us. The snow kept falling. And the agents, now with the body bag open, had no trouble at all lifting James from the ground and placing him in the bag and enclosing him in the plastic shroud.

42

The Henry Hudson Parkway was mostly deserted, and with the SUV's four-wheel drive, Agent Njeim had us going nearly fifty miles per hour. We had left the Freedom Tower only a few minutes ago, and the sight of James's body was still fresh in my mind. Every time I blinked, an afterimage remained just as stark and imposing as the real thing.

I stared out the window as Agent Njeim drove.

"Can Nate and the other analysts back at the Vault track where we're going?"

"Yes."

"Can you disable the tracking?"

She hesitated.

"We're not going to your daughter's, are we?"

I looked at her now.

"Can you disable it?"

"Yes."

"Then do it."

"First tell me where we're going."

I gave her the address of a place in Harlem.

"What's there?"

"Hopefully everything."

The apartment building off Edgecombe Avenue looked just like it had thirty years ago. Not much had changed about its red brick façade except that there was a green overhang over the front entrance. When I had lived in the building with Shalissa and the kids, that overhang had been red.

Agent Njeim asked, "In there?"

"Yes. The basement."

"Why the basement?"

"That's where I trained James when he was younger. The super put a lock on the basement door, but it was always easy to pick. There was a lot of room down there for us to move around."

"How do we get inside?"

"I'm thinking the back way will be best. Fewer people around. Besides, the entrance to the basement should be just a door away."

It turned out we didn't need to break into the building. Someone, probably a child, had left the door propped open with a glove.

We slipped inside.

Fortunately, the hallway was deserted. The basement door was right where I remembered it, only the cheap lock had been replaced. Made sense. Thirty years had passed, and no doubt there was new management. Tenants probably actually got proper maintenance nowadays.

"Can you pick that?"

Agent Njeim reached into the pocket of her jacket and pulled out a small black device. She held it over the lock, pressed a button, and the next thing I knew she had turned the knob and the door eased open.

We headed down the steps.

Just like it had when I was down here last, the space was used for storage and maintenance. Racks against the wall held extra supplies, such as doorknobs and hinges and even two toilets, one of which looked new, the other used. The ceiling was high, which had made for a good place to train, as I would need to teach James how to jump and flip.

Agent Njeim looked around the room.

"So what are we looking for?"

"I'm not sure yet."

"You said you hoped everything would be here."

"That's right. My son's house was torn apart. The people who killed my daughter-in-law and grandchildren were trying to find something."

"And you think that something is down here?"

"I'm hoping it is."

"Why?"

"Because if it's not down here, I don't know where else it could be."

"But why do you think it's down here?"

"Like I said, this was where I trained James when we lived at home. Then when he moved out to his own place, we would still train here. Sometimes we would miss each other, so we left notes."

"Where did you keep the notes?"

I pointed at a thick pipe in the ceiling.

"Right up there."

It took Agent Njeim a minute to climb up to the pipe, but nothing was hidden there.

I looked around the basement.

"Maybe he hid it somewhere else."

"What if there isn't anything?"

"Those people were looking for something."

"Yes, they were looking for your son. And they found him. What if that's all they wanted?"

"Then why tear the house apart?"

"Maybe they found what they were looking for."

I thought about it for a moment. The truth was the possibility had crossed my mind, but I didn't want to accept it.

"Or if they didn't find it, what if your son placed whatever it is someplace else?"

I was quiet.

"Mr. Shepherd, I know you want to believe that there's something more to this, but what if your son didn't know anything about what was going on? That your son had nothing these people wanted?"

It was completely silent in the basement. Except for the heater running full blast in the next room, of course. I remembered how hot that heater had made it some nights when James and I trained, sweat soaking our bodies, that sometimes we just wanted to beat the shit out of it.

"Let's start looking."

We looked. We looked everywhere. All that we found was that we had wasted nearly twenty minutes. It was clear to both of us early on that nothing would be here, but neither of us voiced it. Agent Njeim didn't even bother trying to reason with me.

She just went along with it, as if humoring a crazy old man. Which, in a way, I guess I was.

Then Agent Njeim's phone buzzed, the disposable Roger had given her. She answered hesitantly.

"No, sir, I don't know what happened to the GPS."

She paused, listening, then turned to look at me. Into the phone she answered again.

"You called Mr. Shepherd's daughter's house to see if we were there? Well, yes, sir, we're currently in Harlem following up on a lead."

Another pause as she listened.

"I see. Yes, give me one moment."

She held the phone out, hit the speakerphone button.

"Okay, sir, go ahead."

I said, "Hello, Roger."

"Mr. Shepherd, I hope you'll fill me in on what you two of have been up to at some point, but for right now I want to inform you what they've found with your son's body. Bear in mind, there's still not much that can be done until he thaws out completely, but one of our techs noticed some mineral under his fingernails. All his fingernails, actually, as well as his toenails."

"What mineral?"

"It appears to be something called Wollastonite. It's a silicate mineral that's used mostly in tile factories."

"What does that have to do with my son?"

"That's the thing—we have no idea. Wollastonite is only found in a handful of countries, such as China, India, and Finland. The mineral is also mined in three towns in upstate New York."

"What towns?"

"Give me a moment."

Soft clicking came through the speaker as Roger typed at his computer.

"The towns appear to be Willsboro, Conway, and Gouverneur."

I was silent. Suddenly I couldn't speak.

"Mr. Shepherd? Agent Njeim, are you still there?"

"We are."

Agent Njeim focused her gaze on me.

"Mr. Shepherd, what's wrong?"

I looked at her but wasn't sure what to say at first. Then I glanced down at the cell phone in her hand. At the other end of the invisible line, Roger sat in his office, waiting for me to speak.

"Roger, we need to go to Conway as soon as possible."

"I don't understand. Why Conway?"

"Because the people who killed my son didn't put that mineral under his fingernails by mistake. They wanted it found. They wanted me to know."

"I still don't understand. What's so special about Conway?"

"It's where I was born."

43

onway is in Essex County, just under three hundred miles north of New York City. Because of the snow, it took us two hours by helicopter to reach Conway, which put us close to three o'clock in the afternoon.

Agent Njeim and I flew in one of the helicopters along with two other men, not including the pilot and copilot. Two other helicopters accompanied us, each consisting of a team of four. The teams didn't know exactly what the mission was— even I didn't know what we would be walking into—only that there was a possible terrorist threat in this sleepy New York town.

Because of the possibility of our communication being intercepted, Roger agreed that the only communication would be between the three teams. No one at the Vault knew about this impromptu mission.

The pilot alerted us that we were approaching the town.

I glanced out the window. Conway borders with Lake Champlain, and now the lake was completely iced over, a flawless carpet of white stretching between New York and Vermont.

Agent Njeim had checked the weather on the way up and found that Conway had already gotten three feet of snow.

Now she leaned forward and tapped my leg. We all wore headsets to hear over the roar of the rotors, but none of us had spoken this entire time.

"Where?"

"Near the edge of town. I still can't remember the address, but I'll remember it once I see it. Assuming the house hasn't been torn down."

It wasn't much to go on, but we didn't have anything else. All we knew for certain was that a mineral had been placed underneath my son's fingernails, a mineral that was mined in three upstate New York towns, one of which I had grown up in.

It was more than coincidence.

Something was waiting for us here. We just had to find it.

Conway had been one of the few upstate towns with a black community. I remembered that the house in which I'd lived was on the outskirts of town. There was an ice cream place three miles away, the Conway Creamery, and my mother and I had walked there at least once a week during the summer. We had walked down our road to the main road and walked up that road until we reached the creamery. The lake had been toward our right as we walked up the road, which put the house toward the east.

This was how I directed the pilot. Our house had been on the corner of the lane. From several hundred feet up, even with the snow, I recognized the house the moment I saw it.

I pointed.

"That's it."

Agent Njeim checked our location on her tablet.

"That's Woodlawn Lane. Which means that house is 19 Woodlawn. Does that sound right to you?"

It did. It had been almost sixty years, but I now remembered my father would write us letters, and on the envelope I could see that address in his almost illegible handwriting. When my mother sent letters back, she never put a return address, on the off chance the government or someone else might determine our location.

Agent Njeim typed on the tablet.

"The house was purchased fifteen years ago by a Frank and Norma Greene. Both retired. Mr. Shepherd, are you sure this is the place?"

"Yes."

Agent Njeim nodded at one of the men.

"Scan it."

The man had a rifle with a large scope on top. He aimed down at the house and stared for several long seconds.

"No heat signatures."

The other man said, "Maybe the Greenes are vacationing down South."

Agent Njeim stared down at the tablet and shook her head.

"According to their phone records, they were active as of yesterday. They should be home."

She motioned to the pilot.

"Put it down."

But the pilot couldn't put it down because of the height of the snow. The state road a quarter of a mile away had been plowed and it was determined the pilot could land the chopper there, but we didn't want to waste time. So the pilot lowered us down as far as he could, just so that the skids kissed the top of the snow, and Agent Njeim and I and the rest of the team climbed out of the helicopter before it rose back up in the air so the second helicopter could drop off the other team. The third team stayed in the air to cover the area.

None of the houses along Woodlawn Lane were impressive. Our entrance had no doubt caught the attention of the neighbors. The team in the third helicopter would monitor emergency calls, so if one of the residents called 911, they would intercept the call and give us time to investigate the house.

The teams spread out along the road. Each carried M-16s. The man with the large scope scanned the house again.

"Still nothing."

I asked, "Can that detect a bomb?"

"You think there's a bomb in there?"

"At this point, I don't know what to think. But I wouldn't put it past these people."

"If you think a bomb's in there, we need more equipment."

He turned to Agent Njeim.

"Just why are we here, exactly?"

"We're following up on a lead."

"Three teams for a lead? Listen, my men and I have been patient this whole time because we were told this is a top secret mission and that we would be briefed once we arrived, so clue us in. Like who is this guy?"

He indicated me. Of course he did. The two men in the helicopter had been wondering who I was from the moment they boarded back in New York.

"He's a civilian consultant."

"Bullshit."

Before Agent Njeim could respond, I spoke.

"Enough."

I stared at the house. No lights on inside. According to the man, no living bodies.

"I'm going inside."

Agent Njeim said, "We don't know what's in there yet."

"Only one way to find out."

I started up the driveway. I took my time. The snow kept falling around me, heavier than back in the city, and it didn't help that the helicopters continued to circle above us.

The house next door was maybe twenty-five yards away. The front door opened and a man stepped out. He held a rifle at his side. He squinted out at the men lined up on the road and the helicopters in the sky and then his gaze settled on me.

He shouted, "What's this about?"

One of the men started up his driveway.

"Sir, put the rifle down and go back inside."

The man's voice grew with anger.

"It's my goddamned right as an American to own this rifle and you won't tell me otherwise!"

I stepped up to the front door. The snow was up to my knees. I knocked on the door, but there was no answer. Not surprising. I tried the knob, thinking it would be locked. It wasn't.

I opened the door.

My daughter-in-law and grandchildren stared back at me.

44

Mr. Shepherd? What's wrong?"

Agent Njeim shouted through the snow and the roar of the helicopters and the neighbor who demanded to know what was going on here.

I glanced back at her, at the men lined up on the road, and held my hand up for her to wait. I turned back to the doorway. Already some snow was cascading inside.

The heads of my daughter-in-law and grandchildren were lined up on the couch inside the front door. My daughter-in-law's head in the middle, my grandchildren's heads flanking her.

I stepped inside, closing the door behind me.

Despite the three choppers outside, the house was silent. In a room somewhere nearby a grandfather clock ticked.

"Hello?"

No answer.

I started deeper into the house. The next room I came to was the kitchen. Norma Greene lay on the floor with a single bullet hole in her head. She stared at the wall nearest her with wide, glassy eyes. Her blood had spread across the linoleum floor.

Behind me, the front door opened and Agent Njeim stepped inside.

"My God."

"Norma Greene is in here."

"How long has she been dead?"

"Looks to be in the past twelve hours."

Agent Njeim closed the door behind her. She stared at the three heads on the couch for several long seconds without speaking. Finally, she blinked and looked up at me.

"Who knew that you grew up here?"

"Outside my father and mother and grandparents? Nobody. This was my grandparents' house, you understand. My grandfather worked at the paper mill most of his life. My mother was born in this town, but she had always wanted to live in New York City. That was why she ended up there."

"What brought her back?"

"Me. And the Reaper, though by the time I was born the Reaper had been killed. But my father didn't put it past the military to send someone else after him, and he wanted to keep my mother and me safe, so he sent my mother to live up here with her parents. This was where I was born, in this house. My grandparents knew a local doctor who delivered me and who managed to get me a birth certificate. My father's name wasn't on the certificate. As far as the entire town was concerned, for those who noticed such things, I was born out of wedlock. My father sent money whenever he could, he wrote, but he never visited."

Agent Njeim stepped into the kitchen. She crouched down next to Norma Greene, being sure to keep out of the circumference of blood. She stood back up.

"So nobody knew you had grown up here?"

"No. I went to school here until I turned ten. That was when my father decided it was time for us to come to the city."

"When did you … start to display your powers?"

"Probably much sooner than I remember. My mother watched me carefully from the moment I was born to see whether or not I was different."

We started through the rest of the house, Agent Njeim with her gun in hand.

"My mother had told my grandparents because she felt they had a right to know. My grandparents were good people. They helped raise me. Then I turned ten and my grandfather died of a heart attack. A couple months later, my father wanted us to come back to the city."

"Did you have friends?"

"I was friendly with some of the kids at school, but nobody who was close."

The bathroom was empty, as was the dining room. Down the hallway, the bedroom door stood open.

"My mother had explained to me early on how I was different. She told me I had to do whatever I could to keep my differentness to myself. I knew about Temple then—every kid my age did—but she didn't tell me the connection because she feared I would brag about it at school."

"Anything odd ever happen to you while you were here?"

"What do you mean?"

"If the only people who knew you lived here were your parents and grandparents, I'm trying to figure out how these people knew about the place. Why they would go to all the trouble of bringing your daughter-in-law's and grandchildren's heads here."

We continued down the hall. Neither of us was surprised to find Frank Greene in the bedroom. Based on the way his body had fallen, it looked as if he had run into this room. Away from his wife. Letting his wife die first. Or maybe he had been in the bedroom when the intruders broke into the house. If so, his body had more bullet wounds than his wife. Three in the back, one in the head. His hand was outstretched toward the bed.

I stepped into the room.

In my head, I pictured him rushing into the room for some reason, bullet holes already in his back. He stumbles, falls to the floor, but still keeps trying to crawl forward. Reaching for something on the bedside table when the shooter enters the room and places one final bullet in his head.

Agent Njeim prompted, "Nothing unusual happened to you?"

"No."

I stared down at Frank Greene and the layout of the bedroom.

"Well, yes, something unusual did happen. The reason my father decided it was time for us to come back to the city, now that I think about it."

"What?"

"I decided to walk into town by myself one day. My mother had given me money for the corner store and I wanted to buy candy. The shopkeeper had always been friendly to Negro kids. And there was this boy who stopped me on the way. He didn't say anything, just pushed me. I tried to walk past him, and he pushed me again. Then when I tried to walk past him a third time, he punched me in the stomach. It … it didn't hurt, not like being punched in the stomach hurts most people, especially kids, but still, it was the first time it happened. It surprised me, and I fell to the ground. And the boy, he started kicking me as hard as he could. And despite his size and age, he was strong. And mean. He never said anything. There was nobody else around. But then a car stopped and someone shouted at the boy and the boy took off. The person in the car got out, maybe to try to help me, but I jumped up and ran back home. My mother wanted to know what was wrong, so I told her, and that was when she sent a letter to my father, and he decided it was time to bring us back to the city."

"Who was the boy?"

"No idea. I had never seen him before. I didn't know him from Adam."

I stepped over Frank Greene's body to inspect the bedside table. There was nothing on top except an alarm clock and a Blake Crouch paperback and a glass of water.

I opened the top drawer. Inside was a large Bible, nothing else. I closed the drawer, went to open the bottom drawer, but paused and opened the top drawer again. I picked up the Bible. Held it in my hand for a moment, weighing it, and then opened the cover.

The Bible had been hollowed out. In fact, it wasn't even a Bible. Just the outside was meant to look like a Bible. Inside was a Smith & Wesson pistol.

I took the pistol out, dropped the magazine. The thing was fully loaded. Which meant Frank Greene was coming to protect himself against the people who had broken inside to kill him and his wife.

The house was so quiet and still that we both heard the front door open. One of the men shouted.

"Agent Njeim?"

I put the gun back in the Bible and put the Bible back in the drawer. We returned to the front of the house.

The man was staring at the heads on the couch.

Agent Njeim said, "What do you have for me?"

"The neighbor says an SUV showed up here six hours ago. Two men got out, one of which was carrying a large black bag. They went inside and came back out ten minutes later and left."

"What did the neighbor do then?"

"Nothing. Turns out he doesn't believe in getting involved in other people's business. But when we showed up, he thought he should say something."

The man looked back at the couch.

"Who do the heads belong to?"

I said, "My family."

"Why are they here?"

Agent Njeim said, "We don't know. That's what we're trying to figure out."

The man shook his head. He muttered as he headed back outside.

"Goddamned wild goose chase."

I turned to Agent Njeim. I could see in her face she was thinking the same thing I was.

I said, "Three teams. We took three teams away from the city."

Agent Njeim nodded. She reached into her parka and brought out her disposable. She flipped it open and punched the only number programmed into it.

Time seemed to slow. The grandfather clock in the next room was extraordinarily loud.

Agent Njeim listened to the phone, and relief crossed her face at once when she spoke.

"Thank God, Roger. Yes, we made it, and we found ... well, the heads of Mr. Shepherd's daughter-in-law and grand-children. But has anything happened there?"

She listened for a long moment, then shook her head at me as she spoke into the phone.

"Good. We just wanted to check."

I asked, "Al-Naser is still at the black site?"

"Roger, please check that al-Naser is still in custody."

She waited. A minute passed. I watched her face the entire

time. I could tell the instant Roger spoke again. I saw her eyes widen slightly, and her lips part. She spoke quietly before closing the phone.

"We're on our way back now."

"Al-Naser?"

Her face had gone ashen.

"He's escaped."

45

We didn't learn much more on the flight back except that the people who had broken Abu Muhammad al-Naser out of the black site went directly through the Chinese place next door.

Despite the harsh weather and the fact most people stayed home, Mojo's was still doing steady business. Their phone rang nonstop for delivery orders. Customers were asked if they would agree to a five-dollar "blizzard delivery fee." Most said yes. And so young kids came and went from the restaurant all afternoon. There were a few patrons who had ventured out into the cold, however, and it was these patrons who died first.

When the men entered the restaurant, they didn't make any wild declarations. They simply opened fire. Killed a couple in a booth near the door before a trio at a table near the back was gunned down. The servers were caught in the crossfire. The gunmen continued to the back and entered the kitchen where they killed the staff. With no one else in the restaurant, they went to work in setting charges around the kitchen. Somehow they knew that the corridor was directly beneath the kitchen floor, and they set the charges so that when the charges blew, a large hole opened up granting them access to the black site.

That was all Roger was able to tell us. All surveillance cameras inside the black site had been shut down, and what had been there was erased. All surveillance cameras within a five-block radius had been shut down, too, so the coming and going of the men were concealed.

Every man and woman in the black site—eight total—were killed. The only body not found, once Roger sent a team over to verify, was al-Naser. There had been no other prisoners.

Roger said that when a team first entered Mojo's, the phone was ringing. Potential customers dialing in to order moo shoo pork and chicken lo mein and probably wondering whether the restaurant had closed due to the snow while the staff and patrons lay dead in pools of blood. The phone kept ringing until someone finally pulled the cord.

Agent Njeim asked if Roger had any idea where al-Naser may have gone. Despite the five-block radius outage, the analysts must surely have seen something. If not by surveillance camera, what about satellite?

Roger said they were checking but he didn't sound too hopeful, not with the heavy cloud cover. It went without saying a blackout like that had occurred on the night my daughter-in-law and grandchildren were murdered. The team across the street taken out first, then my son's house raided.

We landed an hour later. The teams wondered what the true purpose of the mission had been. Yes, they were aware three heads had been found in the house, the old couple who resided there murdered, but they knew there was more going on and didn't like being kept in the dark.

Agent Njeim proposed stopping by the black site but then decided it would be best to return to the Vault. An SUV was waiting for us. I didn't recognize the driver.

I pulled Agent Njeim aside before we got in and whispered into her ear.

"Can we ditch this guy and go on our own? I need you to disable the GPS again. There's one more place I want to check before we go back."

Her gaze turned stern.

"Mr. Shepherd, I can't—"

"Please. Just humor an old man."

She stared at me for several long seconds before shaking her head.

"I can't. I'm sorry, but we need to return to the Vault."

Agent Njeim opened her door and started to get in but paused when she realized I hadn't moved. She turned back around.

"You're a stubborn old man, aren't you?"

"There aren't many more stubborn."

She pursed her lips, thinking about it.

"Okay, give me a second."

I waited while she spoke with the driver. He did as Agent Njeim asked without question. He handed her the keys, and a minute later we were inside, Agent Njeim behind the steering wheel, me in the passenger seat.

"Where to now?"

This time, there was no need for subterfuge. We parked on the street, right in front of my son's house, and marched up the walkway to the front door.

"They locked it before they left last night, didn't they?"

She nodded and produced that small device of hers. Within seconds, she had the lock disengaged and we stepped inside.

Once again I had that foreboding sense of loss. I had

known my daughter-in-law, if briefly, but I had never met my grandchildren. Had never listened to their voices. Laughed at their jokes. Pushed them on a swing set.

Agent Njeim said, "Now what?"

I headed straight for the kitchen. Everything was still scattered all over the place, as it had been last night. Cans everywhere, boxes bent and crushed with their contents spilled across the floor.

I stepped carefully through the mess.

"Frank Greene's Bible reminded me of something."

Agent Njeim stayed in the doorway.

"Which is?"

"When we lived in our building there had been some break-ins. Minor stuff, just petty theft, and at the time there was more for Temple to worry about. We got an extra lock for our door, but my wife still wanted an additional layer of protection, so she found one of those fake cans of Lysol that was hollowed out to hide money and other valuables inside. Someone broke into our place, she figured, they wouldn't bother with the cleaning supplies under the sink."

"So you think your son did the same thing here?"

"I know for a fact he did."

"How can you be so confident?"

I found the can I was looking for. I picked it up and held it toward Agent Njeim so she could see the label.

She squinted to read the label in the dark and frowned.

"Lima beans?"

"My son hated lima beans growing up. His wife did too. They had joked once it was one of the few things they had in common."

"What if they found a shared love for lima beans later in life? Or what if their children liked them?"

"Only one way to find out."

With the can of Del Monte in one hand, I used my right hand to twist the top.

Nothing happened.

I shook the can and heard the condensed beans inside.

Agent Njeim was quiet for a long moment, watching me.

"I'm sorry."

I closed my eyes. This … this couldn't be right. My son had to have died for something more than just terrorists wanting his blood and brain. He had to have stumbled across something that made him a target. Or did he? Maybe I was reaching for straws. Hoping for a conspiracy that didn't exist because I wanted to believe there was more to what happened to my son and his family than just senseless death.

With my eyes closed, my other senses became heightened. I heard Agent Njeim's slow and shallow breathing. I heard a car pass by outside. And I heard the clock on the wall tick. The stupid Temple clock my son had bought despite the fact he hated all Temple merchandising. Why had he bought it? No doubt for the kids. It made me think about Agent Palmer and how he had always wanted to tell his kids about his job protecting Temple and how he would never be able to tell them anything, and it made me think about everyone else who had died today, and before I knew it my grip on the can began to tighten.

But then I opened my eyes, dropped the can to the floor. Stared at the clock on the wall.

Agent Njeim said, "What's wrong?"

"My son never would have allowed a Temple clock in his home."

I stepped over the scattered cans to approach the clock. I reached up and took the clock down off the wall and turned it over. Taped to the back was a small object. I tore the object from the tape and held it up for Agent Njeim to see.

"What is this?"

She smiled.

"A flash drive."

46

On the way back to the Vault, I called to check in with Sanchez.

"Everything all right?"

I could hear the shrug in his voice.

"It's okay. Not really doing much but sitting here. I'll tell you, Aisha's boyfriend is kind of a dick."

"Kind of?"

He laughed and asked how things were going on my end.

I glanced down at the flash drive in my hand. I didn't want to leave my friend in the dark, but the truth was I didn't know if there was anything here at all.

"We're getting somewhere, I think. When I know more, I'll let you know."

"Want to talk to Aisha?"

I did, but I wasn't sure what to say to her. She hadn't been thrilled to see me initially, and even if she was warming up to me, she wasn't thrilled to have Sanchez stay in her home as a bodyguard. My sudden appearance had disrupted what harmony existed in her life. Until this was all sorted out, I didn't want to mess with it any more than I already had.

"I will when this is all over. Thanks again for everything."

The men in the garage searched us before we got in the elevator. New protocol, one of them said, which made sense after the revelation about Taylor but which put a wrinkle in the new plan if they found the flash drive. Which they did, quickly enough, when one of the men waved a wand over my coat. The man nodded at my pocket, and with a slow hand I reached in and withdrew the flash drive.

"What's that?"

"What do you think it is?"

Impatience strained Agent Njeim's voice.

"Guys, I appreciate the extra level of security here, but we're dealing with some things right now that can't wait and, no offense, you're slowing the process. So … shall we?"

The man clearly didn't like being questioned, and it may not have helped that Agent Njeim was a woman from the Middle East. But in the end she outranked him and that was all that mattered, especially after everything that had happened today.

The man stepped back and told us to head down.

Agent Njeim pressed the button for the elevator.

Like last time, nobody met us in the corridor when the elevator doors opened. We headed straight for the control center and found Nate at his station, his computer screens open in front of him. Taylor's station had been shut down, all her computers dark.

Agent Njeim nodded at Taylor's station.

"Find anything?"

Nate answered while he typed, his focus on the screens.

"Nothing on the surface. Whatever she was doing, she was hiding it well."

"But you managed to figure out she was the mole."

"Yes, but I wasn't looking specifically at her when I did it. The way I did it, I followed some breadcrumbs into a back door she hadn't even known existed, let alone forgot to close and lock."

"Now what are you doing?"

Nate kept his focus on his screens, his fingers typing a mile a minute.

"We've widened the net for al-Naser to the entire state. We're searching every database for any irregularities. Facial recognition is in full force too, but with most transportation shut down because of the snow, I'm not sure what good it will do."

"He's probably holed up somewhere."

"Probably. But he can't stay holed up forever. The instant he shows his face, we'll have him."

Nate's desk phone beeped. He hit a button and spoke into the microphone on his headset.

"Yes? Yes, sir, right away."

Nate hit the button again and glanced up at Agent Njeim.

"Roger wants to see you."

Agent Njeim and I both turned and glanced up at the office above us. Despite the dark glass, we could see Roger standing behind his desk. His shadow motioned for us to come upstairs.

Agent Njeim waved up to him, nodding, and then turned back to Nate and leaned down, lowered her voice.

"We found a flash drive at James Shepherd's residence. We

tried to access it on the computer at the house, but the thing has been encrypted."

This made Nate pause. His fingers, now frozen, stayed on the keyboard, but he finally looked up at us, his head doing a slow turn.

"The house was searched. Nothing was found."

"This was hidden."

I inconspicuously withdrew the flash drive from my jacket pocket and placed it on the table. I kept my hand there until Nate leaned forward and moved some papers to cover my hand. I slipped my empty hand away.

Agent Njeim said, "Right now this is for your eyes only. Report back to me when you find out what it says."

Nate shook his head.

"I won't be able to access this here. I mean, I could, but the system will log the activity."

"Any way around that?"

"I'll see what I can do. For the time being, what do you—"

Behind us, Roger's office exploded.

47

The blast sent the dark glass spraying out all over the room. Almost everyone hit the ground at the same time. Only one analyst turned toward the explosion and was rewarded with several slivers of glass tearing into his face. He cried out and hit the ground.

The explosion itself had sounded like the boom of a firework. Only this firework had been set off in a room two floors underground.

Roger's office was now just a crater.

Strobes started flashing around the room, and an alarm sounded, and seconds later two more explosions went off in the corridor.

I sprinted over to the corridor now filled with dust and smoke and debris. The dust and smoke came from both directions.

Agent Njeim ran up behind me, her hand cupped around her mouth and nose to keep out the dust.

"We're trapped."

"Are there any other ways out?"

She shook her head.

The lights flickered. They grew dim and then strong again and then flickered once more before going out completely. A second later emergency power kicked on, or at least the backup lights came on. Their harsh white beams speared the thick dust.

We returned to the main room. Most of the analysts looked around frantically, not sure what to do. Very few of them had been trained for a situation like this. The man whose face had been peppered with those slivers of glass was on the floor, being treated to by two other analysts who may or may not have known what they were doing.

All the computer screens were dark.

Nate's headset had tumbled off his head when he hit the floor. He picked it up now, put it back on, and hit the button on his desk phone several times before shaking his head and flinging the headset aside.

"Phones are down."

Agent Njeim pulled the disposable from her jacket. She flipped it open and checked the screen. She shook her head.

"I'm not getting any service."

I glanced back up at Roger's office. Smoke still poured out of it.

Without a word, I headed for the stairs. Agent Njeim followed.

Up the stairs we went, but cautious, in case another explosion went off. That had been known to happen in the past. In fact, Prometheus had done it once during his short-lived reign of terror over the city. He had blown up an office building and watched and waited for emergency personnel to arrive, and it was only after they sent in the bomb squad to search for any other explosives that he set off the second bomb. Not in the building, but out in the parking lot, right where all the bystanders were watching to see what would happen next.

Twenty-three people had died that day, over forty wounded.

The corridor outside Roger's office was empty, though his door had been knocked off its hinges due to the blast. We stepped over it and into the smoke-filled room.

Agent Njeim shouted, "Roger!"

No answer. Not that one was expected. Not after an explosion like that.

Debris littered the floor. Most of it was from the ceiling and walls. Hardly any glass, as the blast had sent that out into the control center.

From somewhere inside the smoke came a cough and then a groan, both faint and weak.

"Roger?"

The cough came again. It was over toward Roger's desk. Or where Roger's desk had once stood.

We circled what was left of the desk, slowly, expecting to find Roger's dying body trapped by rubble. We were half right. He was trapped, but he wasn't dying, at least not yet. He had a gash on his forehead and part of the desk lay on top of him. He must have been sitting at his desk when the explosion occurred and dropped to the floor at the right moment for the desk to have taken the brunt of the blast. In many ways, he had gotten lucky.

Roger's desk was solid wood, fine oak, the kind of wood used to build ships back in the day. Certainly sturdy enough to protect him from the bomb and save his life.

"Roger, don't move."

Agent Njeim and I got in position to move the desk off him.

The desk was heavy, but with two of us working we managed to lift it just enough to give Roger the space he needed to squeeze himself out. He grimaced as he did, favoring his right leg, which had taken much of the impact.

When he was clear of the desk, Roger tried to sit up but grimaced again, holding his injured leg.

"Is ... is everyone okay?"

Agent Njeim shook her head.

"We don't know yet."

"Was this ... this the only bomb? I thought ... I thought I heard others."

"There were two others, at least from what we can ascertain. Roger, they've trapped us down here, cut our power. Cell service is also down."

Roger squeezed his eyes shut tight, either from the news or the pain, it was difficult to tell which.

"Goddamn it."

Then his voice rising even more.

"God*damn* it."

Agent Njeim and I helped Roger to his feet. By then the smoke had begun to clear and we could see the entire room. The blast's origin point appeared to be in the corner of the room, on the opposite side of where we now stood. Which explained how Roger had managed to survive.

I said, "I thought your people had searched this room."

"They did."

Roger attempted to put weight on his foot, and when he found that he could, he limped forward.

"But they were searching for bugs. Some kind of secret surveillance equipment. Not a bomb."

I glanced at Agent Njeim.

"They were waiting for us to return to the Vault."

"What do you mean?"

"Whatever they have planned next, they want us trapped down here until they accomplish their goal."

Roger dabbed at the gash on his forehead, which was still fresh with blood. He bent and picked up his glasses off the floor, but both lenses were cracked.

"You said the elevator and stairwell were taken out as well?"

Agent Njeim nodded.

"Yes."

"Have you verified both are inaccessible?"

"Not yet."

"Do that first. But if there isn't a way to climb to the top using the stairs or elevator shaft, there may be another way out."

48

D espite having escaped the blasts, the chef was frantic. His eyes wide, his large hands shaking, he paced back and forth through the kitchen, mumbling to himself about how they were going to die and there was nothing anybody could do about it and who was going to take care of his two cats, Bert and Ernie, and what about his mother, she needed to be reminded to take her pills at night and why did this have to happen *today*.

Roger said, "Relax, Louis. Everything will be all right."

But Louis didn't listen. He kept pacing, kept mumbling, and barely even noticed when Roger led us past him toward the back of the kitchen. There were two doors here: one which led to what was presumably a large walk-in refrigerator, another door into which Roger inserted a key to open.

A storage closet, filled with boxes and plastic containers of food. But it was past all of this, deeper into the closet, where a large panel in the wall caught our attention.

Agent Njeim took the lead now. She approached the panel and lifted its handle and pushed it up into the wall.

"What is this?"

"A dumb waiter. Essentially a small elevator. It's how the fresh food and other kitchen supplies arrive daily."

"Without power, the thing won't work."

"Of course not. But you could climb up."

Agent Njeim slipped a small flashlight from her pocket and shined it at the space and then stepped back and shook her head.

"There's no way that will work."

Roger said, "It's going to have to."

"If it were more narrow, maybe I could manage it. But it's too wide. I wouldn't be able to keep the pressure the whole way up. Roger, we're talking two stories at least, and who knows if the panel on the other side is even easily accessible from the inside. For all I know, I do manage to make it up there, I can't get out. Not to mention that the dumb waiter itself will probably be blocking the way."

Roger turned to me.

"What about you? Do you think your ... powers could get you up to the top?"

"In my prime, maybe, but now as I am, no."

I stepped forward and poked my head into the narrow space. Something tapped my shoulder, Agent Njeim offering me the flashlight. I took it and flicked it on and shined it up the shaft.

It wasn't cramped, but it wasn't roomy either. Maybe three feet wide, five feet across. Too wide for Agent Njeim, yes, but maybe not too wide for Agent Njeim and someone else.

I stepped back, turned off the flashlight, and looked at Agent Njeim as if for the first time. I assess everybody I meet in the first couple seconds, attempting to determine their strengths and weaknesses, but now I assessed Agent Njeim on her size, her weight, how long her arms and legs were. Just how strong she appeared.

She frowned at me.

"What is it?"

"I have an idea."

"Are you sure this will work?"

Up until that point, I had never heard fear in Agent Njeim's voice. It didn't make me feel any better about our current predicament, but at the moment I had to fake confidence.

"We'll make it."

Her back was to me, but still I sensed her head shift to the side as if to look at me.

"How can you be so sure?"

"I just know."

Nate said, "You guys are crazy."

Roger glared at him.

"Stop it."

They were standing outside the dumb waiter, Roger still favoring his right leg, Nate waiting with a laptop. If this went according to plan, he would be the first analyst we'd bring out. He needed to be ready the moment we made it to the top.

Agent Njeim and I stood straight up in the shaft, our backs to each other. Both of us had lengths of rope looped over our shoulders and across our chests. Agent Njeim had found gloves, which would help keep sweat and grease from building on our hands. The last thing we needed was to be only feet away from our target and an errant drop of sweat cause one of our hands to slip.

Three flashlights had been set up on the base of the shaft, pointed toward the top, so we wouldn't be moving in complete darkness.

I stared up at the base of the dumb waiter two floors above us. Twenty-feet, maybe thirty feet high. Wasn't too unreasonable.

I said, "Ready when you are."

With her back pressed against mine, I felt Agent Njeim tense. Then the motion of her body as she braced her hands against the side of the shaft.

This was my cue. I braced my hands against the opposite side of the shaft.

The force against my back increased twenty fold. Agent Njeim was pushing back against her side of the shaft, just as I was.

I said, "Now your feet."

Agent Njeim raised one foot out, her right, and braced it against the corner of the shaft. Then she did the same with her left foot.

Now it was my turn. My hands braced against the shaft wall, I stretched out my right foot against the one corner, then my left foot against the other corner.

"Let's go."

We didn't move quickly, but we moved surely, which was more important than speed. I let Agent Njeim take the lead. She would move just a little, bracing her hands and feet against her side of the shaft, and then I would do the same, matching her short distance. There was an instance early on when we had just started and were only maybe four feet up the shaft that Agent Njeim's one foot slipped and threatened to send us back down to the base of the shaft. But she managed to keep her grip on the shaft with her hands and reposition her feet to keep us planted.

Her whisper echoed in the narrow space.

"This is probably not a good time to tell you, but I'm afraid of heights."

"If it makes you feel better, so am I."

"Really?"

"No. Just trying to help boost your confidence."

We pushed our way up another foot. Agent Njeim's back muscles quivered against mine.

Agent Njeim spoke between breaths.

"Can I ask you a question?"

"Of course."

"Why Harper?"

"What do you mean?"

Another foot up. Our bodies crossed in front of the flashlight beams and cut shadows at the top.

"How did you end up there? Out of all the towns and cities in the country—in the world—what made you decide on Harper, Colorado?"

"My father."

"How so?"

"He's the one who ended up in Harper. He bought over one hundred acres of land and built a cabin in the middle of nowhere. The land was cheap and he didn't want to be around anyone."

"Did he stay in contact?"

"No. Once he left, I never heard from him or saw him again until one day he showed up and told me about his place out in Harper. Said that when I knew it was time to give up being Temple, I was welcome to join him."

"What about your wife?"

I hesitated, not sure I wanted to talk about Shalissa. Every time I thought about her, it made that black hole in my heart grow larger.

"She was invited too, of course. But then several years went by, and Shalissa started her battle with cancer, and then ..."

"I'm sorry."

"That was a long time ago."

"Why did he think you'd want to live in the middle of nowhere? Why not stay with your family?"

"Because by that point he understood the most basic principle of being Temple."

"Which was?"

"That once you become a hero it's impossible to stop. The desire to continue helping people is always there. And when the realization hits you that you've grown older and can't save people like you had before, a sort of ... depression hits you. My father realized this early on, and that's why he bought that land and built a cabin in the middle of nowhere. To stay as far away from the world as he could. The farther he was from people, the more the desire to save them went away. I know because it was the same for me."

"What did he say when you showed up?"

"Nothing. He wasn't there when I showed up. The cabin was empty. There were things in it, like his bed and other furniture, even some canned goods, but that was it. I waited a day, then a week, then a month, thinking that at any moment he would pull up in a pickup truck, but he never did."

"But what about the land?"

"It was completely paid off. And my father had squirreled money away in a bank account that would take care of the taxes every year. There was no electricity to worry about, no utilities. I had more than enough money to keep myself going for the rest of my life, so I decided to stay. After having been there a couple months, I couldn't think of going anywhere else. By the way, Agent Njeim, we've made it."

"What?"

She had been concentrating so hard on my words that she barely remembered what it was we were doing. I could feel her body shift as she looked up and saw the dumb waiter directly above us.

"Don't look down."

I said it quickly, afraid that any slight glance might cause her hand or foot to slip and, as a consequence, send us both tumbling down the shaft.

"I won't. But I was right earlier. The dumb waiter is blocking us from the top."

"Yes and no."

"What does that mean?"

"It means you don't see what I see."

49

Because of the position of the flashlights beneath us and our bodies blocking almost all of their illumination, it was difficult to see the grate in front of me. But my eyes had since adjusted to the dark during the long minutes it had taken to climb up this far, and my night vision was still far superior to others, even at my age, so I saw the grate without any trouble. It was a duct, and judging by the grate it looked as if it would be large enough to fit a single person. Which was a problem, of course, as there were two of us currently braced in the shaft and any slight misstep may cause us to fall to the bottom two stories below.

Agent Njeim asked, "What is it?"

"The panel grate to an air duct. It looks big enough for one of us, but not both."

"How is that supposed to help us?"

"I need your knife."

"It's in my pocket."

"Which pocket?"

"My left-hand pocket."

With my feet braced against the corners of the shaft and

my left hand braced against the side of the shaft, I carefully lessened the pressure on my right hand, little by little, to ensure that without the pressure it wouldn't cause us to fall. If there was any chance taking my hand away would weaken our support, I would put it back and we would have to figure out something else. But it seemed as if we were okay. So far so good. I reached back and lightly touched Agent Njeim's hip, moving my fingers over the side of her pants until I found the bulge of the knife. Thankfully the knife was longer than her pocket, so part of it stuck out. It made it easier to slip it from her pocket.

"It's a switchblade. All you need to do is press the button on the side."

I pressed the button on the side. The blade slid out with a soft snick. Four inches long and sharp. Good.

I asked, "How are we doing?"

"Oh, you know. Just hanging out."

Agent Njeim tried to put some humor in the tone, but it was clear she was scared.

"Give me a minute or two and this will be over."

I worked the blade on the side of the grate, first carefully, just trying to feel it out, and then with more force. Back and forth, back and forth, until the blade slipped underneath the panel. Now I had more room to work the blade. I withdrew it and did the same to the top of the grate, then the bottom, then the other side. Finally, at one point, I'd worn the grate out enough from the screws holding it in place, and with one final back and forth motion with the blade, the panel fell.

Three seconds, that's all it took, and the panel smashed into one of the flashlights beneath us with such force that it caused the shaft to vibrate.

Nate shouted up at us.

"What the fuck was that?"

Roger shouted, "Are you okay?"

I said, "We're fine. Almost there."

Agent Njeim whispered, "Are we?"

"We'll find out in a second."

Still with my left hand braced against the side of the shaft, I reached into the open space the fallen panel had revealed and felt around the edges for something to grip. Nothing.

"Shit."

"What is it?"

Panic in Agent Njeim's voice.

"What's wrong?"

"This might not work like—"

Agent Njeim lost her grip. I didn't know whether it was her hands or feet that had slipped, but suddenly the pressure against my back began to weaken. I heard the short intake of breath as the realization hit her what would happen next, and without thinking I grabbed the bottom edge of the duct with my right hand and swung my left hand down and grabbed Agent Njeim's hand as she began to fall.

Agent Njeim weighed maybe one hundred thirty pounds, much of it muscle. Considerably less than my nearly two hundred pounds, and in my prime, pulling her back up to safety would not be a problem, but I wasn't the young man I used to be, especially in terms of strength.

"Stay calm."

Agent Njeim's entire body trembled if her hand inside my grip was any indication.

The gloves thankfully gave me a tight grip on the edge of the panel, enough that the over three hundred pounds did the trick in keeping us secure. At least for now.

"I'm going to pull you up. When you can, use your other hand to grip the side of the duct and climb inside."

"What about you?"

"We'll worry about that when we get to it. Now, are you ready?"

She was quiet for a long moment. Then she answered, her voice soft and quiet.

"Yes."

I closed my eyes, took a deep breath, and began to lift Agent Njeim. My feet didn't have anything to support themselves on, as the shaft was too wide, but still I tried to make Agent Njeim's path to the vent as open as possible. Higher ... and higher ... and Agent Njeim said, "I'm almost there," and still I lifted her higher until first her hand gripped the edge of the vent, then she was almost able to lift herself, and my muscles began to relax as the weight dissipated.

But my grip on the vent was starting to weaken.

The gloves had done a great job keeping me in place during the time it took to lift Agent Njeim into the vent, but now my grip was starting to falter.

Above me, Agent Njeim had squeezed the top of her body into the vent, only her legs sticking out as she began to crawl forward. If her knee or foot accidentally hit my fingers holding me in place, there was the chance I might let go.

Her knee or foot did not accidentally hit my fingers. They managed to pass by my fingers as she moved deeper into the vent. I could hear her as she moved about, and at first I wasn't sure what she was doing as it seemed to take much longer than it should, and then her gloved fingers wrapped around my arm. I looked up. Her face peeked at me from where she had evidently twisted around in the vent.

She said, "Stay calm."

Then with a slight smile on her face.

"Ready?"

50

After Agent Njeim had helped me climb up into the vent, after we traversed the vent maybe thirty yards to another grate that Agent Njeim needed to kick at several times before it broke away, we found ourselves in a utility room where there was even more ductwork. The emergency lights were the only lights working here too. The place was dusty and smelled of grease and oil. The exit door opened into a corridor to the back of the building and led to an exit to the street. The room next door would be the access to the dumb waiter. Just like in the utility room, the only lights were the emergency lights along the walls.

We found a secure place to tie one of the ropes and tied the other rope to the end of the first rope, ensuring that it would be long enough, and then Agent Njeim climbed back through the vent with the coiled rope, and once she reached the end she let it drop down to the bottom of the shaft. Nate, who wore a bag with his laptop inside slung over his shoulder, tied the rope around his waist. Not the most ideal harness, but it would have to do. Once I heard from Agent Njeim that Nate had been secured, I began to pull him up the shaft. The gloves helped the rope from digging into my hand, but it still wasn't easy. Agent Njeim stayed where she was in the shaft to monitor the rope to ensure it didn't fray. When Nate was close enough, she took his hand just like she had taken mine and helped pull him up into the vent.

Once Nate was in the utility room, he untied the rope around him and handed Agent Njeim a radio to communicate with Roger. She radioed down to Roger. Roger said we needed to get back online and contact the president ASAP. He said the explosions had happened for a reason and we needed to find out what that reason was as soon as possible.

Nate was still massaging the sides of his body where the rope had nearly choked him on his way to the top. Then his eyes lit up as a thought crossed his mind.

"Have you checked your phones?"

We pulled out our disposables. Flipped them open and checked the screens. Mine had a signal, as did Agent Njeim's. Just one bar, but it was something.

Nate said, "Let's get closer to the street. There's a chance the blocker won't reach that far out."

We followed him down the corridor as he explained— probably more for my benefit than Agent Njeim's—how it was possible to create a sort of invisible barrier that blocked cell phone reception. He posited that the same thing had happened here, as before the explosion cell reception had been working like normal.

As we neared the exit door, the bars on our disposables increased to two bars, then three.

Excitement entered Nate's voice.

"Sweet!"

He slipped a laptop from his bag as he dropped to the floor, sitting with his back against the wall, flipping open the laptop's lid and powering it on.

Agent Njeim glanced back down the corridor as if someone might be coming in our direction.

"Do you have the flash drive?"

His focus on the laptop screen, just like on the screens back at his workstation, Nate nodded.

"Of course I have it."

"Then access it before you check the system."

This made Nate pause. He looked at her, his face tight.

"That might not be a good idea. Roger's right—those explosions were no doubt coordinated with something on the outside. I need to get back online as soon as possible."

I leaned forward.

"But there's a chance whatever is happening is *because* of what's on the flash drive."

Nate turned his attention back to the laptop.

"Yeah, and there's also a chance the flash drive has nothing at all to do with it."

He typed for several seconds in silence, then realized Agent Njeim and I were staring at him and looked up at us, all at once uncomfortable. He groaned.

"Christ, fine, I'll check it first. Gimme a sec."

He withdrew the flash drive from his pocket, flicked off the top, and inserted the drive into the laptop.

"If this fucks up my computer, you can explain it to Roger."

As before, once the drive was accessed, a screen was brought up asking for a password. This didn't seem to worry Nate, who opened another program and typed a mile a minute and moved his finger around on the pad to move the cursor on the screen, clicking here and there, and then after a moment the screen asking for a password went away and a new screen appeared. Only it was impossible to tell what was on the screen because it all looked like gibberish.

"Shit, this is some heavy-duty encryption."

Agent Njeim asked, "Can you break it?"

He gave her a look.

"Please. Do you know who you're talking to?"

"Yes, someone who's getting on my nerves."

"I can break it, and there's actually a good chance I can open the system and make sure it doesn't know about this new file."

"Are you sure?"

He hesitated.

"Pretty sure."

"This could be life and death, Nate."

"I know. But first I—"

He paused, squinting at the screen.

"Monarch."

On the screen was still that gibberish, all letters and characters jumbled in a nonsense pattern, but near the top only that one word was legible.

Agent Njeim said, "What's Monarch?"

"No idea. But that's what this file must be named, or where it's from, or whatever. I need to keep working on it, but first I need to get us back online."

Nate closed out the programs, or at least he hid them from the main screen, and he typed more on the laptop, moved his finger around on the pad to move the cursor, and a new window popped up. None of it made any sense to me, so I stepped away as Nate did his thing and Agent Njeim watched. Finally Nate sighed, resting his head back against the cinderblock wall.

"Sentinel hasn't been compromised. Thank God for small miracles. Let me see what else might—"

I cut him off.

"How do you know?"

"What?"

"How do you know Sentinel hasn't been compromised?"

"All of them are online without any distress markers."

"Is there any way one of them could be taken offline without you knowing it?"

"Absolutely not."

Another pause.

"I mean, not unless ..."

His expression changed as he realized he might have missed something. He refocused on the laptop, typing faster than ever. For a solid minute he was quiet, just typing, his focus intent on the screen, and then he sucked in air between his teeth.

"Shit."

Agent Njeim said, "What is it?"

"Sentry Number Six. It's been taken offline. They set it up so that no alarms would sound and that from the outside it looked like everything was okay and it was still online, but I'm looking at the security feed right now. Four guards are down, all of them dead. And both missiles—"

He swallowed and looked up at us. His eyes wide. His face pale.

"The warheads are gone."

51

Nate checked the rest of the Sentry locations around the city and confirmed that they hadn't been compromised. Agent Njeim told him to double-check the locations.

He said, "Sentry Number Six is the only one."

"Are you sure?"

"Positive."

"Can you access the feeds from security cameras around the block?"

"Already on it."

Several seconds passed where the only sound was Nate's fingers tapping at the keyboard, and then he swore.

"Fuck."

"What is it?"

"They shut down the cameras for a five-block radius. It looks like it was just for fifteen minutes, but that was enough time for them to be invisible."

"Can you expand the search?"

"I'm doing that now."

More ultra-fast typing, the laptop's glow reflecting off Nate's glasses.

"I'll track any vehicles headed in or out before and after those fifteen minutes, but it's going to take a while."

"How much time?"

"If I wasn't the only one working on this, maybe five, ten minutes. Now with just me? I can't say."

I said, "What if they're not on the streets?"

This made Nate pause, but only for a moment, before he started typing again.

"What do you mean?"

"Say they accessed the building by helicopter. Landed on top of the building, loaded the warheads, and took off. Can you check for any helicopters with your computer?"

"Yes, but it will take even longer. Listen, let me concentrate on this and I'll let you know as soon as I know something."

His gaze flitted toward Agent Njeim.

"For now maybe you should let Roger know."

Agent Njeim said, "I know. I was hoping to give him good news before I told him."

"What kind of good news?"

"Like that we have an idea where the fucking things went."

She turned away, put the radio to her mouth.

"Roger, come in."

Silence.

"Roger, come in."

More silence.

She turned back to us, her face all at once apprehensive. There was no telling what could have happened in the past five minutes. Maybe another piece of the building had fallen, caused by a delayed tremor from the blast, and sent a chunk of concrete crashing down on Roger. Or maybe he had gone to check on the others and there was too much concrete between us for the radios to communicate. Over a hundred different possibilities, none of them good, but before any of us could voice those concerns, the radio crackled and Roger's faint voice came through.

"Yes, what is it?"

"I don't have good news, sir."

"Spit it out."

"They breached Sentry Number Six and took both missile warheads."

Silence again, only this time it wasn't because Roger wasn't there. He was obviously there, had obviously heard Agent Njeim's words, and was now attempting to process those words. Losing Abu Muhammad al-Naser was bad enough, but now two warheads?

Agent Njeim said, "Sir, we need to notify the White House as soon as possible."

For a long moment, Roger didn't answer. Then the radio crackled again.

"Yes, of course. Actually, I just checked another cell phone. I have a signal. I'll make the call right now."

I withdrew the disposable from my pocket. Where before there had only been three bars on the screen, now there were five. Which meant that the invisible barrier blocking cell phone reception had been lifted in the past several minutes.

The radio crackled again.

"Are there any others?"

Agent Njeim said, "Others, sir?"

"Sentry locations, goddamn it. Are there any others?"

"No, sir. Nate checked and double-checked every location. Only Sentry Number Six has been compromised."

"Do we know who and how this was done?"

"I'm afraid not, sir. Security cameras in a five-block radius were taken out during the breach. Nate's checking before and after that time period to try to find something."

"Good. At least I can tell the president that much. Not like it's going to help the situation any. God*damn* it."

It wasn't clear whether that last part Roger had meant to communicate through the radio.

Agent Njeim said, "What do you need us to do right now?"

"Right now wait where you are. Try to find out where these people went. We need to find those warheads, Agent Njeim."

"Understood, sir."

She dropped the radio to her side. She turned back to us—me standing next to Nate, who had continued to type a mile a minute—and opened her mouth to say something when, from the exit door behind us, there came a sudden and piercing blast as someone blew the lock.

52

was standing closest to the door, which was maybe twenty yards away down the corridor. At once I turned, putting my back to the door, and grabbed Nate's arm with one hand and his laptop with the other and yanked them both up and shoved Nate toward Agent Njeim, who was already stepping forward, her gun raised.

Nate protested, but I propelled him forward, telling him to hide. He was aware of the explosion, of course, but he was more focused on his work to care. Like he was protected inside a digital cocoon and what was happening was nothing more than a slight irritation.

Two seconds had passed, maybe three. The door was shoved open. Heavy footsteps followed.

I pushed Nate inside the utility closet, tossed him his laptop, and then slammed the door shut and turned back to the men pouring into corridor, each aiming assault rifles at us.

The first man shouted.

"On the floor! Put the weapon down and get on the floor!"

Agent Njeim held her ground. She didn't lower the weapon. I didn't have a weapon, but I wasn't going to let these men know that. I kept my hand behind my back, hidden, as if concealing a gun.

There were only three of them, but the firepower between them was enough to tear our bodies to shreds. They didn't appear to be Army or National Guard. Not the typical uniforms I was used to seeing. Then again, it had been decades since I had bothered to notice anything, so maybe they were proper military. But right now that didn't change the fact the Vault had just been attacked by terrorists.

The men, seeing that Agent Njeim wasn't going to lower her weapon, began to advance.

Agent Njeim said, "That's far enough."

The men paused, maybe surprised at the confidence in her voice, considering that she had one gun versus their three assault rifles. She might get off a few shots, might take out one of the men, but the other two would surely kill her. The fact that she knew this and didn't care was enough to give them a moment's hesitation.

"Get down on the ground."

The first man said this while the man on his left looked at me again with renewed interest. The lighting was bad in the corridor, just the few emergency lights near the ceiling, so we were mostly in shadows. The men had clearly seen me, but this man was now studying my face.

He said, "Are you Elijah Shepherd?"

I said nothing.

Now the other two men tried to make out my face in the dark.

Agent Njeim said, "Who are you?"

The first man lowered the barrel of his rifle slightly.

"Special Forces. We were called in by the president to secure Mr. Shepherd."

"Identification?"

The man held Agent Njeim's gaze.

"We don't carry identification."

"We'll need to check with the White House first."

"That's fine, but we're wasting time. We need to secure Mr. Shepherd now."

Agent Njeim didn't move for a long moment, her weapon trained on the three men. Past them, through the open door, snow continued to fall on street.

The first man seemed to make a decision. He relaxed his shoulders, stood up straight, and lowered his rifle. After a moment the other two men did the same.

Agent Njeim lowered her weapon. She raised the radio still in her left hand to her mouth.

"Roger, come in."

Silence.

"Roger, come in."

The radio crackled, and Roger's voice came through.

"I'm on the phone with the president. What is it?"

"Three men are here. They claim to be Special Forces. They want to secure Mr. Shepherd."

The radio crackled again.

"Yes, apparently the president sent them to do just that. Other men are right now working to open the stairwell and pull everyone up. We're almost back online."

As if on cue, the regular lights in the ceiling flickered on.

Roger said, "Ah, there we are. Listen, I need to get back on with the president. But yes, those men are fine."

The first man motioned at me.

"Let's go, Mr. Shepherd. We don't have time to waste."

Agent Njeim turned back to me.

"You should go with them."

I nodded. But instead of taking a step toward the men, I

turned and opened the door to the utility room. Nate sat on the ground just inside the door, the computer on his lap.

"Anything?"

His head shook.

"I'm still looking. Can't seem to find anything several blocks out. I mean, yeah, I see some vehicles, but nothing that looks right."

"What about a helicopter?"

Another shake.

"Doesn't appear so. I found a camera on Sentry Number Five that was pointed in the direction of Number Six. Nothing came or went during that time."

I was quiet for a moment, thinking about this.

"What about the subway?"

"What about it?"

"They could have gone underground."

When Nate shook his head this time, it was with much more force.

"All the trains are shut down."

"Are you sure?"

"Positive."

By this point Agent Njeim had wandered over to the utility room. The three men stayed back near the door, one of the men now outside keeping watch, the other two men patiently waiting for me.

I said, "Is there a chance that—"

"Look, Mr. Shepherd, no offense, but this is what I do. This is what I'm good at. I appreciate you wanting to help, but right now I need to focus."

I turned back to Agent Njeim.

"Good luck."

Then I stepped past her toward the two Special Forces guys.

"I'm ready now."

53

The lead guy introduced himself as Novak. He motioned at a Humvee parked across the street.

On the corner, right next to the bank and garage entrance, were two other Humvees. Two men stood on the sidewalk, keeping watch. They wore the same black uniforms as Novak and his men.

As we headed toward the Humvee across the street, another Humvee turned the corner and halted beside the bank. Men piled out, their uniforms declaring them National Guard.

One of the men shouted at us.

"Who are you with?"

One of the two men by the garage entrance approached him, telling him they were Special Forces and that everything was under control. Another National Guardsman—a young guy, maybe twenty-five—veered toward us.

"What happened here?"

Novak answered as he led me toward the Humvee.

"Explosion. My men are digging everyone out."

"We didn't hear about any explosion."

Novak opened the back door for me, turned back to the kid.

"Like I said, my men are taking care of it."

The Guardsman nodded at me.

"Who's he?"

Novak ignored him, turning back to me.

"Let's go."

I started to get inside but paused. Something was bothering me. Two warheads had been taken, yes, but warheads didn't just disappear.

I said to Novak, "Where's the closest subway station?"

"Why?"

The Guardsman said, "Three blocks south, one block over."

Novak's voice went gruff.

"Mr. Shepherd, we need to leave now."

"I understand that. First, though …"

I gazed down the block.

"I need to check something."

"It can wait."

I stepped away from the Humvee, shut the door.

"No, it can't."

I started down the block. Novak called after me, telling me to come back. When he realized I had no intention of listening, he started after me. I heard the crunch of snow as Novak began to follow, and the Humvee's engine turning over and its wheels digging through the snow as it headed my way. Another set of footsteps started up, too, a somehow lighter set.

Novak said, "Go back."

The Guardsman said, "I'll stay with you for a bit."

At the corner of the block, I glanced back at the Guardsman and pointed west.

"That way?"

He nodded.

We started down the block. The Humvee moved at a crawl, maybe five miles per hour, as we trudged through the snow. Down to the end of the block, then south again toward the subway station. One block away.

The Guardsman said, "What's this about, anyway?"

Novak didn't answer. All I heard were their boots crunching through the snow until, all at once, both sets of footsteps stopped and there came a faint gurgle.

I glanced back.

Novak withdrew a knife from the Guardsman's throat, which was gushing blood. The Guardsman's hands went to his throat, as if to keep in the blood. He stumbled back, fell to one knee, then dropped to his side.

Novak wiped the blood from the blade using the sleeve of his jacket.

"He should have minded his own business."

The Humvee slowed to a halt, only feet away from me. The passenger door opened and one of the men stepped out. He aimed a gun at me.

Novak said, "No more fucking around. Get in the vehicle."

I said, "You're not going to kill me."

"Maybe not, but that doesn't mean we won't shoot you. Get in the vehicle or else we'll—"

The gunshot sounded an instant after a chunk of Novak's face disappeared. He stood for a half second, then fell to the ground.

Agent Njeim hurried up the block, her weapon aimed.

The shot had distracted the Humvee's passenger for a second, but a second was all it took for me to step forward and shove the Humvee's door into him. It surprised him enough to cause him to drop to his knees, and I shoved the door into him again. This time the side of the door struck his head and sent him stumbling back into the snow.

I leaned down and grabbed his gun from the street and brought it up just as the Humvee's driver raised his weapon. One bullet to the driver's head, and then I turned and placed another bullet in the passenger's head as he reached for another weapon.

Agent Njeim approached the Humvee. She held the gun at the ready, checking the vehicle for anyone else, then looked up and down the block.

"What the hell was that?"

Before I could answer, a sound caught my attention. It was a faint sound, barely audible, but my ears were able to pick it up.

"Do you hear that?"

"Hear what?"

I turned back down the block, toward the subway station. I stood there motionless for a second, then started moving.

Agent Njeim said, "Where are you going?"

I started jogging as the sound increased. Agent Njeim waited a couple seconds before she followed.

We reached the entrance to the subway station at the moment the sound began to fade. When I'd heard first it, it was starting up, and as we'd run down the block most of the sound had traveled past, but now it was just the trail of the noise.

Agent Njeim said, "Was that ..."

I nodded.

"We need to go down there. Do you still have the radio?"

She pulled it from her jacket pocket.

I said, "Call Roger. Tell him what happened."

She hit the talk button, said Roger's name, but the only thing that came back was static. She tried once more but with the same result.

"I don't like this. Maybe we should go back."

"We need to check down there first."

Agent Njeim pulled the disposable from her pocket. She opened it, stared at the screen, then closed it.

"If those men were part of this, then there's a good chance the other men back at the Vault are part of this too."

I weighed the gun in my hand. Glanced up the street, at the bodies and the Humvee.

"Go back. I'll check this out first and then meet up with you."

"I'm not letting you out of my sight. Not after what just happened."

"Then let's make this quick."

I started down the steps. At the bottom was a metal barrier.

It took two bullets to destroy the lock, and then I rolled up the barrier and we slipped through.

Despite being closed, all the lights were on inside the station.

We jumped the turnstiles onto the platform. It was deserted.

"I'm not imaging things. You heard what I heard, right?"

Agent Njeim nodded.

"It was definitely a train."

"Makes the most sense. They used the blackout time to take the warheads to the nearest station. From there they probably had a train already waiting. If they were able to override the system and breach the security for Sentry Number Six, beating the metro's security would have been a piece of cake. Nate probably wouldn't have noticed anything wrong even if he'd tried looking."

"Where do you think they're taking the warheads?"

I walked over to the large subway map on the wall.

"Sentry Number Six is located in Hell's Kitchen, right?"

"Yes."

"According to the map, this is the blue line. Which means—"

I paused as my pocket vibrated. Or no—it was the disposable in my pocket that vibrated. I frowned at Agent Njeim as I withdrew it. There was no number on the screen on the outside of the phone, just the words INCOMING CALL.

I flipped open the phone and placed it to my ear.

Roger said, "Are you okay?"

"For now. Where are you?"

"Are you still with those men?"

"No."

"What happened?"

"One of them killed a National Guardsman. They pulled a gun on me. Agent Njeim and I killed them."

"Agent Njeim is with you now?"

"Yes."

"Mr. Shepherd, listen to me carefully. Don't give anything away with your face or posture."

"What's wrong?"

"Since the power came back up, I've had two of our analysts scouring the system to try to find out what happened and, well, there's no other way to say this. We found the other mole. It's Agent Njeim."

54

Agent Njeim stood directly in front of me, watching my face. She had her gun in her right hand, pointed at the ground.

I turned away from her, back to the large map on the wall.

"We think they're using the subway system to transport the warheads."

Roger was silent for a beat, probably confused by my change of subject, and then he understood.

"Ah, yes. She's there with you now, isn't she?"

"Yes."

"Is she armed?"

"Yes."

"Are you armed?"

"Yes."

"Then it's simple. Shoot her before she shoots you."

I said nothing. Just stared at the different colors showing the different lines on the map crisscrossing Manhattan.

"Elijah, I can have men there within minutes, but there's no telling what she plans to do in that time. Granted, I would prefer you take her alive so that we can question her, but I don't want to take the chance. Not after everything that's already happened."

Behind me, Agent Njeim shifted her weight from one foot to the other. The soft swish of the fabric of her jacket as she moved. I watched her reflection in the glass. She kept still, the gun at her side.

"You need to take her out. Right now. There's no telling what she plans to do with you."

I continued to watch her reflection. Agent Njeim continued to stand still. The gun at her side. Very quickly she could raise the gun and put a bullet in my head. It would take less than a second.

"Goddamn it, Elijah, are you there? Do you hear me? She's part of this conspiracy. She's a part of the group who killed your son and his family. She's with the people who came after you in Harper."

Still I said nothing.

"My God, Eli, she's with the people who killed your *dog*. You need to put her down before she puts you down."

I watched Agent Njeim's reflection shift again from one foot to the other. The gun stayed at her side. A simple flick of the wrist, a simple squeeze of the trigger, and a bullet would go straight through the back of my head.

I said, "I understand. I'll do it now."

Roger was quiet for a beat.

"Good. I have men on the way."

I closed the phone but didn't move. Just stood there, watching Agent Njeim's reflection.

She said, "What's wrong?"

I turned around and aimed the gun at her face.

She didn't move. Didn't even attempt to raise her weapon. A frown creased her brow.

"What are you doing?"

"What was my cat's name?"

"Your what?"

"My cat."

"I ... I don't know what you're talking about."

"Back in Harper, at my cabin, I had a cat. What was his name?"

Her face was blank. Her gaze shifted from my face to the gun and back to my face.

"I have no idea what you mean. I didn't even know you had an animal."

I stared at her for a moment, reading her eyes. Then I lowered the gun to my side.

"Exactly. Nobody did. But Roger somehow knew about my dog."

"Wait—you had a cat *and* a dog?"

"Just a dog. And again, I never told anyone about her. But Roger knew. He tried to use it to play on my emotions."

"To do what?"

"Kill you."

She was silent, processing my words. Her head began to shake in short jerks from side to side.

"Why ... why would he want you to kill me?"

"Because he says you're the other mole."

"He's lying."

"Yeah, I think we've established that point already."

I flipped open the disposable, dialed the number I had memorized, and placed the phone to my ear.

Agent Njeim said, "Who are you calling?"

The phone rang and rang and rang, but nobody picked up. I counted ten rings before I disconnected the call.

"Sanchez isn't answering his phone."

"Do you think your daughter—"

"At this point I don't know what to think."

I glanced past the gate and turnstiles toward the two sets of stairs leading up to the street.

"Roger said he has men coming."

Agent Njeim followed my gaze, then looked across the tracks at the opposite platform. Over there were two sets of stairs leading up to the street. Four ways Roger's men could enter the station. Actually, no—there were six ways if you included the tracks themselves.

She said, "They'd be at a disadvantage. We could pick them off as they came down. It would be like a kill box."

"Not unless they threw down tear gas first. Besides, Roger's under the impression I've killed you by now."

I glanced down at the phone in my hand.

"Roger said these can't be tracked, but can they?"

Agent Njeim nodded, already pulling hers from her pocket. She clamped her gun beneath her armpit to free her other hand and quickly stripped off the back of the phone, tore out a tiny chip, tossed it aside, and then broke the phone in half.

"Give me yours."

I considered trying Sanchez once more, but I knew there wasn't any point. If he were able to, he would have answered the first time I called. Which meant he wasn't able to. Which meant something terrible had happened.

I handed her the phone and stepped past her, the gun at my side. I stared up at the steps, then turned to stare across the tracks at the opposite platform. Any second, men would be swarming down the steps. Any second, we would be surrounded.

After withdrawing the tiny chip and breaking the phone in half and tossing the pieces aside, Agent Njeim looked at me.

"Now what do we do?"

I glanced at the large subway map. At those different colors showing different lines crisscrossing Manhattan.

"I'm going to head west and work my way toward my daughter's place. I need to check on her."

"What about me?"

"I suggest you head the opposite direction. Once they realize I haven't killed you, they'll be looking for both of us. Better to force them to put out a wider net."

"They'll know where you're headed. You could be walking into a trap."

"Most likely. But I can't not do this."

"What about Nate?"

I hesitated. Nate had the flash drive, what may or may not be the key to all of this. I didn't want to give up on it, but there wasn't much choice otherwise.

"Nate's on his own for now."

I walked to the edge of the platform. Dropped down to the tracks and held the gun up at my side.

Agent Njeim dropped down next to me.

"Good luck."

I nodded.

"Same to you."

We parted ways, and each hurried into our own tunnel of darkness.

55

By the time I emerged from the subway station four blocks from my daughter's brownstone, night had fallen and the snow had stopped. Not that it discouraged people from staying inside—there were even more people out and about, trudging through the snow, a few cars slowly moving up and down the street.

Like the previous subway station, this one had a gate keeping people from entering—or, in my case, exiting. It took two bullets to disintegrate the lock, which caused a few stares from passersby as I climbed the steps to the street. But when they saw I still had a gun in my hand, they quickly turned and headed in the opposite direction.

I stuffed the gun and my hands in the pockets of my jacket and headed down the block. Minutes later, I turned onto Aisha's street. Cars parked on the street, all of them covered in snow, but that was it. No people. No men in black uniforms with assault rifles waiting for me.

Of course not. They'd be waiting inside.

I withdrew the gun and held it by my leg as I continued down the sidewalk.

The lights were on inside the brownstone.

I paused for a beat. Looked up and down the street. Up at the trees and the roofs of the houses along the street.

Stillness.

Silence.

I climbed the steps to the brownstone. A curtain blocked the view of the parlor room just off the door. That was where I had last seen Sanchez. Where I shook his hand. Where I ignored his apology and told him to keep my daughter safe.

I didn't bother knocking or ringing the doorbell. I knew the door wouldn't be locked, and wasn't surprised when I turned the knob and pushed the door open.

The smell hit me at once. It wasn't a strong smell, and most people probably wouldn't have even been able to tell there was a smell at all. At least not until they moved deeper into the house. It had always helped me as a detective, my heightened sense of smell, to know just how long a body had been dead. We'd still need to wait for the official word from the ME, but by that point I was already working on leads that often ended up with a solid arrest.

Two people were dead inside.

I closed the door behind me and stomped the snow off my boots. No sense being quiet—the house was empty except for the two bodies. If Roger's men had wanted to take me out, they would have done so by now. Which meant ... what, exactly?

Billy was in the parlor. He lay on the floor, a bullet between his eyes. The Oriental rug had absorbed much of his blood. The blood didn't look too fresh, but it didn't look too old, either. By the smell, it could have been two or three hours old. Which meant Billy had been killed around the same time the Vault was bombed. The same time the warheads were stolen from Sentry Number Six.

I moved deeper into the house, toward the scent of the

second body. I knew before I even saw the body that it belonged to Sanchez. These people wouldn't have killed Aisha. At least not yet. They wanted something from me, and they were going to use whatever they could to get it. Sanchez had been my partner, had been my friend, but he wasn't family.

He lay on the kitchen floor. The spaces between the tiles had pooled his blood like rivulets. Unlike Billy, who had been shot once between the eyes, Sanchez had been shot multiple times. Three times in the chest, once in the throat. I could almost picture the scene: the intruders barging in, killing Billy first, and Sanchez taking Aisha to the back of the house for cover, his gun in hand. Judging by several of the shells littering the floor and the holes in the wall toward the front of the house, Sanchez had gotten off a few rounds. But it hadn't saved him in the end. It hadn't saved Aisha either.

Sanchez began to chirp—only it wasn't him, of course, but the phone in his pocket.

I stared down at his body for several long seconds before kneeling down beside him and extracting the disposable from his pocket. I opened the phone and placed it to my ear.

"Where is she?"

A slight pause on the other end, the person maybe surprised my first question was so direct. Then Roger spoke.

"She's safe."

"Let me talk to her."

"Not right now."

"Yes, right now. Otherwise, I assume she's dead and whatever it is you want from me is off the table."

Another slight pause.

"She's not currently with me."

"I don't care. Unless I talk to her, this is over."

"Fine. Give me a minute."

The phone clicked off. I held it away from my ear, stared at it for a moment, then closed the phone and stood back up. I stepped over Sanchez's body and leaned against the counter so I had a good view of both the front and rear of the house. The disposable in my left hand, the gun in my right. Waiting.

A minute later the phone chirped.

This time when I answered it, I didn't speak first.

Sobbing on the other end. Soft, distant sobbing. Then my daughter's voice.

"Hel ... Hel ... Hello?"

"Aisha."

"Dad? Dad, is that you?"

"I'm here."

"Dad, they killed Billy! They killed Uncle Hector! I—I don't know what to do. I'm so scared."

Before I could say anything, the phone disconnected again.

I closed the phone and waited. This time, it took only thirty seconds before it chirped.

Roger said, "Satisfied?"

"Why are you doing this?"

"Believe me, Eli, this is nothing personal against you. It's business."

"So now you're a terrorist?"

"I'm not a terrorist. I'm a patriot. And like any patriot, I'm doing what's best for my country."

"You killed my son and his family."

"Not me personally, but yes, my people did."

"Why?"

"The reason doesn't concern you."

"I beg to differ."

"You can differ all you want. Tell me, what gave me away?"

"You knew about my dog. I never told anyone."

"Ah, yes. I guess that would have tipped you off."

"What do you want?"

"You, of course. It's always been about you."

"You had me. I was in your office. I was in your headquarters. I was in the SUV when you took me to see Sentry Number Seven."

"Yes, but unfortunately none of those instances were an opportune time to take you out. The best shot we had was the Manhattan Bridge, when you were headed into the city, but that didn't work out so well."

"What's your plan for the warheads?"

"That doesn't concern you."

"Once again, I beg to differ. The same with Abu Muhammad al-Naser—what's your plan with him?"

"That doesn't concern you."

"Whatever game you're playing, it's not going to work. I'll contact the president and tell him what you're up to. He'll shut you down."

Roger actually laughed.

"A good idea, yes, but the president is currently under the impression that Agent Njeim has taken you hostage. If you contact him, he'll believe it's under extreme duress and will not believe a word you say. Trust me, Eli, this has all been worked out. Every contingency has been evaluated and examined. We know what we're doing."

"And what are you doing?"

"Nice try. Had my men taken you back in Harper, all of this could have been avoided. Had that even happened, though, the end result would still be the same. A dangerous terrorist would have escaped the black site, one of the Sentry locations would have been breached and the warheads stolen, and Agent Njeim would have been ousted as a mole. Hell, why do you think I hired her in the first place? We've been working toward this day for a very long time, Eli, and nothing is going to stop us."

"I wouldn't be so sure about that."

Roger laughed again.

"What are you going to do, Eli? You're an old man, just like me. Sure, you may have at one time had great power and strength and speed, but those days are far behind you. You won't be able to stop this, just as your son didn't."

"Monarch."

Silence.

"I know all about Monarch, Roger. So does Agent Njeim. She's taking that information to the proper authorities as we speak."

Roger's voice was tense.

"How do you know about Monarch?"

"My son hid a flash drive. I'm assuming that's what your men were trying to find when they ransacked the house. They didn't look close enough."

Roger was silent for another moment, and then he sighed.

"Not like it changes anything. Yes, your son did steal a flash drive. He'd become aware of our operation, somehow. He was a bright kid, your son. His snooping was what caused us to accelerate the plan. If it were up to us, we would have waited at least another six months."

"Sorry to disappoint."

"Yes, well, shit happens. Now do you want to save your daughter? Of course you do. It's in your nature to save people. Why else do you think we took her?"

I said nothing.

"Central Park. Ninety minutes."

"Where in Central Park?"

"You know where."

Roger didn't wait for me to respond. He didn't need confirmation that I would show up. Like he said, it was in my nature to save people, and I would do whatever it took to save my daughter.

He clicked off.

I stood motionless for a moment, then flung the disposable at the nearest wall. It didn't shatter into a hundred pieces. It didn't even break apart. It just hit the wall with a thud, clattered to the floor.

I kneeled back down next to Sanchez.

"You did what you could, my friend. Thank you."

In response, the front door opened.

56

The front door didn't open suddenly, but slowly, so slowly in fact it didn't make a sound. But ever since I'd stepped inside the brownstone, the house had felt like it was holding its breath, and the second the door opened, even just a bit, the house released that breath, a drop in pressure. That's what I sensed first. Then I heard an engine outside, a vehicle idling in the street.

I stood back up and stepped over Sanchez and continued silently through the kitchen, the gun now held at the ready.

Footsteps farther down the hallway. Slow, calculated footsteps. The floorboards didn't creak with the added weight, but still there was a slight moan as the person entered the house.

I stepped through the doorway and aimed down the hallway.

Agent Njeim stood inside the foyer. Her body was turned slightly, her gaze directed into the parlor room and at Billy's body lying dead inside. She held her weapon with both hands, and when she saw movement from the corner of her eye, she spun and brought up the gun. Saw it was me and lowered the gun.

"Your daughter?"

"Gone."

"Hector Sanchez?"

"Dead."

"This is your daughter's fiancé?"

"Yes."

I started down the hallway, glanced past her at the street and the idling sedan. Someone occupied the passenger seat.

"Who's with you?"

"Nate. After those men had come to take you, he got suspicious. After what happened, his paranoia kicked in and he packed up his things and took off."

"How'd you find him?"

"He found me, actually. He searched the city for me using facial recognition. One of the subway cameras picked me up."

"If he found you that easily, Roger's people can find us just as easily. Hell, he knows I'm here. I just talked to him."

"What does he want?"

"Me. That's all he said. He'll trade my daughter's life for my own."

"You don't believe him, do you?"

"I believe that I'm the one he's after, yes. But will he spare my daughter's life? Probably not."

"Nate managed to access the flash drive. He knows what Monarch is. More importantly, he thinks he knows why Roger wants you."

Agent Njeim drove. Nate stayed in the passenger seat, huddled over his laptop. I sat in the back and listened as Nate told me how he managed to override the entire citywide security system.

"It was pretty easy, actually. All I needed to do was access—"

Agent Njeim cut him off.

"We're all very impressed, Nate, but tell Mr. Shepherd what you learned about Monarch."

"Right, so Monarch seems to be a private security contractor. It's only in its infancy right now, but it's looking to become the next big thing in private security. It's just waiting for the right moment."

"What moment?"

Agent Njeim said, "Mr. Shepherd, are you familiar with private security contractors?"

"No."

"They're essentially soldiers for hire. Companies in other countries, usually those in war zones, use private security contractors as bodyguards. Many are employed by the U.S. government on a contractual basis. Soon after the 9/11 attacks, President Bush tasked the CIA to create a top-secret assassination unit to find and kill Al-Qaeda operatives. He went over Congress's head when he did this, and Congress didn't even know about it until seven years later, when it was revealed that the CIA had hired Blackwater to help run it."

"What's Blackwater?"

"A private security firm. Ex-military, or in the case of Blackwater, ex-Navy SEALs. These are highly trained operatives that work beyond the rules set forth by the Geneva Convention. They have no accountability. In 2007, Blackwater operatives shot at Iraqi civilians killing seventeen and injuring twenty in Nisour Square, Baghdad. Only four of them were tried and convicted—one for murder, the other three for manslaughter. But those at the top? Nothing. If anything, they were rewarded."

"Rewarded how?"

"Hundreds of millions of dollars. And that's just the tip of the iceberg."

"How so?"

Agent Njeim glanced at Nate.

"Tell him."

Nate shifted in his seat to look back at me.

"Based on the documents I read, Monarch plans to offer something no other private security firm can offer."

"Which is?"

"Super soldiers. Men like you and your son. Imagine if there were a dozen of you. Imagine if there were a *hundred* of you. The United States—or whoever hired Monarch—would be unstoppable. Every country would fear us. And, more importantly, the government would not have to send so many people into war. They wouldn't even have to deploy soldiers."

"But these soldiers, even if they're somehow given my powers, wouldn't be invincible. A grenade could take them out."

Agent Njeim said, "That's not the point. Monarch is basing its entire operation on the *potential* of these super soldiers. Yes, they may not become invincible, but they'll still be stronger and faster than ordinary soldiers. That's all that matters to investors. We're not talking about millions of dollars. We're talking about *billions* of dollars."

I was quiet for a moment, thinking about this as Agent Njeim drove us through the near-deserted city streets.

I said, "That's why Roger stole the warheads. That's why he broke Abu Muhammad al-Naser out of the black site. When I spoke to him, he said they had planned this for years. He said that's even why he hired you, Agent Njeim, so that you would be ousted as a mole."

"What's his plan?"

"Another attack in the city, this one conduced by ISIS. Like

Roger said yesterday, the 9/11 attack renewed this country's resolve to go to war. He said nobody likes war, but that it's a necessary evil. He said the U.S. has essentially never stopped being at war with one country or another, but everyone has begun to feel fatigued. But a major attack on U.S. soil would revitalize everyone for war. The people would demand it."

Agent Njeim said, "And Monarch would be waiting in the wings to step in. Once they showed the government what they could do, the money would pour in nonstop."

Nate kept typing on his laptop.

"That's not all. Roger Davidson is not even his real name. At least according to the documents on the flash drive, so I searched and found out that it's true. He has such a high-security clearance that he can do pretty much whatever he wants. For some reason, ten years ago, he changed his last name to Davidson. He worked as a top secret operative and convinced the government to let him change it to protect his family. Not too long after that his wife died, and his children moved away and, from what I can tell, he no longer has any communication with them."

I asked, "What did he change his name from?"

"That's the weird part. His original name is what comes up as the chairman for Monarch. He has four board of directors, and they're already receiving funding from a handful of investors."

Agent Njeim prompted, "Nate, tell him the name."

"Ah, yes. Sorry. So Roger Davidson was once called—or is still called?—Malcolm Strickland."

Nate shifted again in his seat to look back at me.

"Does that name mean anything to you?"

My initial response was to shake my head and say no. But then I thought about it for another moment, and I realized that it did mean something to me.

"Agent Njeim, I need you to drive us somewhere."

I gave her directions.

She asked, "Why there?"

"There's someone that might be able to help us. As is, we're three people going up against what is potentially an army."

Nate shifted again in his seat, only this time it was more like a squirm.

I said, "Two people."

Nate shook his head.

"No, I'm with you guys, but I just ... I mean, this isn't what I do. I don't *kill* people, you know?"

Agent Njeim asked, "Why don't we contact the president directly about this?"

"Because Roger already thought of that. According to him, the president is currently under the impression you've taken me hostage, and that if I contact him, it will be under extreme duress."

"The vice president, then. Or the Joint Chiefs of Staff. Anyone at the White House. Or, hell, we could take this to the *New York Times*."

"We don't have time. Whatever Roger plans to do, he's going to do it soon."

Agent Njeim said nothing to this. Her hands tightened around the steering wheel.

Nate was still typing on the laptop. A map had popped up on the screen, and he glanced back at me with a frown.

"Why are we going to a parking garage?"

The Mercedes was gone. There weren't even any recent tire tracks. The whole top level of the parking garage was one flawless carpet of snow.

The sedan idled behind us on the next level down, where Nate stayed hunched over his laptop. Agent Njeim and I stood just below the top level on the rise, weapons in our hands.

Agent Njeim glanced at me.

"Now what?"

I stared at the empty space where the Mercedes was yesterday, Roman Vyhovsky locked in the truck.

"Now we make a house call."

57

Maksim—the restaurant Roman Vyhovsky owned as a cover for his illegal activities—was doing steady business despite the hard winter weather. At least from the sidewalk it looked like there were several people inside, some at the long bar along one side of the room and the tables and booths scattered about.

Normally a bouncer was stationed outside the main entrance, but because of the frigid temperature, the bouncer had planted himself on a stool just inside the door. Even so, he was still wrapped up in a winter jacket, a wool cap on his head. When I stepped inside, he stood from the stool and blew on his hands as he rubbed them together and asked if I had a reservation.

I shot him in the foot.

As the bouncer fell to the ground, he attempted to pull his piece out from its place near the small of his back. The bulky jacket slowed him down, and within a second I took possession of the gun.

Now with a weapon in each hand, I headed deeper into the restaurant.

Inside, everyone heard the shot. All conversations halted. Some men rose to their feet, pushing their women to the floor as each reached for weapons.

A quick scan of the room showed me five men in total, including the bartender who had a shotgun. I took out the bartender first, two bullets to the shoulder. I moved as I fired, weaving through the tables, using both guns to fire at the four other men. None of them were kill shots—I had no intention of killing them—and the bullets ended up in either their shoulders or their legs. Some of the men managed to squeeze off a few rounds, but none of them were within a yard of me.

The whole thing took less than seven seconds from the moment I shot the bouncer in the foot and then, once the men were down, all was silent.

I shouted, "Roman, I need to talk to you!"

Heavy pounding on the stairs near the back of the restaurant. Two men appeared, both with Heckler & Koch MP5s strapped around their necks. For a second they took in the scene, their fallen friends, and then they aimed the MP5s at me.

I set the guns on the nearest table, raised my hands.

"I'm here to see Roman."

As if all it took to summon him was uttering his name twice, Roman appeared. He didn't scramble down the stairs as quickly as his men. He took his time, one slow, steady step after another. He held a gun in his hand, but it was at his side, as if an afterthought.

Like his two men, Roman took a second to drink in the scene before focusing his attention on me.

"Kill him."

I kept my hands raised.

"Wait."

The men paused.

I said, "Roman, if I had wanted to kill any of your men tonight—or even you last night—I would have done so. You know that."

"Am I supposed to be grateful to you?"

"I'm here to talk business."

"The only business I have with you is to see you dead."

"Maybe so, but what I have to tell you may cost you millions. You're a businessman, Roman. Tell me that doesn't worry you."

He stared at me for several long seconds. The room was completely silent except for those men on the floor, groaning in pain.

Finally, Roman said, "Bring him upstairs."

The men with the MP5s led me up the stairs and down a hallway to Roman's office. It was located near the back of the restaurant, with a wide window overlooking the street on that side.

Roman's desk, just like Roger's, was much too big and bulky for its intended purpose other than to show those who sat in front of it that the person who sat behind it was important.

Roman lowered himself down into his leather chair, leaned back, placed his hands behind his head.

"Now tell me why I shouldn't have my men kill you right now."

Besides the two men with the MP5s, there were two other men in the office. One of them was Viktor. He sat on the leather couch, his arm in a sling, his leg wrapped. His glare burned into me.

I said, "Like I told you—business."

Roman sighed.

"I have no business with you."

"No, but what I'm currently involved in will affect your business. It will most likely affect all business in the city."

"Why should I care?"

"Like I said. You're a businessman, Roman. You know exactly why you should care. How did your men find you, by the way?"

He held up his gold Rolex.

I said, "Nice watch. What does that have to do with anything?"

"There is a GPS tracker inside this watch. My men always know where I am. In case—"

He stared at me blankly.

"—someone decides to abduct me."

"That's helpful."

"Just so we are clear, you are not leaving this building alive. My men will kill you, and they will drag your dead body down the stairs so that my guests will see who ruined their evening."

"Maybe you should offer them free drinks to make up for everything."

Viktor said, "Let me do it."

I looked at Viktor for a second, then turned back to Roman.

"I don't have much time. I need to be in Central Park in a half hour."

"You will not make it."

Roman nodded at Viktor.

Viktor jumped up from the couch, or at least jumped up as fast as his wounded leg would allow. He wobbled for a second, steadied himself, and then pulled his gun out from the small of his back.

I held up a finger.

"Point that at me and you'll never walk again."

Viktor grinned. Started to chuckle. Aimed the gun at me, and the window behind him cracked as a bullet tore through it and then tore straight into the base of his spinal column.

He cried out, hit the floor, and I stepped forward and sat down in one of the two leather chairs facing Roman's desk. These chairs weren't as nice as the one Roman now sat in, but they weren't meant to be.

"There's a sniper on the rooftop across the street. She'll take out you and the rest of your men if I give her the signal. I don't want to give her that signal, Roman, but I will if I have to. Because time is running out. I now have twenty-eight minutes to be in Central Park, and I can't be late."

Behind me, Viktor screamed in pain.

"Have I taken out some of your men? Yes. But I didn't kill any of them. If you want to continue doing business in this city, you're going to listen to what I have to tell you."

Roman said nothing.

"Tell me, Roman, what was business like directly after 9/11? I imagine it wasn't good. I imagine your business suffered for months. Shipments of your product into the city alone were probably stalled for weeks, if not longer. Am I right?"

Roman glanced past me at Viktor on the floor, then at his other men stationed around the room, before focusing on the bullet hole in the window and the building across the street where Agent Njeim was positioned, her sniper rifle focused on him.

Finally, he leaned forward and folded his hands on the desktop.

"I'm listening."

58

Several years after Prometheus set off the bomb that killed seventy-six people and injured one hundred fifteen, a memorial had been erected just outside Delacorte Theater. I'd never seen the memorial in person, as I had left the city right after the bombing, but I had read about it in the papers. Back then I still read the papers on a daily basis until I realized there was nothing I could do about all the terrible things I read about. A large marble memorial contained each victim's name. Now, at almost midnight, the memorial was almost entirely covered in snow.

An SUV was parked beside it. Its engine idling, its running lights on. No other vehicles were in sight.

I walked down the drive toward the SUV. I kept my hands held at my sides, showing that I wasn't carrying a weapon.

When I was fifty yards away, the SUV's headlights blinked on.

I paused.

The back door opened and Roger emerged. As before, he put most of his weight on his left foot and seemed to hobble about as he slammed the door shut.

A man stepped out of the SUV's front passenger side. He opened the rear door and pulled out a struggling Aisha. She had duct tape over her mouth. Her wrists were bound. The man gripped her arm and shoved her forward, but she pulled away and tried to run. The man yanked her back, slapped her across the face. She hadn't even noticed me until that moment, and when her eyes fell on me, she attempted to shout through the tape.

Roger said, "Put her back."

The man shoved Aisha back inside the SUV and slammed the door shut.

Roger turned back to me.

"Now I'm hoping we can cut the shit."

I said, "When you bombed your own office, did you expect you would be injured?"

"It would be more suspicious had I not been injured."

"I know who you are. Malcolm Strickland."

If this surprised Roger, he didn't show it.

"Your father was Colonel David Strickland. Which makes you the son of David. Davidson. Was that meant to be cute?"

He shrugged.

"When I created the division of Homeland Security to oversee Temple, I knew I had to change my name. I figured I would one day encounter you, or at the very least your son, and there was an excellent chance you both would know about my father. It would be my way of dangling the truth in front of your nose until I was ready to kill you."

"If you wanted to kill me, you would have done it already. But you don't want to kill me, at least not yet. Like my son, you need to get me into your lab. You need to drain my blood and spinal fluid and everything else so you can create your super soldiers."

Roger hobbled forward so that he stood beside the front of the SUV.

"Close. We already got your DNA from your son's blood and spinal fluid and brain. We believe we have what we need for our purposes, though there is concern of the Xerox Effect. Are you familiar with the Xerox Effect? When something becomes replicated so many times it begins to lose it … purity, so to speak. Granted, your son was only two generations from his grandfather, the original, but it's still a concern. Yes, we will take what we need from you at some point, but that's not the reason we haven't killed you yet."

"I know what your plan is. You want to set those warheads off and kill people so that you can blame ISIS. What I don't get is why steal the warheads in the first place? Why not just set off one of the Sentries to blow up something?"

"We certainly could have done that, but it wouldn't have been nearly as dramatic. Think about the narrative, Eli. A dangerous terrorist escapes a black site, manages to steal two warheads from a top secret program only a handful of people in the world know about, and then detonates those warheads on U.S. soil. It's going to be a shit show. Congressional committees will be created to investigate what happened. The media will talk about it nonstop for months. And, most importantly, the public will demand an even greater response to the ongoing war against ISIS. That's where Monarch comes in."

"Sounds like you have it all figured out."

"Of course. I told you we've been working on this for a long time."

"You're going to kill people."

"I'm not a monster. The warheads will go off, yes, but no lives will be lost."

"Then how do you expect to create this shit show you so desperately need?"

"Remember, sometimes symbols are even more precious than lives. Now, are you going to make this easy or difficult?"

"What do you think?"

"I think you came alone. But I think Agent Njeim and her analyst buddy are out there somewhere. Clearly Nate was the one who told you about Monarch. To be honest, I'm not too worried. I thought you might have some trick up your sleeve, but we've been monitoring the park for the past hour. No heat signatures except yours have entered the park. Which means you're alone."

A rumbling started up around us. The lamps on the front of several snowmobiles winked on and the men riding them steered them out of the trees and down the slopes. They fanned out and slowed the snowmobiles and cut the engines, and then each grabbed the rifles strapped over their shoulders and aimed those rifles at me.

Two SUVs came down the drive too, each with their running lights on. They parked at the end of the drive, fifty yards away. The back doors opened and men stepped out, also aiming rifles at me.

I was surrounded.

Roger said, "Check him."

The SUV's passenger started toward me. As he approached, I held my arms out to my sides.

The man patted me down. He searched my pockets. He turned away and nodded at Roger and returned to his place beside the SUV.

I said to Roger, "I'm here, just like you asked. Now let Aisha go."

Roger smiled. It wasn't a cold smile or a flat smile. The smile said that he was clearly amused by my statement.

Behind me, there was a slow, steady crunch of snow. Even

with my back to the sound, I could tell it was past the SUVs. Someone walking down the drive.

Roger's gaze shifted past me.

"Look who it is."

I didn't look.

"Let Aisha go."

"If you defeat him, I'll let her ago. I'll let you both go."

For some reason, this surprised me. I had always thought there was a chance—a slim chance—he might let Aisha go, but not me. No way would he ever let me go. Except … if I defeated *him*.

Behind me, the slow, steady crunch of snow stopped.

I turned around.

Standing directly in front of the two SUVs, bathed in their headlights, was Temple.

59

The outfit had changed over the years, from the one Vanessa Clark created in 1943. Just as styles evolve, so had Temple's. He still wore all black, from head to toe. Kevlar was added to protect him from bullets. The ski mask transitioned to something much more comfortable and breathable. But still there was no opening to see the skin of the person hiding behind the mask. Black goggles stared out at me.

I unzipped my parka and pulled my arms out, letting it fall to the snow. This at least gave me better control. I was an old man, yes, but my skills were still better than anyone else's one-on-one. At least it had seemed that way the past couple days since I had needed to start using my skills again.

I stood motionless in the snow, waiting for this Temple to make a move.

He didn't move. He waited for me to make the first move. Normally I would have waited him out, but I was impatient. The sooner this ended, the sooner Aisha may be able to walk away from all of this.

I took a step forward, and as I did, Temple launched

himself at me. We hit the ground and Temple was immediately on his feet, circling me, waiting for me to get back up. I rolled over and got to one knee, and then I was flat on my back again after Temple kicked me in the jaw. The back of his boot came at my head and I rolled away, springing to my feet and throwing a punch at the masked face. Temple dodged it and threw a punch into my solar plexus. He spun and knocked me back down with a roundhouse kick. I rolled away again, managed to gain my feet, and circled Temple, aware that the dozen or so men were still training their assault rifles on me, aware that Roger was watching and that Aisha was in the SUV, duct tape over her mouth.

Despite the adrenaline pumping through my system, my breathing slowed. My heartbeat slowed. Everything slowed.

This time, I waited for Temple to make the first move. When he stepped forward, I launched myself at him. He stumbled back, fell to the ground, me on top of him. I tried to grab the mask, pull it off to see his face, but he shoved me off. He was back on his feet within a second. As he kicked at my head, I grabbed his boot and yanked it forward. He lost balance and fell, flipping through the air. I jumped on him, my knee to his chest. He tried to shove me off again but I kept punching at his face, both fists moving at once. I felt like I was never going to stop. I felt invincible.

Something hit my shoulder. The force wasn't great, but it was enough to knock me off Temple.

One of the men had shot me. Not a kill shot, just a round in the shoulder to give Temple some help.

Temple was on his feet in an instant. He turned toward the man who'd fired his rifle, stared for a moment, his hands balled into fists, then turned back to me. Whoever wore the mask, he wasn't happy about the interruption.

As I climbed to my feet, Temple launched himself at me again. I fell back, turned, scrambled to my feet, but he was already in front of me. I raised my fist to punch him, but he grabbed it, twisted it hard enough to force me to spin. He pulled up on the arm, trying to dislocate it, but I fought with everything I had to stop him. He was right behind me, and I threw my head back into his face—or at least I thought it was his face. The back of my skull hit something solid, and the pressure on my arm let up. I spun back around and raised another fist, but he kicked me in the stomach, punched me in my face. Before I knew it, I was back on the ground and he was on top of me, and I tried to shove him off but he was unmovable, too strong, and his fists rained down on my face and my chest and I tried to fight back, tried to do *something*, but there was nothing I could do, absolutely nothing.

I felt my body trying to heal itself from all the places where it had been bruised and bloodied, but my body was old and was having a hard time trying to keep up. Eventually, it would get to the point where my body realized it was a lost cause and shut down. When that happened, nothing would save me.

I was faintly aware that Temple was not going to let up. I was faintly aware that I was going to die here in the snow, just yards away from the monument that had been placed for the people who died because I hadn't saved them. I was faintly aware that Aisha was close by, watching this happen, and that soon she would see her father die. I was faintly aware that someone had approached, was now standing right over us.

"Enough."

Roger whispered it, or maybe he shouted it.

"Don't kill him yet."

Something pricked my neck, something long and thin. A needle.

Temple had stopped punching me. His weight on me lessened as he stood up, but I just lay there on my back, staring at the night sky.

Then, seconds later, blackness.

INTERLUDE
ORIGIN STORY (III)

We stood on the rooftop of a building on the Upper East Side. The building was thirty stories tall. Not a monolith like many of the other buildings in the city, but still tall enough for us to see most of the city laid out like an intricate model. It was the middle of the night and lights flickered in distant windows like stars.

My father said, "How do you feel?"

"Fine."

"Not nervous?"

"No."

He smiled and chuckled and clapped me on my shoulder.

"Of course you're nervous."

It was September 3, 1973. My father had been Temple for almost thirty years. He had more stories than he could ever share with me. He'd only shared the important stories—like how it all began—but the lesser stories he kept to himself. Told me very soon I would have lesser stories of my own. Instances when I helped stop a robbery or mugging. The city still had its issues with crime, and I would be the one to help clean it up.

My father had been Temple for almost thirty years and now

he was walking away. He had already packed his things, loaded his car, sold his apartment. By that time my mother had passed away nearly a decade ago.

"Where will you go?"

"I told you—I don't know."

"Will I ever see you again?"

"I certainly hope so."

"I still don't understand why you need to leave. Why you just can't stay here in the city. We're going to have children at some point. It would be great if they met their grandfather."

My father shook his head slowly, looked away.

"Don't make this harder than it has to be, Eli."

"I just don't get it."

"You will some day."

"What does that mean?"

"You'll eventually get to a place where you'll realize there isn't much more for you to do. That it's time to let your son—or daughter—take over if they so choose."

"I understand that part. But I don't understand why you have to leave."

"It's this city."

"What about the city?"

"It ... it's like a magnet. It draws on me. This need we have to help people, to save people, it will never go away. And being here in this city, it sometimes become too much. That's why I have to leave."

"Wherever you go, there will be trouble. People will still need help."

My father smiled again.

"The world got on before Temple, and it will get on after Temple."

"What if I don't want to do it?"

My father didn't even blink.

"Then you don't have to do it. I was never forced to be Temple. I wanted to do it. I needed to do it. If you don't feel the same need—"

"Of course I do."

"Then why did you ask?"

I said nothing.

My father clapped my shoulder again.

"You're nervous. I understand. Believe me, I understand. I was in the same situation as you were a long time ago. Only I didn't know what I was doing at the time. You, on the other hand, have had training. You know everything you need to know."

"Shalissa is terrified."

"As she should be. Your mother was terrified for me as well. It kept her up at night. But she understood it had to be done."

We stood there then in silence, watching the city again. Finally, my father said it was time for him to go.

I asked, "Any parting advice?"

My father smiled.

"Of course. Try not to do anything stupid."

"Gee, thanks, Pops."

My father embraced me. At first I wasn't sure what to do. My father had always been standoffish when it came to signs of affection. He had grown up without a father himself and hadn't had any male role models in his life. He once told me he had been terrified to learn he would be a father because he was certain he would mess it up. Maybe that was another reason why he had sent my mother to live with her parents upstate for the first several years of my life. Even when we eventually came back to the city and my father was around, he never hugged me. He told me he loved me, would clap me on the shoulder, but that was it. No hugs. No kisses on my head.

I said, "I'll miss you."

My father stepped back, wiping at his eyes.

"I'll miss you too."

We were silent for another moment, and then my father turned and started toward the stairs. I watched him go, afraid this was the very last time I would ever see him. But then he turned back, raising a finger.

"There is one more thing, now that I think about it. I'm sure at some point there will be a situation that will be too much for you. You'll probably tell yourself you can't win. If that situation occurs, remember you can always walk away."

"But ... wouldn't that make me a coward?"

"That depends. You need to ask yourself what's worse— being a coward or being dead."

"Have you ever walked away?"

"No."

"Then why are you telling me it's okay?"

"Because you're my son and I love you."

"I'm never going to walk away."

My father smiled.

"I know you won't. You're not one to start something you can't finish. That's what I admire about you. That's why I know you'll do great. You don't quit. You'll see a challenge through to the end, whether you live or die."

PART FOUR
SUPERMAN IS DEAD

60

The first thing I became aware of was the light shining in my eyes.

My first impulse was to open my eyes, but the light was right there, burning through my eyelids. I turned my face away, but the light was just as strong no matter where I tilted my face. I opened my eyes, slowly at first, until my eyes began to adjust and I realized that the light was a large, bright lamp.

I was on an operating table.

At least that was my first thought. I was naked except for my boxer shorts. The table was steel and very cold. I wasn't lying flat, but resting at an angle, maybe forty-five degrees. My arms were clamped. My ankles were clamped. There wasn't even any give—they were clamped down as tight as they could go. I tried to lift my head to look around the room but couldn't —my neck was clamped as well.

Machines surrounded me. I could hear their beeping. I realized there were wires on my body—my chest and arms—no doubt monitoring my vitals.

Nothing was over my mouth. I could call out if I wanted to, shout as loud as I'd like, but I knew it would be no use. Wherever they had taken me, it was no doubt a secure location. No matter how loud I shouted, nobody other than those who were watching me would hear.

Footsteps sounded in the silence. A soft, hollow tapping. Footsteps on concrete.

The lamp in front of my face was swiveled away.

My eyes adjusted in a second to see the man standing beside me.

I spoke between clenched teeth.

"Where's my daughter?"

Roger said, "If it means anything to you, your son put up much more of a fight than you have. He was secured to a table very much like this one with his arms and legs clamped tight, but still he fought. Maybe it's because he was younger. More in the prime of his life. What do you think?"

I said nothing.

"My techs will be in momentarily. The process shouldn't take more than an hour."

My eyes had adjusted now to take in the rest of the room. It wasn't very large. Besides the machines around me and the table itself, there wasn't much else. In the corner of the room, standing on a tripod, was a video camera.

Roger noticed me looking at the camera.

"Our investors require us to keep everything monitored. That way they can check in whenever they please to make sure their money isn't being wasted. I've tried explaining how dangerous it is, keeping a record of our proceedings, but they don't care. I guess if I had the money they did, I wouldn't care either."

"Why are you doing this?"

"Money, of course. More money than you could ever imagine."

"So it has nothing to do with your father?"

Roger frowned.

"Not really. Sure, I could tell you part of me wants to complete what he started, but the truth is he was a military man and did exactly what the military told him to do. He conducted the experiments, and when one of the test subjects escaped, he did everything he could to capture and kill that subject."

"The Reaper."

"That's right—the Reaper. He sent the Reaper after your father. He figured sending another test subject to hunt your father would be the best bet. Unfortunately, it didn't work out the way my father had envisioned."

"Your father almost died."

"Almost. He didn't, though. He managed to get away, but as you can imagine the military was less than happy with him. He became their scapegoat. They stuck him with a desk job at the Pentagon. I was only three years old at the time, so I only heard about all of it decades later. Your father was much smarter than the military anticipated. They realized they couldn't hunt him in the traditional sense, so they switched tactics."

"How so?"

"In 1954, they had Joseph McCarthy claim Temple was a communist. By that point the public had begun to see Temple as a hero. The hope was branding him a communist would stop that. It didn't."

"What else?"

"There were several other things they tried, the most notable having a Congressman try to pass legislation that would force Temple to turn himself over to the federal authorities. Unfortunately, President Kennedy was a huge supporter of Temple and threatened to veto any such legislation."

"Was that why he was assassinated?"

Roger smiled.

"My security clearance is high, but not that high."

I said, "Where are my things?"

"What?"

"Besides my clothes, I had a car key and a watch. What did you do with them?"

"Don't worry about them."

"I am going to worry about them. The key belongs to a car I'm borrowing from a friend. I need to return it to him."

Roger smiled again. He motioned at a table against the wall beyond the camera. My clothes and the car key and watch sat on top.

"There are your things, but I wouldn't worry about returning the car to your friend Darrell if I were you."

At the sound of Darrell's name, my body tensed. I glared back at Roger.

"What have you done with him?"

Roger smiled again but said nothing.

"Did you kill him?"

Roger said, "I think our time here is done."

"Where's my daughter?"

Roger reached out, patted me on the shoulder.

"Take care of yourself, Elijah. When it's time, don't fight it. It will only make things worse."

He swiveled the lamp so the brightness shined in my face before he left. His footsteps echoed off the concrete floor. The door opened and closed. For a second there was more silence. Then the door opened again. Another set of hollow footsteps echoed. These were somehow sharper. As if the person wasn't wearing rubber soled shoes, like Roger had been, but heels. At first it was just a shadow past the light, and then the lamp was shifted away again and a face materialized.

Aisha.

61

Here was a time where I loved and respected you. You were my role model. You were my hero. Guess when that changed."

I said nothing.

"You know when it changed. You know exactly when I began to hate you."

Again I said nothing.

Aisha's face darkened.

"Say it. Say her name."

"There was nothing I could do."

"You lie."

"It's true. Nothing would have saved your mother."

She slammed her fist on the operating table.

"Bullshit! You were only thinking about yourself."

I said nothing. There was nothing for me to say. Twenty years had passed and she had held onto this all that time. While I had entered into a kind of depression, Aisha had let the loss open a hole in her heart that grew wider and wider through the years. Now she had become enraged at the mere notion that her father could have saved her mother but instead chose to do nothing.

I asked, "What are you getting out of this?"

"What do you think? I'm getting the only thing that matters."

Despite the metal clamp restraining my neck, I moved my head slowly from side to side.

"It won't work."

"You don't know that."

"I do."

"For decades, they've been trying to find a cure for cancer, and now I will bring them one. And not just cancer—all diseases. Imagine that: a world where nobody gets sick. Where nobody is forced to watch their loved ones wither away in a hospital bed. No more reason for people to feel helpless anymore."

"You'll become a billionaire. Buy all the brownstones you want."

"This isn't about money. I made that clear to Roger at the start. I don't want anything from this. I plan to make the treatment free. Or at the very least cheap enough that it'll be affordable to everyone. I understand pharmaceutical companies won't be happy about it. They'll do whatever they can to stop the research, to keep the cure out of everyone's hands. But I'm going to make it work."

"Interesting how you justify your actions."

"Fuck you. You have no right to judge me."

"I think I do. You killed your brother."

"No, I didn't."

"Roger's people did, and I assume it was because you gave them the idea of using James's DNA to create Monarch's super soldiers."

She shook her head.

"You have no idea what's going on."

"What about Yolanda and the kids?"

Aisha said nothing.

"I'm guessing you were the one who went there that night. Not by yourself, though. No, you went with a few of Roger's men. But you were the one Yolanda saw when she looked out the window. That's why she opened the door, invited you in. But Roger's men, they came into the house too. They were the ones who killed Yolanda and the kids. Tell me, Aisha, did you watch when Roger's men cut off their heads?"

Despite her best effort to steel herself, Aisha looked away. Stared at the wall for several long seconds, then sighed.

"In case you're wondering, I was never jealous of James. Him being Temple, it was never something I ever wanted to do. I want to help people, yes, but not like that."

"You allowed your fiancé to be murdered."

She shrugged.

"He was an asshole. The only reason we were together was because I needed his money to start my foundation. There was never really any love between us, at least on my end."

I stared at her. This wasn't my daughter. The one who had wanted me to tuck her in at night on those rare occasions I was actually home. The one who sat on my lap when we watched cartoons. The one who told me she wanted to be a doctor when she grew up.

"Your fiancé may have been an asshole, but what about Hector?"

The light in her eyes dimmed at the sound of his name.

"That was unfortunate, but there was no other option. If anything, it's your fault—you made him stay there to watch after me. I told you I would be fine."

There was a silence, both of us watching the other.

I said, "When did Roger approach you with this?"

"What do you mean?"

"You said you didn't bring the idea to Roger. So he must have brought it to you. How long were you both planning this? Did you talk to your brother in the meantime? Did you play with his children?"

"I actually brought up the idea to James. I asked him if he'd let me test his blood. I told him there was a chance that we could potentially find a cure for cancer. That we could save the world. But he wouldn't listen to me. He said it wouldn't work."

"He was right."

"Shut up."

"Neither you nor Roger know what you're doing. You're just working on speculation. You *think* you understand what it is inside my body—inside James's body—but you have no idea. Roger said because James started sniffing around they had to take him out. Which means they had to come for me. Which still doesn't make sense, because there was no way you or your brother knew where to find me."

Aisha said nothing.

"You must have tested this beforehand. Roger wouldn't have gone to this length unless there was substantial evidence this could work."

I paused.

"Aisha, who was that at Central Park? Who was Temple?"

For an instant doubt crept into her eyes. Like she was beginning to second-guess everything. Maybe the little girl who used to give me hugs every morning was still there, trying to break past the woman whose heart had grown cold. But just as quickly as the doubt flashed in her eyes, it was gone. She shook her head, started back toward the door leading out of the room.

"I killed her."

Aisha paused at the sound of my voice, her back still to me.

"I couldn't bare to watch her another second. Her suffering ... it was too much. You and your brother had left—to get some coffee or to take a nap in the lobby, I don't remember which—and I was alone with her and I just wanted the suffering to end."

Aisha turned, slowly, her glare burning into me.

"What did you do?"

"I used a syringe. I found a vein in my arm and I filled that syringe with my blood and I inserted that blood into one of her veins. I had the same thought as you did—I thought that I could somehow save her. I'd been so hesitant, knowing in my heart that it wouldn't work, but I couldn't live with myself if I didn't at least try."

She took a slow, unsteady step toward me. When she spoke, her voice was barely a whisper.

"What happened?"

"At first nothing. A whole minute passed and there was no change. Then another minute passed and there was still nothing. I thought maybe the blood wouldn't do anything after all. Or I thought maybe I needed to give her more. Then ... then she began convulsing. Violently. I tried to hold her down, tried to calm her, but she wouldn't stop. She started foaming at the mouth. The blood vessels in her eyes burst. She had a seizure right there in my arms. I called for help, and the doctors and nurses came running. They did what they could to save her, but it was no use. Minutes later you and your brother arrived. Do you remember?"

Aisha nodded, the movement so slight it was almost imperceptible.

"You ... you looked stricken. I thought you were blaming yourself for not doing anything. I thought ... I thought that's why you were so upset."

"No. The reason was because I *had* done something. I killed her."

"But she was dying. If anything, you put her out of her misery."

"I didn't see it like that at the time. All I knew was that I had somehow accelerated her death. That's why I didn't stay for the funeral. Not after what I'd done. Especially not after what I had done to Prometheus."

"You murdered him, didn't you?"

"He had killed too many people. I figured he deserved to die."

Aisha said nothing. She just stared at me. Again I thought I saw the little girl in her eyes, the one that knew the difference between right and wrong. But then she shook her head.

"It may not have worked for Mom, but it *will* work. I'll make sure of that."

She turned, having finally steeled herself, and exited the room.

I was alone.

Until, a minute later, he appeared again. Temple. He stepped inside the room and slowly approached me. There was something familiar about him, a distant smoky odor. Then he was standing beside me, in the same spot Aisha had stood just minutes before, and without a word he reached up and pulled the mask off his head.

Holding the mask at his side, Darrell smiled down at me.

"Hey there, brother."

62

have to hand it to you, Eli, being Temple must have been a pain in the ass. It's one thing to have to run around the city saving people, but in *this* getup?"

Darrell shook his head, held up the mask.

"How are you even supposed to see out of this thing at night?"

Just like with Aisha, I said nothing at first. I stared back at Darrell, trying to figure out where this new piece of the puzzle fit.

Darrell grinned.

"Didn't expect to see me again so soon, did you?"

I said nothing.

Darrell frowned.

"Gonna play it tough, huh? All right. So let me get right to the chase. My mother? Vanessa Clark. Does that name ring a bell?"

It did. Of course it did. My father had told me the story. About the young woman he'd saved from the alleyway, the one who let him stay in her apartment and who helped make the first outfit. He had fallen for her, that much was obvious, but he had left ...

"How?"

Darrell frowned again.

"What do you mean, *how*? You had children. You know how it works."

"But my father never—"

"He did."

"No, he—"

"*He did*. The last night they were together. He took advantage of her and left her and never returned. Nine months later I arrived."

I just stared at him.

Darrell said, "She died giving birth to me. There was no other family to take care of me—well, there were her parents, which I guess were my grandparents, but they wanted nothing to do with a bastard grandchild—so I ended up in an orphanage. But I didn't stay there long. I ran away and lived out on the streets. Tell me, Eli, at what age did you start to realize you weren't like other children?"

I said nothing.

"For me it was three years old. That's when I first sensed him."

"Who?"

"Our father."

Our father. The phrase sent a chill down my spine.

Darrell studied my face, searching for any clue the surprise no doubt in my eyes was false.

"That's the one, well, *power* you never had, isn't it? The ability to sense others like yourself. Granted, there aren't many of us. For me it was just our father, and then you, of course. Then when you got older and had children, I was able to sense your son. Not your daughter, I'm afraid—Aisha wasn't given the same abilities we have, but I learned that she possessed an uncanny ambitiousness. Seriously, Eli, you should be proud of your daughter. Most people claim to be ambitious, but few actually follow through with their ambitions. Your daughter has always been determined to save the world, and it's going to happen."

Darrell tossed the mask aside, leaned closer to me.

"In case you haven't figured it out yet, Eli, your daughter hates you. She admitted to me it started on the night her mother died, but I wonder if it started even sooner. There was a time when she was just a girl she got very sick and was in a lot of pain. And you did nothing to help her other than take her to the doctor. Granted, there really wasn't much for you to do, but try to see it from her perspective. Her father and her brother never get sick. They get hurt, yes, but they heal immediately. But Aisha and her mother get sick. They get hurt and it takes a while for them to heal. It's a theory of mine, but I think her resentment toward you started in her childhood."

Darrell grinned at me again, patting me lightly on the head.

"My mother kept a journal. That's how I knew about our father. My grandparents had kept it along with some of her stuff in the attic. I found it after I'd killed them. In the journal my mother wrote about her encounter with our father. It finally made sense who this man was. And it became a game—I would sense him on one side of the city and I would race there to watch him save someone or fight criminals. Not too longer after, of course, I began to sense you. You were farther away, but you were stationary. I was young, just a boy, but I was streetwise and I knew exactly what had happened. I knew you were my brother. That's when I made my way up north to find you in your little town, and I watched you. What's more, I watched your mother and your grandparents. I realized your mother was still in contact with our father. I realized our father had sent her away—had sent *you* away—to keep you both safe. And this realization made me furious. So furious, in fact, one day I decided to do something about it."

"You were the boy outside the store."

Darrell nodded.

I said, "You ... I had never seen you before. It was such a small town, everybody knew everybody else, but you ... were an outsider. And you were just there, waiting for me. Because you wanted to beat me up."

"I wanted to do more than beat you up. Truth is, I wanted to kill you."

"Thanks to you, my mother contacted my father and he brought us back to the city. We were a proper family again."

"I know. Sorta backfired on me, didn't it? Oh well, I suppose it was meant to be. I still followed your father from time to time, though. I followed you as well. It became an obsession."

"For what reason?"

Darrell shrugged.

"Boredom, mostly? Truth is, I can't even remember. Sure, I was jealous at first, but the more I thought about it, I realized I didn't want to be Temple. Too much responsibility. Too much work. And then before I knew it the day came when your father decided it was time for him to pass on the mask to you. So when he left, of course I followed him."

"Did you kill him?"

"Not right away. I bided my time. He didn't even seem to know where he wanted to go at first. He bought a car—a 1970 Dodge Charger, surprise, surprise—and took off driving across the country. It was almost a year before he ended up in Colorado. Before he ended up in Harper and found the land cheap enough and started building that cabin. Even then I wasn't sure what I wanted to do, but I watched him from a distance. I waited until he had finished the cabin, and then I followed him back to New York where he spoke with you."

"He told me about Harper. He told me about the cabin. He told me that one day I would get tired of being Temple and would want to leave all of it behind, and that I was more than welcome to stay with him when that day came."

Darrell nodded again.

"Yes, that's what I assumed he told you. Once he returned to the cabin, I realized that he meant to stay there. I was tired of waiting, so I approached him. He must have been surprised, as he was in the middle of nowhere. But then … he recognized me. Or not me so much as my mother—our eyes, he said, were the same. I told him about what I knew. About how he had taken advantage of my mother. His face fell when he heard this. He even started to tear up. He claimed that it wasn't true. That yes, they had made love once, but that that was it. He said he knew he could not stay with my mother, that her family would never forgive her if she married a black man, and so he left. He said he had wanted to stay more than anything, but for her he left. He said he thought about her often, a couple times even tried to track her down, but never saw her again. When I told him what happened, how I was his child, he hugged me. Can you believe that, Eli? He *hugged* me."

Darrell stared past me, as if into a distance only he could see. Maybe he was picturing that day, standing alone by the cabin with my father. The sky clear, the sun bright. The air so crisp it was like an illusion.

"Remember that hate I mentioned? The one that's been growing inside Aisha ever since she was a girl? I'd had the same kind of hate growing inside me. Hatred toward our father, mostly, but also hatred toward you. Because *I* should have been the one who had a mother. *I* should have been the one to take the mask once our father decided it was time to give it up."

This contradicted what Darrell had said only minutes ago, but I didn't think it mattered. Whether or not he was jealous of me becoming Temple instead of him, the simple fact remained: he had killed our father.

"What did you do?"

"When he hugged me, I didn't do anything at first. I just let him hug me. Then when he stepped back, smiling at me, wiping the tears from his eyes, the anger bubbling inside me became too great. I lashed out at him. He wasn't expecting it, but as you know, that didn't matter. His senses were heightened enough he could see what I planned to do even before I did it. And that would have been just fine for anybody else, but I was his son. I had the same DNA and I knew exactly how he thought, so while I made it seem like I was going to do one thing, I did another. It caught him completely off guard. I got in a position where I had a tight grip on his throat. And I squeezed. I squeezed so hard eventually he stopped trying to fight me. I squeezed so hard eventually he just lay motionless. I squeezed until I'd crushed his windpipe. I wanted to make sure his body would not be able to heal. I wanted to make sure he was dead."

"Then what did you do?"

"I doused him with gasoline and burned his body. Part of me worried that even with a crushed windpipe he might somehow return from the dead. So I burned him until all that was left were bones, and then I took those bones and I scattered them up in the mountains. I stayed at the cabin for a few years. I always sensed you out east, and part of me wanted to go find you, but I kept telling myself it wasn't time. In retrospect, I think I was scared. The last time I had faced off against you, you were just a boy. Now you were a man. I didn't think I could defeat you so easily. Until I then sensed someone else just like me."

"James."

"Yes. Once you had a son—and a daughter too, as it turned out—I knew that someday you would leave the city. You would become an old man, just like your father, and you would pass the mask on to your son. And I knew that when that day came, it would be time for us to finally meet."

"Were you ever even in Vietnam?"

"No. But I read about the war. I knew you had gone to the war, and I wanted there to be some kind of, well, shared experience between us. I knew you would eventually leave home, and I figured you would end up in Harper. After all, by then I had come to understand why our father decided to live in the middle of nowhere. After being Temple so long, I figured you would want to do the same. Of course, I also knew that when you did show up, all that you'd find would be an empty cabin, long abandoned. There would be no trace of our father. But I suspected you might stay anyhow. That's why I bought that house and opened the store. I wanted to be there for when you arrived. Had you gone elsewhere, I could have easily closed up shop and followed you. But you did come to Harper. And we ... we became friends."

"Your children and grandchildren. Do they even exist?"

"None of it existed, Eli. Just like my gimp leg and my need to use that cane, they were created just for you."

"But why? Why go to all that trouble?"

"Truthfully, I have no idea. My ultimate goal has always been to see you die. Well, okay, maybe that's not true. Maybe not at first. But after I killed our father? That's when it started. When I realized that I *liked* having that power. Which was odd, because I hadn't felt that way when I killed my grandparents, though in retrospect I think it's because they were just ordinary people. They weren't special like our father. So I knew in the back of my head that you were always going to die. I just didn't know how I was going to go about it. You had cut yourself off from the rest of the world, but I hadn't. I kept tabs on your son and daughter. I was impressed by your daughter and all she wanted to do. And I saw an opportunity. I had you believe I never left Harper, but I did often. I went to Manhattan to watch your daughter and son. And during one of my trips, I realized that your son and daughter were already being watched. It took me a while to figure out by whom, and by then I started doing research of my own. I learned about Homeland Security's special task force to watch over your family, and I learned about Roger, and after even more research I figured out who Roger really was. And so I had an idea, something I thought might appeal to both your daughter and to Roger. And guess what, Eli—it did. The idea of using Temple's DNA to further both of their agendas appealed to them just fine, and now here we are, you and I."

"Why not take me out by yourself? Why have Roger's men come do it?"

"Because killing you was never part of the plan. In fact, much of this hasn't been part of the plan. This wasn't supposed to happen for at least another six months, but your son got nosy and had to be taken care of. And because of that, it accelerated everything. Despite your age and the fact you were retired, you were still viewed as a threat. Roger wanted to make sure you were neutralized, so that's why I put together that little test."

"What little test?"

"The fox. I had to bring you down off the hill somehow. I knew the fox would get you to come down, because naturally you'd want to see what you could do to save it. You'd take it to your vet friend over in Durango, and on your way back you would swing by to see me, as you always did. And when you did arrive, what did you find?"

"Those two punks with the motorcycles."

Darrell laughed.

"Yes, they were fun, weren't they? Those two kids were always stopping by the store. I told them I wanted to play a prank on a friend of mine. I even offered them one hundred dollars each. They did a splendid job, didn't they?"

At first I wasn't sure what job it was they were supposed to do, but then it hit me. Of course. What was the one thing that would prove, at least from an outside perspective, that my powers had faded?

"I flinched."

Darrell nodded.

"Exactly. But in retrospect, I realize now that you flinched on purpose. Because that was what you were expected to do. You thought the situation was real. You didn't want it to escalate any further than it already had. That's why the team that came for you that night didn't succeed. They expected your powers had faded. But then you showed up at my house, and I wasn't sure what to do."

"You did look surprised, but I figured the surprise was simply because I'd shown up in the middle of the night."

"While you were in the shower, I contacted Roger. I told him you were at my house and asked what he wanted me to do. I asked him if I should keep you there, but he said no. He didn't want to have a new team arrive with civilians in the area, as that would cause a scene. I told him I thought you were going to head back to New York. He said that would be fine. He said he would make it work. And, well, I guess in a way he did make it work. You're here, after all. Not quite the plan, as I had said, but the end result was the same."

"Now what?"

Darrell glanced toward the door.

"Now I think it's time for me to go. Roger's techs should be in here soon."

"What do you get out of this, anyway? What's your end game?"

"You. Simply seeing you dead. Like I told you, it's that hate and resentment I've felt in my own heart all these decades. Your death—*Temple's* death—is all it needs to be satisfied. Money, power—I don't care about any of that. Let Roger and your daughter enjoy all the success."

"What if they double-cross you? After all, if they need my DNA, why not just take yours?"

"The thought has entered my mind. But I have an understanding with Roger and your daughter. I can confidently say at this point I don't believe that will be a problem. Of course, after all their testing, they might find that none of it works. That's always a possibility, and then they might want to dispose of me in the same way—after all, in terms of the Xerox Effect that Roger likes to talk about, I'm the closest to the original—but by then I plan to be long gone."

There was a knock at the door. A man in long white lab coat entered.

Darrell said, "That's my cue."

"'Brother from another mother.' It was always there, right in front of me. Just as you always said you never knew your old man."

Darrell smiled.

"The craziest part? You were actually a good friend. There were times when I even debated telling you the truth. But I knew that if I did that, I would be betraying not just myself, but my mother."

"You did all this for your mother? She would be so proud."

The smile in Darrell's eyes faded. He glared hard at me for a long second, and then without another word he turned and started toward the door and the doctor holding it open. He only paused when I called out to him.

"Before you go, Darrell, don't forget the key to the Charger."

He turned back to me, frowning. When his gaze shifted toward the table against the wall, his frowned deepened.

"What is that?"

"It's a car key. You mean to tell me you don't remember what they look like?"

"Not the key. Whose watch is that?"

"You mean the expensive gold Rolex? It's mine."

He stared hard at the table and the car key and the watch for a long moment. Then his gaze focused on me.

"You never wear a watch."

Now it was my turn to smile.

"You're right. The watch isn't mine. I'm just borrowing it from a friend."

I looked at the camera positioned on the tripod. There was a chance Roman and his men had not been able to track the watch to this location. There was a chance Nate had not been able to hack into the system and was not watching me now, waiting for the signal. Only one way to tell.

I shouted, "Now!"

A second later, the lights went out.

63

Complete darkness. Everything had gone dark, even the machines surrounding me. They had gone silent, too. Everything was silent for a second until Darrell shouted for the man to get Roger and then, a second later, the emergency lights kicked on. The emergency lights weren't nearly as blinding as the normal lights, but it was still bright enough to see the shocked expression on the man's face.

An alarm went off. It was impossible to say what kind of alarm it was—fire, intruder, or just emergency—but a heavy screeching started up, echoing first in the hallway and then in the room itself. Strobes immediately followed, and as Darrell started for the door, it looked as if he was moving in slow motion.

Darrell pushed the man out into the hallway. He turned back to glare at me.

I smiled.

Past him, somewhere in the hallway, came gunfire. And shouting. And more gunfire.

Darrell exited the room.

Beyond the closed door, the gunfire and shouting continued, only now muffled.

A minute passed.

The strobes kept going and the alarm kept blaring and the shouting and gunfire became intermittent. I struggled with the metal clamps keeping my wrists and ankles bound, but there was no give. Like Roger had said, even James couldn't break them, and he had been much younger and stronger than me.

The door was flung open and someone entered, a weapon in his hand. Just like Darrell, he seemed to move in slow motion, so I easily watched as he ran toward me, raising his weapon. Halfway to me, though, a gunshot sounded out and his body suddenly stopped, his eyes going wide, his mouth dropping open. He stood motionless for a second, and then fell forward to the ground.

A man standing in the doorway lowered his weapon. He glanced back out the hallway, looked left and right, shouted something in Ukrainian, and then entered the room. He stepped over the man he'd shot like the man didn't exist, like he was only an afterthought, and then he was standing right beside me.

He raised his gun and placed the barrel against my head.

"So easy."

"Don't."

This was from Roman, stepping into the room. He had an H&K MP5 strapped over his shoulder. He glanced at the body on the ground and then glanced around the room and spotted his watch and made his way over to the table. He slipped the watch around his wrist, stared down at it as if to check the time, and then came over to the table, withdrawing his handgun holstered to his belt.

Roman pushed past the man and pressed the cold barrel of his gun into my chest, right above my heart.

"We shoot him, we shoot him here. This way the superman dies slowly. Painfully. A headshot will serve no purpose other than immediate death. Is that what we want, Ivan? Do we want immediate death?"

Ivan shook his head.

"No, we do not."

"That is right, we do not want immediate death for our friend here."

I said, "Have you found the warheads?"

The barrel didn't waver from its place over my heart.

Roman said, "My men are searching for them as we speak."

"Where are we?"

"A warehouse in Tribeca. The basement of a warehouse, to be exact. We will find the warheads."

"What about Roger Davidson?"

Roman said nothing.

"You need to cut me loose. I need to get in contact with Nate and Agent Njeim as soon as possible. If Nate hacked into this building's system, then he's hacked into the surrounding area. He'll see if Roger tries to leave."

Roman stared at me for another couple of seconds while the strobes kept flickering and the alarm kept blaring and, outside in the hallway, the gunfire and shouting continued.

Finally, the barrel of the gun lifted from my chest as Roman stepped back. He shifted his gaze to take in the rest of the table.

He asked Ivan, "You have a flashlight?"

Ivan pulled out a small flashlight and flicked it on. Roman motioned with his head for Ivan to inspect the table. Ivan glanced under the table and then stepped back and nodded.

"The clamps can be loosened underneath."

Roman said, "Do it."

Ivan didn't look happy about it, but he did as his boss instructed.

Stepping onto the concrete floor, I looked first at Roman, then at Ivan.

"What about a weapon?"

Roman shook his head and started for the door, Ivan following close behind.

"Find your own, superman."

Their weapons raised, they entered the hallway, and a whole new cacophony of gunfire started up.

64

didn't bother with socks or a T-shirt. I threw on the pair of jeans and the sweatshirt and boots and started toward the door but paused and turned and ran back to the table. I snatched the car key and stuffed it in my pocket and headed back toward the door, bending and scooping up the dead man's gun as I went.

The gun was a Glock 9mm. I ejected the magazine to check how many rounds were left—eight—and then I slammed the magazine back in and jacked the slide and placed my hand on the doorknob. There was still gunfire out there, though it was sporadic. The last thing I wanted to do now was step out into a frenzy of flying bullets.

A moment passed and there was a lull. I tore open the door and stepped out. I took in the mayhem in an instant: the dead bodies on the ground, the alive bodies moving down the hallway. I raised the Glock but paused when I realized the two men headed toward me were Roman's. They raised their weapons too but then realized I wasn't a target and continued past me, jogging at almost a leisurely pace.

I watched as the men turned a corner. From that direction,

more gunfire started up. I glanced at the bodies on the ground and spotted an MP5 from one of Roman's fallen men. I bent and scooped it up as I started down the hallway. Stepping over dead bodies and scattered pieces of concrete.

I paused at the end of the hallway to peek around the corner. Nothing but two more dead bodies. These wore white lab coats. Roger's techs. Not quite Roger's soldiers, but still I didn't feel sorry for them.

I spotted a camera toward the ceiling. I had to assume Nate was already in the system and monitoring the action. He no doubt saw me, but there was no way for us to communicate.

I continued down the hallway. The gunfire was coming from behind me. Maybe I'd have to head back that way. Still, for some reason, this felt like the right direction to go.

I turned the corner and found three more bodies. One Roman's, two Roger's. I hurried past them toward the end of the hallway and turned another corner.

And there stood Aisha.

She had a gun in her hands, aimed right at me.

I hesitated, and that allowed her the extra second to pull the trigger.

The bullet tore into my stomach.

I stumbled back, tripped over one of the dead bodies, and fell to the ground. The Glock fell from my hand, clattered away.

Aisha advanced. The gun in her hands shook, whether from adrenaline or fear, it was impossible to tell. Had she been in more control of her functions, that first bullet may have hit my head or my heart. As it was, her nerves sent the bullet low.

She stepped up close. Aimed the gun at my face.

"You were lying."

A slight tremor in her voice, but otherwise her eyes were full of resolve.

"You didn't do anything to help save her."

"I did."

From the corner of my eye, I saw the Glock. Maybe four feet away.

"I did exactly as I told you. I tried to save her, but it didn't work."

Her head started shaking slowly from side to side.

"No. That ... that's not possible."

Gunfire exploded farther up the hallway. It was enough to cause Aisha to glance up, the gun suddenly unsteady in her hands, and that extra second gave me the chance to reach out and grab the Glock. I aimed it up at her as she steadied the gun in her hands, the barrel once again pointed at me.

Neither one of us fired. This seemed to surprise Aisha, whose expression relayed that she had expected to die just then. Her grip tightened around the barrel of the gun. Her eyes hardened.

"You missed your chance."

I shook my head.

"I can't kill you. You're my daughter. But that doesn't mean I won't stop someone else from shooting you instead."

Confusion filled Aisha's face. Then she sensed movement behind her and spun right as Agent Njeim fired a round into her leg. Aisha screamed, dropping her gun, and fell to the ground.

Already my body was healing itself from the bullet wound. Unfortunately, the bullet was still in my stomach.

Noticing this, Agent Njeim slipped out her switchblade and tossed it to me.

I popped the blade and dug it into my stomach. A couple seconds, that's all it took, and then I'd worked the bullet out enough for me to pluck it out with two fingers and fling it away. I wiped the blade off on my pants and closed it and handed it back to Agent Njeim.

She said, "Keep it."

I rose to my feet, slipping the knife into my pocket.

"The warheads?"

"Nate's still looking for them."

She unclipped a small radio from her belt and handed it to me.

I hit the talk button.

"Nate?"

Brief static, and then he spoke.

"That looked pretty nasty."

I glanced up at the security camera farther down the hallway. Watching it, I spoke into the radio.

"Any word on the warheads?"

"I'm tracking Roger and two of his men right now. They're in a van headed toward the river. Whether they have both warheads, I can't say for sure, but nobody else has left the warehouse."

As we were in Tribeca, that would be the Hudson River. I thought about it for a moment. If they were headed toward the Hudson, there was a chance they would be headed toward the Holland Tunnel. But that wouldn't make sense. Unless …

I spoke again into the radio.

"Nate, where are they now?"

A brief pause on Nate's end as his fingers no doubt flew over his keyboard.

"They're headed to the docks. Why … why do you think they're headed to the docks?"

I glanced down at Aisha.

"Do you know what Roger plans to do?"

She just glared up at me, her face twisted in pain.

I thought about it again, trying to remember everything

Roger had told me, not just tonight but since I first met him twenty-four hours ago. There was one thing that kept going through my head. How Roger intended to start a war, but how he claimed he wasn't a monster, that he didn't want to kill anyone. Which meant …

I asked Agent Njeim, "Is Roman on this frequency?"

"He should be."

I hit the talk button again.

"Roman, can you hear me?"

Silence for a moment, and then Roman answered.

"I heard—the warheads are headed toward the river. My men are on the way."

"Hold off on that."

A brief pause.

"Why?"

"You said earlier you have access to a helicopter?"

Another brief pause.

"I do, yes."

"How long before you can get it here?"

"No more than ten minutes."

"Get it. Also a parachute."

I turned to Agent Njeim.

"Could a helicopter land on the roof of this warehouse?"

She thought it over for a moment.

"It probably could, yes."

I spoke into the radio again.

"Roman, get the helicopter here ASAP. Have it land on the roof."

"What is this about, superman?"

"I'll tell you once the helicopter gets here. Make sure it's quick."

I turned back to Agent Njeim.

She said, "Let me come with you."

"No. You need to keep an eye on my daughter. And you and Nate need to try to collect as much evidence as possible. There's a chance this may not turn out like we hope, but at the very least you can get evidence to use against Roger and Monarch. Find out who the investors are, any research, stuff like that. Find *something* to try to clear your name."

"What are you going to do?"

"Try to stop Roger."

"But do you even know what his target is?"

"Yes. The Statue of Liberty."

65

I took the extra radio and headed through the corridors toward the stairs. Nate, watching from wherever he was hunkered down with his laptop, guided me. I found the stairs and started up to ground level. I headed up to the second floor, then the third. I turned the corner for the stairs leading to the fourth floor when suddenly I went sprawling back toward the floor.

I landed on my back and immediately rolled to the side and sprang to my feet, but Darrell was right there in front of me, having already advanced from where he'd been on the stairs to kick me in the chest. I raised the gun to fire at him, but he swatted it from my grip. The Glock clattered across the floor. I went for the MP5 strapped over my shoulder but Darrell stepped in close, elbowed me in the face. I stumbled back, and he grabbed the MP5 and yanked the strap from off my shoulder. I expected him to fire several bursts into my chest, but he tossed the MP5 away. I watched it skid across the concrete floor and then looked back at him.

Darrell said, "I can't let you stop him."

The radio on my belt crackled, and Nate's voice sounded.

"Mr. Shepherd, I've lost track of you. Are you okay?"

I held Darrell's gaze.

"I answer this and tell him no, and there will be men here within seconds."

"Then don't tell him anything."

Darrell took a step toward me.

"Don't you ever wonder about that day when we were boys? Had you known your true potential then, would I have beaten you so badly?"

I gauged the distance to the Glock, which was maybe twenty yards away. Only it was maybe fifteen yards from Darrell. Which meant if I broke for it, Darrell would likely beat me. The same with the MP5, which lay a bit farther away.

The radio crackled again.

"Mr. Shepherd?"

Darrell said, "Roger may be crazy, but this needs to happen."

"I thought you didn't care about Roger's plan."

"I don't. But I do care about Temple not being able to stop him."

The space between us was less than ten yards. I could charge Darrell, but it wouldn't do much good. Even if I attempted to feint a punch or kick, his heightened senses would catch it and he would block me. The same if he charged me. We were brothers, which mean we shared the same strange DNA.

The radio crackled once again, only this time it was Roman's voice that came through.

"Superman, where are you?"

Darrell said, "Looks like you're going to miss your ride."

I started toward the stairwell leading up to the fifth floor. I didn't even bother looking at Darrell, who stood silent for a moment, stunned. He certainly hadn't been expecting this. The truth was, I hadn't been expecting to do it. I was allowing my body to move on autopilot. What happened next would not be something I planned.

As I stepped past Darrell, he reached out to grab my neck. I ducked and spun and threw my elbow into his throat. He stumbled back, issuing a guttural sound, and I dove for the Glock. I hit the concrete hard but managed to grab hold of the rubber grip, and I rolled and fired at Darrell who was already hurrying toward the stairwell. Two bullets caught him in the back but he didn't slow, just kept going. Not up the stairs, but down.

This was what he wanted—for me to make the decision, Darrell or Roger.

I climbed to my feet, keeping the gun aimed with my right hand as I withdrew the radio with the other.

"Nate, Darrell is headed down to the third floor. Follow him. Don't let him escape. Roman, I'm headed up now."

I scooped up the MP5 from the floor, threw the strap over my shoulder, and started up the stairs.

The helicopter was waiting on the roof. The first thing that struck me was that it was painted red. And that there was a Caduceus—a short staff entwined by two serpents, wings splayed above them—inside a six-pronged cross.

I poked my head inside. Roman sat the controls, along with another one of his men as the copilot. A third man waited in the back.

I said, "This is a medical transport chopper. This is for emergencies."

Roman was already moving the instruments around on the dash. The engine started up, the rotors beginning to turn.

He called back, "Is this not an emergency?"

"Where did you get it?"

"I know people. Hey, you wanted a helicopter ASAP, yes?"

I climbed up into the chopper and slid the side door closed. A large black pack sat on the floor. I picked up the pack and hefted it.

Roman said, "Do not worry—there is a parachute inside."

He glanced back at me.

"I do not want to kill you just yet."

He pulled back on the stick to lift us into the air.

The chopper's communications were patched into Nate, who confirmed that Roger and his men had gotten on a boat at the docks and, from what he could tell, they were headed toward Liberty Island. It didn't take long by boat to reach the island on a normal day, but, fortunately, the river was choppy with ice. They needed to take their time. Plus, I suspected they didn't want to draw too much attention. From what Nate said, they were going without any running lights.

I told Roman to take us up as high as he could. I said that I didn't want to stay too low, in case the clatter of the rotors gave us away. I'd played with the idea of flying low, using a sniper rifle to take out Roger and his men, but there was no telling what Roger might plan to do then.

And so we rose, higher and higher above the city. Roman understood the reason we didn't want to get too close and waited to move us toward the Hudson until we were at least 3,000 feet, and still he kept rising. There was some cloud cover, which made it nearly impossible to track the boat out on the river. The man beside me gave me his night vision scope. It took several seconds before I spotted the boat.

It was already halfway to Liberty Island.

I told Roman to go up even higher and to try to hover above the island. I wanted to come at the boat head on if possible. It took two minutes, and then we were in position. Roman kept the chopper in a hover. By that point, I had strapped on the parachute. It had been over forty years since I last made a jump. I figured the basic principles still applied.

Before I slid open the side door and let in the roar of the rotors, Roman shouted at me.

"Superman! Do not fuck this up!"

I slid open the door, and as expected the helicopter's rotors raged sound at us. I hoped we were high up enough that Roger and his men didn't hear us from down on the boat. Hopefully, they were dealing with their own engine, and besides, there was the wind whipping into their faces.

I didn't need the night vision scope anymore. My eyes had adjusted just fine. Even at this distance. I hadn't let the boat leave my sight all this time.

I handed my headpiece to the man in the seat beside me. I made sure the Glock—which was now fully loaded—was holstered, just as I made sure the MP5 was secured.

I closed my eyes, took a breath, and jumped.

66

Just like in my dreams, I was flying. Only that wasn't right. In my dreams, I had control. Here I was just falling. The wind whipping at my face. I wasn't wearing goggles, so part of me wanted to close my eyes, while another part wanted to keep the distant spot that was the boat in sight. Then that spot grew larger and larger, and when I was 1,000 feet away, I pulled the cord.

An opening chute is never a pleasant experience. That was one of the things I learned from my time in Vietnam. The chute opens, grabs the air, and suddenly your momentum halts. It's enough to break your neck if you're not careful.

There was wind blowing across the river, so I needed to be conscious of that as I used the straps to steer toward the boat. Some of the water was frozen, though in pieces, and the boat was slowly making its way through the slush. I spotted two men out on the deck, both carrying weapons. So far it didn't seem like either one noticed me.

That would change soon. In seconds, really. I didn't want to let go of one of the straps, as that would cause me to lose control of the chute. At the same time, I needed to grab one of my weapons. If I was lucky, I could take out both lookouts before even landing on the boat. Of course, after I fired my first round, the second lookout would be alerted, as would everyone else on the boat. In that instant, I would lose the element of surprise.

When I was less than five hundred feet away, a gust of wind knocked into me. I pulled at the straps to stay on course. The wind had pushed me toward the starboard side of the boat, and I needed to steer back. I decided to loop around, coming at the boat from the rear. One of the lookouts was there, watching everywhere but the sky. But then he must have heard the rippling of the parachute, or maybe an echo of the helicopter hovering in the sky, because he tilted his gaze up at me. For an instant there was surprise in his face. Then he raised his weapon.

I let go of the strap and grabbed the Glock and brought it out and fired a single round.

The man's head snapped back as the bullet smashed through his nose.

Another gust of wind hit me, carrying me now off to the right. I didn't want to risk dropping the Glock, but I couldn't afford not to steer the chute, so with the Glock in hand I grabbed for the loose strap.

Two hundred feet away.

The other lookout hurried to the back. Saw his dead counterpart, then looked up at me as I came in fast.

I'd grabbed the loose strap at the last moment and managed to give it enough pull that I didn't land right in the water. Still, I ended up on the edge of the boat, right on the stern. I almost lost my balance and fell over, but another gust pushed the parachute forward a bit. The second lookout fired at me. I ducked and returned fire, three rounds, two of which landed in his chest.

My feet now planted on the boat's deck, I undid the straps and threw the pack off as another man stepped out from inside the cabin.

He never had a chance.

I dropped him as I advanced, placing a bullet in his forehead. I stepped over him and into the cabin. The lights were off, but that didn't matter. I spotted Roger at once. Also the warheads. Also Abu Muhammad al-Naser. Al-Naser lay on the deck of the cabin, ankles bound, wrists bound behind his back. He had duct tape over his mouth.

Roger aimed a gun at me with his right hand, while he held something black and small in his left hand. A detonator.

"I'll blow us both up."

I held the Glock on him.

"What makes you think I care? Like you said, I'm an old man. I have nothing. My son and his family are dead. Sanchez is dead. My daughter hates my guts. And my dog—*you* killed my dog. I have nothing to live for except to make sure you don't succeed."

Because nobody was now controlling the boat, we were no longer moving forward. Just drifting in the water among the pieces of ice. Behind Roger, through the window, the Statue of Liberty stood 1,500 yards away.

When Roger spoke next, his voice was soft, almost reflective.

"Temple has always been a curse on my family."

"It's too late, Roger. We have evidence on Monarch. We know exactly what you plan to do. The president will see it soon, if he hasn't seen it already. Even if you manage to follow through with your plan, it won't do anything other than to destroy a national landmark."

Roger's face was blank at first. Then he smiled, barked out a desperate laugh.

"Then what should I do? If what you say is true, it's all over for me."

He raised the detonator.

"This is already primed. I set it the moment you landed. I let go of this button, the warheads explode."

Roger glanced down at al-Naser, shook his head.

"It would have been perfect. *Everything* would have been perfect."

He was a man coming to a conclusion, one he had known was there but didn't want to accept. Now he had begun to realize there were no other options. Which meant I had no other choice. There was no saving al-Naser, even if I wanted to save him. So I shot Roger in the face—one perfectly placed bullet, right between the eyes—turned and sprinted toward the side of the boat. It was only a second, maybe two, but it was enough for me to try to escape. Roger's mental capacity wouldn't be enough for him to let up on the detonator on his own. With a bullet in his brain, there would be no more mental functioning. It would all come down to gravity.

I didn't look back. I ran and jumped off the side of the boat —as behind me the world exploded.

67

For the first second after I jumped from the boat, nothing happened. I was weightless. Then the blast came and its shockwave propelled me forward at such great speed I had no control. I landed headfirst into one of the pieces of ice floating on the water. Consciousness began to ebb and flow. My body lay on those pieces of ice, but the explosion had also caused the water to begin rocking and those pieces of ice broke apart and my body slipped down into the water. I kicked my legs and scrambled with my hands at the ice above me, but it seemed no matter how hard I tried there was no escape. My consciousness kept ebbing and flowing, and I wasn't sure if the darkness around me was from the night and deep water or from my mind losing focus. And so I sank, deeper and deeper, the darkness scrambling to take hold.

Thumping overhead. Bright lights. My body still sinking toward that darkness, but I was half-aware of noise above the water. Somebody splashed down into it. Somebody looking around the darkness and then spotting me and swimming hard to reach me. Somebody reaching out a hand. And me, in the last few seconds before the darkness took over, reaching out my hand to grip his.

———

A flash of being pulled up out of the water. The clatter of rotor blades. Being laid out flat on the vibrating floor. Somebody pounding on my chest. Somebody else breathing into my mouth. Again, and again, and again. Until, finally, I coughed up water and was able to breathe again. Then Roman shouting to give me the shot. The shot? A needle in my neck, just like back at Central Park. A second later, darkness again.

68

A hand slapped my face.

I jerked my head up, blinking away the darkness.

I couldn't move. I sat in a chair, naked except for my underwear, and I couldn't move. My legs secured tightly to the chair legs. My wrists and arms secured tightly behind my back. Not with ropes or straps, but with chains.

Roman stood in front of me, a gun at his side. Beyond him were two of his men. We were in a small room, the walls cinderblock, the floor concrete. Maybe another warehouse. Another basement. It didn't matter. Standing off to the side were two more of Roman's men. Each was armed with MP5s. All aimed the MP5s at me.

"Glad you are still alive."

Roman's voice was flat.

"I was worried we had lost you in the water."

I looked around the room once again before meeting his gaze.

"You saved me?"

"I did."

"Why?"

"Because like I told you before—"

He leaned in close, placed the barrel of his gun against my chest.

"—I am the one who gets to kill you."

He said nothing else after that. He just pulled the trigger. Three times. The first bullet pierced my heart. As did the second bullet. As did the third. Each of them exited through my back. My body convulsed with each round.

I stared up at Roman, my mouth slightly agape. But there was nothing for me to say even if I could speak. That blackness that had almost claimed me in the river started to come again. The edges of my vision blurring. Darkening.

For the first time Roman's stoic expression changed.

He smiled.

"Superman is dead."

My head dropped as the blackness rushed in.

69

Roman stepped back. He tilted his head from side to side, stretching the muscles. He turned away and holstered his gun and started for the door.

"Make sure to collect the shell casings."

His men were silent for a moment. Then one of them spoke.

"What about the body?"

"Dispose of it in any way you see fit. Cut it up into a thousand pieces. Burn it. Soak it in acid. I do not care. Just make sure the place is spotless when you are done."

He continued toward the door. His footsteps were strangely loud for some reason. Maybe not to him, or to his men, but they were to me. Each footstep like a firework explosion. I heard it in the blackness as my body ... as my body healed itself.

Because the three bullets had torn my heart apart, my heart no longer beat, hence there was no way for blood to flow through my body. But for some reason, this wasn't the case. My blood was working overtime, more so than it ever had before.

Within seconds, it had repaired my heart—which immediately began beating again. The itching sensation was everywhere. Healing my chest and back, yes, but also every other scratch on my body.

It all happened in the course of seconds, and then I breathed in air as if for the first time.

Roman, almost to the door now, paused.

Without even seeing him, I knew this. Just as I knew the four other men were now watching me. Suddenly my senses had become heightened more than they ever had before, even during my prime. I heard each individual man's breathing, just as I heard each individual man's heartbeat. The one to the right of me had an irregular heartbeat.

Roman turned away from the door.

"Impossible."

I opened my eyes, looked up at him.

For the very first time, I saw fear in his face.

He shouted, "Kill him!"

The men raised their MP5s. It happened all in less than a second. But less than a second was all the time I needed.

Chains kept my legs and wrists secure, but I broke them apart without any trouble, like they were paper, and I stood up from the chair and flung the chair at the man on my left as I jumped over at the man on the right, the one with the irregular heartbeat, and I punched him in the chest so hard it actually stopped his heart, and as he slumped to the ground, dead, I extracted the MP5 and spun and fired at the two men flanking Roman, both returning fire at me, but dodged past their spray of bullets, kicking off the wall and flipping through the air and taking out both of the men, and then the fourth man, still trying to bounce back after having the chair flung at him, raised his weapon at me, and I slipped up behind him and jerked his neck so hard that I nearly tore his head off his shoulders.

The fear was still in Roman's face. He scrambled for the gun still holstered to his belt. I advanced on him, taking my time, and when he managed to draw his weapon and fired at me, I easily shifted from one side to the next, judging the placement of the bullets nanoseconds before they were fired to ensure I wasn't in their trajectory. Then, quite suddenly, I stood in front of Roman just as he exhausted his magazine.

His eyes were still wide.

"How?"

"Simple. I'm Temple."

And I kicked him in the chest, so hard that he went flying into the door and knocked the door from its hinges and continued into the cinderblock wall outside. I heard each and every one of his bones snap at the impact. Then he was slumped on the floor, still alive but paralyzed.

I started forward, meaning to finish the job, when I heard someone out in the corridor. There had been hurried footsteps that paused when Roman went crashing through the door. Silence for a long second, and then the footsteps started up again, only this time with much more caution.

I stepped out into the corridor, my finger on the MP5's trigger, and placed a bead on the approaching intruder. Then I lowered the MP5.

"Hello, Agent Njeim."

She stood there for a moment, staring at me. Her gaze shifted from me to Roman and the smashed door against the wall before returning back to me.

"You look ... different."

"I feel different."

"What happened?"

"Roman shot me in the heart. Three times."

She frowned.

"Then how …"

"I have no idea. I think somehow the extra stress on my body caused it to go into overdrive. It repaired my heart and the rest of my body like when I was in my prime. In fact, I feel even better than I did when I was in my prime. Stronger. Faster. How did you find me?"

"I had Nate monitor the helicopter from the second it took off. He gave me the location of where it landed and told me where Roman and his men had taken you. I headed straight over to save you."

I smiled.

"I appreciate the thought. How long since the boat exploded?"

"Almost an hour."

"My brother?"

She shook her head.

"Nate has no idea where he went. He said it's almost like he disappeared."

"Were you and Nate able to gather enough information to clear your name?"

"More than enough information. The president has been told everything. I could tell he didn't want to believe it at first —Roger was a trusted ally—but the evidence was irrefutable."

"Do you trust him?"

"Who—the president? I do. I believe he'll do the right thing."

"You don't sound so confident."

She hesitated.

"The White House is already spinning the story. They're going to claim Abu Mohammad al-Naser managed to sneak into the country with a weapon, and that his plan was to destroy the Statue of Liberty."

"Who will the White House say stopped him?"

She hesitated again.

"Based on the fact that your son is dead, they're going to claim Temple stopped him. And that in doing so, Temple was killed."

I said nothing.

Agent Njeim said, "It's complete bullshit, I know, but there's no other way they'll be able to explain it to the American people. They need heroes and villains, and it's unacceptable to them when those villains are their own people."

"So Roger?"

"I'm not sure yet, but I wouldn't be surprised if he won't some day be honored for dying in service to his country."

"What about Monarch?"

"It's gone. Without Roger, there's nobody to run it."

"But its investors?"

Agent Njeim said nothing.

I nodded, filling in the missing pieces.

"Billionaires and politicians. Their involvement can never come to light, otherwise it will look poorly on the country."

"As Roger told you before, the world has changed. The good guys and the bad guys change hats all the time."

I glanced back at Roman, who was still alive, but barely.

"Where are we, anyway?"

"The basement of a warehouse in Chelsea."

There was a room off to the right with a few items. My clothes were in there.

Agent Njeim said, "The president will be thrilled to hear you're still alive."

I entered the room and bent down next to the pile of my clothes.

"I'm sure he would, but that's not going to happen."

I checked the jeans pockets. Found what I wanted and stood and faced Agent Njeim again.

"I need to change into some clothes that aren't wet and freezing."

I held the car key up in my hand.

"Then I need a ride."

70

I t was five o'clock in the morning, another hour before the sun rose, and the parking lot of the Third Quarter was completely deserted except for the Charger parked near the end of the lot. Or at least I had to assume it was the Charger that was buried under three feet of snow.

Agent Njeim helped me clear it off. I climbed in and inserted the key and said a silent prayer when I turned the ignition. At first it didn't seem like the engine would turn over, chugging a couple times, and then, on the fourth try, it worked. I revved the gas a few times to make sure it wouldn't crap out and then turned on the heat and stepped out to let it warm up.

Agent Njeim said, "You could stay."

"I could."

"But you won't."

"No."

"Why not?"

"Like you said—like Roger said—the world has changed. My father always knew there would come a day when Temple would no longer be needed. When he would overstay his welcome, as the saying goes. I think that time has come."

"But ... you're different now. You said so yourself. That you feel even better now than you did in your prime. There's no reason you couldn't continue the legacy. Especially with Nate and me backing you."

"I appreciate all your help, Agent Njeim, but I'm afraid Temple's time has come to an end. The world managed to get on before Temple, and it will manage after Temple."

Beside us, the Charger's engine purred.

I asked, "What will happen to my daughter?"

"To be honest, I'm not sure. She can't very well stand trial, not after what she was involved in. There's a good chance she'll end up in one of the black sites around the country."

"I wouldn't call that justice."

Agent Njeim shrugged.

"Would you call any of what's happened justice?"

She had a point there.

"So what about your brother?"

"He's out there somewhere. He waited all this time to get back at me, he won't just give up now."

"And your plan?"

"I'm going to make sure he comes for me. And I'm going to kill him."

"What if he kills you instead?"

"Then I die. But after having been shot three times in the heart, I think I have an advantage."

Agent Njeim opened her mouth, started to say something, but then stopped.

I said, "What?"

She shook her head.

"Nothing."

"Say it."

"What if your brother had children of his own? What if there are others like you out there?"

"That I will have to worry about when the time comes."

I held out my hand.

"It was a pleasure, Agent Njeim."

She shook my hand.

"Take care of yourself, Mr. Shepherd."

"You too."

I watched her drive away in the SUV and then got into the Charger, which wasn't nearly as warm inside as it should have been for having the heat on full blast.

I hit the wipers to clear the residual snow from the windshield and realized that I'd parked facing New York. The river was several blocks away, and there were several buildings between me and the river, but still I had a great view of the city's skyline. It looked so quiet in the dark. So peaceful. So vulnerable.

I shook my head and put the Charger in gear.

Time to go.

71

I had gotten on I-95 and was headed south for a mile—the highway deserted—when I spotted a van in an embankment. As I neared, a man climbed out of the van and hurried up the slope, waving his arms.

The Charger was moving at a crawl. Stopping the Charger would be no problem under the current conditions. But did I want to stop? Suddenly I had the suspicion that this was a setup. Either Darrell was in the van or he was somewhere nearby, waiting for me to step out of the car so he could make his attack.

I coasted to a stop as the man approached. He was heavy-set, bundled up in a jacket and wearing a New York Mets baseball cap. I had to lean across the passenger seat to the lower the window enough for the man to poke his head inside. There was hope in his face for an instant, but it vanished when he realized I was just an old man.

"Slid off the highway, I see."

He nodded.

"My own stupid fault. Should've known better than to drive in this weather, but we wanted to get an early start."

"Where are you headed?"

"To my wife's family in Ohio. It's a bitch of a drive, which is why I wanted to do it with hardly no traffic. Stupid me."

"Need help?"

"Thanks, but I don't know what you could do. We called for a tow truck an hour ago. They said it would be at least two hours before the tow came. I was hoping maybe you were it."

I glanced at the rearview mirror. Nothing behind me. The highway was empty besides myself and this man and his family.

"Let me see what I can do."

"No, really, it's okay."

"You and me. Maybe we can give it enough of a nudge to get it back up on the highway."

The man looked at me like I was crazy but didn't say a word. He stepped back, maybe hoping I would continue on. Instead, I drove the Charger several yards forward and parked on the side of the highway. When I stepped out, the man hadn't moved from his spot.

He said, "Really, it's okay. We can wait for the tow truck."

I started down the embankment. As I reached the van, the passenger's side window lowered. A woman looked out at me.

I said, "Hello."

She forced a smile.

I glanced in at the back of the van and saw a young girl in a booster seat and a ten-year-old boy. Both were asleep, covered with blankets.

"Ma'am, your husband and I are going to try to push the van back on to the highway. Can you move behind the wheel and give it some gas?"

She looked at me dubiously.

The man said, "Really, sir, we appreciate the gesture, but we can wait for the tow truck."

"Either you help me or I'll try it on my own."

The man sighed.

"Babe, mind giving it some gas when we're ready?"

She nodded, positioning herself behind the steering wheel.

The van's engine was idling, keeping the children in back warm. The boy began to stir awake. He blinked, looked out at his father and me, and asked his mother what was happening.

She said, "Shh. Go back to sleep."

I asked, "Are they buckled in?"

She nodded.

The man said, "I know it doesn't look too far—"

Meaning the distance between the van and the highway.

"—but believe me, I tried everything I could to get us moving. The wheels just spin."

I walked to the back of the van. I planted my feet, squared my shoulders, and placed both hands on the rear panel.

The man didn't move at first, baffled by my insistence, and then stepped up beside me and placed his hands next to mine.

The woman watched us in the rearview mirror, waiting for the signal.

I nodded at her.

The van's engine began to whine as the wheels started spinning.

The man groaned as he pushed, and I waited a few extra seconds before I gave the van a solid shove, just enough for the wheels to connect and for the van to start back up the embankment.

The man lurched forward, landing in the snow. He wiped the snow from his face and watched as the van moved up onto the highway.

I helped the man back to his feet, and we trudged up the embankment to the van which now idled behind the Charger.

The woman jumped out of the driver's seat and circled the van, her voice filled with excitement.

"I can't believe that worked. Thank you so much!"

Surprisingly, she hugged me.

"You're our hero. You have no idea how long we've been waiting. Thank you, thank you, thank you!"

"It was nothing. Just a bit of luck."

The woman, exhilarated to be out of the embankment, climbed into the passenger seat.

The man stared at me for a few seconds, as if he wasn't sure I existed. Then he seemed to shake it off, blinking, and held out his hand.

"Thank you."

I shook his hand.

"I'm just glad it worked. You still headed to Ohio?"

He laughed.

"No, I think we'll head back home and wait until the roads are a little less dangerous. Thank you again."

I waited until the man got back into the van, until the woman waved at me one last time, until the van pulled away, moving at a slow, cautious speed, before I walked back to the Charger. Before I slid inside, though, I stared out at the New York skyline several miles away. The sun was beginning to rise, cutting beams of light through the darkened skyscrapers. Among the skyscrapers, the Freedom Tower stood the tallest. Its light at the very top flashing like an SOS.

ABOUT THE AUTHOR

Robert Swartwood is the *USA Today* bestselling author of *The Serial Killer's Wife*, *No Shelter*, *Man of Wax*, and several other novels. He created the term "hint fiction" and is the editor of *Hint Fiction: An Anthology of Stories in 25 Words or Fewer*. He lives with his wife in Pennsylvania.